EverAfter Romance
An Imprint of Diversion Publishing Corp.
443 Park Avenue South, Suite 1008
New York, New York 10016
www.DiversionBooks.com

This is a work of fiction. Names, characters, places and incidents either are the product of the author's imagination or are used fictitiously. Any resemblance to actual persons, living or dead, events or locales is entirely coincidental.

For more information, email info@diversionbooks.com

First Diversion Books edition May 2015.
Print ISBN: 978-1-62681-8804
eBook ISBN: 978-1-94283-306-2

SHUTTERIRL

CD REISS

*everafter*ROMANCE

Prologue

Los Angeles is mine.

From the ports of San Pedro to the base of the Angeles National Forest, from Santa Monica Beach to the trench we call a river, I own this city. And like mother and daughter locked together, the ownership is reciprocal. I've been nurtured in her arms, brought to adulthood as if pulled by the roots of my hair, sung to sleep with a lullaby of car alarms and freeway traffic.

I grew up in twelve neighborhoods, the ward of foster parents who didn't give a shit if I stayed out most of the day, as if they knew I was the city's child. I learned how to fold myself between alleys, how to hide, how to appear in unexpected places, how to whisper my intentions to the city and stand still long enough to listen to her directions. I didn't finish high school. I didn't need to. The only lessons I ever needed came from the throb and hum of this wide-open, sexy metropolis.

Every greased-palm-coated street leads to opportunity. Lights turn green when I approach. Traffic parts like the Red Sea. When I stop, a parking spot opens up before me. The city speaks in my gut, whispering the way to go. I should rob banks for a living, or drive a cab. I should be a cop or a paramedic. But that's not how it worked out. That was never Los Angeles's plan for me.

I am a paparazzi. Or, if you want to split hairs, paparazza. With an *a*.

I can get to a mark and get away with the shot faster than any of them, in heels and backward. I'm prettier, I smell nicer, and I take exactly zero bullshit from celebrities. I don't work for them. I don't kowtow or suck up. If they're in public, their ass is mine.

This is the story of one celebrity, and as much as the city, he is mine.

Chapter 1

Laine

My butt hurt. My feet were fine, even in heels, and my shoulder didn't ache, even with the twenty-pound camera bag slung over it. But my ass, which leaned against a railing not meant for leaning, throbbed like a dance floor.

Tom, my foster brother, stood next to me, his camera hoisted like a javelin. He had a scraggly beard and a hipster's idea of grooming. Even in broad daylight, he was so sallow, he looked like a black-and-white picture pasted into a Kodachrome world. At night, he was barely even visible.

"My phone's buzzing," he said.

"Mine too."

Our phones always buzzed. It was the Muzak of our lives. I checked my screen.

—Britt's at NV—

Too little. Too late. At one in the morning, we'd already been staking out the back of Club NV for three hours, waiting for Britt to walk out with Maryetta, her longtime lover. The back exit faced the parking lot and was manned by two huge Armenians in leather, standing behind a velvet rope. I was on a first-name basis with both of them.

I might know the city like the back of my hand, but I didn't have a line on when some self-hating actress would get tired of a club and decide to go the hell home. So we waited in the weed-bitten corners of the alley, under the hard shadows of the street lamps. Anyone would think the alley was empty but for the two Armenians, but paps were hiding in the corners and behind the SUVs, wedged between buildings and cars. Two were on a garage roof three doors west. They'd rented it just to keep their lenses on Club NV.

Tom poked his phone. "Kill Photo."

He still used an agent, and they sent him calls. I was past giving someone a chunk of my money for their connections. What had been great while I was with Kill was that the outlets looked at their pics first. When a mag got upward of forty thousand frames a day, you needed to be fast, and you needed to be verifiable. Kill's photos were fast-queued. Head of the line. Seen first and paid on time.

But I got to the point where my frames got ahead of everyone else's at Kill, and I didn't need them anymore. I kept telling Tom to ditch them. I'd help him get fast-queued, but he was too timid to go out on his own.

"I told her we're already staking it out on your hunch." He scrolled down Kill's text. "Britt. London. Michael. Blah blah."

In an unreciprocated intimacy, everyone in Hollywood called anyone who was someone by their first name. Michael was a name I loved hearing, partly because his pictures netted me a nice take, and partly…mostly, because he was Michael Greydon. There had been times, maybe three or four in the past years, that I imagined he saw me past the lens.

"Is Michael snorting anything?" I asked. "Because America's Boyfriend cutting lines would be a million-dollar shot."

I was being snarky, but the fact was, I didn't want to hurt him. He was perfect, from the breathtaking smile that implied sex but never stated it, to the sharp green eyes that didn't look at but through, from the way he moved as if carried on his own jet stream, to the body that made me shudder. I wanted him to stay exactly as he was. Stunning. Captivating. Catching the world, and me in the tractor beam of his personality. Bringing him down with a photograph would have been criminal.

The valet pulled a Ferrari up to the velvet rope. Paparazzi crawled out of the dark corners, their cameras up like shields. Only the VIP room could call ahead to the valet. Like clockwork, the back door slapped open, and Britt Ravenor, with her pixie cut and big hoop earrings, stumbled out of the club. The valet held the driver's door open for her. Michael Greydon—with his walnut hair and wicked smile, lithe body and immeasurable talent—came out behind her. Every time I saw him in person, he blew me back, and I had to pause before putting the camera in front of my face. I heard the cadence of his voice in my head, the way his mouth moved, the way his face lit up when he smiled. And his hands… God. A tingle went up my back, and I put the camera in front of my face to stop it. I had work to do.

SHUTTERGIRL

Lots of stars had entourages, but Michael Greydon didn't. His isolation made him less accessible because he wasn't surrounded by people I could connect myself to. Charming and only slightly aloof, he was so adept at managing his career and public image that everyone assumed he'd gotten more than talent and looks from his movie-star parents, Gareth Greydon and Brooke Chambers.

I didn't assume. I'd known him in high school, and he'd been as gorgeous as he'd been a workaholic. I imagined he was much the same as an adult.

The valet handed Britt her keys. She swiped for them and missed but got them on the second try.

Britt had been a victim of the beauty pageant circuit, the daughter of an ambitious single mother who'd pushed the girl until the family broke. Britt broke slowly, over the course of a decade, from drinking too much and driving while doing it. It was the mother who was wrapped up in a straightjacket at Westonwood. I sympathized with Britt, understood her life, but that didn't stop me from making money off it.

Flashes went wild as Britt got into the car. Not mine. I held my shutter back. That wasn't money. Not yet.

Britt was halfway in the Ferrari when Michael went for her keys with a quick, decisive move that came from years on varsity tennis. Britt giggled and bent over, hiding them. He pushed her out of the way, trying to get behind the wheel instead. She wrestled him aside, and he put his arms around her, tickling her to get her away. It was delightful and charming, and it would make fantastic copy.

That was my picture. I got my manual focus going, because they were moving, and no auto-focus lens could think faster than I could.

Click. Money. *Click.* Money.

I kept them in frame, head to toe. The money was in what they were wearing, from shoes to hair bobs. Even when Britt held her arm out and Michael reached for it, I moved with them, keeping all appendages in the frame.

I realized, even through the lens, that Britt was drunk and Michael was trying to keep her from driving. They were working together for a big Oscar-season thing, a remake of the 1970s classic *Bullets Over Sunset*. Big feels. Big tears. Big money. Michael's father had played the green gangster then, and now he was to play the role of the old mob don his son had to kill. It was marketable to a fault, especially since Gareth hadn't made a movie in a decade.

Through the frame, where everything was clear, there was a touch of desperation on Michael's face, even when it looked as though he had his co-star under control. Unfortunately for him, she'd shot all of *Zombie Apocalypse* drunk, so when she twisted away from him, she was skilled at it.

I pushed against Roger, the pap next to me, to keep them in the frame, digging my heel into his foot.

Michael went for the keys again, smile gleaming as if he was simply doing a sight gag, and Britt twisted, dropping her hands. Michael caught the keys, but Britt put her knee between his legs. Her aim was perfect, and Michael took two steps back, letting go of the keys.

Even the dog pack of paps went *ooohh*. I got a couple of shots then put my camera down.

Michael Greydon, an A-lister's A-lister, was crouched over in pain while everyone else shot Britt. I should have been shooting. It was money, and I only had four pictures. Yet I'd stopped because he was looking at me through the lens. Not just looking but appreciating. I felt a warm tingle over my skin, as if hands had gone up my shirt. He *saw* me.

I'd shot him a hundred times over the past years, yet I had always been convinced he didn't know I was there. Did he recognize me? Shit. I'd considered the possibility every time we were on the same block, but it had never seemed so likely.

The glance must have been the length of a shutter snapping, because by the time I got the camera down, his attention had shifted back to Britt. She slipped into her Ferrari, and he held the door open, saying something I couldn't quite decipher. It sounded like *don't do this*. The engine revved to life, and the tires peeled against the cracked pavement, sending scree flying. I got caught in the rain of rocks and moved just before she skidded off with the door still open.

She came to the T at the end of the alley and cut the right too close, and the centripetal force shut the door as it scraped the corner of the building. The Ferrari missed a parked Civic, blew by two girls in sparkly outfits, and took off. Britt was gone.

"That's gonna be the end of her," Tom said.

"Shame," I said. "She had talent. Did someone call the cops?"

"Raoul has a contact. They'll pick her up before she gets to Venice." He turned, and his eyes went wide. "Oh my God."

I craned my neck toward the entrance but only saw the sparkly-shoe girls hustling away from the dented driver's side door. They went around the corner to the front of the building.

"What?" Was he talking about Michael looking at me? I still felt undressed from it.

"Nothing," Tom said.

The rest of the paps were taking pictures of the Ferrari's rear lights getting smaller in the distance, but I had my camera back on Michael Greydon. He laughed with one of the bouncers and hobbled inside. The big Armenian had his phone to his ear. I hoped he was calling the cops about the drunk in the Ferrari.

I jabbed Tom's calf with my stiletto. "Talk to me."

"Randee. That's her. She just walked in."

"With the sparkly heels?"

He nodded as if the rest of his body was paralyzed. Tom had spoken about Randee from the band Razzledazzle. He had a huge crush on her but had been unable to cross the photographer-artist barrier.

Any time he wasn't making money with me, he was shooting hip stylings in Silver Lake or rock bands playing in parking lots. He had a knack for catching a musician's passion and a deft hand at retouching. He should have been doing clubs and performers full time, but there was no money in that. The money was in one-in-the-morning stakeouts and chasing celebrity drunks. I'd stopped promising him he'd get a big break doing a candid celeb shot. I'd stopped trying to convince him it was photojournalism. I just called it money, and he heard that.

"Come on." I pulled his sleeve. "Let's upload from the Exploder while these douchebags chase a dead story."

We trotted over to Cordova Court, where he'd parked. We cut through a residential driveway I'd discovered when I was eleven, through a little-used gate, over a chain-link fence, and through a narrow space between buildings, cutting seven minutes out of our walk time.

Tom's Explorer smelled like camera grease, fast food, and armpit. I'd driven it before, and it shimmied to the left so badly, I'd barely been able to make right turns. Since then, I called it the Exploder. We got in and, as if we were EMTs on a scene, immediately unpacked and laid out our equipment: wifi routers, laptops, cables, cameras, and cell phones.

"I don't have my USB cable, damn," Tom mumbled.

He was a chronic forgetter of parts and pieces. I carried extra around just for him. I reached into my bag for the extra USB cable he needed every couple weeks.

"Thanks, Laine." He plugged in. "You're all right for a girl."

"You'd starve without me."

He shrugged as if he knew it was true.

I brought up my shots, did a quick edit on the best ones, and got them up on my server. Then I emailed my contact list the link and told them I was selling the four pictures on the server: one of Michael trying to get the keys away from Britt, one of Michael getting kneed in the groin, one of Britt hitting the side of a building, and one of Michael Greydon looking through the lens at me. I took a second with that one. He couldn't have been more inaccessible, yet the photo was so intimate, as if his eyes felt places only hands could reach. But that was what he did, wasn't it? That was his talent, to expand the space of the frame until you thought he was looking at *you*, touching the places that needed healing, when in fact, he was only looking at himself.

I changed my email before sending. I had three pictures. That last one made me tingle, even if I'd imagined it. That gaze was mine.

I snapped my laptop shut. "What now?"

"Kill servers are so slow." He stared at the screen, tapping the edge of the machine as if Kill Photo's servers would hurry up to a rhythm.

"Let's go in," I said. "We got the shots. Let's chase your future girlfriend."

"What? We can't go in there."

"We'll go in the front. It's different bouncers."

"I can't."

"Does she even know you exist without a camera in front of your face?" I flung my laptop into the backseat. "Have you said one word to her as a man, not as a guy who takes pictures of musicians?"

"Irrelevant."

"Answer me."

"I'm not going in there."

"You'll never get that girl if you always have a camera between you," I said, unzipping my thigh-high stiletto boots.

"Jesus, Laine, what are you doing?"

"Okay," I said, yanking off my boots. "Number one, anyone who'll give us a hard time is in the Emerald Room." I unbuttoned my jeans. "Don't look."

He averted his eyes as I peeled off my pants.

I continued, "We're just regular schlubs. We're not Emerald Room material." I yanked down my shirt. It was a black knit tunic that, when not bunched, could serve as a very short dress. "Number two, Britt's probably failing a breathalyzer right now, and Michael just got kneed in the balls. They left. I'm sure Brad followed with whichever girl he was in the mood for. Dollars to donuts, there's not an A-lister to be found in there."

I convinced myself all that was true because the idea that I wanted to go into the club to see Michael was utterly ridiculous, not even worth considering, even if the thought of him putting his eyes on me made the skin between my thighs feel awake and alive.

My tank top straps tied over the shoulders. I pulled them under my arms and twisted the shirt around until it was a tube top with a bow in the front. "No one in there knows us or cares that we've been in the parking lot for three hours. Period."

"What are you doing?" he asked when he turned around.

I rooted around in my bag. "Getting you into a club." I found an old tube of lipstick and picked the dust and crumbs out of the crease between the bullet and the cap.

"What's your angle?"

"What's that supposed to mean?" I pressed my lips together to smooth the color.

"You always have an angle. I've never seen you do something just to do it."

I wrestled my boots back on. What was my angle? Should I tell him that having Hollywood royalty like Michael Greydon look at me as if I was sexy and beautiful made me feel alive, excited? It was almost as good as chasing a mark down Rodeo or getting a tip and realizing I was only a block away from the action. I wanted to be in the center of something stimulating, and I wanted Tom to get the girl. I didn't want to just collect bids for my pictures and go to bed. I wanted to make something happen.

"We'll leave the rigs in the back. Just lock up." I handed him my camera.

He held it for a second, feeling its heft. It cost twice as much as his, and he did appreciate beautiful things.

I opened the door and stepped out.

"Does everyone need to be your gynecologist?" he called.

"We're not getting past the rope in what you're wearing, and I'm not

13

risking leaving my rig in this car just to get turned away at the door. Come on, Tom. For once, chase something." I slammed the door before he could argue.

He was a good guy, Tom. He'd saved me from myself when I'd needed saving, and he was the family I'd never had. I'd never had a father, and my mother went to prison when I was five. Tom's mother had had a boyfriend who was, let's say, unabashedly stupid and cruel. We latched on to each other young and made life up as we went along. He was my rock, my world. Anything I did, I wanted him with me, because he was more of a brother to me than any shared set of parents could create.

He never approved of what I did, because that was the only thing he knew of family. He was especially hard on the few guys I'd dated. They weren't safe or mature enough. I mean, if I wanted a guy who would take me to the farmer's market, pick up some organic kale, and eat it lightly sautéed before making afternoon love in a squeaky little bed, then sure, he'd approve of that guy. But I wanted a man who'd climb fences with me. Trespass. Steal from the rich and give to the poor. I had a fantasy of a man who got arrested with me, pleaded innocent, and kissed me on the precinct steps when we made bail.

I was too much of a hustler for most men. I ran too fast, broke too many rules, and stayed on the right side of the law by too thin a margin. My ambition was scary, even to my friends, but I didn't feel safe unless I had something to work for.

I walked up to the velvet rope, ignoring the line, putting my long boots in front of me as if they were the sum total of who I was. Tom schlubbed along beside me, handsome but morose, a study in monochrome, and looking away from me as if I embarrassed him. The bouncer didn't break my stride or the rhythm of his conversation as he opened the rope and let us in at exactly the right moment. He didn't clip it shut until Tom was past the rope with me. We were in.

Now we just had to find the girl with the sparkly shoes. Then I got the twisting feeling in my gut that things were going to change. I ignored the desire to run back to the car. I put my chin up, added swagger to my step, and decided I owned Club NV.

Chapter 2

Laine

I'd been to every club in Los Angeles. I'd paid off waiters, bartenders, and cleaning staff. I'd seen the rooms lit in fluorescent in the afternoon, filled with the blare of vacuum cleaners and Spanish music coming from a boom box. But I worked at night, so though I did my share of socializing, I rarely saw a club functioning as it was meant to.

Even so, one could count on a few things in any LA club west of La Cienega. Industry douchebags, tall girls with perfect skin, and surgically modified bodies and faces were just a few items on the smorgasbord. Club NV had an outdoor courtyard open to the sky, potted palms, a few trees growing from the floor, white couches, and an all-male staff that flirted as if their jobs depended on it. It had been very different five years ago. Now? Yawn.

"What are you having?" I yelled over the throbbing techno.

"A beer," Tom said. "Do they have beer? In a bottle? That's all I want."

I leaned on the bar and snapped my credit card onto the granite, where it could be seen. "Listen to me." I put my finger in his face. "When you see this girl, do not go negative. Do you hear me? I know you're out of your element, but if you're tense and snappy, you're only going to make it worse. Take a breath."

He pressed his fingertips together and said, "Ohm, Mom."

I flipped my pointer finger down and put my middle finger up. He didn't even see it. He was looking past me and upward. A necklace of wrought-iron railings circled the courtyard on the second floor. I followed his gaze to Sparkly Shoes and her friend, frou-frou drinks in hand, leaning over the railing and looking down on the courtyard.

"Crap," I said. The indoor part of the club was accessible on the first floor, but the second floor, where she was? That was the Emerald Room.

"Can we go home?" Tom asked.

"One drink, then we go."

The bartender leaned over. "What can I get you?" He winked at me. He looked as if he was wearing mascara.

"Leo?" I said, recognizing a particular twang in his voice. "Are you Leo?"

"Sure am."

"We met once. You're one of my tips." I showed him my business card. I'd given it to him already, many months ago, and he'd tipped me off to the comings and goings of a few marks. I paid him through PayPal when I sold the picture. It was clean and discreet, and I always paid very well.

"Oh, yeah. Hey, Laine. How's it going?"

"Good. I'll have a glass of something white and dry. And, uhm, who do I have to blow to get upstairs?"

"That's a rhetorical question," Tom growled.

Leo smiled a half moon of caps. "I know." He poured chardonnay into a huge stemmed glass. "Look, guys, no cameras upstairs. I'd get blackballed out of every club on the west side."

"Strictly personal. I don't have my rig. My brother here is clean too. I know the rules."

"I can't."

I took a hundred-dollar bill out of my bag and laid it on top of my credit card. "You have my word. We're only customers tonight, not paps."

"Laine," grumbled Tom.

"You're a good tip, Leo. I'm not about to ruin our friendship. And by friendship, I mean our ability to make money together."

He slid my wine across the bar. "If it wasn't for your reputation, I wouldn't even consider it. But everyone knows you're the most honest pap in the business, so let me see what I can do." He turned to Tom. "What can I get you?"

Tom tapped his fingers, looked at Leo, then Sparkly Shoes, then back at Leo. "Three shots of tequila. One, two, three. Line them up right here with a beer at the end."

"There's a man who knows how to party!" Leo shouted.

I sighed into my glass, disappointed. I had the feeling that despite my best intentions for Tom, I'd be driving the Exploder home.

The Emerald Room wasn't a lick special. Same shit but indoors and looking down at the goings-on in the courtyard. I bailed on Tom as soon as I could. As long as I was with him, he wouldn't get near Razzledazzle Girl. So I went to the bathroom and took a different route back.

I picked a spot at the bar, and after three minutes, I had a perfect view of him on the patio, pivoting his beer bottle between two fingers. The tequila had done its job. Now he just had to keep it from coming up his esophagus.

A man came up next to me, leaned an elbow on the bar, and spoke as if we were in a spy movie. "Has anyone mentioned to you the length of your skirt?"

"Too long?" I kept my eyes on the patio. I knew who he was.

"Magically, it shows everything and nothing."

"You're not getting under it, Mister Sinclair. I'm not one of your screaming fans."

I looked around, and he was indeed Brad Sinclair. Twenty-eight. Six one. Two Oscar nods but no wins. His last film took in twenty million opening weekend, landing the skiing movie in a solid second for three weeks running. He wore a jacket, corduroy shorts, and sunglasses. A douchebag's douchebag. I sighed into my second glass of wine.

"Want to play a game?" he asked.

I didn't know what kind of face I made—probably something that looked as if I'd eaten a lemon—but I didn't have anything better to do. I got the distinct impression he didn't know who I was, and that was its own flavor of amusing. "What kind of game?"

"Guess what I'm drinking." He finished the last of what was in his glass and put it on the bar. "And I'll buy your next one."

"There won't be a next, but I'll play."

He smirked. People paid good money for that smirk, and my hand itched for my rig.

I placed my phone on the bar and cracked my knuckles. "Do I get to ask a couple questions?"

He put his pinkie and thumb together. "Three." He was enjoying himself. It was all over his posture.

I admitted to myself that I was enjoying this as well. I glanced toward the balcony, where Tom had initiated a conversation with Randee. I peeked into Brad's empty glass. A quarter-inch of clear, condensing fluid draped over the low rolling hills of ice.

"Carbonated?" I asked.

"Yes."

I leaned in, sniffing. A maraschino cherry was wedged between two chunks of ice, and I caught the distinct scent of almonds. "You on any kind of diet? Like super restrictive or to lose weight or anything?"

"No."

That ruled out diet mixers and meant allergens weren't a problem.

"How much was it?"

"Free."

That had been a filler question. Those guys never paid for their drinks. I put my glass down and leaned back, elbows on the bar. "Amaretto and Coke."

He slapped his hands together. "Nice!"

In that moment, he didn't look like a manly-man superstar who could take down an evil overlord but a seventh-grade dork moving up a level in Mario Bros. He poked the bridge of his sunglasses, pushing them up his nose a quarter of an inch.

I wasn't impressed by celebrities, since I worked with them every day. Well, I didn't work "with" them. I more worked "at" them. But they were a way for me to put food on my table and pay my mortgage. Like fish in a pond, I might admire their grace or color, but in the end, I ate them.

In that same way, though I wasn't impressed with Brad, I was. Because I knew not just anybody got to do his job. It was tough in its own way. For some, it was a hard job to *get*, and for some, it was a hard job to *do*. It required talent (for some), hard work (for others), and enough genetic entitlement to qualify for nepotistic pushes, like a daddy with a gold statue on the mantel (for the rest). I believed a person needed two out of the three to make it, and even one was difficult to the point of impossibility.

So I respected Brad for having talent and for working hard to overcome the fact that he'd grown up in a small town in Arkansas. What he'd achieved was no small feat, but what he did with his success wasn't too impressive. As he looked at me through his sunglasses, lips tightened in a flirty smile, I had to remind myself of that, because he was a beautiful man, and I was single to a fault.

"Who's the guy?" he asked, tipping his chin toward Tom. "He ditching you for the skinny girl?"

I thought about saying yes and feigning a broken heart. I was chronically lonely, even if I didn't admit it, and a night with Brad had its appeal. It might even feel good, but all I could see was the dampening effect on my career if word got out that I'd spent a minute alone with Brad Sinclair. A pap depended on tips, and if I started playing for the other side, the tips would stop. Known fact. Ask Lorenzo Balsamo. The guy had spent a weekend in Diane Falston's bed and wound up taking wedding pictures for a living.

So I decided not to play with lies, because as famous as he was, I was famous in my world. I'd forgotten that for a moment. "Oh, come on, Brad. Take the sunglasses off. You might recognize me."

He made a little grunting sound, as if I'd suggested I was on his level, but he didn't take off the glasses. I wondered if he thought he'd keep them on when he took me to bed, or if he was just playing with me. I leaned in, hooking my fingers over the top of his sunglasses. I smelled the soak of amaretto and stale dance-floor sweat, and I felt sorry for him. Even with his entourage and all his fame, was he as lonely as I was?

"Hey, hey. The shades stay on," he protested, smiling and moving my hand off him. He picked my phone up off the bar. "Want a selfie with me?"

I put my hand over his. "No."

"Why not?"

I didn't want anything like that committed to digital. I couldn't believe he hadn't identified me. Was it the vision-killing sunglasses or general obliviousness? Or did they never see us with our big lenses and tendency to hang in packs? He pulled the phone away, and my hand went with him.

"Are we about to start wrestling for my phone?" I asked.

"Let's wrestle, gorgeous," he said with a smile, yanking the phone away.

I got closer so I could reach it. "You're pissing me off, Sinclair."

He smiled and bit his lower lip. I pressed into him, and he loosened his hold on the phone. I snatched it away.

"You want me to take your damn picture?" I said, holding up the phone. "You got it."

I saw better through a two-dimensional square, and once my vision was limited to what would be in frame, I saw that Brad was wobbly, stoned or drunk or something. He didn't look ready to be photographed. He'd most certainly regret it in the morning. I was still looking through the glowing screen when a hand popped up in front of Brad's face, getting bigger in the frame before the phone was snatched away.

"Back up," said a voice.

Without the phone limiting my view, I saw the man standing in front of me. Michael Greydon, arms taut between us, was half-turned toward his friend. Oh, I remembered that jaw. Someone would dig it up in fifty thousand years and call it a perfect specimen. The shape of his hand on Brad's bicep, the way it articulated as if every finger had purpose. And cinnamon. The sharp, spicy scent went from my nose to the base of my spine.

"We need to talk," he said to Brad. Michael was taller than I remembered, and he had an even stronger presence.

"Give me my phone," I said.

He turned, and well, I gasped. I'd seen him a hundred times from ten feet away or blown up on a screen to a hundred times his normal size. But I hadn't seen him that close in a long, long time. Even in the half light, he was terrifyingly perfect, the result of a few generations of movie-star couplings. He was precision folding in on itself, without adornment, simple brown hair just long enough to be accurately untidy, eyes the color of jade and so clear they looked right through me.

"My phone," I repeated, holding out my hand.

"You," he said.

I think my heart shrank as if it was a night animal exposed to bright light. Which was bullshit. I didn't shrink from anything. I sucked my cheeks in and stood up taller. "Me."

He indicated the phone. "What do you have on here?" He was worried about me taking pictures. He couldn't have recognized me. Same as any other day.

"Shouldn't you be home nursing your aching balls?"

"It was a stage kick."

"Yeah, Mike," Brad said. "Go see Britt and make her apologize."

"She went to Christian's place." He turned to me, fingering my phone with a rueful look, and passed it over. "I'm sure this'll ring in a minute with the same information."

I took the phone, and he walked out to the patio, where Tom and Randee were talking. I looked back. Brad already had a new drink in his hand.

"Messed up," Brad mumbled. His glasses dropped all the way down his nose, and he looked at me without them. "Hey, you're Shuttergirl."

"So?"

Brad pushed off the bar, wobbled a little, and leaned back, holding his hand up for the bartender. Michael stood with his elbows on the railing. I wondered if the folks in the courtyard had noticed him yet and if he wanted to be seen, yet distant. His posture said he was trying to get away from his friend's drunkenness.

"Hey, asshole!" It was Gene Testarossa, the agent from WDE who managed Britt, Brad, and Michael; he was a card-carrying entourage member.

Gene slapped Brad's back and shook his hand. As they spoke, I brushed past them to the balcony. The music blasted from the courtyard, painting a thick coat of noise over conversations. The occasional shot of laughter drifted upward.

I should have left Michael Greydon alone. Shoulda just gone to the dance floor and given my booty a few good shakes and flirted with a boy or two before going home by myself, or waited in the Exploder for Tom to show up with his schlubby scowl. But I had a perverse compulsion to remind him of me. Maybe it was because he thought of me as a dirty pap, even when he'd seen me up close and without the rig. That bothered me.

"You really looked like you were hurt out there," I said from a few feet behind him.

He looked over his shoulder at me. "Shuttergirl."

I stepped forward, putting my hands on the railing. "Is that the only name you know me by?"

"It's the name I can repeat in company."

"I deserve that." I'd come with my wine glass, but it was empty. A poor prop to hide behind and a loaded gun of bad judgment. I put it on the railing. "Here." I handed him my phone. "There's nothing on there. You can check yourself. I promised I wouldn't take any pictures up here. I just came for a drink and to get my brother laid."

He took the phone. "I see you got the drink. How's it working out for your brother?"

"He's behind me."

Michael looked over my shoulder and leaned an inch closer. His neck was made of sinew and stubble, and he still smelled like the Christmas mornings I never had. "He's face-locked with an Asian girl."

I spun around. Tom was indeed attached at the mouth to Randee from Razzledazzle so tightly I could barely see his face. I fist-pumped.

Michael was looking at my glowing screen, bathed in its blue light, and he smiled at my fist-pump. "Mission accomplished?"

"Yes."

"I wish I had a sister like you." He smiled that million-dollar smile, the slight one with only a few teeth showing, and I noticed that spot in his short beard where hair didn't grow. It was the size of a small pumpkin seed, and it was the sexiest thing I'd ever seen in my life.

I didn't melt. Not a bit. I never felt insecure or overwhelmed. I was the master of my realm. I owned the space around me, the city, the—

Jesus Christ. If he smiled like that again, I would have a coronary.

"I've had about twenty brothers and sisters. Tom is the only one who stuck," I said.

"That's a pretty crappy average."

"You never met my foster sibs."

Before he could say whatever he was about to say next, my phone lit up with a notification from *YOU* magazine. I knew it by the buzz. Probably a buy, and if I knew the notifications at all, they'd include the subject line of the email. The first words would be Michael's or Britt's name in all caps.

I put my hand over the phone. My fingertips touched his wrist, and his touched mine. I was tempted to keep them there. I guessed I did keep them there too long, because he looked into my face, and I realized how close he was. I curled my fingers over the phone. His fingers tightened around my wrist. Skin on skin, for the second time in so many years, sent the same electricity, the same current from my hand to the neglected space between my legs.

"Oh, right." He waved his finger as if recalling the hours we'd spent telling each other everything. "I forgot. I mean, I didn't forget. It's been a long time."

"Never mind, superstar. Sob stories are for losers."

He smiled that way again but with a nod, as if he understood and agreed. Then he tilted his head a little.

"Sob stories are for losers," he repeated pensively, looking at me more closely. "Been a long time," he repeated. "But I remember the bleachers."

I touched my nose with my forefinger. His smile was heartbreaking. I wanted to look away, because I was going to fall under the weight of his eyes, but I didn't. I wouldn't let him cloud my mind, or admit it when he did.

Our hands separated, but he kept the phone.

I was feeling cheeky. Maybe it was the wine. "Remember? Or never forgot?"

"What's the difference?"

"Expectations. Did I just jog your memory, or have you recognized me the whole time? And you never said 'hello.'" The phone stopped buzzing in his hand, and I relaxed. *YOU* magazine could wait.

"The opportunity never presented itself," he said.

"Talking to me would hurt you. People wouldn't approve. I know how that is. I forgive you." I was flirting. What a silly fool. I turned away and looked down into the outdoor courtyard so I wouldn't feel the disorientation of his gaze.

"So," he said, "you became a photographer."

"I became your worst nightmare."

"You used to be my friend."

"Things change."

Like paper floating in a developing tray, he softened, rubbing his bottom lip with his thumb. I imagined them on my body, and I stiffened, because a shock of desire had shot through me. How could he do that to me? How could I allow it?

We paused on that. I had been his friend. Before he was anyone, he was still someone, parting the reeds wherever he walked in a school where I was no better than an outsider, fostered by a studio exec and his wife to save their dying marriage. I'd been unable to keep them together, unable to fit into their world of privilege. I was an outcast in new clothes and almost held back a year because of my scant education. My foster parents wouldn't hear of it, so I was put in the class that fit my IQ, not my education, and I floundered. I was set up for failure, but I tried. Damn, I tried.

I'd needed quiet, so I went to the tennis court bleachers every day to study subjects I'd never been prepared for. I studied to the rhythmic *thwock-pop thwock-pop* of yellow balls as Michael Greydon, a senior to my sophomore, practiced that brutal serve over and over. *Thwock-pop thwock-pop.*

He'd thought I'd been there to watch him. I hadn't been. Not initially.

"How's your serve?" I asked, looking into the courtyard at NV, then back at him.

"Tore a ligament in college." He bent his elbow in my direction. "Haven't played a tournament since."

"You called that playing? I called it watching you suffer through three hours of frustration every afternoon." He laughed a good, hearty laugh, so I continued. "No, really. You, cursing heaven and earth. Loudly too. It seriously undercut my study time."

"You distracted me."

"You should have asked me to leave." I shrugged coyly, because after a couple months, he'd shaved half an hour off his cursing and I'd shaved thirty minutes off my study time so we could sit together and talk.

"Did they adopt you?" he asked.

He must have known the answer. I was sure he'd worked with Orry Hatch or been to one of his parties.

"Nah. They didn't want a kid, especially not a troublemaker like me. They wanted some fantasy family they were too busy to have. But stop"—I held up my hands—"we're getting into loser territory. Sorry about what happened with that blonde chick." I waved my hand as if I didn't know exactly who I was talking about, but I remembered Lucy clearly. Once she saw Michael and me talking, she'd started leaving dollar-bill encrusted G-strings on my locker with a sign that said "Career Counseling at Polecat State."

"She runs her own modeling agency now." He shrugged. "The engagement was short, let's just say."

"You're still friends though," I said. "I see you around."

That was silly, because he had a reputation of staying friends with everyone. From A-list talent to cocktail waitresses, no one had a bad thing to say about him, and he never spoke ill or well of the women he dated.

"Yeah. You know, I kind of feel like an asshole. I should have said hello when I recognized you the first time."

I shrugged. I'd assumed I'd meant nothing to him. When I'd sold my first photograph of him, when my copyright line appeared next to the picture, I'd hoped he'd remember. The nineteen-year-old me had stayed up late, worrying and hoping at the same time, but over time, I stopped caring or worrying at all. If I meant nothing to him, I meant nothing.

I stopped thinking I was insignificant to him on the balcony of Club NV.

No. My throbbing, unattended sexual desire was making that up. He and I had nothing in common. Zero. So despite the liquidation of my spine, my buzzing, glowing phone reminded me of the worlds that separated us. I had never hated that chasm as much as I did that night. It yawned before me, no smaller for his physical proximity, and I wanted to leap over it so badly I tasted cinnamon in the back of my throat.

"How about a do-over?" I said.

"Of our meeting?"

"Pretend you haven't seen me since that last time in the bleachers."

"All right. You first."

I looked over the balcony at the outside part of the club then back at him, with my finger pointing. "Hey, aren't you… let me place you." I tapped my chin. "You're the guy from Breakfront with the serve. Michael?"

"Oh! Hey, you're the girl in the bleachers. Gayle? Dolores?"

"Nope."

"Apple?"

"No! Let me give you a clue. Lover's…" I spun my hand at the wrist.

"Laine! Nice to see you again."

I held out my hand, and he put my phone in it but didn't move away. We held hands, the vibrating, brightly lit device sandwiched between us. I felt as if the energy passing between us lit the phone up, and the connection of our eyes locked our fingers together.

Brad and Gene burst onto the balcony like cops at a drug lord's.

"Britt's at Sequoia Hospital," Gene said, as if picking up a conversation that had never happened. "Broken clavicle."

Michael held up his hands, letting go of the phone. "What?"

"She told you she was at Christian's so you wouldn't get upset," Brad said, pointing. "This is you, Mike. She's scared to disappoint you."

Gene mumbled, "How you gonna shoot? How's she gonna do the movie? What the hell, Mike?"

"Okay, you guys need to calm down," Michael said.

"Calm down?" Brad shouted, ten percent more sober. "You can't shoot without her. And your dad, what's he going to do? What are *you* gonna do? This'll hold up production. And your *dad.*"

Was he talking about the *Bullets* shoot? He must be. I suddenly felt as if I was eavesdropping, which didn't bother me as much as the fact that I was right in front of them.

"Dad will be fine," Michael growled.

My phone jangled and lit up. The number was my contact at Sequoia. It seemed as if a hundred things happened at once, all vying for everyone's attention. Michael shot me a glance, but Brad continued, undistracted.

"That's weeks. You don't have wee—"

"Shut up!" Michael said.

"No!" Gene was a raging bull. "I told you Britt was a liability."

Michael seemed to be coming apart at the seams, swallowing whatever was in his throat: pride, anger, a dose of frustration, possibly. Meanwhile, I was backing away, trying to get my phone to shut up.

"No pictures!" Michael shouted.

"I know!" I shouted back. I didn't know how I'd become their focus, but I felt their attention physically, as if it ripped me open so they could look inside me. I was a well-lit billboard in a traffic jam, stuck under everyone's eyes. I couldn't stop feeling it as I tried to get the phone to stop jangling. I was shaking and pushing the wrong buttons.

Of course I had a QikPic app on my phone. Pictures on the fly were my job, after all. So while trying to get the call to go away, I pressed the home button. The phone thought I wanted it to calibrate the light and focus, so it did that in a split second. In the next split second, the flash went off, and the tiny digital excuse for a shutter opened.

The three angry men were bathed in light.

"Oops," I said. Maybe I'd seemed coy. I was as embarrassed as hell.

"I knew I couldn't trust you," Michael said.

"It was an accident."

"I'll get a bouncer," Gene said.

"Go to hell." I was pissed off. Partly, I was angry at myself. I knew how the damn app worked, and I'd let myself get flustered because I was listening to an insider conversation while trying to tamp down a high school attraction while wrangling a stupid app that worked all too well.

What really piqued my rage was that Michael thought I'd taken that picture on purpose. Not that it mattered what he thought of me. Despite that moment of connection and silly encounters in high school that had never amounted to anything, he and I would be separated by velvet ropes and bodyguards in the morning.

"My word is good," I said with my fists balled. He could look at me and see a dirty pap, but I couldn't let him see a liar.

Los Angeles stopped with the next sound.

Clickclickclick. The sound of a shutter, like a hammer coming down repeatedly, froze me. I watched Michael's face change from overwhelmed to angry, his mouth a tight hyphen, as he reached for me then past me.

Behind me, Tom grunted. His voice was a call from my childhood, and the rest went up in chaos. I backed up and fell ass over teakettle on Tom. Michael stood over me with my camera in his hand.

My camera.

"What the—" I didn't get a chance to finish.

I scrambled to get off Tom, skirt hiked over my underpants, and watched Michael throw my camera over the balcony. When I righted myself, Michael was gone, and Tom kneeled behind me. Randee stood behind him with her lipstick smeared.

I turned on him. "What the hell, Tom!"

"That was a money shot!"

"I promised we weren't carrying!"

Below us, in the courtyard, my camera was smashed all over the stones.

As my foster brother went to retrieve the rig, I watched Michael get pulled across the courtyard by his agent. In seeing him through a lens for so many years, I'd forgotten him. Maybe it was circumstance, or maybe it was self-preservation, but I didn't think remembering would do me a bit of good.

Chapter 3

Michael

My name is Michael Greydon. Try not to hold that against me.

I've never wrecked a car, never knocked a girl up and paid her off, never screamed at my driver, never never never.

I think I became a series of nevers, and those nevers made me more valuable to the people who hired me. So I kept it up, and there I was, not wondering why I might grab a camera and throw it off a balcony, but what kind of person did that. I was a paper cutout of a man, blank and ready for anyone else to draw on.

When I first got into the business officially, at eighteen, I was told repeatedly that I didn't need to like my agent. I was told that, as a matter of fact, liking my agent would not only make the task of firing him more difficult but necessary. Agents weren't meant to be sincere, ethical, or good company. Agents were meant to tear out their grandmother's throat and eat her esophagus for a deal.

I was sure Gene Testarossa had used his grandmother's hide for the seats in his Mercedes. At Club NV, I wasn't uncomfortable with the centripetal force on my douchebag agent's moral center. By the time he pulled me away from the scene in the Emerald Room and out to the parking lot, I started to question everything I had been taught.

"Get off me," I said, yanking my arm away.

"What were you doing with her?"

"Talking."

"This is going to cost you more than a camera."

This was a mess. Between Britt breaking a bone and my temper tantrum, we were internet fodder for the rest of the week.

Gene got me into his Mercedes SUV, whipped a U-turn out of the alley, and peeled east as if his ass were on fire, and in a way, it was. His eyes were bugging out, and his finger jabbed at me, clicking the pink gold of his watch.

"Were you doing blow tonight?" he asked in a completely businesslike manner, as if the culmination of his job was in that question.

"What?"

"Were. You. Doing. Blow?" He peeled onto the 10 freeway toward downtown.

"No." I didn't know what he was getting at. I didn't do drugs, and he knew it.

"Then what's with the behavior?"

I leaned back in the seat. I didn't feel right. I felt down, as if the adrenaline spike had drained me of energy. I stepped outside myself and watched the emotional toll of my physical distress. I could use it some time to inform a scene, or a word, or a glance.

I'd been photographed constantly since I was a baby. I had plenty of privilege, but that came with plenty of responsibility. I couldn't show what I was feeling, ever. I had to be nice to everyone all the time, and I couldn't be sick, not really. If I was shooting, my sick day cost everyone millions. If I didn't work every single day I was contracted to, people could lose their jobs. That's what my father had taught me. He said if I insisted on selling my life, if I insisted on getting into the business, then I was accepting responsibilities that weren't to be taken lightly. Everything I did, right or wrong, was seen under a looking glass, disseminated, analyzed by the public, then ignored. And all I ever wanted to be was right.

"You are so lucky I caught you," Gene said. "You looked like you were going to punch someone."

"What was I supposed to do?"

"Act like a goddamn grown-up."

"I cannot believe who this is coming from."

"I'm going to be frank." He changed lanes on the 10, zipping east in a blaze of headlights.

"Good. Be Frank. Because Gene's a dick."

"Tonight, everyone's going to be looking at you. After Britt's fucking meltdown, they're going to wait for *Bullets* to sink. Is that what you want? I mean, no one cares what DMZ says, but once *Variety* starts in, then you start losing the confidence of the studio. Then you know what happens? Money gets pulled. Notes called in. The schedule is screwed, and the bond goes up. Then you have a reputation. You end up not working."

He was talking about my father, who hadn't made a movie in ten years because no one would book a drunk. Gene wasn't a subtle guy, but when it came to my dad, he knew to shut the hell up.

"Where are we going?" I asked.

"Ken."

Ken was my PR guy, a powerhouse rotating in the same moral universe as my agent. But as little as I thought of him, he didn't throw stuff when he got angry.

I stated the obvious. "It's late."

"You can tell him that when we get there."

Downtown appeared over the horizon, a smattering of star-drowning lights. Glass-encrusted shafts hung together in a huddle, and we twisted right into the middle of them.

I knew what I looked like to the public. I looked as if I had all the freedom in the world, but as Gene handed the night valet his keys with an admonition to take it easy and not change the radio stations, I realized I hadn't done a damn thing I wanted to do my whole life. I shut my eyes and tried not to curse repeatedly, drowning out my anger with thoughts of work. Football. Food. But the only thing that washed away the frustration was my curiosity over Shuttergirl.

Chapter 4

Laine

Tom had picked up the pieces of my camera like a baby, then he took Randee's hand. Her eyes lit up like strobe flashes. He yanked her, and we all ran to the Exploder so fast I couldn't keep up. For a guy who had his head up his ass whenever he was working, he seemed competent and together, even purposeful, as if he'd woken up from a long sleep.

I was pissed at him. Livid. But we were on autopilot. I didn't know how to stop the process and bitch out my brother. I only knew how to stop everything and upload the pics. Everything went on hold between the picture getting shot and the upload, because the lapse between the click of the shutter and the pic going online—complete with negotiation, photo retouch, and edited copy—was all of ninety minutes. A ten-minute delay to bitch at Tom could lose the sale.

I stood at the driver's side automatically, hand on the handle and waiting for him to lean over and pop the lock. Randee stood with her hands in front of her.

"He's not driving," I said. I wasn't getting in the back because he'd locked lips with her for fifteen minutes. That was already more explanation than she'd earned.

Pop.

I got in, and Tom and I did our thing. I snapped the camera from him and did quick forensics on the damage. The Canon was busted. The scratches and dings were nothing, but the hairline fracture across the front meant I'd have to buy a new body, and the lens was cracked. This would hurt to the tune of about seven thousand dollars.

"The memory card is shredded," I said, reaching for the laptop and wifi.

Randee sat crammed against the door, hands in her lap. I still hadn't heard her speak.

"I ran it through the internal." He looked into the back. "There's food and water in the cooler if you want." He plugged in the cable. "You gross industry douche, I got you."

"He's not," I said.

"Who are you defending?"

The picture came up. The angle could not have been more perfect. Michael was caught mid-camera grab, looking like an enraged, entitled little prince. The public loved seeing them rise and loved seeing them break. Tom was about to make a couple months' rent and then some.

"Wait, Tom."

He didn't look up from his screen. "What?"

"I'm in the picture."

He hit Send. "You wanna sign a release?"

"Tom!"

"What?"

"You don't talk to me? You don't ask me? It's my camera, my face—"

"Your back."

"You are an asshole."

I knew Randee was back there. Her presence loomed like a video camera in a bedroom.

"It was a shot," Tom protested. "You told me—"

"Don't—"

"Get the shot if the shot can be got. That's what you've always said." He tossed me the keys. "Drive."

"I told Leo we didn't have our rigs."

"You lied," he said.

"*You* lied. You 'borrowed' my rig, and you lied. That is not cool. He could get fired."

I'd never spoken to Tom like that because I'd never had to. He was fragile and passive, which explained too much of his childhood.

He straightened up and got onto the freeway. I faced front and stewed. He knew I wouldn't cut him off, not for this infraction at least, but I didn't know what to do with this level of rage. One, because he was my brother, but two, because the picture was going to net him a bundle, and I wouldn't stop him from making a bunch of money. I was trapped by my own loyalties. But

I wanted to punch him in the face because I was who I was.

"So what?" Tom said. "I'll make a nice take on this, and I can buy you a new camera and dinner."

"I lost my appetite," I said, pulling away from the curb. "I am so mad at you. Do not speak to me again."

"Come on, Laine." He flicked my knee. "Let's meet Irv. You can get mad at him."

The sad thing was, Irv, our mentor, had joints that ached late in the night. He was probably already awake and would be happy to meet us at three in the morning.

"Oh, Irv is going to eviscerate you good."

From the back, Randee snickered. I turned around. She just sat straight.

"You all right back there?" I asked.

"Yes. Thank you." She smiled.

I did not trust that girl. I'd wanted to make things happen for Tom, and I had, but I determined that I'd never do that again. Nothing good could come from this.

We waited for his upload, and the calls started coming in. The heat on the picture and the story of the temper tantrum surrounding it was so hot, we had to pull over three times while Tom and Kill Photo negotiated the sale. Even though I wanted to strangle him, I made hand movements to communicate when he could ask for more money. If he was going to screw up, he should at least get paid for it.

It took us over an hour to even get to downtown, and by the time we hit club traffic on Olive Street, the picture was just about to go viral.

"Poor Michael," I said.

"He broke your camera," Randee said from the back.

I shrugged. "Still. It didn't belong there." I punched Tom in the arm for the tenth time. "You're lucky about that nice payday."

"Maybe the guy who threw it should replace it."

"Don't even…" I let myself drift off. Tom had to replace it, because there was no way Michael Greydon would lower himself to speak to me ever again, and that shouldn't have bothered me. I didn't need to talk to him to do my job. But he'd touched me, and I still felt the electricity of it. Jesus, I wanted him, and I hated myself for it.

Chapter 5

Michael

Kenneth Braque, LLP, was the biggest public relations firm in Los Angeles. He did politicians, doctors, lawyers, corporations, and industry types like myself.

His expansive lobby was quiet at that hour. The floor had been cleaned and buffed, the plants watered to a glisten, the glass and metal polished, and the sound system silenced. The night watchman looked up from his book. His face was blue from the bank of screens. I'd never seen him before, but then again, I'd never shown up at three in the morning.

"Sign in, please," he said.

Gene snapped up the clipboard. "Did Ken Braque get here?"

"Yeah," he said then pointed at me. "You're the guy from *Dead Lawyer*, aren't you?"

"Yes, I was in that."

"Man, that was, like, the worst I've ever seen. When that building collapsed, I was like, man, you have got to be kidding."

"Yeah, well…" I shrugged. "No one tries to make a bad movie."

"You were good though, man. You were good."

"Thank you." I shook his hand and shot him a smile.

We got two steps away before I heard him say, "Hey! Can I get a picture?"

I never denied a fan a picture. Ever.

I stepped toward him, but Gene got between me and the guard. "Dude, no. Get behind your desk."

The guard got behind his desk, and Gene and I got into the elevator.

"Think." Gene poked his head so hard his stupid watch rattled. "That guy posts your picture to Facebook, and in fifteen minutes, everyone knows you were at your publicist's in the middle of the night, an hour after you threw a tantrum at a pap."

"Has anyone heard from Britt? Is she okay?" I wanted someone else to worry about. Worrying about myself wasn't any fun.

"She's fine. But your movie is screwed."

I didn't care about the movie, but my father did. I'd wanted to do it for him. I wanted to rescue him, but it was harder than it looked.

Gene put his hand on my shoulder. "We're going to get you out of this, buddy."

I had to swallow the words *get your hand off me*.

The elevator doors opened into a huge, empty lobby with an unmanned reception station. Ken's offices had always impressed me. Tucked into the corner of a building made of glass, it made me feel as though we'd walked onto a precipice. No paper, pen, computer cord, book, or tchotchke was left unattended, undusted, or unorganized. It was always like that, even for surprise visits.

The lights were out, except for the absolute necessities, and the space was dead. Ken stood at the reception desk, wearing plaid pajama pants and slippers, a laptop illuminating his face. His hoodie said Harvard University across the front in grey felt.

"Greydon," he said without further greeting, "were you on coke?"

"Come on, man."

He looked at me over the top of his reading glasses. "Drinking?"

"Hey, Ken." Gene held out his hand. "I was there, and—"

"Not that much," I cut Gene off when Ken ignored his hand.

"Then what the hell were you thinking?" Ken asked.

"That I needed to give you something to do. You know, earn your retainer."

He slid off his glasses. "Save the smart mouth routine for the ladies." He turned the laptop toward me.

He was on DMZ, looking at a picture of me in all my rage, my fist pushed forward. I looked vicious and brutal. A director couldn't have constructed a better shot to make me look as if I was on the edge of sanity. The violence of the moment was stark. My jaw clenched. My fist tight. The color drained from the scene by the low light. I had been grabbing a camera, not hitting anyone, but that didn't matter. The picture didn't show my thoughts, as few as they were.

"I suggest you don't read the comments," Ken said. "They had no business up there." Gene pointed at the screen.

"Apparently they did," I grumbled.

"And nobody gives a shit." Ken snapped the laptop shut.

"These paps are out of control," Gene said. "They worked like a team. She softened him up, and he took the picture."

"This is Tom Schmidt and Laine Cartwright. They don't have to work that hard."

"She was flashing her tits and he was taking the picture," Gene protested.

"The one he threw?" Ken replied dryly.

"I'll replace the camera," I said.

"They better not try to sue him." Gene held up his hand, showing off his ten-pound pink gold watch.

"You stink at this, Testarossa," Ken grumbled.

"You know what, Gene?" I said. "Thanks for the lift. You should go." He looked about to say something, but I cut him off. "I'll call you when we're done."

He glanced at Ken, who said, "I'm sure you have other clients. We've got this, bud. Go take care of Britt."

"Yeah," Gene said. "Cool, cool." He shook my hand then Ken's at the door.

After Ken was gone, my public relations guy didn't waste a second before getting down to business. We hadn't even left the empty reception area.

"Tom Schmidt is easy. We'll work something out with his agent. Laine Cartwright's dicier. If she so much as skinned her knee, you're in for it. She's super tough. Twenty-five. Been at this since she was seventeen. She gets the dirty laundry big money pics: Tawny, London, Lindsay, you. She's extremely aggressive, the pap other paps follow. Got a way of landing in shit. Stop me when I'm telling you things you already know."

"I know her name, what she does, and you should know… about the laundry…" I paused, and he raised an eyebrow. "She and I were at Breakfront together."

"Oh, God. No."

"Oh, God. Yes."

"You were intimate with her."

"No. I mean, yes, but…" I rubbed my eyes. I'd been tired before I left the club. This was more exhausting than anything I'd ever done.

"Get to the point," Ken said. "I have Britt's lawyer flying into LAX in two hours."

"It was nothing." Saying that felt deeply wrong, as if I was telling a whopper of a lie. "It was nothing actionable."

"Was there penetration? Just tell me so I can earn my retainer. Are you her baby daddy?"

I laughed. "No."

"You swear?"

I made the Boy Scout sign. "On my Eagle Scout pin. It was worthy of the Hallmark channel."

"Why didn't you finish the job?"

"She was fifteen, and I had a girlfriend."

His eyes flickered, and I knew he was doing a quick subtraction problem. "Statutory."

"Jesus, Ken, I held her hand."

"Spare me the boring details," Ken said, "Did you tell her anything she doesn't need to know? Does she have anything to hold over you?"

"No."

"And the guy she was with? You know him? He got anything?"

"No. I never met him before."

"All right." He zipped up his hoodie like a punctuation. He lived for this. "Let me see what I can dig up."

"You going to tell everyone who she's sleeping with?" I joked.

"If it'll help us." He was serious.

I felt as if I'd forgotten who I was talking to. I'd hired my public relations person using the same metrics I'd used to hire my agent.

"I want to replace the camera and be done with it," I said. "Right now, I'm more worried about Britt holding up production."

"You and me both."

"I want to wake up Steven and get some rewrites. Put her character in a chair—"

"Done already. I have a call in to Gareth as well." He turned back to his laptop. "Go get some sleep."

"Ken," I said, and he turned from his computer to look at me over his glasses. "Do I have to worry about this?"

He sighed as if I were asking a question so stupid, a four-year-old would have dismissed it. "You're a nice Midwestern boy who was born in the wrong city. That's what they love about you. You're a born-and-raised Hollywood actor with Midwestern morals and Midwestern manners. Go home, and go to bed. Rest like your life depended on it. And don't look at the internet."

Chapter 6

Laine

Los Angeles had a reputation for being warm all the time and brutally hot sometimes, but the facts were more complex. In early November, the days hung around room temperature, but as soon as the sun set and the sky faded to the color of the cold, deep sea, a wall of still air proved that Los Angeles wasn't a warm place. It was a cold place with a hot sun.

Tom called Irving as we drove east, shimmying left the whole way. We were night owls, hovering over the city, and as tired as I was, my schedule didn't include going to sleep at three a.m. It was dinner time.

"He'll meet us at Carnosa," Tom said.

"Drop me at home."

He was sullen. More monochrome than usual. If I kept on him, I would turn him off to making money. Maybe that wasn't a bad idea. He was terrible at it.

"I'll get you a new camera," he mumbled.

"That's not the point."

"But—"

"Forget it," I said. "Just give me a minute to stop wanting to kill you."

I had to figure out a way to stop being mad at Tom, because without him, I had friends and tips and working relationships but no family.

We'd almost stopped speaking completely once, when he was dating an actress whose name I'd forgotten. She was a waitress, to be honest, and always would be, but she took issue with him working with me. She didn't like the stakeouts or the chases, and she railed on him about privacy every time I walked into the room. Tom had the roof over his head because of his celebrity shooting, and he was able to pay for dinner whenever they went out, but she didn't like the way he made his money. He started to believe she was right.

When he was nearly broke and still refused to spend a few hours across the street from Ute Thurnam to put food on the table, I finally broke down and told him this girl (whose name still eluded me) was worried about the privacy of her dream celebrity self, who would dump him the minute she became worthy of a paparazzo, which she never would. She was one of the useless romantics who thought saying "I am successful! I AM an actress!" would make it happen. But it wouldn't. Not without talent and not with her head in the clouds. Not unless she worked her ass off and beat the streets. She was a failure before she'd even started, a game player, a cockeyed dreamer, a waitress for life. She thought stuff just happened without working for it.

We hadn't spoken for three weeks after that, which was exactly as long as his relationship continued. In that time, I felt broken, wavering between staunch refusal to move from my position and the quivering need to apologize. I hated myself for needing him. He was a pain in my ass, but he was my only family, and without him, I felt unsure of my place in the world.

In the end, he'd called and said I was right about everything. The Nameless Waitress was horrible and useless, a cheating, lying whore. I agreed of course, because she'd turned out to be as faithless as any dreamer, and I gave my sympathies while feeling warmth and relief. Everything was back to normal.

Irving met us at the Carnosa food truck, which was in its usual spot in a downtown parking lot. They'd set out a few chairs and tables, and Irving had already staked us out a corner. We gave Tom money, which he refused, and he and Randee went to order. Irving fished my laptop and my busted camera out of Tom's bag.

At sixty years old, give or take, Irv looked about seventy. His right arm was skinny, permanently bent, and missing a pinkie finger. As a teen, he'd been in a car accident outside the Wiltern Theater, and that arm had never healed properly. Only the thoughtfulness of a photojournalist who had been shooting the band had helped his family find the driver who had hit him.

"Nice mess, this," he grumbled when he found the picture of Michael on my laptop. "Probably the best picture your brother's taken in his life."

Irving had picked me out of a crowd of kids my last semester of Breakfront. As a storied portraitist, known for his work with celebrities and politicians, he was one of the school's many featured teachers. When I'd disappeared for a week after Mister Hatch filed for divorce, Irving found me in a squalid home in Westlake, back with Tom as a matter of luck. He offered to mentor me, and I said Tom came with the package.

"I can't believe I'm in it," I said. "Now I have to either let it go without a problem, which makes me an accessory to him bringing a rig where he shouldn't have, which destroys my reputation, or I tell everyone he stole my camera and destroy his. Either way, the focus is on me, which isn't good for my prospects."

"Maybe it's time your brother started making his own way."

"He'd starve."

Irving laughed, showing his rough teeth. "Laine." He always pronounced my name with the *e* at the end, and he was the only one I let get away with it. "I keep waiting for your wake-up call."

"Well, this wasn't it."

"You could do some damage as a real journalist."

"Is this why you got in the car at the crack of dawn? To give me a hard time for making a living?"

"I gotta tell you, sweetheart, I can't let it go." He rapped his lame knuckles on the wood table. "This is the exact right time for you to get out."

Irv had been like a father to me when I needed guidance, and though he'd earned the right to say whatever he wanted to me, I wasn't used to getting scolded. I was used to simply going where my gut instructed.

"You taught me this job," I snapped. I was tired and trapped and still smarting from the remembrance of Michael. I felt worthless enough without Irv poking my raw places.

"I taught you how to take pictures. I didn't pick you out of a few thousand so you could stand outside clubs in the middle of the night. You have a gift, and you're throwing it away on trash. You were meant for better."

"You're full of it. You've encouraged me since I was fifteen. You mentored me to hustle Hollywood, and if hustling means something different to me than it means to you, that doesn't change the facts."

"You're wasting your life. Think about it," he said.

"'Don't think.' Isn't that what you said? 'Shoot with your eye, not your brain?'"

"I was talking about the art, not the business."

"It's still good advice," I said.

"Youth. Swear to God, it's wasted on the young."

I sighed. "I'm sorry, Irv. I'm not trying to throw your words back in your face."

"But you are." His eyes were sunken, and his skin was ashen.

I hadn't thought about Irv getting old until that moment, but even his voice had aged. His transition from kooky middle-aged guy to concerned old man had happened while I wasn't looking.

"I'll think about it," I said, tapping my phone, as if my attention on it would make a tip come through it. But there was no tip.

Tom was on his way back with a tray and a girl in sparkly shoes. She had her arm looped in his.

"God," I said, "I hope she's better than the last one."

"You and me both."

Chapter 7

Michael

What had it been about her? And why did I care?

I had problems on top of problems. I had neither the desire nor the time to let a woman get under my skin. It wouldn't be fair in any case. I was going to do the movie and get my father back on his feet, and I didn't have a minute for anything else.

But once I'd retrieved my car from Venice and started the drive home, my concerns over the movie and my PR problems were replaced by excitement. Laine. Right in front of me. She had gone from a beautiful and sullen teen to a stunning and witty woman. I'd felt explosive, like a test tube of nitrous, ready to detonate at the slightest agitation, as soon as she was within reach. I had to pull over at a bus stop and see if I still had her number. I synched my phone and scrolled through ancient backups. My head was down and clear of worries about anything but what the girl in the bleachers thought of me.

This was a one-eighty. I was supposed to run from her. I had a bizarre relationship with paps, so intimate and so distant. A one-way mirror through which they could see me, but I couldn't see them.

Her number was gone, of course.

Even at three something in the morning, I could text Monie and have her dig up Laine's number. In my world, a ridiculous request was almost normal. I pressed the phone to my lips then just did it. If Monie didn't want to answer the text, she didn't have to.

I didn't wait for an answer. Sitting in a bus stop, even in the middle of the night, was an invitation to be seen by strangers.

As I snaked up the hill, I checked for SUVs parked across the street from my house. Nothing yet. Even paparazzi slept sometimes. I hit the gate remote and turned into the drive. Little holes the diameter of camera lenses had been poked into my hedges. In the end, I'd just covered the inside of them with tarp, turned my gate into solid metal, and tried not to be home, ever.

I stopped inside the driveway and pulled the emergency brake. When the gate closed, I took out my phone. Monie had messaged me back.

—213-343-5529—

I fist-pumped. Monie was getting a fat bonus. I dialed the area code then stopped. I'd forgotten what Laine had become. Had she put a hole in my hedge? I had a career that left me no time for relationship maintenance. If I was going to be irresponsible and get involved with a woman, I probably couldn't pick anyone worse than Laine Cartwright.

But when she'd given me a do-over at Club NV, it was like a drop of sugar water on a dry tongue. Even after Britt, and Ken, and everything that had happened between meeting her and sitting in my car in my driveway, I wanted to experience the excitement of her again.

I had no reason to step outside my path. I was set. It was like senior year all over. Everything was a go.

Back then, I'd been tightly scheduled and ready at the gate. I had Lucy, who I loved as much as an eighteen-year-old can love anyone, and I felt settled there. Acting was the least risky career path I could have chosen, but to calm my father's disapproval, I'd majored in English lit, knowing full well the drama department was ready to switch me. I'd gone and auditioned for two features behind my dad's back but with my mother's approval.

I hadn't known the girl who started sitting in the tennis court bleachers in October, and as I tried for that inside corner over and over, she didn't seem to be there because she knew me either. Her face was buried in a book, legs akimbo over the seats in front of her as if she were ready to spring.

"Do you know her?" I'd asked Lucy one night when she came by at the end of practice.

My girlfriend looked at the bleachers and wrinkled her nose. "That's the new Hatch kid. Sophomore, but she's way behind on everything. Dumb as a post. And cranky. I mean, they pulled her out of the gutter. You'd think she'd be happy. Hello?"

I was fascinated. The gutter? What was it like in the gutter? What kind of person did it make you? And how could something so beautiful, even from twenty feet below, come from the gutter? Who was she? Inside. I think I looked up at her—with a sneaker leveraged against the seat in front, the other knee draped over the armrest to the side, a book in her lap, and impossibly long hair waterfalling over her shoulders—for one second too long.

Lucy had tugged on my jacket. That long look had caused no end of trouble for the gutter girl.

It was either that, or months later, when I lobbed a ball up there to get her attention.

"Thank you!" I called. Tennis etiquette dictated that I say "thank you" instead of, "Hey, can you get that for me?"

She put her book down, untangled herself from the seats, and grabbed the ball.

"Do you talk?" I shouted.

She folded her arms. "When I have something to say."

She'd been so hard, so impossibly distant. Her unavailability was thrilling. I had absolutely no control over my curiosity.

"And you have nothing to say?" I shouted.

"I do. Your coach says to give it a rest twice a week. You should listen."

I could have said the same to her, but she probably needed to study more than I needed to practice.

She threw the ball down. It went wild and landed on the other side of the court. "Sorry," she called down. "Can I have a do-over?"

I lobbed another ball up to her. "Thank you."

She scuttled for it and threw it back. It landed close enough to me to be called a successful throw. She'd waved and sat back down, twisting her legs around each other and getting back to her studies.

I realized I'd been in the front seat of my car and stroking the edge of my phone for way too long, remembering her. She was a vortex. I'd avoided getting swallowed up in her once, and now, more than ever, I needed to avoid it again. I would replace the camera, finish the movie with my father, and do whatever I had to do afterward.

I tapped the little garbage can by Monie's text, and the DELETE key came up.

Chapter 8

Laine

Tom slid in next to Irv with his tray of tacos and horchatas. Randee waited at the head of the table for a second before slipping in next to me. She gathered up a greasy waxed bag of fries and a packet of ketchup.

Tom doled out the food. "Kill wanted to know how I got into the Emerald Room."

"How *did* you get into the Emerald Room?" Irving asked.

"Laine got us in."

"Please tell me you won't make that public," I growled.

"No," Tom said, smearing green salsa all over his burrito. "I told them I went in as a civilian. That's my story, and I'm sticking to it."

"You might get sued," I said as I noticed Randee drawing a perfect red line of ketchup across a single fry.

"Or Kill could get sued," Irving said. "They go after the deep pockets."

The color drained from Tom's face, if there had been any there to begin with. "I didn't realize."

"I'm not saying I told you so." I pointed my straw at him. "But I want to. I'm saying, if you act docile, they'll drop it."

"How do you do it?" he asked. "How do you chase so hard and never get into trouble?"

"I know where the lines are." I said it self-righteously even though I shouldn't have. I kept in the career lines, but I hadn't gone into the Emerald Room so my brother could meet a girl. My ass had been on fire to see Michael again, to talk to him, and I had been looking for an excuse to make it happen. Why did I only realize my motivations after the fact? I shook my head. "I wouldn't worry about it. America's Boyfriend won't rock the boat hard enough to get in on the lawsuit, and everyone will be bored of it in a week. In the meantime, lay low."

"What am I supposed to do for money?" He pushed his food away. "I made a good take on this, but a couple of *weeks?*"

Randee spoke up. "We'll get you some work with the band. It'll be fun!"

Tom shrugged as if that was nothing, but I saw the tension melt off him. For the next half an hour, we talked about anything else: what movies were being made where, the best spots to shoot, what kind of camera Tom should get me.

"Seven grand?" he said, his face puckered.

"At least. Unless you can get a discount from Merv. I'm sorry, but I'm not letting you off the hook for this."

My phone rang with a number I didn't recognize. Usually that meant a good tip, and usually I'd get a shot of adrenaline and reach for my rig before I even answered. But this time, I wondered for a split second if it was someone corroborating whether or not I had been on the balcony with Michael.

I knew right then that I wouldn't lie for Tom. "Hello?"

"I'm sorry, I just realized it's the middle of the night."

"Excuse me?" I said.

"Is this Laine Cartwright?"

"Is that who you dialed?"

There was the pause that usually came after an aggressive reply to a request for immediate self-identification.

"I hope so, or I'm going to have to apologize to a complete stranger."

I didn't recognize his voice until he was in the middle of that sentence, and my knees turned viscous.

"I know it's irregular, but my assistant got your number," Michael said. "I hope you're not upset with me."

I glanced at Irv then Tom. If they could see the quivering in my gut, they gave no sign.

"How did she get it?" I said, stalling.

"I can ask her in the morning. I don't want to wake her again."

"Can you hold on a second?" I slipped off the bench. It was rude to talk on the phone at the table, but more importantly, I needed to hear what he had to say without Irving watching me and Randee listening like a boom mic. I tried to keep my head as I crouched on the curb of the parking lot. It was relatively quiet, and the smell from the dumpster wasn't so bad.

"I'm sorry I left like that," he said.

"Don't be. Tom should be apologizing. He crossed a line. And me too. I didn't mean to take a picture on the balcony. It was an app fail."

"I'll get your brother a new camera."

"It was mine," I said, "so don't worry about it. I have a good spare."

"I want to replace it."

I smiled a little. "You were always so decent. But no. He wasn't supposed to bring it into the club, so he's got to shell out the cash."

"My father would be disappointed if I didn't take responsibility for my actions."

"It was a nice rig." I leaned against the cinderblock wall and rolled a half-empty beer bottle with my heel. "I don't want to put you out."

"I'll borrow money from my parents if I have to."

I smiled. I couldn't help it. The fact that he'd thrown my camera from a balcony clamored for my attention and told me I should be mad. I was mad. I was boiling mad. But then again, I wasn't.

"I can't come to your office to pick it up. People will talk." I kicked the empty beer bottle until it rolled a few feet and clattered. I hoped he couldn't hear it, or he'd know I was in a filthy parking lot.

"I'll bring it to you."

"That works both ways. If I'm seen with you, it's bad. No one wants to tip a pap who's friends with A-listers. You can just call Merv's Photo and have them leave it for me."

That was the most obvious solution. His assistant or whomever would make a call, I'd walk into the photo store, see a hundred people I knew, pick up a camera, and get away clean. It was the best and only way to manage this, but I didn't want that. I wanted to suggest it, but at the thought of seeing him again, I felt heady and excited. I prayed just a little that there was a reason that wouldn't work.

"Is that how you think of me?" he said. "An A-lister?"

How I thought of him? I hadn't stopped thinking about him since we'd crossed paths. I thought about how he would taste, how he would sound low in his throat, how he'd touch me.

"I gotta make a living." I didn't think about my auto-answer until after I said it. Then I had to backpedal. "But it was nice to meet the guy with the bad serve again."

"I had a great serve. I just couldn't hit the inside corner."

"You should have listened to your coach," I whispered, snickering. God, what was happening to me? Was I *giggling?*

A busboy came out of the back of the restaurant with a bucket of onion leavings. His apron dripped with raw chicken gunk, and his gloves were caked with who-even-knew.

"How about this?" he said. "I have an event at the Breakfront School tomorrow night. They're great at locking the joint down. I'll get you in, and I can give it to you there."

"You'll get me in?" I said, assuming he could hear my sarcasm.

"Why? Did you have an invitation?"

"Oh, screw you, superstar."

Of course I hadn't been invited. I'd been a student there for fifteen minutes and made nothing of myself that anyone thought was important. Even the people who bought my pictures did it in the shadows. No one invited me to a party unless there was a velvet rope for me to stand behind.

But Michael and his parents went every year. That had always been a temptation for me.

"Are your parents going this year?" I kicked myself before the last word was out of my mouth.

"Oh, I remember now…you have a Brooke thing."

He called his parents by their first names, of course. So Hollywood. It was almost charming on him.

"It's not a big deal. I'm sorry. Forget I asked."

"I was going to introduce you to her when we were in school, but you never let me."

Because I'd die, obviously. I wasn't a fan of anyone. I wasn't a follower of the stars unless following them could make me money. I didn't care one way or the other what happened to any of them. Except Brooke Chambers. I'd seen Michael's mother in *Love in Between* when I was eleven, and I'd never been the same. Her dewy goodness, generosity, and kindness broke my heart. I didn't want to *be* her. I wanted to be near her in a way I couldn't explain. I saw every movie she was in, and when I met Michael, I spent an hour explaining her virtues as an actress.

"Well, if your mother's not going," I said, "I'm not going."

"See you there, Shuttergirl."

I hung up without saying good-bye but smiling nonetheless.

Chapter 9

Laine

Every year I managed to avoid photographing the Breakfront Autumn Gala. The guys with the press cards stood in the front to shoot what they were told, and the paps stood in the back, getting the gritty shit at night's end.

I didn't avoid conflict; I ran headlong into it. But Breakfront? Photographing the comers and goers was some aggravation I didn't need, because not everyone there would be a celebrity, and at my old school, that could be a problem. Actors tended to look at the camera as a partner, even when they weren't working. Non-celebs had a way of looking at the person holding the rig, not the lens, and if someone—say, model-turned-agency-head Lucy Betencourt—saw me in a crowd of paparazzi... well, I might as well be wearing a G-string with dollar bills taped to it.

"No," I said to my girlfriend Phoebe, who sat at my dining room table with a Starbucks and an open copy of *YOU BRIDAL* magazine. "I'm not going. I have a bad feeling."

"I can't believe you're going to miss the gala." She snapped the brakes off on her wheelchair and put the magazine on her lap before she rolled out. "Everyone goes."

Everyone. What a loaded word. Everyone to the exclusion of anyone. But Phoebe had spent her whole childhood in doctors' offices, flipping through celebrity magazines. Eventually she became an entertainment lawyer with plenty of access to the people in those magazines, yet she never lost her girlish fascination with them. I loved her.

"You should go and get my camera. That's the answer. You go."

"Me?" She pointed at herself then opened her magazine again. "What's the point of that? Why are you pushing this off? Why can't you just go have fun?"

I paced the concrete, the sound of my boots echoing against the high ceilings. "I love that you think everything's about fun. I really do. But I have a bad feeling."

Phoebe snapped the bridal magazine pages with intent. "You always have bad feelings when things might change."

"I like the way things are."

"Mm-hm. What are you wearing?"

I sighed. "Help me pick, would you?"

She rolled toward the bedroom as if she was in a race. "I thought you'd never ask."

We went through my clothes and shoes and chose a simple thing from the back of my closet. I ignored the gut instinct that something was going to go wrong.

Usually, I listened to my gut. Until the night at Club NV, it had been a rule. If I had a feeling something would go wrong, I just stopped doing whatever it was, and the feeling went away. So all I had to do to be safe was not go. I blamed Phoebe for my willingness. She had everything I lacked—a good family and a fiancé who loved her—and I had legs and an invitation to a hot Hollywood party.

"You need to shut your phone," Phoebe said, choosing just the right bracelet and slipping it on my wrist. "It's nothing but temptation to split."

As if on cue, my phone lit up. It was my contact at Sequoia.

I answered. "Yeah?"

"Britt Ravenor's being released in an hour."

"Thanks," I said, but she'd already hung up.

I'd get a nice take for that shot. I could make it to Sequoia in forty minutes, more than enough time to find out which exit they were using, and get very, very close. I could dig up my spare rig, go get the shot in my good clothes, and go to Breakfront late. Maybe then the bad feeling would pass. Or more likely, night would come, and my phone would rattle, and I'd use money as a reason to avoid the gala.

I was all right with that. I didn't need to go to a fancy party. Though it had been a pricey camera, I could still get Tom to dig deep into his pockets and replace it.

I talked myself out of going to the party as I helped Phoebe into her car, then I went back upstairs to my huge, empty loft. All I had to do was text

Michael my apologies.

**—Hey, sorry I can't make it. We can either
forget the camera or do the Merv's thing—**

The bad feeling went away as soon as I hit send. Even as I yanked off the dress, I found myself hoping that he'd text back that he wanted to see me anyway. I didn't have a chance to question my girlish desire, because three seconds after I hit send, the text was bounced.

Of course. He was a superstar. He couldn't get incoming calls from numbers outside his little goddamn list. I wanted to throw the phone out the window.

Not counting the bedroom, which was separated by a wall of shelves, my loft was a huge open space with fifteen-foot ceilings, a few exposed brick walls, and one huge wall that was smooth and plastered. On it, I'd put a custom mural of a map of Los Angeles. Even though the street names were so small I had to get nose-close to see them, the map took up the entire wall. It stretched from the Pacific to the easternmost points of the San Gabriel Valley, from Flintridge, which was only visible with a ladder, to San Pedro, touching the floor.

I cursed it, claiming ownership of every street, and stopped on the west side, just south of Brentwood. In a tiny green patch behind a hedge was a school for the specialest snowflakes money could raise.

The tennis courts were the size of memory chips and just as green.

Why was I so enraged? Why did that make me wrestle myself back into the fancy black dress with the lace trim? Why did I poke the dangling silver earrings into my ears as if I was stabbing myself, and why did the feeling that something was going to go wrong just get stronger and stronger when I jammed my feet into red-soled pumps?

Because I didn't want to go to a stupid party. I wanted to see the guy with the serve again, and there was a pretty good chance that if I didn't go tonight, I'd never see Michael again without a lens between us.

To hell with it.

Let it all go wrong.

Chapter 10

Laine

I had a black Audi that I kept spotless. If I wanted to park outside fancy clubs and restaurants, if I wanted to stop in some of the best neighborhoods in the city to shoot out the window, my car needed to fit in to the point of invisibility. A Mercedes would have been even more inconspicuous, but sometimes a girl has to make a concession to her own taste.

I pulled up to the Breakfront guard and told him my name. He looked on his little clipboard. He was a nice-looking kid with light brown hair finger-spiked at the top, which had been the style two years before. Clean-shaven with a sweet mouth and a rock-hard body under his generic blue shirt, he smiled at me with caps, and I knew he was an actor biding his time. I smiled back.

"Hang on for a second, ma'am."

I tapped the wheel, looking inside the grounds. I'd always gone in through the student entrance, and this entrance, for parents and benefactors, was older, more elaborate, and verdant within an inch of its life. It had been designed to provide a feeling of peace and safety. During my first visit through this entrance, during the interview with my new, and quite temporary, parents, I'd felt safe, as if I was returning home.

I didn't have the same feeling as the blond guard tapped my name and creds into the computer, but I remembered it. I remembered how real it felt and how fake it had been.

"Miss Cartwright?" he said, leaning down.

"Am I not on the guest list?" I flicked my eyes at the clock. Could I still make it to Sequoia?

"You are, but I hate to say this—maybe I should get a supervisor?"

"Just tell me."

"Well, you're on the guest list, but our system pulled you up on the 'no entry' list. It's kind of like a 'no fly' list that the TSA keeps but—"

"Did it say why? Did I commit an armed robbery?"

"It just says you're a photographer-slash-journalist. This list carries over year after year, so maybe someone with the same name had a problem with a benefactor or board member years ago?"

I didn't say anything. I was too stunned.

"I'm happy to get you a supervisor. I'm sure it's a mistake, but he has to sign off on it."

"It's fine." I rolled up my window.

He raised the gate behind me, and I backed out. I felt nothing, not even disappointment. No, I didn't care at all. I was going to get my head-to-toe of Britt getting out of the hospital and—damnit, if I cried, I would totally mess up my mascara, and that was not cool. This was *not cool.*

I'd gone to the Breakfront School, same as anyone. Michael was on the board at twenty-eight, as was Lucy Betencourt. But me? I'd gone there, and it was mine, board or no. As much as Los Angeles. As much as Balonna Creek or the Arroyos. Mine, mine, mine. I would not ask permission to be a citizen of my own damn city.

I turned off San Vicente and parked on a side street, trying to breathe normally without gulping for air. The tennis courts were across the street, behind fences and hedges, like the camera I didn't care about, and Michael, who strangely, I did care about. I wanted to show him what kind of woman I'd become, what kind of woman he'd left behind. I wanted to show him my heels and my long legs and everything he'd missed. I wanted to see him up close again, to dissect how he'd changed, how his soft skin had become rougher, his jaw more defined, his jade eyes more mature with concerns and thoughtfulness. His hair had gotten darker and a little wavier, and I wanted to inspect it for change, to ask what had happened in the years past. And now, poof. Never.

A text came in.

—Fiona Drazen's at Tinkerbell's with a new guy—

Nothing in my life had changed. I just had to continue as always. I couldn't make it to Tinkerbell's, not with my spare rig across town, but it was Thursday night. My phone would light up like a Christmas tree in an hour.

I checked my passenger-side mirror so I could pull out. I could see down the block and across San Vicente. The green-tarped gates of the tennis courts were centered in the oval of the mirror, objects closer than they appeared.

I'd studied in the tennis bleachers partly because they were relatively quiet and unpopulated in winter, but also because I could exit the school from there without being seen by anyone who would hand me a professionally printed Future Prostitutes of America application. I could slip out unseen and unscathed through a patch of trees and a little-known gate meant for emergency crews. It set off an alarm for half a second until the gate shut behind me. From there, I just cut across the golf course and onto San Vicente.

I still felt the gnaw of something going wrong. With it, excitement flowed through my veins like a drug.

I shut the car and got out. Breakfront was mine.

Chapter 11

Michael

"Here's what I want," I told Steven in my most modulated tone. "I want you to play with that schedule so we're shooting for the next three weeks. This delay cannot happen."

We stood in the foyer outside the ballroom, our anti-social postures a temporary bulwark against intrusion. I'd tried to get an appointment with the director of *Bullets*, but the fallout from Britt's accident had kept him busier than me.

"We frontloaded the schedule. We can afford it and still make release," he reassured me.

"I don't care about the release."

"You should. It's your Oscar."

"This delay cannot happen." I was shouting down an alley. More than twenty-four hours had passed, and the delay was happening.

"What's the problem, Mike?" Steven put out his arms, the ice clinking in his whiskey sour. "Gareth looks like shit on a cracker. He needs the time off if you ask me."

I leaned a little closer, my eye contact transmitting seriousness and secrecy. "Look, have you talked to him?"

"Yes?"

"He's holding himself together with spit and chewing gum."

"He's not on the bottle. I'd know," Steven said.

He wasn't. Not yet. But he had a failing liver and an addiction that would only be slowed by work.

"He's not," I said, "but I know the patterns. He needs this movie. He needs for it to happen, and he needs to get treatment or fall off the wagon. Soon."

The director thought he was just dealing with a Britt nightmare. I'd promised him my father would stay sober for production. That was the deal.

I glanced over Steven's shoulder to break eye contact. Through the layers of guests milling and mingling, I saw Laine, neck craned to catch my eye, carrying an aura all her own.

I hadn't felt more than curiosity when we met all those years ago, and though the curiosity had a mile-wide sexual streak, I wasn't ready for it. But this woman, right now? I was ready, and she looked delicious, soaked with the sweet, tart sticky juice of the forbidden. It must have been all over my face, because Steven looked around in the middle of a sentence.

"Do I know her?" he said.

"Do you?"

"I feel like I do, but I can't place her."

I hadn't foreseen a problem when I put her on the guest list and paid for her ticket, but that had been stupid and naïve. The room between us was full of people she'd shot, whose images she'd sold for an amount commensurate with their invasiveness. There was too much room between us. I saw Theo muscle through the crowd toward her then Janice, who'd had a sex tape foible only weeks before.

"Steven," I said, wanting to close the conversation before I got sucked into her sphere, "we talked about this. The cirrhosis will kill him."

"Let me ask you something," Steven said pointedly, even as I wanted to break away and head for Laine. "Let's say Britt didn't break something. What were you going to do after we were done shooting? He's going to drink again."

"I don't know," I said. "I figured if I could show him thirty days wouldn't kill him, he'd get treatment."

Steven patted my shoulder as if comforting me and encouraging me at the same time. There was something slightly patronizing in it, but I didn't care. Laine needed me.

I painted on a smile and walked to her. With her little clutch in front of her, chin up, she walked straight for the bar, where we triangulated and met.

"Glad you could make it," I said, putting my hand on her arm to let everyone know she was with me and thus safe from harm.

"Just came for the camera."

"You're wearing a dress. You look stunning."

"Some rigs are worth dressing up for. What's your excuse?" She smiled, looking me up and down.

I touched my tie. Which one had I worn? I forgot. "Occupational hazard. I don't get to dress down."

"It's working for you."

"Can I get you something to drink?"

A glass of white wine appeared at her elbow.

"Thanks, Robert," she said to the bartender.

I ordered something for myself while a waitress came around with a silver tray of stuffed endive leaves. Laine pressed her lips together in refusal, and the waitress left.

"Do you ever get this feeling," she said, eyes darting around the room, "that people are looking at you?" She laughed almost immediately. "Never mind."

She cleared her throat and picked up her head, straightening her shoulders as if she'd always told herself she'd act a certain way when she was in my shoes, and this was the way. In attempting to look comfortable, she looked incredibly uncomfortable.

My inner delight darkened when I saw two men in navy suits walk in and scan the guests. *Oh, no.* Laine was there because I wanted her there, and if they took her out, I didn't know if I'd see her again. The compulsion to stand between them and fight to the death was physical, as if I'd be losing more than nice chatter at a party. I put my hand on her arm to keep her by me.

Chapter 12

Laine

Some of them recognized me. That, I knew. The question was, what would they do about it? I was on their bad girl list, but when Michael touched my arm, that list stopped mattering. I had to hold my head high. I belonged there as much as anyone else, even if I was only there to pick up a replacement camera. The string quartet, the dark wood, the wool rugs, and the three-ton lead crystal chandeliers—all of it was my birthright as much as theirs.

Only Lewis, the caterer, had stopped me in the kitchen amid the shouts of the staff and the bang and clatter of pots and plates. The fluorescents seemed brighter than the human eye could bear.

"Laine?"

"Hey, Lew." I hadn't even slowed, but he'd grabbed my arm.

"What are you doing?"

"I need to get in. I'm on the list, I just…" *I just have to sneak through the kitchen.* "I don't have a camera." I held up my bag, which couldn't fit more than a raisin and a rolled up dollar bill.

"Laine, come on," he said as if he would pry something from me with his sarcasm.

"Have I ever lied?"

"You've never needed to lie," Lewis said.

"I'm a guest, whether you believe me or not. If you don't get out of my way, everyone's going to know you have me on speed dial."

He'd surrendered, but I felt in the depths of my belly that that hadn't been the last of it. When Michael smiled after looking across the room, I knew that this was going to go terribly wrong. He was stunning, and irresistible, and a one-way ticket to nowheresville. But the stunning and irresistible parts were not to be ignored. He stood straighter when he saw me, as if I was the only woman in the room, and I shuddered.

"You do look nice," I said. "That's why people look at you."

"It's not my talent?" He didn't seem offended, just playing.

"Try letting your beard go mountain man and running around in sweats. See who wants to look at you then."

I didn't mean it as an insult, and he didn't seem to take it as one, but he did get serious all of a sudden. It was only a slight shift in attitude.

He leaned toward me just a little. "Would you rather be known for what you do, or who you are?"

I leaned in a little as well and whispered. "I'd rather not be known."

"Okay, well," he leaned in closer, whispering, and my eyes fluttered closed from how close his lips were to me. "You're about to be known as the pap who got escorted out of the Breakfront Gala. And I'm about to be known as the guy who didn't let that happen."

I looked behind me. The security guys weren't wearing cheap uniforms with patches on the shoulders, but I knew them by their heavy gait and the authority on their backs. They were across the room, looking for someone. Me.

I put down my wine. "This was a bad idea. I'll just go."

He put his hand over my wrist with confident authority, as if he had a right to touch me. "No, you won't."

"I'm not going to embarrass you."

He looked at me, nothing but warmth in his eyes, and a little of the anxiety that had followed me into the room melted away. He tightened his grip on my wrist. He could have led me anywhere, and I would have followed.

"You're the most interesting person in this room right now," he said. "And they want me to stay more than they want to get rid of you."

"I doubt that."

"Let's find out."

I didn't know Michael Greydon much better than the millions who didn't know him at all, but I knew a few basic truths. He drove sober, got in at a decent hour when he was shooting, always smiled, didn't sleep around, and hammed for any lens pointed at him. But what I saw in his face then was something I'd seen on a few of the men in my life and more than my share of friends and fake family. It was the look I was told I got before I did something rash.

He looked as though he wanted to get into trouble. Any normal woman, recognizing that, would have tried to steer him to safety, but my neck burned hot with the thought. I didn't know if it was from the idea of trouble or the sexual streak in his recklessness.

"Michael Greydon?" I said. "What is on your mind?"

"I have no idea." The words rolled around his tongue as if he loved having no idea.

I should have been excited. Thrilled. I should have jumped into his arms and suggested something reckless that sat at the very edge of legality. But I didn't, because unlike most of the people I'd climbed fences and broken things with, he had something to lose. A lot to lose. If I created a scene with him, I'd lose something as well. My anonymity, which was already compromised by my gender, would be non-existent.

So though temptation twisted me in knots, I pulled my hand away.

That was when Lucy Betancourt showed up. The story of their breakup a year after he entered Yale was well known, but from her bitter expression, knowledge of the torch she carried for him was less common.

"Laine?" she said. "Laine Cartwright?"

"Laine, this is Lucy—"

"Hello, Lucy. It's nice to see you again," I lied. The last time I saw her, she'd been slipping a *Cosmo* article entitled "How to Fellate Him Like a Porn Star" into my jacket pocket.

"Well, it's nice to see you!" She tucked a perfectly blown-out blond lock behind her ear. Her suit was a conservative Chanel two-piece, and her pearls were triple-looped around her neck. "We all wondered what happened to you."

"I left."

"Well, we knew that! Of course, but no word on why? We worried terribly."

"Things happened."

"We all knew the Hatches got divorced, but we didn't think—"

"I bet."

Michael spit out a laugh then looked over my shoulder. Lucy followed his gaze to the security guys then touched his arm. I wanted to bite off her hand.

"I'll take her," she said softly to him.

I nodded and stepped toward her. I didn't trust her as far as I could throw her one-handed, but I needed to save Michael and myself the grief of a fight.

"No, you won't," Michael said. "I have this."

"No. I'm putting my foot down. I. Want. To. Go." I stared him down, chipping at the resolve in his jade eyes. He might have been an actor, but I was a pretender and good at it. I was going to protect him from me, even if it meant giving up any hope of feeling his touch again.

"Come," Lucy said.

I hesitated. My gut roiled, but I wasn't sure whether it was because of Lucy, the guys coming to escort me out, or the idea of coming so close to Michael and losing him.

"The camera's in my car," Michael said. "Don't go too far away." He brushed by me to intercept the security guys, and I grabbed his arm.

"Forget the camera." I was one hundred percent sure I never wanted to see him again, even if I knew I'd change my mind as soon as walls were between us.

I let Lucy pull me through the crowd. Did anyone notice me? I recognized a couple of faces, mostly people who dined or hung out with the characters I chased. I made eye contact when they did, and they looked away every time. I was the center of attention. I wished to god they'd all stare outright.

But they didn't. I'd never been so uncomfortable in my life. When I followed Lucy to a small side foyer that didn't have any guests looking-not-looking at me, I felt like a drowning woman yanked to the surface for her first gulp of air.

"You all right?" she asked.

"I'm fine."

"The security guys here don't care," she said. "They'll escort you out in front of everybody. I thought I'd save you from that. But if you want to go back—"

"No, I'm fine. Really."

"I have to go in. Do you remember the way?" she asked.

"Yeah."

"If you're seen, they'll escort you to your car. Just don't make a big deal about it, and it'll be fine."

"I was thinking of going all limp and letting them carry me."

She paused, warmed, and said something it looked as if she had to think about first. "We did worry about you."

"Really? I'm surprised you didn't hunt me down in every strip club in Vernon."

"How do you know we didn't?" She smiled curtly. "You'd better get going." She walked back toward the ballroom.

"Lucy?" I said.

She turned slightly, waiting.

"Thank you."

Chapter 13

Michael

The air went out of the room as soon as she left. As if someone had taken the knot out of the bottom of a balloon, everything flattened.

She was nothing to me, and chasing after her was irresponsible. But I had a camera in my car with her name on it, and as I made small talk about the industry, the school, and the city, I wanted to give it to her whether she wanted it or not. Me. Hand to hand. Not my assistant or my agent or my publicist. I'd invited her to the gala to get something done, and it was getting done.

I texted her but heard nothing back. Ten minutes later, in the middle of talking up *Bullets*, I realized I hadn't approved her number for incoming. Suddenly, the room felt stifling hot as the air pressed in on me. I didn't want stupid small talk, and I didn't want to be me for another minute. So I smiled and excused myself.

It was cold outside, but I felt better.

The smart thing to do would have been to go home and rest. Taking weeks off for Britt's foibles might screw my life, but I didn't have to help it along, did I? I didn't have to ignore everything I was told by people who knew better.

"Michael?"

It was Lucy, striding out alone in her low heels.

"Hey. I was just thinking about going home," I said.

"You should." She took my elbow in a way that was too familiar. She'd never touch me like that if people were watching. "You look tired."

"Thanks for helping out with Laine."

"I never knew what happened to Little Miss Guttersnipe."

"Don't call her that."

"Laine, then."

"She's very successful at what she does."

"I'm not surprised. She was quite industrious."

"You treated her like shit."

She shrugged. "What do you want from me? I was sixteen, and she was after my man. She's lucky she didn't make it to prom. It would have been my mission to send her home crying." She brushed a fleck of something off my jacket. "What's been happening with you lately, Mister Greydon? You're distracted. I can't get a smile out of you. Is Gareth on your case?"

She had grey eyes that never looked warm or inviting, and it was only her voice that told me she was truly concerned. I didn't want to lie to her, but the truth wasn't an option.

"I like pretending nobody's watching," I said. "New hobby. You should try it."

"Sorry, no. Do you want to slip out and get a bowl of soup?"

She smiled at me. Our first date had been outside a soup truck, during the short window between the dark tunnel of puberty and the oncoming train of my public life.

"I'll take a rain check. I'm going to go home and go to bed."

I walked her to the door and let her go back to the party by herself.

Even as I decided to make an early night of it, I walked west across the campus with my hands in my pockets. The valet was east, and I'd left my coat in the coat check, but I had no desire to brave the company to retrieve it. No. I wanted to do something else entirely. I walked on autopilot through Humanities Quad, and up the short jump of steps into the small tennis stadium. The lights were down, and the crickets' mating calls were the only accompaniment to the traffic on San Vicente.

As if she'd heard my thoughts, Laine waited in her old seat, sitting cross-legged with her arms over the backs of the chairs on either side, face up to the sky. She was so inappropriate in her fancy dress and relaxed posture, sitting on the hard plastic seat as if it were a couch.

"Hello," I said.

"I had a feeling you'd come." She spoke without opening her eyes.

"You should have let me fight for you."

She opened her eyes and turned to watch me come down the steps. "I don't want you to fight for me."

I sat next to her. "You robbed me of the opportunity to tell everyone to kiss my ass."

She showed me her palms. "Wait, wait, wait. Hold on there, big guy. If you want to tell everyone to pucker up, you have exactly the platform to do it without me, okay?"

"You think it's that easy?"

"I do. You call a press conference and everyone—"

"My agent has to and—"

"So Gene Douchearossa does it. What's the diff—"

"He asks me first what it's about—"

"And you just make something—"

"Everyone will know I lied and then—"

"So you want to tell people to kiss your ass, but you don't want them to think you're a liar?" she said with finality.

"I'm not a liar."

"Even when you lie?"

I didn't know what came over me. The way her eyes glinted in the moonlight. The mischief in her voice. The boldness of her argument. The dress. Those particular bleacher seats. The bleat of a car alarm from the parking lot.

But something definitely came over me.

Chapter 14

Laine

I couldn't go to my car. Yes, I wanted to protect him from me. Yes, I cared about everything I'd built, and he was a walking, talking career bulldozer. But I couldn't walk out. I kept imagining his body under his clothes, the way it moved, his hands on me, his lips, *those* lips.

Some base instinct told me he'd show up, and an even baser one wanted to see him so badly, I felt the blood flowing through my veins when I thought about it.

And he did. I thought I'd explode from the unexpected relief in my chest. But something came over him, as if a mask he was wearing came off. I didn't know what it was about. At first I thought he was angry that I'd called him a liar, which technically, I hadn't. I'd only meant to say that you either care what people think or you tell them to kiss off. There was no in between. I was ready to explain all that, but he put his finger up to shush me.

"Work with me," he said, taking my wrist and pulling me up.

"Where are we going?"

He pulled me down the stairs, my skirt flying and my skill in heels more useful than ever.

"You watched me practice every day for six months," he called over his shoulder.

"Partly true."

He stopped when my feet hit the court and turned to me. "Your point?"

"For the last two, you kept me from studying with your yack yack yack."

"I offered to teach you to play, and you didn't want to."

"I'm not an athlete."

"I disagree."

He took my hand and pulled me again, lacing his fingers through mine. He walked toward the clubhouse, and I followed, so distracted by his touch I almost tripped over my own legs. The small building had a tunnel through it, an underpass with trophy cases of memorabilia and a water fountain.

"All that time," he said, his voice echoing in the small space, "I wanted to volley with you. Just talk without talking, and you wouldn't."

He got to the equipment closet door with a little keypad with ten buttons above the doorknob. He let go of my hand to push a combination while his other hand pressed the lever.

Nothing happened but a soft beep and a little red light.

"Michael, seriously? You think they didn't change the combination in all these years?"

"You don't know this school very well." He tried it again with the same result.

"I should be going. It's late," I said, even though I didn't want to go. Not at all. But I didn't feel aggressive or demanding, and I felt as though Michael needed a little space.

He approached the trophy case and put his phone up to it. The blue light fell on racquets and balls used to win meaningless championships and pictures of kids who later became famous as players or magnates. Some were winners, and some only qualified for a mention because of what they did later in life.

"Here," he said, motioning me over.

He put his hand on my back and directed his phone light to a black-and-white photo of his younger self with a championship trophy, next to another photo of his gorgeous body stretched in the air for a mother-of-a-whore serve. The line of hair between his navel and his waistband distracted me from the grimace on his face. I wanted to trace it to its logical end as much now as I had when I was fifteen. The black graphite racquet and yellow ball he'd been using when he won leaned on the side wall behind the tempered glass.

"Are we reliving past glories today?" I said, feeling as though that was too harsh only when it was halfway out of my mouth.

But if he was offended, he gave no indication. He just scanned the underpass by the light of his phone. When he found a garbage can, he removed the lid by grabbing the edge of the center hole. "Back up, Laine."

"What are you...?

He swung the heavy lid at the case and shattered it. Glass tinkled to the concrete.

"Jesus! Michael!"

"It's my racquet." He took it out of the case, shaking shards off it.

"But—"

He plucked up the ball. "I'll put it back." He bounced the ball once, twice, then smacked it into a vibrating mass using the racquet. "The strings need tightening, and the ball is only half dead. Come on."

He pulled me again. No alarms went off, and no security guards came running. It was just us grinding broken glass under our feet.

He went out to the court, and I followed.

"So, not for anything?" I said, "But what's gotten into you?"

He pointed the racquet at me, handle first. "You're a lefty, right?"

I couldn't believe he remembered. My hand went to the work leather handle as if guided by an invisible force.

He smacked the ball to the ground and snapped it into his fist on the way up. "I wanted to do this when you and I were talking up there in the bleachers. Talking was nice, don't get me wrong, but this is too. Just try to get it over the net."

He bounced the ball to me. I swung and missed.

"It's gonna be a long night," I said as he retrieved the ball.

"You'll be a pro in fifteen minutes." He smiled from ear to ear. "Just swing, don't swat. Like, who do you hate the most in your life?"

"Right now?"

"Sure."

"I want to kill my brother," I said.

"Why?"

"Because he brought my rig into a VIP room after I'd told someone he wouldn't. Then it got thrown off a balcony, which if you ask me, was totally fair considering it didn't belong there, and then he sold the picture, which had me in it."

"You were in it?"

"My back, but that's not the point. The point is he's leveraging the fact that I love him, and I do not like being leveraged."

Michael threw the ball. It bounced right at me, and I pulled that racquet back and swung as if Tom's stupid head was a little yellow sphere.

It went flying.

"Oh," Michael said while it was midair. "Wow, it's…"

It landed on the flat roof of the clubhouse.

"It's the only ball we had," I said.

"Short lesson."

I didn't see disappointment in his face as he looked up though—only some kind of exaltation, a basking in something wonderful. A release, maybe. And maybe I was wrong. Maybe I was projecting how I felt at that moment and he was just passing time until he got to do the next thing famous rich people do. Maybe it was dark except for the streetlamps a block away, and that smile was really a grimace, and his posture wasn't relaxed but slouched.

I didn't even know the guy, really, and I could have been wrong about a lot of things, but I wasn't wrong about the release in my own ribs, the glorious wonder I felt at the stupid stolen ball getting lost on the roof, or the flutter I felt seeing his pleasure.

I felt fifteen again, and he was a senior holding my hand on the armrest, and this minute at Breakfront was my big chance at redemption. The whole of life opened up before me. A life where I didn't have to chase. I only had to make someone happy for a few minutes a day, and sometimes, not always, but sometimes good things didn't have to be chased down. Sometimes they'd come to me.

"I want that ball," I said.

He tilted his head. "Really?"

I leaned the racquet on the net. "I want that ball, and I'm going to get it."

"We've been losing balls on that roof for years."

"That was your last lost ball."

I'd climbed fences, trespassed on roofs, broken things, run in front of traffic, been arrested and not charged, and sped down the freeway and Santa Monica Boulevard. But never had I ever been so thrilled as when I went behind the clubhouse and found the utility ladder attached to the building. I got up the first step. Michael stood beside the ladder, and I turned my head to him. My eyes were a few inches above his.

"You're going to crack your face with those heels," he whispered.

"You have no idea who you're talking to," I whispered back before I headed up the ladder. I felt him behind me in the stability his weight added .

"Are you looking up my skirt?" I called back.

"Yes. Yes, I am. And if I may say so—"

70

"Don't even make something up. It's pitch dark."

"You're beautiful. I'm not making that up."

I stopped and looked down at him. "Do not even."

"I'll say what I like."

He put his hand on my ankle, lightly at first, looking at me. Our eyes locked, me from above, him tilted upward. I didn't move my foot, and he moved his hand up my leg slowly, over my calf, lingering on the back of my knee before ever so gently moving a few inches upward and brushing the inside of my thigh.

My legs lost the ability to hold me, and my other foot slipped. His grip tightened to hold me up, and his touch sent shockwaves through me.

"Jesus," he said, hand still inside my thigh. "You all right?"

"I'm fine."

"Good. Get moving." He slapped my calf, and I got moving.

When my head crested the roof, I saw a flat surface littered with hundreds of yellow orbs arranged randomly, like stars in the sky. Scooting to the ledge, I spun on my bottom and dropped onto the tar surface. Michael came up a second after.

"This is a pretty good view for being only one story," I said, walking to the north side, where the city laid itself out for me like a quilt on display, from my feet to the blackened strip of sky where the mountains ended.

"The best view in the city is from the courthouse rooftop, downtown." He touched my bare shoulder, fingertips laced with intention.

I kept my eyes on the skyline, because if I looked at him, I would lose myself, and I couldn't. Not today. Not ever. Not with him. What was I doing up there? His fingertips traced my collarbone, his breath on my ear, and I was going adrift.

"I know the best views," I rambled in a last ditch effort to keep the career I'd worked so hard for. "I went up to the top of the library once, tallest building in LA. Of course, it was as illegal as hell, but I knew this guy who... he..." I turned. I had to. We were kiss close and getting closer. "We came here to do a job."

I pulled away. He took the side of my face and yanked me back toward him. A second went by, his green eyes black in the night. His intentions were broadcast through his posture, his energy, enfolding me inside it.

If I ever had a real actor this close, I'd never trust him. But this wasn't acting. Or if it was, I was fooled. I swallowed and pressed my lips together.

"We'd better get to it," he said with a smirk.

How could I be relieved and disappointed at the same time?

I stepped back, picked up a tennis ball, and threw it east toward the practice court. It didn't clear the length of the roof. It bounced off another ball and flew sideways, disrupting the pattern and sending a bunch of other balls skittering.

"Told you I wasn't an athlete!" I cried, laughing.

Michael shot two over the roof, and I heard them plunk onto the court. "Put your back into it, Laine. Throw it like you mean it."

I grabbed one in each hand and threw them. They barely cleared the edge of the roof, but I put up my arms and cheered, claiming victory.

"Faster!" Michael said, lobbing a blitzkrieg of tennis balls.

I scuttled along the roof, knees bent, chucking balls and laughing as I tried to keep up with him and failed. I didn't know if we were even making a dent in the roof's tennis ball population. I didn't even know if half of mine were making it to the court. I started throwing balls to Michael, and he caught them and lobbed them. He picked up more between my poorly aimed tosses, moving his body like an instrument.

I moved back toward San Vicente, conscious of the edge of the building. I was high on the rhythm. I couldn't disrupt his poise, even when my toss was so bad I didn't think it would reach him. We were laughing so hard I was blind and barely able to walk and throw at the same time. He lunged, caught a ball, and I stepped back. My foot landed on top of a tennis ball, and it rolled. I lost my balance.

The ledge of the roof was only two feet high, and as I tried not to fall, my body was pitched left with the torque of my shoulders. If I'd have been on the ground, I would have taken a step left and taken a deep breath before I stood straight. But I didn't have the ground under me, just a two-foot-high ledge I was about to fall over.

The wind dropped out of my lungs as I was yanked back. Michael pulled me straight, his grip definitive and almost painful. I steadied myself on him, gulping for air.

"You really aren't an athlete," he said.

He still smelled like cinnamon, and I had to know immediately if he tasted of spiced cider.

I didn't wait for him to move or even breathe. I put my hands on the sides of his neck and pulled my face up to his, smashing our lips together in the most graceless, artless kiss in the history of kisses.

I was so clumsy, I kissed his teeth, and it took him a full century and a half to align his mouth to mine, putting lip to lip, skin on skin, slipping his tongue to mine. Oh, yes, he tasted like sunshine and smelled like cinnamon. Like a different world. The other side of the city. Deep brown and layered in cardamom. Drenched in sepia. His tongue filled my mouth like a flood, and my belly twisted with a rolling current.

It was better than I'd ever hoped. More intense than I'd imagined. More real than the roof under my feet and more divine than the heavens above.

He stopped, putting his nose astride my nose, and I thought of that pause as my last chance to save my career.

Screw the pause. Screw the career. Screw Michael Greydon.

We kissed again with renewed passion. I threaded my fingers through his hair, and he moved his along my back. He drew the pin out of my chignon.

"That hair," he groaned before putting his lips to mine again.

His erection pressed on me, and my knees went jelly. He pulled me to him, holding me close to keep our lips together. My body overrode every firing neuron in my brain. That erection was mine. I owned it. I wanted it to be a part of me, moving inside my body with gentleness and violence and everything in between. Him. I wanted him, with his hands slipping around the side of my dress to touch my breast and his hips pushing against me, with the taut body I stroked under his jacket, with the motions of a man on the edge of losing control.

I didn't even have a brain. I was simply a velocity. A direction. Zero to desperate for him in three point two seconds.

I would have let him take me on that roof, though I didn't know if that was what he had in mind. I would have gone home with him or taken him back to my loft. I would have given him every inch of my body without a hope of seeing him again. Stupidly. Definitively. Recklessly.

But it wasn't to be. A light flashed, diffused to orange by my closed eyelid. Then another. Though I couldn't hear past the white noise of the busy street below, I knew that each flash had a *click* to accompany it, and each click was a hammer on a nail on the coffin of my dead career.

I believed love was forever. I knew people should always choose love over a job, but this wasn't love. This was a set of circumstances that led to real heat between two people. I wasn't choosing between two worthwhile objectives.

At twenty-five, I'd been a photographer for almost a decade. I'd done nothing but work. I'd had a bad few years with men after leaving Breakfront, then I had a sprinkling of short, unsatisfying romances I didn't take seriously. I lost my virginity just to get it over with. The only thing I'd ever cared about was taking pictures, and giving it up for a moment's pleasure didn't seem like something I'd be happy about in the long run.

I mean, we existed in the world. On a rooftop surrounded by lost tennis balls and a good fifteen minutes of laughter, I might have felt as if we were the only two people in the universe, but the fact was, we weren't an island. If we were ever destined to become a unit, to fall in love or even some half-shaded version of it, we had to exist in the larger world together first.

And that wasn't going to happen.

Not with the paparazzi dog pack huddling on San Vicente like, well, dogs. As soon as we stopped kissing and stood there staring at each other, they started calling our names, because sure, he was famous, but they all knew me.

"Just say this wasn't your plan the whole time," he growled.

"Go to hell."

I pulled my hand back as if I was getting ready to slap him, and he held it gently. He must have felt me shaking or seen the tears welling in my eyes, because his suspicion disappeared.

"It's going to be fine," he said, touching the side of my face.

Even as my mind told me that he didn't know what he was talking about, my heart was soothed. It was going to be fine. I believed him.

He didn't look down at the paps, but in that moment of confidence, I did. I saw Jerome and Terence, Raoul with his bald head and chunky gold chains.

I pushed Michael away.

"Listen," he said, putting his finger up as if he was going to school me on how to handle a crowd of paps.

I couldn't speak to him about anything that mattered. I couldn't even form words. I felt slapped repeatedly by the shutters.

"I didn't ask for this," I said.

I turned and walked to the ladder, kicking yellow balls. He grabbed my arm when we got to the edge. We were still visible from the street, and the photographers had moved down the block like a school of fish.

"Let me go," I said.

"I'm going first so if you fall, I can catch you. Now you can either wrestle me to the ladder first and give these guys more to shoot, or you can let me go first and give them nothing."

My face screwed up as I realized what he was saying. We would get shot going down no matter what, but what we gave them was up to us. I was frozen.

He took me by the shoulders and looked me in the eye, but all I could see in my mind was the angle of the cameras below, what we looked like together and what would sell. I couldn't think past that.

"Laine, listen."

I couldn't even look at him. I only had eyes for who was in the street and what they were getting.

"Look at me." He shook me almost imperceptibly, and I turned enough to put him in my field of vision.

He leaned in, one eye clear jade in the streetlight, one dark in the night, his mouth set to make a point. The little *pepita* of a hairless spot on his chin was a comfort, a memory of times "before." I breathed once, then again, focusing on him. I would have told him he was beautiful if I hadn't been somehow cleared of any kind of rational thought.

"Just follow me," he said. "Don't look at them."

The desire to look down was overwhelming.

"I'm going to go first," he said, "but I'm going to be with you the whole time. Right?"

I nodded.

"Just look at me, Laine. When we get down, I'll show you the way out."

Like a poke in the pride, what he said woke me.

"I can get out without you," I said.

"Challenge accepted. Now come on."

As soon as he put a foot of distance between us, I felt the loss of his presence. He stepped onto the ladder, and I watched him, unmoving, until only his chest and head were visible.

He waved me over. "Come on. Don't look. Just come here."

Carefully keeping my dress over my legs, I stepped onto the ladder. He was close to me, too close to look up my skirt. I had a hundred wisecracks at the ready that I couldn't utter, because he was blocking me from the lenses, and I needed him. In three steps, we were below the hedge, blocked from them completely. We got to the ground seconds later.

Michael took my hand and headed for the court and the front door.

I pulled back. "I'm going this way."

"There's nothing that way."

"Michael, in about a minute, they're going to put holes in that hedge big enough for their lenses. We need to be on opposite ends of the city by then."

"Come out with me. We'll deal with it tomorrow."

"That's too late. I'm sorry. I've worked too hard." I let his hand go and stepped backward.

"Where are you going?" He looked like a man slapped in the face.

I didn't want to hurt him. I didn't even think it was possible.

"I want you to know," I said, "I've never been kissed like that."

Before he could respond, I ran into the trees.

Chapter 15

Laine

When I'd gotten to my car the previous night, I had two choices: see if I had any tips on my phone or sit there and cry. Crying wasn't an option. I didn't cry over anything, especially not some guy and a pack of stinking paps, so I checked my texts.

I'd had messages from all over the city. The last one came in seconds earlier and was close enough to the loft that I could grab my spare rig. So I did that without thinking about a thing. I went to the Starlight, put the camera to my face, and realized I'd only checked the camera for battery power.

There was a reason it was a spare: it was busted. The shutter was broken.

I'd stood there in my evening dress and pumps, ignoring the jibes from my peers as I tried to get the shutter to snap. I'd chased like a dog but missed the shot of Thomasina Wente leaving the club with a broken heel. I went back home and fell into bed, still feeling the press of Michael's lips on mine and the ache of longing between my legs. It was a living thing, buzzing for attention, taking blood flow and fluid. When I slipped my hands beneath my underwear, I was soaked and my clit was hardened to a furious stone.

So I did what millions of women had done and would do—I rubbed myself to orgasm thinking of Michael Greydon. Finding that wasn't enough, I did it again, until I stiffened from toes to throat, thinking of nothing, feeling everything, lost in him. I fell asleep cursing his name and breathing deeply of his cinnamon scent on my hair.

I woke up to the phone ringing and his spicy scent still in my nose. I'd wash my hair, for sure. Just as soon as I answered the phone. Or maybe tomorrow.

"Hello," I mumbled without looking at the caller. I'd left the blinds open, and the morning sun punched me in the face. I rolled over.

Tom said, "What the heck, Laine?"

"It's nine in the morning. What the heck is right."

"Michael? Michael Greydon? Really?"

I groaned. The pictures must have gone up. I had no idea what Tom was doing up so early, but the first thing any pap did in the morning was look at the gossip sites to see what marks were doing, who'd gotten the shots, and what were trending subjects. Tom, as much as he denied being a pap, did it every day.

"We happened to be at a party together."

Why was I lying? Not to protect myself but to protect Michael. Stupid and pointless.

"Laine, it's all over the feeds."

I jumped out of bed, flipping back the covers. I scuttled to my desk, still in my fancy black underwear. I knew what Tom had seen. I knew exactly what those pictures looked like, but I couldn't go another second without seeing them.

"It's not a big deal," I said, sitting down.

"If you say so." His tone said he didn't believe the words or the woman who uttered them.

I found the pictures immediately. They were exactly what I thought they'd be, from the angle to the strength of the flash. Rows of consecutive frames of us kissing on the roof, and me turning so my face was toward the cameras. I couldn't deny it. I couldn't pretend it wasn't me. And of course, no one could pretend it wasn't Michael, because the public had memorized his face long ago. I felt an odd ownership of it, as if they were sharing something of mine without my permission. It was an ugly, jealous feeling.

"Shit," I grumbled.

"He's got his hand on your ass."

I scrolled down. They'd all sold it. From Raoul with his blown-out strobe to Terry who couldn't frame to save his life, and each photo made my thighs quiver with the memory of how every nerve ending from my waist to my knees had been on fire. That kiss, hand on ass or no, had been worth recording. I couldn't stop staring at the angle of his chin against mine, and his fingertips pressing into my biceps as if he wanted to crawl into me. My hand inside his jacket, feeling for the hardness of his body.

My phone buzzed in my ear.

"I have to go." I clicked off with Tom and checked my called ID. "Pheebs, don't get on my case."

"Michael Greydon? Michael *freaking* Greydon? The most gorgeous—"

"Really? Pheeb? Really?" If Phoebe's clients heard the way she spoke about celebrities, they'd never guess she was a lawyer.

"—unattainable—"

"Stop."

"—talented—"

"It's not that big a deal."

"—charming—"

"I'm going to hang up." I scrolled down my computer screen. DMZ had drawn hearts and camera flashes all over us.

"Gorgeous. Okay, that's the last thing I'm saying."

"Here's what I'm saying, and I quote, 'Michael Greydon, the prince of the Hollywood system, caught kissing the lady frog and known paparazzi, Laine Cartwright, on a rooftop at the Breakfront School. Who will photograph the wedding? And with paparazzi on the invite list, how much of Hollywood royalty will attend?'" I read.

"What was it like? Kissing him?"

I leaned back in my chair and put my bare foot on the desk. "Like kissing any guy." I flexed and released my knee so I rocked in the desk chair. "Kissing any guy who's the best kisser in the world."

"Oh, God." Phoebe was swooning. I knew the swoon. She swooned like that over a cycle of ten actors, some dropping out so a new one could replace him. "How did it happen? Tell me everything."

My phone vibrated again. I looked at the screen quickly and put it back to my ear. "I can't. I have another call. Two, actually."

"Call me later!"

I had Irving and an unknown number. I picked up the unknown number. Maybe it was a tip, and I'd have an excuse to run out the door without brushing my hair. "This is Laine."

"Hello, Laine, this is Brenda Vinter from the *LA Post Almanac* section. How are you today?"

How was I? I'd been fine, very fine, excellent even, until a reporter called. I'd worked with the *Post* often enough but only with editorial acquisitions. Never reporting.

"What can I do for you, Ms. Vinter?"

"Well, as you know, we're an old-fashioned paper, so though we can't catch stories as quickly as you can, we have the ability to put together meatier pieces, so—"

"You're comparing what you do with what I do?"

Was I being hostile? Yes, I was being hostile. I didn't even know what I thought that would get me, but I was watching my life get pulled away from me. Being hostile seemed like the only way to get it back.

"Do you have time for a few questions about these pictures on the roof last night?"

"The *Almanac* section is industry news. How is who Michael kisses industry news?" I asked.

"He's kissing the industry. You're a star in your own right."

No, I wasn't. I was a frog, and she was stroking my slick green hide to get me to jump.

"Thank you for calling," I said. "I have no comment."

I hung up as if the phone were on fire, and in a sense, it was. I was in way over my depth, and a buzzing sense of disorientation deafened me to any other thoughts. The only way to quiet it was to pace my loft, saying what I always said when I felt unsure, but I felt like a liar for the first time.

I own this city.

I own this city.

I own this city.

Chapter 16

Michael

I slept on the couch when I slept at all. Most nights though, I didn't sleep well, and I could be found in the big empty room in my guest house, watching movies.

"Watching" might not be the exact right word. I analyzed them. Primarily, I analyzed the acting, the way the story was revealed in postures, glances, and small movements. I could watch a great movie a hundred times and every time peel off layers of the actors' preparation.

If I'd told Laine what I did when I got home from kissing her, I'd be embarrassed. I captured the feeling in my heart and mind and ran home without thinking of much outside it, and I put on *Casablanca*.

There was a single kiss, told in flashback. Humphrey Bogart kisses Ingrid Bergman in Paris, and that powerful alpha male we met in the beginning of the movie, who was leathered with experience and fermented in whiskey, closes his eyes and surrenders completely. He seems to be in such rapture that he loses track of the kiss, and his mouth slides off Bergman's for a second then returns.

I thought, as I kissed Laine, that that feeling was what Bogart was channeling when he shot the scene. Complete surrender to the moment, to another person, to a kiss.

When I got home, I didn't go into the main house. I went right to the guest house. I didn't even close the door or take off my jacket. I cued up the projector. *Casablanca* came on seconds later. I knew where that kiss was in the chapters, because I'd spent hours trying to peel it apart, wondering how I could catch that feeling and put it on the screen.

I didn't sit on the leather couch but stood in front of the projected image, watching for that moment. That feeling I held... I let it go. I let myself feel that heat of excitement, that twitch of need. It was on the screen. Even with his eyes closed, Bogart had it. People lived and died for it. Gave up everything to feel it.

I plopped on the couch and let it run without sound, because the words were just distractions. I saw how his hand moved on her for the first time, and I understood the possessiveness in every twitch of his fingers. The love scenes in *Bullets* were coming after Britt's break. I was going to nail them.

I sat on the couch, leaning back in the cushions, and let the movie run. The whole thing became clear to me. It wasn't even acting. Bogart was living that character. I wished I could go back and reshoot every love scene I'd ever done. They'd been all affect and indicating. What a waste.

I fell asleep and woke when the couch cushions tilted and I went off balance. I opened my eyes, still foggy.

"If people only knew," Ken said, "Michael Greydon doesn't sleep on a feather bed with a leggy blonde but craps out in front of old movies in his dress pants. Are you still wearing your shoes? Jesus, kid."

"How did you get in here?"

"You use my old cleaning lady, and I greased her wheels. Answer the door next time." He slapped a manila envelope and a stack of pictures on my lap. "I've been up all night."

I didn't want to open the envelope, but I couldn't avoid the pictures. She was stunning. That hair was going to make me crazy. I wanted to twist it into shapes all over her body.

"I assume that's the last of her," he said. "But it's still got to be managed."

"No." I tossed the stack in Ken's lap and got up to stretch my legs. These days off were going to kill me. I couldn't make it a habit to sleep past seven. "That's not the last of her unless she turns me down. Which she won't."

"How am I supposed to spin this?" Ken asked.

"It's not my job to make your job easy."

Casablanca had been on a loop, and Bogart was on my wall, saying something clever and manly at the bar. On his face, with the sound down, I could see every second of heartbreak.

"I don't mind difficult," Ken said. "I mind impossible."

I scooped up the remote and shut off the player. "The public doesn't care what she does for a living. They'll think it's cute."

"The public? The public has to know who you are, or you don't have a career. It's the industry you have to worry about. Do not underestimate their influence." He counted off his fingers. "The press, who hate paps even when they pay them. The agents, who have clients who can't get work because of what these assholes get on camera. Publicists, yes, that's me—"

"Whose job is to spin it. Spin it, Ken. Get off my back."

"You don't go to bed with paparazzi. That's nuts. No one even talks about that. You don't let the wolves into the hen house."

"This is my personal life. You're as bad as they are."

I felt encased in clay, trapped by Ken's intentions against my own. I walked out into the yard, squinting against the winter sun.

My house sat on a hill. The yard was small considering what I paid for the place, but the scope of the back view could wipe out a man's personality for seconds at a time. That was why I'd bought it. It didn't make me feel grandiose. It made me feel small and essential at the same time.

"This is not about where you're putting your personal dick, Greydon," Ken said from behind me. "This is about three generations of men in this business. It's about the fact that you don't know how to do anything else. You want to end up like Gareth? You want to spend ten years drinking because no one wants to hire a moody, temperamental ass who loses bond? And what could he do besides say tough guy lines? Nothing. He was trained to do nothing else. Like you. Outside the business, you have nothing. No skills. No assets. No training."

"And my father managed to keep me in private school and a big house."

"That's how you judge his success? Let me ask you, how would you handle not working then leaning on your son to get a movie made so you can have your great comeback?"

I looked back at him. He had his hands in his pockets as if he was staying humble and non-confrontational.

"Lay off my father. You don't know what you're talking about." I think I growled low, the words gurgling from my gut.

Ken put his hands up as if showing me he was unarmed. I knew better.

"You're right. It's not about your father. What does she mean to you? You've seen her twice since you were kids. What *could* she mean to you?"

"Not the point."

"What is the point?" Ken could have gotten tight or irritated, but he didn't. He was the picture of reason.

"I like her. That's the point."

"You can like a lot of girls."

"I like her. Period. I don't have to explain myself."

He looked out over my view, squinting at the horizon. He put his sunglasses on. "You're right."

"I'm right?"

"You know what? This spins like a top." He swept his hand over the landscape. "Michael Greydon. Hollywood's new rule-breaker. Perfect. No one tells you what to do. You'll date the foster kid with no family. The commoner. We don't play her as the Hollywood underbelly. We play her as the sexy underdog. You'll be America's Boyfriend times a hundred."

"I don't think she's open to being played."

He flicked his wrist. "Irrelevant."

"It's totally relevant."

"In a couple of weeks, you're going back to shooting. Steven's going to double down on the calendar, and you're going to have zero access to anyone off set for a month." He stepped down the flagstone path, and we walked to the front, where he'd parked his Mercedes. "You might want to check out that envelope I left on your couch."

I put him in his car and watched him pull past my tarp-covered front hedges and out the gate.

I texted Laine.

—I still have your camera—

Chapter 17

Laine

A tip hadn't come through in hours. Nothing. Nada. That hadn't happened in years. I'd have liked to think my phone was broken or that I had no signal, but when I'd refused the seventh call from unknown extensions of known celeb mags—meaning, the lifestyle reporters were calling me, not the editorial acquisitions department—I knew my phone had a virus. The name of the virus was Greydon.

I didn't have much of a life outside work, which I'd never thought about because I was too busy working. It didn't take long for me to get antsy.

"Hey, Phoebs, what are you doing?"

"Setting up for my niece's baptism. Oh my god, she's so cute. What are you doing?"

"Nothing."

The weight of silence nearly broke my phone.

"You should come!" she said.

"I—"

"You can take pictures."

Baptism pictures. Weddings next. No doubt I'd soon be competing for jobs with Lorenzo Balsamo. I almost choked on my horror when my phone vibrated in my ear.

Phoebe's voice cut into my thoughts. "And Rob would love to see you." Rob, her fiancé, was as happy and gregarious as she was.

"I have to go. I'll call you tomorrow."

The text sat on my home screen after I cut the call.

—I still have your camera—

I sighed.

Could things get worse?

Yes, indeed they could. This could all blow over, but it wouldn't if I continued to see him. I shouldn't have answered the text, but figuring it might bounce back anyway, I did.

—Keep it—

It didn't bounce. I paced. Looked at my map.

Still it didn't bounce.

Okay, fine. He'd put me on his short list, and as much as that gave me a flutter of excitement, it ate at me. I had to get out of the loft. I had to find some action. I would die if I didn't move.

The last decent tip I'd gotten was at Sequoia. It was deader than dead. Britt had left the hospital with one arm in a sling and the other over Maryetta, smiling and waving to the cameras.

Back in the day, when I was still too young to drink or even vote, my phone didn't do a damn thing but sit in my pocket. I still hustled. I still got out the door and made it rain. So though the car was nicer and the parking lot I kept it in was more expensive—I was still the same girl with the same fire under her ass.

I approached my car with my phone plastered to my ear.

"Tom?" I said, jangling my keys.

"Hello, Mrs. Greydon."

"Shut up, asshole."

"Where have you been?" he asked.

"Staring at my phone, that's where. Has all of Hollywood gone and died?"

"Shoulda kept your lips to yourself, big sister."

I stopped in the stairwell, my hands gripping the steel handrail. "It's not that. It's just slow today." I knew that wasn't true before I was done saying it. Gossip was never slow. "Please, it's not like I can go out until the camera's fixed anyway."

He could have turned into a real dick. He could have tormented me. With the right jab, I'd have been reduced to a puddle of powerless rage.

Instead, he asked, "Fiona's at her trainer's. Should be out in a couple of hours. Maybe more, depending. Think you'll have it fixed by then?"

I could have chased anyone, shown my face and my continued viability.

I could beat the street same as always as if nothing had happened. That was the smart thing to do. Be seen with a camera, doing what I did.

"Can you pass me her twenty?" I asked. "When you know it, I mean."

I'd never asked Tom for a damned thing. I'd never had to. I should have been happy about the flip, about the chance for him to lead the waltz, and in a very distant, big-picture kind of way, I was. But he was my closest friend, and we had a relationship that I understood. I felt it changing. It wasn't that I needed to be his boss or in some sort of superior position, but a thread of uselessness ran through me, as if my identity showed a crack. If I wasn't helpful to him, what was I?

There was a moment of silence on his end then the strum of a guitar and the murmur of female voices.

"I'm working," he said.

"I can hear that, Razzledazzle Boy."

He laughed softly. "I'll let you know when I know."

"Thanks, Tom."

"Don't thank me until I come through. And, Laine?"

"Yeah?"

"Don't sweat this. It's temporary. They forget."

Sure. They'd forget. But would I?

"I'll be at Irv's fixing my rig if you need me."

We hung up. By the time I got to the car, a text had come in. Had Tom gotten Britt's twenty so fast?

—Is this a special actor-chasing camera?—

I smiled and leaned against my car.

—It takes fine pictures of flowers and shit—

—Teach me how to use it—

—There's a manual in the box—

—It doesn't kiss like you do—

I'd typed a few replies—some sweet, some snarky, none truly honest enough to send—when another came.

—I want to see you again—

I felt as though my insides were transported to the sky while my eyes stayed on Earth and stared at those letters. But as much as I smiled remembering our kiss, a part of me stayed firmly planted on the ground. He made me feel nice, he truly did, but with every word he used to rope my heart, my brain screamed foul.

—I can't. It's career suicide—

The pause was longer than they'd been before. Had he given up on me? On the one hand, if it was that easy, he wasn't worth it. On the other, if I meant what I said and said what I meant, and if he respected me enough to hear that, I should be relieved. I should be able to move on, repair whatever damage had been done, and remember him well.

I got in the car confused. When I started it, I got another text.

—I'm not going away so easy this time—

I didn't want to be relieved. I wanted to be annoyed. I wanted to text him back and threaten to call the cops, but I couldn't be that dishonest with myself. I didn't want him to go away any more than I wanted to forget him.

The phone rang while I was on Temple.

"Hello, Miss Cartwright?" said a woman's voice.

"Yes?"

"I have Kenneth Braque on the line."

I knew who Kenneth Braque was. Everyone knew. As much as I wanted to believe he was calling to represent me, I knew he represented Michael. I stiffened at a click from the other side. I was totally unprepared for this conversation, but that was how I'd rolled my whole life.

"This is Ken Braque, Laine. How are you?"

"Fine, thank you."

"I own the public relations firm of—"

"I know who you are," I said.

"I represent Michael Greydon."

What was this? Did Michael know about Ken calling me? Did he arrange it? I shouldn't have picked up. I was driving, for Chrissakes.

"I'm aware. And I saw the pictures."

"Good. I think I can help you," he said. "I wanted to discuss how you intend to speak to the press about last night."

"However I want." I felt bitchy and tight. Though I knew he could do more for me if I played ball, all I could imagine was him talking to Michael about how I needed to be managed. Was this a baby-sitting call to see if I was going to cause trouble? "I'm a big girl."

"Of course," he said, as if he'd never, ever try to tell me what to say despite the fact that spin control was his job. "And I'd never expect you to tell anything but the truth. But in representing my client, I do have to help the people he's involved with and try to get a line on how they're going to talk about him. It's my job."

"So you can craft a response."

"You can put it that way."

I wasn't taking him seriously, and I should have. But I was annoyed. I didn't want anyone to know how I felt or what that kiss had meant to me. I didn't want anyone between Michael and me, even though a world existed between us already. I was weak, thoughtless, and the fact that Ken had talked straight rather than blown smoke up my ass put me off guard.

"Did Michael tell you to call me?" I asked.

"No, he did not. But nonetheless, I think I can help you. You've been getting calls from reporters, I assume?"

"Maybe."

"I can help you with a response," he said.

"I don't want my response crafted. I don't want to make any response at all." I felt as if I was making decisions without thinking things through. I pulled over, parking in the red.

"I can help you with that as well," he said. "Look, I know this can be overwhelming, especially for someone with one foot in the business and one foot out. I'm not trying to sell you anything—"

"I can pay you," I said. I didn't want to hire him necessarily. I didn't want to *not* hire him either. I just didn't want him to think I couldn't pay him if I wanted to.

"Why don't you come around, and we can discuss it?"

"Fine."

"Until then, if anyone asks, I'll say you're not responding," he said.

"All right."

He transferred me to his assistant, and I made arrangements with her for two afternoons hence, which seemed late to me. The whole thing could blow over or explode in that time.

I was suddenly terrified. This was bigger than I was, and I wasn't thinking. Everything I said would be put through the amplifier of the media. I didn't know what I'd say next, and that was a problem. I needed to step back and think, for once, before I shot my mouth off.

I got three more calls from unknown numbers in the next three minutes. As unused as I was to taking any kind of levelheaded action, I did the only sensible thing. I didn't answer any.

Chapter 18

Michael

"Were you drinking?" my father asked, popping a yellow ball with his racquet so it would bounce up into his hand. His question seemed almost self-directed. He wasn't drinking, and it was making him tense.

"I don't need a drink to kiss a woman."

"You're going to botch this." He thwacked a ball to me. I caught it and put it in my pocket. "Your friend Britt already delayed production long enough to screw everything. Steven says we almost lost bond."

He thwacked me another, and I almost missed it. My father was a belligerent prick when cornered, and with everything about *Bullets over Sunset* being held together by PR departments and sneaky scheduling, he was a thrashing mess. I'd stopped listening to his negativity and growling aggression a long time ago and learned to see the man under it.

"Lucky genius frontloaded the schedule," he said. "You know why? Britt. He knew something would happen with Britt. So, smart guy, but not so smart. Because now you're becoming a risk."

"Since when will kissing stop production?" I said. "You're talking crazy. The studio buys a bond note to insure a film against catastrophe. An actor dying, or falling off schedule too far, not the lead kissing a paparazzi."

"Public relations." He poked the racquet at me. He'd had the only red clay court in Los Angeles installed right in his backyard. It was the most difficult surface in the world to play on, and he liked it that way. "You date a paparazzi, you look bad, and the movie looks bad. The studio can call in the bond guys. You do not want that, and I can't afford it. This is my comeback."

Gareth had played cowboys, soldiers, and cops his entire career. Those personas became steeped in alcohol, fermenting until they became the embodiment of who he was. Playing the staid don of *Bullets Over Sunset* was a stretch, but he was doing it. He would get his Oscar, and he knew it.

"What was this with you breaking a display case window?" he asked.

"I paid for it."

"You've never paid for anything. And here's what I'm saying—don't start paying when you're on my movie." He got on his side of the net. "I'm tired of saying it over and over—you don't get free time. You don't get discretion. You need to wake up, kid." He held up a finger like a weapon.

I might have grown up a golden boy, but when he held up his finger like that, I was seven again.

"I never wanted this for you, but since you chose it, you live it," he said. "You do not show them you can't handle a role, or they'll make sure you're right. Trust me on that."

"You need to step behind the line." I tossed up the ball.

"No, I don't," he said as I served.

Of course he didn't have to get behind the line. I faulted the center line.

"You've never faced consequences," he shouted as I set up my second serve. "Well, keep it up, mister, and you will."

The second serve was supposed to be a gentle way to put the ball in play. It should be your one hundred percent, no-doubt, do-over, least-risky shot, because you didn't get a third chance. But I didn't feel like using my second serve. I felt like a wound coil. I pulled my arm back, and just as I released the tension, I realized he was baiting me so I'd screw up. I served hard to the outside, right where my father was standing.

"Hey!" Gareth shouted when the ball brushed the line and headed for his gut. He got the racquet in front of him just in time to avoid bending over in pain.

I felt a crippling shaft of pain from my elbow to my wrist, and I dropped my racquet. I wasn't supposed to hit so hard, and I hadn't since college. I tried not to scream, and I tried not to even flinch, because that was a sign of not just weakness but incompetence.

"Michael, honey?" My mother's voice came from behind the fence, miles away, across the pool and patio, the rose garden and the barbecue pit.

As if she could sense my pain from the changed vibrations in the air, she traversed the patio in her sensible suit and pearls, just back from a lunch or shopping. As she shaded her face from the sun, the bulge of her lips and the shine of her skin became more apparent. Her eyes perked at the corners, and the skin of her chin was taut around the bone.

"Get your heels off the clay!" Gareth shouted.

"Oh, take it easy, Gareth." She put her hand on my back.

I straightened. "I'm okay." The pain throbbed, but it would go away. I was done with tennis for the day though.

"He's fine," Gareth said.

She rolled her eyes and turned back to me. "I saw those pictures, darling. She's very pretty." She smiled, raising a brow as much as the collagen would allow. "Everyone's talking about it."

"Everyone needs a hobby."

"They have one," Gareth cut in, popping the last ball into the tube. "It's you. You're their hobby."

I stood up. "I know. And you told me so. I'm wrong, careless, and impulsive. Right?"

He patted my back. "But you have a good heart and a mean forehand. Now, is there any lunch? I'm starving."

"Callie put out sandwiches."

"I need a special soda," he said, using his code word for gin and Perrier.

"Gareth," I said, stopping in my tracks. "No."

"I need a drink." He cut the air horizontally with his hand, meaning discussion over. "This delay's eating me alive. And I'm getting a transplant anyway."

"No, Gareth," Brooke said.

"I don't need this liver anymore."

"You're joking to piss Brooke off," I said. "But you're going to piss me off. A lot."

"I'm not joking."

"You take one drink, and you're on your own. Do you hear me?"

"Don't you dare, young man—"

"On your own, Gareth," I said. "Everything I'm doing for you stops. Everything. You can rot. Actually, have a goddamn drink. I'll be glad to get rid of you."

I turned my back on him. I got in the car a few minutes later and sat in the driveway, staring out the window. I hadn't eaten lunch with them. I couldn't watch him drink again. Without a movie to hold over his head, I was powerless.

How fast can I drive an Aston Martin? Should I get a faster one? My skin itched and tingled. I wanted to get out of my body and not just feel a thrill but be it. To exist only as a levitating mass of risk and unsurety.

The blue bag from Merv's photo that my assistant had brought me was still on the passenger seat floor.

I couldn't risk my body. I had to keep that together, but everything else was fair game. Something, anything. A change. A shift toward meaning. I wanted to touch something with the blood of life coursing through it.

I was going to chase Laine.

Chapter 19

Laine

Tom could take ten minutes or ten hours to get me a twenty on some action. I had to get out. I had to move. At the same time, I knew moving would get me into more trouble than pacing the loft with the TV on. I wasn't looking for problems, but I was looking for something, and that was always trouble.

I got in the car and headed south.

I'd denied Michael Greydon had an effect on me when I was fifteen. He'd held my hand. We hadn't even kissed. What *should* he mean to me? He'd come up to the bleachers at four thirty every day, bouncing his ball with his racquet on each step, forearms taut and tanned. He was wealthy, secure, an example of the clean life I thought was closed to me.

He'd sat next to me, same as always, his presence sending shivers over my skin. The twenty-five-year-old me laid my hand on the arm rest of my Audi, remembering the position of my hand and the way his fingers trailed down my hand and grabbed mine. Thank God I was sitting, because my breath stopped. My heart didn't do much better.

I'd known he liked me when he took my hand in those bleachers, and I swore that I would be such a good girl for him. I would be nice and sweet, and from that moment on, I swore my life would change. I'd gotten out. I wasn't a throwaway anymore.

"I won't be here tomorrow," he'd said. "I got that part I was telling you about. That movie. It's shooting in Maine."

I don't know what happened after that. He said something about the logistics of finishing his senior year, but I didn't care about that because he was squeezing my hand. All I heard was that he wasn't coming back. I don't know how I replied, except that I was happy for him and I thought he'd be very successful. I remember being pleased that I'd kept it together, because we were just secret friends. He didn't owe me anything.

He let me go, kissing me on the cheek. "Thank you. I really enjoyed hanging out with you."

"Me too" was all I could choke out. "Good luck with everything. And don't forget to take a break once in a while."

He kissed my cheek again. Not a quick peck but a sweet, tender brush of his lips, long enough to let me feel his breath and take a quick gasp of his cinnamon scent. I didn't believe he was really leaving until he turned a corner into the locker room and waved before disappearing.

I waited, but he didn't come back.

A driver took me home at five every day. His name was Jamal, and he always brought me sweet rolls. That day, I didn't get into Jamal's Bentley. I skirted around it and got on the bus. I went to my last foster home in East Hollywood.

Jake had been my last foster family's biological son. He was four years older and sold little packets of brown sticky paste and salt-white powder. His friends called him Jake the Pillow Snake, after the Dr. Seuss character. He was home when I arrived. His room above the garage stank of pot, burning chemicals, and dirty sheets.

That smell… I knew of nothing like it, and as I remembered it, driving across town on the 10, my eyes filled up.

Jake was skinny and hairy. When I lived there, he'd tried to stick his hand up my shirt, and he laughed when I screamed and pushed him away. When I got there the day Michael told me he was leaving, he'd acted as if he didn't want me. I felt so low, so unwelcome that I took my shirt off and put his hand where I'd refused him last time.

"You lose your virginity to some rich guy?" he said, grabbing my other nipple and pulling it long.

"No. Ow."

"Such a pretty girl. Always were. Why you here?"

Maybe I had a doubt at that point about what I was doing there, and maybe I could have left. But to go where? Backward? Or was this backward? Inside my fears about Jake, a little bit of me wanted to just be wanted by someone, and that part of me wore down the bravado. Finally, after years of denying I cared if anyone gave a shit about me, I surrendered to that little kernel of need I'd ignored for so long.

"You want me or not?" I'd said.

"You sure you never been with a man before, sweet angel?" he said, letting my nipple go.

"No."

He unbuckled his jeans. He didn't have any underwear on. He took out his dick, and it was hard. I was pleased I'd done that. It was mine, that arousal. I'd had no idea how easy it was.

"You ever suck a cock?"

Words like that were what I was asking for, weren't they? "No."

He laughed. "Shit, I don't know what to do first." He swung his finger lazily at me. "Get the pants off. I got work to do."

He watched me, and I stood there, naked and looking at the holes in the carpet, while he stroked his dick and thought about what to do with me. I'd hoped, in those moments, that he'd give me some sort of reprieve, as if it was no longer my choice to just put my clothes back on and go home. But that didn't happen. Not at all. Because I had no home to go to, as far as I was concerned.

He gently and sweetly asked me to kneel, then he put his dick in my mouth. I didn't know what to do. I gagged and choked. I felt incompetent and worthless. Then he put me on my back, pulled my knees way up, and took my virginity like a shoplifter. At least I felt as if I'd somehow gotten that right.

He'd hurt me that day, and he didn't care. Neither did I. He said I could stay as long as I gave him my body whenever he wanted. Fewer hours than a real job for a roof over my head. Because he liked me. That's what he said. He liked me. I told myself that at least I was wanted for something. I had a place, for what it was worth. I had a place, and it was my choice.

I'd shown up at the Hatches' three days later, haughty, proud, and screwed to the gills by my former foster brother and a few of his friends. I didn't know what I wanted out of the rich couple, but I was an outsider. It didn't matter. After that, I left for days, showed up for school when I felt like it. They fought about me. Maybe a stronger marriage would have withstood the battles, but they were already shaky.

I ended up in another home soon after. I had no recollection of it, because I was hanging out with Jake, riding motorcycles, drinking, and thinking the fact that he wouldn't give me drugs meant he loved me.

And it had all started with Michael Greydon's fingers in mine. He did have an effect on me. That son of a bitch. He let me hope. He let me think I'd be something I wasn't. It took me years to get away from Jake the Pillow Snake and Foo Foo the Snoo, with their constant needs and rough hands. It took Tom shoving in my face a stack of pictures that Jake and company had taken with Tom's camera to wake me up. The camera didn't lie. You could retouch a picture and Photoshop it to death, but a piece of trash was a piece of trash.

I knew I could get out. I was just afraid that I had nothing to get out for. I wasn't afraid that I'd be slapped back but that I would still be an outsider.

But I had to try. I had to commit to being better. I ran away to Westlake with Tom, Irving found me, and I finally took his guidance about more than exposure and focal length. I needed to make money, and to make money, I needed to stop playing at being a photographer. I needed to make it a career. I needed to stop screwing around, because screwing around meant I wasn't chasing the picture. I needed to invest money in relationships, which meant going to clubs and being nice to the wait staff. I needed to let my bitten nails grow out and dress like an adult. I needed to make the city my only lover.

I closed my legs and got on my feet. It was the hardest thing I'd ever done.

And now Michael Greydon was having an effect on me again. A different one. I wasn't about to get on my back for all comers. I wouldn't be used by strange men as a repository in the hopes that one of them would love me. But I felt that same need to crawl back into the arms of someone who would accept any part of me.

That was bullshit.

Unacceptable.

I had no time for it.

I almost missed my turn, and I yanked my car across two lanes of traffic to get onto 4th Street.

That was when I noticed the blue Corolla behind me. It cut across three lanes of traffic to get off on Central with me then changed lanes again when I did. Two guys, from what I could see. I stopped my car on Sixth Street and got out, and they blew by me. The guy in the passenger seat photographed me standing outside my car as they passed. They whipped around the corner, into the parking lot, and came around again.

I knew those guys.

They didn't know who they were dealing with. Downtown LA? Those bitches were in my crib.

You know who cares about me? You know where I belong?

I belong in motion on the streets of Los Angeles.

I got back in the car.

If you go north on Central and make a right on Palmetto then another right into a certain nondescript industrial parking lot, you can cross to Factory Place, so named because someone had no imagination and named it after what surrounded it. Once you were in Factory Place, you could approach the Los Angeles Gun Club and use the yearly membership you got specifically for access to the underground parking lot. If you knew a damn thing at all, you knew that the underground lot had a service egress in the back, onto East Sixth.

And if you were cruel, you let the guys following you catch up to you. You pulled into a spot and let them think you were parking outside. You let them stop and get out, then you drove down the ramp and you watched them stare at your car as it disappeared underground.

"Bye-bye, assholes," I said as I turned into the sunlight on East Sixth and headed south. I felt better.

Six minutes later, I pulled up to Irving's place.

Irv lived downtown in a two-story craftsman with chipping lead paint and an overgrown front yard. Even when he taught at Breakfront, his house had looked like an abandoned building. It sat on the corner of a street that had been repaved repeatedly to no avail, because of the eighteen-wheelers rolling by daily. Next door, on the east side, sat a Mexican food warehouse, and across the street was a huge parking lot for the offices of a fashion empire that took up the entire block. Behind him was a small light industrial shop where four sculptors worked in granite and metal. He was the only actual resident in a four-block radius.

You'd think he was some lone holdout who wouldn't sell to developers and thus ended up living in a swirl of light industrial noise, rotting food smells, and toxic dust, but he rented. The developers just hadn't been interested in the property in the eighties, and they left it there. The rent never went up because Irv's landlord knew no one else would want to live there.

"That was some kiss," he said as he opened the door.

"The camera doesn't lie. It was a once-in-a-lifetime."

He snorted and got out of the doorway, letting me into his dark living room. "What's in the bag?"

"I have a broken hinge on my mirror. I thought it was the shutter, but

I'm rusty. I think I need help."

"You know how to fix that."

I shrugged. "Maybe I needed company."

He took the paper bag from my hands and peered in. "Let's take a look."

The house was steeped in his presence, a complete pigsty with an organizational system based in fractal geometry. You could only see it when you stepped back. Boxes of old negatives were stacked on top of files of the same. Every corner, cabinet, and drawer held a piece of dead photo equipment, a file, a folder, or film. Tom and I knew his system from years of interning and working for him, but no one else would.

Irving had set up the second bedroom as a darkroom, boarding up the windows and sealing them with tinfoil. It was painted matte black, and the door had been replaced with a roundabout that kept out light. He'd jury-rigged the plumbing to put in a sink, and the leakage from the pipes, along with chemical spillage, had destroyed the floor to such a degree that some of the boards had rotted right through to the crawlspace.

He led me to the studio next to his darkroom. He laid my spare rig on his table and picked up a screwdriver with such a tiny head that it looked like an awl. "I remember this camera. You're going back to manual?"

I pulled up a stool. "Auto focus is for amateurs."

"That's the spirit." He shook out his hand, cringing.

"Is it the arthritis?" I took the screwdriver and camera from him.

"Hang on." He limped to the bathroom, calling out from the rectangle of light down the hall. "Damn meds wear off all at once. It's like these little men in my joints wait to ambush me."

I worked out the screws. "I think I'm going to go old school and see how I like it."

"You can't do what you do without the auto. You'd have one guy in the pack with something to use and a bunch of part-time editors going through seven submissions a day if it wasn't for autofocus. The technology created the business."

I heard the click of him shaking out pills and the slap of the medicine cabinet closing.

"So, this guy?" he called from the bathroom.

"Michael? He's not a guy. He's a star," I said.

"Is this a relationship?"

"We have a relationship. He runs away, and I chase him." I had the camera open, its guts spread across the table like a heart patient's.

Irving stood in the doorway. I was thankful I'd never told him about the bleachers, or the young varsity tennis player, or anything.

"Are you going to press charges?" he asked from the doorway.

"For breaking my camera? I should sue Tom."

"I think he's serious about that quiet girl."

"You know what she does onstage? Screams like a banshee and pees into a plastic cup," I said.

"No."

"Yep."

"And Tom likes this girl? Our Tom?" He moved a pile of old negatives from a chair and sat down, cringing as he bent and relaxed.

"Irv, can we talk about you?"

"Hell, no."

"Can I be honest?" I said.

"No."

"I'm worried about you."

"Oh, shit—"

"No, listen—"

"Laine—"

"Stop it, okay? You need help," I said. "And before you start, I'm not talking about cleaning this place up. Forget that. It's a hopeless case. You need someone to assist you."

He waved his lame hand at me.

"What?" I said.

"What, nothing. Assistants are for people who have work."

"You could get someone in to go through this shit. You have pictures of celebrities going back thirty years. I can't even imagine what the crap in this house would be worth if everything in it was filed right and sold."

"No one cares about old shit, Laine. People want new stuff. I haven't taken a worthwhile picture in… I don't know how long." He looked out the window, or more accurately, he looked *toward* the window. He was depressed.

I knew his deal. He had plenty of contacts he was afraid to call, because he felt they'd left him behind. He had students surpassing him in every aspect of their careers. He was breaking down physically, and his methods were so dated they were near obsolete. I could count on my fingers the number of my colleagues who knew that stop bath came before fixer.

"How about I make you dinner?" I said.

"I thought you cared about me?" he joked.

But I could cook. Maybe not gourmet meals, but I could put something edible on the table every night, because Jake had added that to my list of responsibilities after a month. So after I fixed my camera, I made him enough food for the week and wrapped it up while he told me about the old days of Hollywood.

The sun went down, and my phone didn't ring. Not Tom with a twenty on Fiona. Not a single tip. And not Michael.

"I have to get out tonight," I said, packing Irv's freezer with meals. "Nothing's come in, and I'm not sitting around. I won't be ignored."

"Maybe you could go to bed," Irv suggested. "You know, take a night off since one's being handed to you?"

"Never."

But once I got in the car, I was bone tired. I went home, showered, paced, and told myself it would all be okay. I went to bed not believing it.

I didn't know what to do with myself. Go out. Watch TV. Pace the loft. I had a feeling, like a vibrating thread through every thought, that something was going to change. With change came hope and hurt.

Every new foster family had that thread. Every time I was let go because another kid was coming on or because I kept going off in the middle of the night, I felt it.

The hippie couple in Malibu, Sunshine and Rover, had been more than a thread. They'd been a thick rope of optimism. At five, I still had the bad habit of hoping for the best. They read me stories with pretty pictures, and when Sunshine pulled me to her I smelled patchouli and sandalwood. Everything they owned was made of beautiful colors. They laughed together and took me walking on the beach in the early morning in winter.

I didn't care when they lost the apartment. I didn't mind the van. It was big enough for us. I would have lived anywhere with them. But the caseworker came and ended it. Rover said they'd come for me when they got a place. He promised.

I'd grabbed his beard and said, "Okay, Daddy. I'll wait."

I'd kept that hope alive through three more homes, avoiding connection with any family because Sunshine and Rover were coming back. I couldn't let myself love another Mommy and Daddy, and most of them didn't want to be loved. They wanted me to do stuff, or go away, or replace a dead thing in themselves.

I crawled under the covers and tried to talk away that thread of hope. I didn't need it. I shot it down, shooed it out the door, burned it away with laser-beam intensity. By the time I fell asleep, it was a thin line of black ash.

Chapter 20

Michael

Brad was an introvert. You'd never guess it from his entourage or his public persona, but in the strictest sense of the word, he was as much an introvert as I was. When he was tired and overwhelmed and needed energy and strength, he retreated into his music, which he'd never share with anyone.

I respected that, and I understood it. Whenever we were seen together, the sober, straight-laced Michael Greydon and bad boy Brad Sinclair, people always noted how different we were. We were more the same than they could see.

Of course, when he felt good and there was fun to be had, he had fun. Tonight, it was a simple dinner and whatever else the night brought. He planned on being out all night without actually making plans.

Me, I was just hungry. I was going to eat and bail.

When I got out of the car, the valet took the keys, and I was subjected to the usual flashes and catcalls. This restaurant in particular was low-hanging fruit for the paps, and I wondered if Brad had chosen it as a joke.

I waved and smiled as usual, but I also did something unusual. I looked at the paps directly, frustrated by the fact that it was too dark, too backlit for me to catch the people behind the cameras. They were all men's voices, but they always were. Laine was stealth silence in her heels.

The feet. I looked at their feet as I walked toward the back of the restaurant. All boots and run-down sneakers. No heels. How many years had she been in those packs and I'd never said a thing to her because it would be too awkward?

I faced them, and the flashes popped like a lightning storm.

"Mike! Mike!"

"You love us now!"

"Over here!"

"What happened with you and Laine?"

"Wanna kiss me?"

The voice on the last pap was deep baritone, and everyone laughed. I caught myself before I said, "Are you going to put out?" That would imply Laine had, and it wasn't anyone's business.

In that second of thought, the pack of them propositioned me.

"Kiss me!"

"Give me a squeeze right here!"

"I kiss better than him!"

"I just brushed my teeth!"

Squeaky kiss noises fell like rain, and I couldn't turn away. I walked right into the pack with my arms out. I grabbed a short guy with a beard and planted one on his cheek. Another guy came at me with his arms out and kissed my cheek. Another just hugged me. We laughed, and the shutters went on and on. With every handshake and testament to my coolness, I looked for Laine, hoping she'd be at the back of the pack, but of course, there were a thousand little stakeouts in the city, and she'd be wise to avoid me.

But still, I looked for her. I didn't know what I expected, but I knew what I wanted.

When the last willing pap had been smooched and the last picture taken, I waved and went into the restaurant. The speeding traffic along Sunset was replaced by music, the hum of conversation, and good acoustics.

Brad sat in the center of a long table in the back with his usual dirty dozen. Guys from his hometown and whatever girl they were with. His manager. A stylist. I knew their names, but they belonged to Brad. He saw me immediately, from half a room away, and waved.

"You!" he shouted. "I want to talk to you!"

After much reseating, shifting, arguing, and joking, I sat next to Brad. He kept one hand on the knee of a German ten-thousand-dollar-a-day runway model who was already half drunk. I said my hellos, using names when I remembered them, and ordered something to eat.

One guy, an obnoxious friend of Brad's from his hometown, held up his phone. A picture of me kissing a bearded pap had already been tossed up. "Too far, Mikey baby. Too far."

He looked like a Hollywood player, with his thick gold chain and carefully placed hair product, but his Arkie accent still hung around the corners of his vowels. Three of Brad's entourage were from home, but this guy was the only ass. I'd forgotten his name, because I couldn't stand him.

"Letting them think you're their friend is too far."

"He was cute," I said. "Here, I'll kiss this asshole too."

I grabbed Brad's head and kissed his cheek. Brad laughed and dunked his napkin in his water to wipe his face.

"Not cool," said Arkie. "These people, they're parasites. You talk to them, and they think they're your friend. They think they have *access*." He flopped the phone down, angry. "They're animals, and they don't have access to us, okay?"

"I'm sorry," I said. "To who? Access to *who*?"

Groans went up, and heads shook. Everyone at the table could feel the tension. Brad's model got up to go to the bathroom.

"Arnie, man," Brad said, reminding me why I called the guy Arkie, "cool it."

But Arnie-slash-Arkie was a sheet to the wind and belligerent even sober. "You cannot fuck paps, okay? That shit is scary. That bitch is scary."

"You didn't—"

"You got fooled by her tits or whatever. Maybe she sucked your dick like a pro, but she's an animal just like the rest of them."

"Shut up, Arnie," Brad groaned.

I said nothing, because the half of my brain that wanted to kill him was arguing with the half that had been trained to be a civilized member of society.

"You can get a blow job anywhere, man," Arnie said while I tried to keep my hands under the table. "Half the girls at this table would suck your dick. Why you gotta get head from a lowlife hooker pap is like—"

I grabbed his gold chain and twisted it so fast, he didn't know what was happening. I tightened it and pulled him over the table. Plates crashed. Girls screamed. Food went flying as I pushed his head into someone's dinner.

"You no-talent piece of shit," I growled, watching his face get red. "You've done nothing your whole life. No one cares what you think."

"Dude." Brad's voice. A hand on my arm.

I looked up to a huge restaurant packed with people standing, phones up. A dance of rectangles, some with flashes, captured me in the act of choking someone with a gold rope. I let the chain go. Arnie hacked, and Brad yanked me away.

I pulled him off me and got my finger in Arnie's face. "Stay away from me."

"With pleasure, motherfucker."

His friends made a show of holding him back, but he wouldn't come after me. He was a coward.

Brad pulled me, navigating the chairs and camera phones, into the kitchen. The adrenaline in my blood made me sensitive to the bright lights and the ambient noise, which was more of a crash bang than a loud hum.

"Dude?" Brad said. "What the fuck?"

I held up my hands. "I'm done with him."

"Cool. Totally cool, but then what? He's always trash talking. That's what he does. Remember what he said about Harriet when you were with her? And you didn't care, dude. You laughed."

"The tone of this was a little different." Was I defending myself? What a waste of time. Choking him with his gold chain was indefensible.

"Sure, sure, I get it," Brad said. "But who cares what Arnie says?"

"I do, all right? I care."

"Duh."

I rubbed my eyes, coming off the adrenaline rush. My apology would have to be public, and the pictures would be discussed by over-coiffed entertainment jockeys in TV studios and insiders over lunch on Wilshire.

The kitchen had quieted, as if the staff had made room for us.

"I knew her in high school," I said, backing into the refrigerator room door. "She scared the hell out of me then, and she scares me now."

"Hey, I get why she scares you now. She's pretty scary with that camera."

"The camera? Fuck the camera. She's got something explosive in her."

"You're the one with the explosive side."

"It's just…" My hands were in front of me, as if clutching something I couldn't explain. Some desire to make things happen, to change, to break the status quo into a million pieces and live in the center of an unknowable, unplanned, unpredictable, boundary-free universe. "I can't keep away, and I won't. Maybe she's going to screw me, but that's my problem."

Brad shoved me into the metal door in a gentle, brotherly way. "You know what? Go for her. 'Cause you're not the guy who gets his balls in a twist for any woman. You feel like this, whatever this is, and I'm cool with it. She seems all right from here. I'll take care of Arnie. I got your back. Just hear this." He held up his finger. "She starts some shit I don't like, I'm gonna tell you. Don't try to choke me across the dinner table. Got it?"

"I got it."

We shook on it.

Chapter 21

Michael

By six thirty the next morning, my night out had been broken apart, analyzed, chewed, digested, and regurgitated. The photos of my affection toward the paparazzi at the back door of the restaurant got the least press, naturally, because I was having fun. The fight was front and center in still and video. Arnie and I had shaken hands over the upturned table. It hadn't been photographed as extensively, but by the time I got up, it was as if the handshake had never happened.

The places that had had enough time to write more than a hundred words about the fight speculated that I was losing my shit because of the break in the *Bullets* schedule. They attributed my rooftop kiss of a paparazza to my tension. I was a workaholic, they said, and without my drug of choice, I was snapping.

I admitted I felt as if I was bending, but it wasn't the schedule as much as what the schedule break might cause. My father would start drinking if the movie fell through. Brooke and I knew it. He was on a thread.

I didn't usually look at the media's reaction to me and what I was doing. It had always been bland and boring. Just me walking or drinking coffee. There had never been any bad behavior to get distracted by, so it had been easy to follow a simple rule... don't look.

The rule was easy until Laine, in that dress, her hair unpinned, her fingers gripping my elbow as I kissed her. I felt alive. And that was a cliché, of course. A phrase directors used that I tossed off as meaningless, representing a feeling that had something more at its core. I had tried to capture it a hundred times by linking it to other feelings that were closer to delight.

But this wasn't delight. It wasn't joy. I'd gotten it all wrong. Life, yes, but inside it sat a precarious tilt toward death, oblivion, pain, and danger. Alive didn't mean happy or joyous. It meant that my relationship with my own existence was unstable, and only in the nearing loss of it did I realize I wanted it so badly.

How had Laine come to represent that? Was it when she nearly fell off the roof and I grabbed her, or was it the look on her face when her brother took those pictures at NV? Or maybe I'd made that connection with her on the tennis court bleachers. Knowing who and what she was, so different from me, brought close enough to touch the side of the world that I never got to see. Was it her survival that caused my fascination?

I sat on the back patio, flipping through the news on my tablet. The pictures of Laine and me still attracted my eye. The *LA Post* piece was ridiculous, because they didn't get it. They didn't know the half of it, but they pretended to until the end.

"It's seven in the morning," Ken said, sounding as awake as always, when I called. "I was waiting another half an hour to call you."

"What the fuck is in the news today?"

"You beating the hell out of a poor kid from Arkansas?"

"How did they find out I knew Laine from before?" I asked.

"What the hell are you doing reading the papers? We have a deal. You don't read the papers, and I tell you what's in them. One, you choking—"

"How did they find out who she was? Her *history*?" I wasn't quite shouting, but I was using a bitch of a tone that only worked through my teeth.

"It's their job."

"No." I pointed at the view of the city below because Ken wasn't in front of me. "The *Almanac* cherry-picks what's easy."

"Jesus Christ, Michael, Britt breaking her shoulder is the worst thing that could have happened to you. I've never met a guy who needed time off so badly and couldn't handle it when he got it."

I knew Ken. He'd deflect until I was apologizing for Arnie, for not being productive on my days off, for not strictly maintaining my image. That wasn't going to wash anymore.

"What did you tell them?" I asked.

"Anything in the public record that would make you look sympathetic. Kissing a foster child as opposed to a slimeball, you know? It works, especially after the incident—"

"With Arnie? Arnie's a moron. If murder were legal, he'd be dead already."

"Can you make sure to not say things like that in public?" he asked.

"Can you never breathe her name again to anyone? Ever? I don't care if it's in the public record. She's mine, and that means she's my problem."

"She can be your asset too."

"Can it be normal? How about that?" I said. "Not an asset or a problem. Not a big deal. Just some girl that I may or may not be seen with again."

Ken sighed as if I was a recalcitrant child he'd explained things to a hundred times. "No, Greydon, normal is not on the menu. Your career would die of boredom on a diet of normal."

I shook my head. "Just leave her out of it, Ken. That, or you let me know what you're doing before you do it. Can we agree on that?"

"Sure, kid. Sure."

We said good-bye and ended it, but his assessment of my choices stuck in my mind. I craved normalcy, and I craved the tingle of life. Could they even coexist? I'd played normal, everyday guys living a life I'd never lived. I'd played them deadened and dull, because that was what I'd been told normal was.

I didn't want normal.

I wanted real.

And my God, Laine was real.

Chapter 22

Laine

I didn't hear from Tom. I slept like a dead thing and could have slept another ten hours. When the sun went down, I could have woken and gone out to the clubs to see who I could catch looking good doing something bad, but that didn't happen.

Sometime in late morning, I was rudely awakened to my ceiling *thumpity thumping* techno music from the loft above. I wasn't just annoyed, I was interrupted.

I gave it thirty minutes, pacing and showering to kill time until whoever was up there split. The space upstairs was unoccupied, so I hoped the cleaning crew was just in to prep it for showing. On the opposite side of my hope, I feared there was a new owner and he was an inconsiderate jerk.

I opened my door so I could stare up the stairwell, which could not have been a more ineffective way to deal with the problem. At my feet sat the *LA Post Almanac* section, without the rest of the paper. I picked it up. Of course the rooftop picture was on the corner of the front page, with Brenda Vinter's byline.

When Celebrities and Paparazzi Share Space

Crap. I read the article, which tried to quickly disseminate whether or not paps and celebs were truly in bed together, how the media feeds on itself, and how the internet played a part in all of it. It said everything and nothing, failing to make its point because it sounded hurried and wanting for space. What they'd really wanted was to show the picture a day late rather than not at all.

But the nugget was in the last few paragraphs. I dialed Phoebe with shaking fingers, trying to shut out the blasting music.

"Did you see the thing in the *LA Post?*" I asked before she could say hello.

"Yeah." She sounded contrite, and her glitter tossing for Michael was gone. "Just now. Where are you? A disco?"

"It says Michael and I were at Breakfront together."

"Yep."

"It says I was the foster child of Orry and Mildred Hatch," I said.

"Yes, it does."

Was that her lawyer voice? I hated her lawyer voice.

"That's invasive. I am not a public figure. I've never hired an agent or publicist to get my name out there. That's the prerequisite. Everyone knows it. That's why I can do my job and they can't touch me."

"Did you talk to Michael's publicist?" she asked.

"He called me. I just said... I don't even remember."

I can pay you.

"Did you know it was his publicist?"

"Yes."

"Did the publicist know you knew?"

I know who you are.

"Yes... so?" I asked.

"Did you ask for his help in any way?"

"No, and I hate your lawyer voice."

"Did he offer it?"

I don't want to make any response at all.

I can help you with that as well.

"Shit," I said.

"If the publicist is trustworthy, then you have a case against the *Post*, but if he told them he was working with you, you're now a public figure."

"That's crap. I haven't even met with him. I could sue him."

"The toothpaste is out of the tube."

"Michael Greydon is poison. If I ever forget that, remind me," I shouted over the thumping beat vibrating through my house.

When a *thop THUP thop* accompanied the throbbing music, I lost my complete and utter shit.

"I have to go," I said.

"Be good," she said.

Maybe she wanted to say something more, but I hung up the phone and jammed it in my pocket. I slung my camera over my shoulder and stormed out the door without locking it. I stomped up the concrete-and-iron steps in my boots and pounded on the upstairs door with the side of my fist.

I was about to kick it when the door swung open. The music got louder, and my breath was stolen right out of me.

"Laine." He smiled his million-dollar smile.

"Michael. What the hell are you doing?"

"I was trying to see if this was a good place to practice. You inspired me the other night." He looked down the hall. "What are you doing here?"

I crossed my arms. "Save it for your audience."

He stepped away from the doorway, and I noticed the racquet in his hand. "Come in then." He looked at my body in a way that was discreet in its speed and warming in its intensity, as if he was trying not to but couldn't help himself, so he decided to do it quick.

I stepped in, arms still twisted over my chest, and he closed the door. He crossed the room to the stereo and turned it off. Other than the musical equipment, the loft was empty but for a table, two chairs, and a gorgeous man I met in high school. His feet were bare, and his sweater was pure white. He might as well have been wearing lingerie with the way the sleeves held his biceps and his ass was cupped in the jeans.

"What do you think?" Michael asked, thwacking a ball against the back wall.

"This is stalking."

"It's stalking if you tell me to go away and I don't." He hit the ball again. He had such control. I would have broken a window already. "Are you telling me to go away?"

"You're an entitled, spoiled brat. What are you doing here?"

He caught the ball in his bare hand with the grace and accuracy of a gymnast. Or a dancer. Or someone hyper-aware of their body at all times. As if he was an actor who worked his ass off to understand his craft.

"I'm afraid to tell you," he said, flicking his tongue over his teeth. His eyes were dirty thoughts, and his lips curved into a breach of etiquette.

"Let me see your hands."

"What?"

He motioned for them, and I stuck them out. He dropped the ball and tucked his racquet under his arm before flipping my hands top-up.

"Before I tell you, I want to see if your nails are long enough to claw my eyes out."

"I can do far worse than that if you don't tell me."

"You're in the *Post*. And they know about where we met."

"Your eyes are safe." I squeezed his hands, and he held them. I didn't know why I allowed it, except for the fact that they felt good. "I saw the paper this morning."

"I'm sorry about that. It wasn't me," he said.

"It was your publicist. I should slap you for paying him to do it."

"That's not why I pay him. But I'm sorry it's too late. Let me make it up to you."

"I want nothing to do with you." With my hands resting on his and the space between us shaped like a fault line, I couldn't have spoken a fouler lie.

"I've made you lunch," he said. "You don't owe it to me to sit and eat it, but you should."

"Always so respectful. Is this the same guy who smashed the trophy case at Breakfront?"

"His nice guy twin."

"I'll sit with you on one condition." I let my hands slide away from his, and the loss was deeper than I expected. It might be the last time I had an excuse to touch him. "That night at NV?" He stiffened, but I wasn't deterred. "You flipped out and smashed my camera, which was… not like you, I guess. Tell me what happened."

A hundred magazines would pay for the story I'd just asked for, even without a picture. He'd never answer it. By the length of his pause and the coolness of his stare, I'd alienated him, and my disappointment was almost physical. Sure, I might avoid drinking the poison that was Michael Greydon, but I didn't expect to feel as if I'd die of thirst.

"Do you like eggs?" he asked.

"Sure."

"Better sit down then. It's all I know how to cook."

Was he going to tell me? Would he make up something? He held the chair out for me and slid it in when I sat. To my right, the huge windows looked over the blue-grey fog of the city from six stories up. Everything was better higher.

"You think I should buy the place?" Michael said from the kitchen island, where he scraped a spatula over a frying pan.

"Are you trying to get me to move?"

His attention stayed glued to his pan. "Salt?" He held up the shaker.

He was messing with me. He knew I didn't give a damn about whether or not he salted the eggs. I stood, clopped over to the island, and leaned back on it, next to him.

"Your dad didn't want you to act," I said. "I remember that. And your mom pushed you to do it. You didn't know who to obey. Personally, I don't know if I could reject your mother either."

"Ah." He shut off the stove. "Brooke Chambers's biggest fan. I think I keep forgetting on purpose." The eggs stood in a nicely gelled yellow pile.

"She seemed so perfect. Perfect actress. Perfect mother. What was she like? I'm sorry, I feel like a dork asking, but I can't help it."

"Same as anyone's mother. Demanding, controlling, and occasionally smothering." He handed me the plate. "But she took it on like she was conquering territory. I have to give her points for ambition."

"Do I get toast?"

"Ah, crap." He reached behind him for a loaf of bread, turned right then left, locating the toaster, which still had Styrofoam flakes on it from the packaging.

"Did your dad see that you were a natural?" I asked. "I mean, in high school, I couldn't tell, but now, I'd like to see you do something you weren't hyper aware about."

He flipped up the loaf, letting it spin in the air, then caught it. "Maybe just bread?"

"That's fine."

"You don't go anywhere without your instrument," he said, laying the eggs and bread on the table. "Your camera. I mean, you brought it to yell at the guy upstairs?"

I swallowed. I'd had a reason or two to bring it, mostly "just in case" and the classic "you never know if…" but the real reason was simple. I didn't feel right without it. "I see better through it."

He pulled the chair out for me again. "I can't leave my instrument home." He smirked, making a blue joke about his instrument without saying a single dirty thing. He was pure sex with a side of fun. And he was warming up. Maybe I hadn't pushed him away with my question. Maybe he'd sate this thirst. I swallowed hard, pushing down my throat the thought of him on top of me, eyes half closed and lost in pleasure. God, was I blushing?

He slid half the eggs onto my plate, his face turned toward me. I wanted to put my flushed skin under a bag. I felt naked, as if he could see my dirty thoughts.

"I have to say," I said to fill the space, "I get it. I get you. But I want to say…" I stopped myself. I'd said that twice, which meant I was hedging. "About that night. On the roof."

He folded his hands in front of him, elbows on each side of his plate, while I pushed my eggs around.

"The instrument thing. I know how it goes. I've known so many actors. And I just…"

"Say it. Whatever it is." My God. How did he make it seem so reasonable and safe to just speak my mind?

"I don't trust you," I blurted. "The other night I kissed you, and it was the kiss of my life, don't get me wrong. Your instrument works fine. And I wake up to my whole history in the damn newspaper. I didn't sign on for that, no matter what Ken Braque says. And I'm not saying this means anything, what's happening here with the eggs and squatting in the penthouse, because you probably just want to seduce me for lack of anything better to do. And okay, I think that's all right, but I'm going to be as honest as I can be. I liked you in high school. I was probably as in love with a person as I could be without having it returned. And I know you had Lucy and everything, but here it is, on the line. I don't want you to hurt me. Because you'll walk away and be fine, and I'll lose everything." I pushed my plate away then leaned against the side of the table and slid out my chair.

Lightning fast, he reached across the table and grabbed my wrists. I took a breath involuntarily and held it without thinking. His hands were on mine again, holding me there, but that wasn't why I was still. His eyes, those clear jade fires, held me in their connection to mine.

"That was brave," he said. "And foolish. And real."

"That's me. Okay?"

"In a nutshell. Yes, that is you."

I didn't want him to let me go, but he looked at me so intently, I needed to leave. I pulled away, and he resisted.

"My father played every movie tough guy like he meant it," Michael said. "He believes that's who he is. That's why he won't get help for the drinking. Because he's too tough. He missed days and flew into drunken rages on set. His career went into the toilet because he was too big a risk to hire. *Bullets Over Sunset* is getting made because it's his last chance and because I could make it happen for him. But he has to stop drinking to do it."

"I'm sorry," I said.

"Don't say that while he lives."

"I mean I'm sorry you have to go through this." I whispered.

He lightened his grip with a smile. "When we were on that balcony together, and I'd just heard Britt was going to delay shooting, I knew he wouldn't make it through. I just… I was on the edge, and I didn't know what to do. That camera, seeing how confused I was, and you, Laine. You. There were reasons I didn't say hello before. I cared about you, and I didn't know what to say to you. When I saw it all fall apart with Britt, I just went over the edge. I apologize for freaking out."

"I get it," I said, even though I didn't get it completely. I only saw his pain, even if I couldn't wrap my head about the motivation.

He let go and leaned back in his chair. "I'm kind of sorry I told you. You're not trained to manage the media. You could be a leak in a watertight drum. But I agreed so you'd stay. It was the deal. And you haven't even eaten your eggs."

I sat back down. I didn't know how to feel. I'd never had a parent I cared about. Irving would be the closest thing, but not a single adult in my life had consistently taken responsibility for raising me into a woman. How could I empathize with the need to save that person?

"And yeah," he said, popping a forkful of scrambled eggs into his mouth, "I'm trying to seduce you."

"You've gotten really lazy then. You should have catered. I mean, no juice even?"

"I can make a joke about my ability to serve after my injury." He pointed at an elbow as if he did it every time he used the word injury.

"You wouldn't dare make a pun."

He smiled that half smile, and the light hit him just right, with a burned yellow tint and a soft halo.

I picked up my camera. "If I ask to take your picture before I do it, am I still a sleazy pap?"

"Are you asking?"

"The light's really good. I won't sell them."

He leaned over and looked at my old rig. The light through the windows was textbook, soft on his cheeks and highlighting the ends of his hair.

"I have your new camera in the car," he said.

"I want to see how this old horse works."

"Is there actual film in there?"

"Yes. It's a terrible pap camera, but for a perfect guy sitting still in perfect light, it's perfect."

"By all means then."

I was reluctant to crouch in front of him and put the camera in front of my face, but once I did, he went into actor mode. I'd never seen someone come through the lens like that. Some people had that thing, that aura, that frame-crowding presence, but until I got him in a shot he wanted to be in, instead of running away, I hadn't understood it.

"You always take so few?" he asked, fingers in his hair, head tilted like a sexy movie star god.

"I take fewer than most. Turn a little toward the window."

"Are you wondering how I found you?" he asked between shots.

"I figure you're rich, so you have rich person superpowers." I meant it. The wealthy could always just get things done in a way the rest of us couldn't. It was an assumption, and a foolish one. It gave him abilities he couldn't possibly have. It set him up to fail me.

"Your name is on your mortgage, and your mortgage is a matter of public record."

I didn't lower the camera, but I stopped taking pictures. Michael leaned down toward me, filling the frame.

"Everything Ken found out is on the public record, and he knew stuff the *Post* didn't publish. Stuff he held back."

I clicked the shutter because my hand got so tight. But the camera? That stayed in front of my face. I couldn't look at him. I felt too vulnerable for that.

"I came here to seduce you with breakfast and to apologize for my publicist and also to tell you that you need to protect yourself."

I remembered the two paps who had followed me downtown. I hadn't even wondered how they'd found me. I assumed it was a tip or something, but what if they'd followed me from my front door?

The frame got dark as he put his hand over the lens and pulled the camera away.

"There's information out there, and it's not a big deal for most people," he said. "But you're out there now. Until they forget and move on to the next thing."

"I don't want to be famous."

"I understand."

"I just take pictures."

"I know." He put the camera on the table.

"And I kissed you. That was—"

He put his finger on my lips. "I'm going to protect you. I'm going to teach you how to do this."

I stood. "No. I don't need to be protected. Who's coming after me? A bunch of smelly paparazzi? Sitting out front in their shitty SUVs waiting for life to come into frame? No. Screw them."

"What about your family? They say screw you too?"

I stiffened. I didn't talk about that to anyone, but I'd told him so much in the bleachers. I'd told him I'd worked in Mister Yi's sweater factory because my hands were small enough for the machines and that he sent me away when the order was done. I'd told him about Sunshine and Rover, who I'd loved and who loved me. I'd told him about the perfectly put-together mom I'd called June Snowcone, her super particular OCD, and how I'd never done anything right for her. I told him about the mom and dad who'd ignored Tom and me, the nights and days we'd spent wandering the city instead of going home. I never expected him to remember it all.

"I told you all about my family."

"Your mother is dead. She died in prison when you were eleven."

"Do you remember that? Or is it from Ken?" I asked.

"Both."

I bit my lower lip, and he reached down to free it from my top teeth. I sat down, toying with my camera on the table.

"This is awkward," I said. "I want to get mad about my privacy, but being who I am and what I do for a living… I can't really, can I?"

"You can if you want. It's just not a good use of your energy."

"I wasn't prepared for this."

"We'll figure it out. Is there anyone else you need to warn? What about your father?"

"You don't remember?" I spun the camera on the table. "He left my mother when she was pregnant. I've never met him. She never told me who he was, not even when she went to jail and I went into the system. He doesn't even know I exist. Why are you even talking about this shit? No one's family is safer than mine."

His elbows rested on his knees, and he looked up at me with big green eyes. "I thought you knew."

Between my intellectual disorientation (What? Who?) and my emotional confusion (Why?) I froze in place. If I'd ever thought of my father as a real person, which I realized had never occurred, I might have been angry at him. But how could I be angry at a man who had never existed? Dead, alive, gone, here, none of it mattered.

Was Michael trying to resurrect the dead? Was he making a man out of a pile of dust or the extra bone of a rib cage?

And his silence. The way he closed his mouth and didn't let his eyes waver from mine. I felt observed, peeled open, and examined in a way that would have been uncomfortable if it hadn't been him. I couldn't explain to myself why it was all right coming from him, why his silent, deadly scrutiny didn't feel invasive but welcome.

"I've seen my birth certificate," I said. "Brian Nordine is nobody. I looked for him. He's gone like the freaking wind. And the wind can have him," I said. "I don't give a shit."

"Really?"

Where did he get that confidence? That ability to say one word that would throw me off my axis and catch me at the same time?

"Really." I grabbed my camera. "Thank you for the eggs. Your apology is accepted, and your warning… I get it. Thank you. I'll keep my eyes out."

Fifteen steps to the door. Why were those lofts so damn big? What was I thinking?

Five steps, and I heard a shuffle behind me, the scrape of a chair. I picked up the pace, and I knew he was behind me. By the time I got to the door, his chest was against my back and his hand was over the doorjamb.

"Don't," he said.

"Don't what?"

"I'm going to get between you and this. I don't like anyone knowing where you are. I don't like you walking around at night unprotected. Especially because of me."

I turned, putting my back to the door. "I haven't seen you in ten years. Now this?"

"I should say it's that I feel responsible for what's happening. But you're in this business as much as I am, so it's not that. It's you. I was up half the night thinking about you in those bleachers. The things you told me. The stuff I told you. How I felt. Back then, I was so confused, and I left you without a call or checking on you for reasons that…" He shook his head. "The reasons were pathetic. No one would have approved of you, and I lived on approval."

He touched my hair, and those long strands became nerve endings for desire. The little hairless spot on his chin shifted, and I wanted to touch it so badly that I did so without thinking.

"Whatever it was I felt before, I'm not hiding from it this time. This time, I'm not going to worry what anyone else thinks," he said.

"What if I'm worried?"

"I'll make you not worried."

His breath warmed my cheek, and I believed he could change things, even as I knew he couldn't. He could only drag himself down. This could only go bad. But I turned my face until my lips touched his, and he stopped being a movie star. He was the boy in the bleachers, the one who worked too hard and cared too much, and I became the girl who could be anything she wanted, the one who was accepted and whose life was about to turn around.

But I'd wanted it then. I'd wanted his hand in mine to be the warning bell for change. In the penthouse loft, with his lips and tongue growing more urgent and his hands on the sides of my face, I didn't want my life to change. I'd done everything I'd set out to do since he'd left, and there he was again, ready to destroy everything I'd built in exchange for a mouth that fit mine like a palm curled over a fist.

I turned to face the door, still trapped by his arms, and opened it a crack. He slapped it shut.

"If you're not busy, I want to take you somewhere."

"I'm always busy," I said, leaning into him.

"Doing what?"

"Taking pictures of Hollywood royalty."

"Bring your camera then."

I held my finger up to him and said in pure mockery, "That kind of thing isn't going to fly, superstar."

He stepped back and took his jacket off the counter. "Today it is. Come on. It's fun. You've never seen this part of the city before."

"Ha! Fat chance of that."

"You'll only know if you come."

The possibility of showing him a thing or two about the city he pretended to rule was too good to pass up. "You're driving."

He opened the door. We went out and strode to the stairs.

"Are we going to get mobbed? Because I'm not up for another *LA Post* story," I said.

"We have ways around you guys when we need them. Today, I needed it."

"What ways?"

He opened the door to the parking lot. "We're not ready for that, Shuttergirl."

I hadn't expected him to tell me the strategies he used to avoid people like me. Or maybe I did. Maybe I'd forgotten who I was for a split second and became no more or less than a girl with a boy, because I was disappointed at the same time as I knew I had no right to be.

He approached a green two-seater Aston Martin and opened the passenger side door.

"This isn't exactly inconspicuous," I said as I buckled in, "but it's super cute."

"One tends to cancel out the other." He leaned in, one forearm on the roof of the car and one on the open door. "You have the very same drawback." He kissed me quickly and closed the door before I had a second to absorb the compliment.

I was smiling like a schoolgirl when he slid in next to me. God, would that be us? Would I do nothing but grin like an idiot around him? I shook it off. That wasn't me. I wasn't impressed so easily.

"If you're taking the 101 anywhere north," I said, "you should get on after the Cahuenga Pass. Time of day, and all."

The engine rumbled to life, and he pulled out, looking bemused. "I should blindfold you, or you're going to just boss me the entire way."

"Good luck with that."

He took my hand at the first red light, drawing his fingertips from my wrists to the webs of my fingers and bending them closed. After everything I'd done in my life with men, after what Jake and his friends had exposed me to—the humiliations, the distasteful acts, all the things I tried to not think about—I couldn't believe that having my hand held could make me feel like four pounds of joy in a two-pound bag.

"Do you want the top down?" he asked, squeezing my hand a little as he headed up Western Ave.

"Will people see you?"

"Yeah, but it's fun. The top, I mean. Not getting seen."

"Next time then."

Damn. I'd said next time, which presumed that there would be a next time. After the *LA Post* story, which was undoubtedly the tip of the iceberg, the last thing we had were guarantees.

"Nighttime's easier," he said. "And anything one lane is good, so no one can get astride, and any cars going the other way can't turn around because it's too narrow. They'd have to pull a K on Sunset by Palisades, and the twisty part of Mulholland."

"Are you telling me your secrets? Because I could be taking notes right now."

"That won't make the road any wider."

"I could just wait until the sun goes down and stand at the side of Mulholland with a motorcycle. All I have to do is wait until I see a good-looking guy in a convertible, then he's mine."

He glanced at me sidelong. "Just call me next time. It's safer."

"But not half as much fun."

Why was I digging this hole? Why was I making this an issue? I was the hunter, and he was the prey. I made money from his work whether he liked it or not, and that was what it was. Maybe I kept bringing it up because it was real. The nagging pragmatist in me wouldn't let the fantasy of our connection exist undisturbed.

But there were our hands, clasped in a double fist, and the longing in my body surged again. I crossed my legs. I was wet. I knew it. Just from this nothing we were doing.

I wanted to say something. I was *going to* say something, but I couldn't find a way to open a conversation without apologizing for how I made my money, and that was the most insincere thing I could do.

At the light at Franklin and Beechwood, just before the psychological barrier of the Hollywood Hills, a horn honked.

"Look at me," he said.

I did. He looked over my shoulder and grinned, making a peace sign out the passenger side window. Through the other car's window, someone squealed.

I didn't blame them.

"You should get a driver," I said.

He leaned back in his seat. He was turned toward me, close enough for me to smell the cinnamon on him. "Driving my own car is an entitlement. Sorry. I'd rather deal with red lights."

He took off, twisting into the park and around the corner, checking his rearview mirror as we went into the deep recesses of the hills. The houses were set back behind foliage, big, well-kept, and selling in the multi-millions. There wasn't a sound up there but the rumble of the Aston's engine and the birds. I was sure he could have put the top down safely.

"I've been up here, you know," I said. "You hardly have to blindfold me."

"Really?"

"Yeah. If you make a right up here and go down a little ways, you'll catch the back entry to the Griffith Park Boys Camp."

"Uh-huh." He kept driving up Deronda, a little curve playing on his lips.

I started realizing that maybe I hadn't been that far up before, because there was nothing there. At the end of the road were two identical gates. One had signs all over it warning against hiking and threatening arrest. The other warned against trespassing.

Michael flipped his visor down and clicked a little beige box that looked like a garage door opener. The trespassing gate creaked open. He looked at me, one eyebrow raised.

"You win," I said. "I have never been past this gate."

"Don't feel too bad about it." He pulled past the gate onto a hidden street of mansions. "I had to do my share of begging to get access today."

The twists and turns of the road were etched into the shape of the mountain, making it impossible for me to keep track of what street we were on. Not that it mattered. I'd never get up there again. "Who the hell even lives up here?"

He put his finger to his lips, taking my hand with his as if he was afraid to let it go, and whispered, "Shh. Lawyers."

I laughed.

The houses fell away, and we drove headlong into the nothing of nature with its fullness of sound. He put the top down, and I looked up, holding my tennis player's hand while watching the canopy of trees, a moving border on the clear blue sky. Still holding my hand, Michael punched the radio. I expected the same techno he'd played in the loft above mine, but something else came out.

"Sinatra!" I yelled over the music.

He sang "I've Got You Under My Skin" with the full force of his voice, and I joined in off key, more joyfully shouting than actually singing.

We made it to the end of the song, entertaining the bugs and squirrels all the way up. A radio tower appeared through the trees. I'd only ever seen that radio tower from the ground, and only then did I know where we were going.

"No way," I said, sitting up straight. "We're past the razor wire!"

A cluster of official-looking buildings appeared, and Michael turned down the radio. "We are."

"Do you know how many times my friends and I tried to get up here?"

"How many?"

"The fence is electrified. And there are cameras everywhere."

"And there's a good reason." He opened the door. "Because troublemakers like you would get yourselves killed." He got out without waiting for an answer, went around the front, and opened my door, holding out his hand.

I let him help me out, and he walked me to the ridge. Below us, from the back, was *it*. The Hollywood sign, standing like an oddly-shaped billboard in the side of the hill, the grid of steel supports holding up the backward letters.

"That thing? That's mine," I said.

"I went to grade school with a kid on Deronda. We came up here all the time. So you're wrong. It's mine."

"Dude, do not even." I took a step down the hill, and the sand and grit slipped from under my shoe.

Michael held me up then slid down a little in a controlled fashion. I took my cue from him and slid a little then steadied myself, gripping his biceps. I wanted to stay still for a moment, just to feel the hardness of his muscles, but he stepped and slid again. Leaning on each other, hands on arms and shoulders, weight on weight, stretching, catching, fighting gravity with only our bodies as a bulwark, we made it to the bottom of the sign.

I looked between the Y and W. "You can see everything."

"To the ocean."

"It's really smoggy."

"It's best the Monday of a holiday weekend." He nudged me, a glint in his eye. "Are you ready?"

"For what?"

He gripped a steel rail on the back of the first O in WOOD. "I could have brought you to any hill in Los Angeles for that stinking view." He put his foot on a rail and hoisted himself up.

"You're going to climb up it?"

"Coming?"

"Oh, hell yes."

He got to the top first. He swung his legs over the side, straddling the letter. He guided me to the same position, steadying me until I was sitting securely enough to face the view. Then he swung his leg over and sat next to me.

"It's breezier than I thought it would be." I closed my eyes then opened them, trying to see that spread of the city for the first time. "Thank you. This was a nice surprise today."

"I used to come up here all the time after I did *Fractured*. Some days, I felt like I was becoming that guy in the magazines. So big. Bigger than I could make sense of. And flatter too. It's hard to explain. But up here... how many people are looking up here right now? None of them can see me. I feel real and unimportant at the same time. I wanted you to see the unimportant me."

"I remember unimportant Michael from high school."

"He couldn't take his eyes off you." His hair flicked in the wind, and the gold of the sunset burnished his skin. "You were a serve killer."

"I'm sorry I was a distraction." I wasn't sorry. Not a lick. All I wanted at that moment was to be a distraction all over again, even though I knew I'd change my mind in the morning.

"It was worth it. *You* were worth it. Every minute. Meeting you, it changed me, and I didn't even realize it at the time. The first time I saw you behind a camera, I didn't acknowledge you because I knew I couldn't walk away again. I wasn't ready to face what everyone would say."

He put his hand over mine, and we sat in silence. After a years-long minute, he slipped his arm around my shoulders and put his face in my hair. I felt him breathing against me.

"It must be hard to keep your head on straight," I said.

"It's not a big deal." He waved it away.

"I don't know what to do," I said. "This is complicated."

"Not up here. Up here, it's very simple."

I wanted to tell him how I felt about him in the simplest language. I wanted to use words like warm and safe and joy, words like admire and appreciate, words that a six-year-old could use. I wanted to use words without guile or hidden meanings, without the weight of everything that could, and would, come between us. But he kissed my mouth, stealing the words and turning them into actions that were complex, layered in desire, and breathing with possibilities a six-year-old couldn't imagine or understand.

Like heat.

And lust.

And the feel of a man's body through his shirt.

And the way the whole of your consciousness can be focused on the way his thumb cruises the ridge of your breast and every thought in your head comes out your mouth in a groan.

That blast of a bullhorn woke me from the dream sleep of the kiss.

"Mister Greydon."

Michael seemed unperturbed. He turned and looked behind us, where a park ranger stood with a red bullhorn. Michael waved.

The ranger put the horn to his face again. "I didn't say you could climb the letters."

"I'm in trouble," he said, but he was smiling. "Come on, let's go back to reality."

He got me down from my pedestal against gravity and let the park ranger give him a hard time. It was obvious he'd been there before and that he'd never brought a guest.

It wasn't until we were headed back down Deronda, and Michael had put the top back up, that I kicked the bag with the replacement rig and realized I'd left my camera at the loft.

Chapter 23

Laine

We went back down the mountain, the pressure of the city growing heavier as we descended. I got caught up on the lives of my old tormentors at Breakfront, his first few movies, and his tennis injury. I hoped I caught it all, but it was hard when he touched me and my skin became a net of electrical currents.

"Where did you land after Breakfront?" he asked.

"Oh, see that church over there?" I said. "It used to be a Ralph's."

"No."

"Yes, look, it's got an oval sign, and there are pictures of vegetables pressed into the concrete."

"Holy crap, you're right. I've passed that a hundred times," he said.

"And that over there? That little strip mall? That building used to be a fire house. You can see the holes where LAFD used to be nailed in."

"Are you avoiding the question? About what you did after I left?"

"You never told me what happened with Lucy," I said. "I really thought you were going to marry her."

"So did I."

"What happened?"

"You didn't read it in the papers?" He glanced at me sidelong while changing lanes.

"I didn't want the CliffsNotes version."

"We were a perfect match," he said then paused. "Her parents loved my parents and vice versa."

"Did I tell you I'm a huge fan of your mother's?"

"You mentioned that."

"She's amazing. She's a goddess. Okay, go ahead. Lucy."

"We looked good in pictures together," he said. "I mean, I know that sounds ridiculously shallow, but half the people rooting for us only knew us from pictures, and at that age, there's no such thing as perspective. So, I mean, we were from the same universe. We had everything in common. We made sense. But I went to college on the east coast, and things got different."

I craned my neck around. "Different?"

"I met people. I expanded, I guess, and it just died."

"No CliffsNotes." I was, of course, guilty of much worse, but I justified it by saying that no one would continue to want me if they knew the full version of my past. I was scared as hell to lose those borrowed moments with Michael.

"Lucy was like a stepsister. I liked talking to her, and we had a lot in common. I thought that was all we needed, but it wasn't that thing. You know? That thing?"

"I've heard of it."

"What's that mean?" he asked.

"It means nothing. So you stayed friends?"

He stopped at a red light and turned toward me. "Tell me about the first boy you ever loved."

I opened my mouth and snapped it shut. Was this more embarrassing than anything I'd done with Jake and his friends? Maybe. Maybe I'd die of shame.

"Besides you?"

"Someone who didn't ditch you before you kissed him," he said.

"The light's green."

"No CliffsNotes, Laine."

Cars honked behind us.

"Go!" I said.

He put the car in park. Someone yelled and honked, but our eyes were locked.

"I'm not going," he said.

I swallowed. Why couldn't I tell him why I'd never felt anything after him? That I'd been taken by men I barely knew, men who shouldn't have touched me? That I'd been bruised, called names, been one body in scenes with many others? I'd wanted to believe that those were acts of love, protection even, because Jake was there setting boundaries. His boundaries, not mine, but something.

Behind us, a car door slammed.

"You have to go," I said. "They're going to recognize you."

"So I'll take a few pictures on Western and Olympic."

I felt pressure to answer, and pressure to not answer, and pressure from the ticking seconds. Michael could have sung "The Star-Spangled Banner" and kept the pressure on with just his posture and his eyes. Damned actors.

Even when the rap of knuckles on his window should have jarred us, he didn't move. The guy looking in the window behind Michael had a beard and slicked back hair. He looked like a few of the guys whose names I forgot, who I hadn't been in love with, all those years ago.

And Michael knew damn well he was there, but he kept his eyes on me, waiting for an answer.

"Besides what I told you in the loft, it just hasn't happened," I said.

"You haven't dated?"

"It's not that I haven't dated. I had one thing last five months. Two things, actually. A cop and an insurance adjuster. It's just, you know, I'm busy, and I bore easily."

I was telling the truth. Two relationships of about five months. Both had bored me into an emotional coma.

"Hey, you asshole!" said the guy at the window, rapping on the glass. "We missed the light!"

"There's more to this," Michael said.

There was more. Plenty more. There were more men than I could even recall.

"I can't," I said. "Not yet. Don't make me talk about it."

Michael's face changed, and I couldn't get a read on it. The bearded guy banged on the window, and Michael turned around to face him.

"Dude!" he said, pointing. "You're Michael Greydon."

"Shit," I mumbled, sliding down in my seat.

The bearded guy turned back to his car. "Earl! Check this out!"

"He's reaching for his phone," I said.

Michael turned back to me. Maybe it was my boneless posture, low on the seat, as if I'd been poured out of a jar of jelly, or maybe it was the fact that the light changed back to green, but he jammed the car into drive and took off.

"Thank you," I said.

"I'm sorry." He turned on Olympic and headed downtown.

"I don't mind a little fast driving."

"That I tried to get you to talk about stuff you don't want to tell me. I can see you're not ready. I'm sorry. I was… sometimes I feel closer to you than I've earned."

How could a person stand up under the weight of such kindness? Especially knowing we couldn't last? That he was the opposite side of my coin, always parallel, never meeting but by some chance bending of the universe? I looked straight ahead as the streets became my own with their worn billboards and cracked sidewalks. The body shops and convenience stores gave way to punk graffiti and hipster conveniences.

I must have looked as shattered as I felt, because he squeezed my hand.

"You all right?" he asked.

"You don't have to explain why you feel that way," I said, "but if you want to—"

"I didn't know what I felt for you. It was new and irrational. I couldn't even process it. And with Lucy and me leaving and everything else…"

"Me not having a family."

"Everything," he said. "I spend a lot of energy worrying about what people think. It's in the job description. But what I felt with you was real, and I didn't have it with Lucy. So I thought I'd just move on and find it with someone else."

"Someone with parents?"

"I was eighteen."

I wasn't trying to press him or make him feel guilty. I was doing worse than that. I was using him as a bludgeon against myself, getting him to list my shortcomings so I didn't have to.

He continued, "And you were barely fifteen."

"I told you my birthday?" I hadn't. I knew I hadn't. He'd known I was fifteen, but if he knew my birthday, then he knew that I was even younger than my classmates.

"Matter of public record."

"Screw the public record. You know too much about me."

"The feeling's mutual."

I didn't know whether to tickle him or punch him. Along with half the world, I knew too much about him because of the choices he'd made. Were we about to get into the age-old argument about the ethical and legal angles of his stardom and my job? Because even though I wasn't as educated as he was, and even though I was starting to cringe at the bitter taste of a life without privacy, I'd wipe the floor with him.

I looked forward to it, because that argument meant we were invested in fitting together. That thought, once it entered my mind fully formed, excited me more than chasing down a mark or getting a once-in-a-lifetime tip. Were we going to have some kind of relationship? Were we going to sit over breakfast together and discuss politics and movies? Could my job coexist with his if we kept it quiet?

He smiled a little, and I knew he was still in good humor. I was building a case in my head and calling up the rulings decided in the paparazzi's—my—favor, when I saw the blue Corolla parked on my block. Then Renaldo's SUV.

"Don't turn into the lot." I shrank in my seat.

"What?"

"They're all over. Left, go left." I peeked at the rearview.

"They don't know this car," he said.

"Thank God. Listen." I shook my head as if trying to loosen something. I closed my eyes and visualized a city block. "My building is connected to the one next door. It shares parking spaces with the Whole Foods."

"You're telling me to go to Whole Foods?"

"Yes."

"Are you nuts? Do you want to be in the paper again?" he asked.

"Trust me."

We made eye contact, and his lips pressed together in a smile. "It's not ever going to be boring with you, is it?"

"Not peaceful either."

"Let's go." He went into the underground lot at Whole Foods.

"Park in the back, by the car detailers."

Way in the back, four guys washed and detailed cars, like little scrubbing gremlins, while shoppers spent their pretty pennies at Whole Foods. Michael pulled up next to a soaped-up Jaguar.

I got out, grabbing the blue bag with my new camera. "Hey, George," I said to the short guy with a grey widow's peak, "can we use your door?"

"You wash car?"

I snapped Michael's keys out of his hand and gave them to George. "Yeah. But the outside only."

He looked Michael up and down suspiciously. "You're Michael Greydon.

Loved you in *Sunday Kill Machine*."

"It's not him," I said.

"I get that all the time," Michael interjected.

I took Michael's hand and pulled him through the heavy white door. The windowless closet stank of soap and chemicals. Bottles of fluid were stacked from floor to ceiling. I opened another door, leading to a stairwell. I ran up it, Michael behind me, to another door with an emergency exit sign.

"Wait!" Michael said.

I slapped it open. "What?"

He laughed a little. "Never mind. You have this under control. I can see that." He took the camera bag from me. "Let me be a gentleman."

"Just this once."

A decrepit elevator door sat at the end of a short concrete hallway. The doors opened right away. I punched my floor, and when the doors closed, I knew I was going to kiss him. But I didn't realize what kind of kiss I would get. It wasn't a sweet brush of the lips but a groping, hungry meeting of bodies. He pressed his hips against me, and when I felt his hardness on my thigh, my body lit on fire from spine to navel.

"I hope you don't have any plans," he whispered as he put his hand up my shirt. "Because once that door opens, you're mine."

His hand went up my back, slipping under my bra. I shuddered and tried to speak, but my lungs had nothing in them. Certainly not the word *no*. I would be his as soon as I could. He ran his hand over my pants and pressed at my crotch.

"Oh, God."

"I want you," he said into my ear. "And when we get back into that apartment, I'm taking you."

I pushed against him in answer, jerking my hips against the flat of his fingers. Yes, yes, and yes. Everything, yes. Months of longing, years of forgetting, and a few days of reawakening were culminating now. He buried his face in my neck, and I reached down to feel his rock-hard dick. His breath got heavy against me, and I thought of him again, over me, lost in pleasure.

Yes, yes, and yes.

The doors sprang open. The distance to my loft was forever with this painful ache between my legs. My floor. My hallway. The open window at the end of it, right by my door. And the huge guy, backlit by the window, recognizable even in silhouette.

It all crumbled.

"Laine?" he said.

Michael turned and got between me and the big guy in the Black Flag T-shirt. I knew him. He looked exactly the same as he had when I knew him between the ages of fifteen and eighteen. Navy bandana too low over his brow. Scraggly hair tied in knots. Maybe his hairline had moved back a bit, and maybe he had a touch of early grey in the beard he tied with rubber bands. He still had a carabiner of keys and rabbits' feet attached to his belt loop.

I'd had an idea, seconds before, that Michael and I could figure out how to be together, but no. I was who I was, and nothing could change that.

"Foo Foo," I said, "how are you?"

He craned his neck to see around Michael, smiling. "I'm good. Still got Gracie."

"Your Harley?"

"It's vintage now. She's so sweet." He shook his head is if pleasantly surprised by something. "You look—"

"What do you want?" I said.

"You should really lock your door." He indicated it with an apologetic nod. He was a two-hundred-fifty-pound cupcake who had no problem pulverizing smaller men over a deal gone bad.

"I'm surprised you're not on my couch," I said, arms crossed. Why was I even engaging him?

"Seemed rude, you know."

"You need to go," Michael said.

Foo Foo looked at Michael, then at me, then back to Michael. "I remember you from *Toledo Spring Break*. Heh."

Michael's character had gotten the crap beaten out of him in that story, and no one in that hallway was under the delusion that Foo was talking about any other aspect of that stupid movie.

"No," I said, pushing past Michael. He held my arm so I didn't get any closer to Foo Foo. He was really getting on my nerves. "He just looks like him. I'm sorry, Foo."

"You were just in the paper with him, sweet angel."

"I was on my way somewhere. Was there something you needed?"

"It's been so long, Laine."

"There are a hundred good reasons for that."

"Jake wanted to say hi."

"So he sent you? And you came like his little lackey?" I shook off Michael and approached my front door, which I hadn't locked in my rage about the loud guy upstairs. Stupid.

"Come on now, there's no reason to get nasty. He saw you with this guy." He waggled his finger as if to say he knew damn well my companion had been in *Toledo Spring Break*. Each knuckle had a faded blue letter tattooed on it. Left hand RIDE. Right hand KILL. "He—well, we both, Jake and I— we were kind of impressed how you moved up."

I was about to give him a piece of my mind. The piece where I told him to get the hell out of my face, leaving me the piece that wanted to cry.

Michael got between us. "It's time to go."

"Hey, man, I was just saying 'hi.' It's nothing."

"You said hi. Now you can go. And don't come back."

Foo pointed his finger like a gun, creasing the K in KILL, his fingertip an inch closer to Michael's face than it should have been. "Hey, I don't care who you are. I will mess you up."

Foo outweighed Michael by fifty pounds of muscle or more, and all I could see in my mind was an incident a decade earlier. Foo had kicked a decent-sized guy down a flight of stairs because he'd stolen a bunch of drugs. I didn't remember the details, only the bloodied condition of the thief's face as he rolled.

I got between them, because Michael wasn't getting kicked down a flight of stairs, and his face was not getting bloody. Not if I could help it. But I was too late. They'd decided in man-language that shit would go down.

Michael acted first, pushing me out of the way firmly but gently, so that he could move a step closer to Foo.

Foo hadn't gone to private school or served on its board before he was thirty. He hadn't played varsity tennis or flown private jets. Foo grew up sleeping on the floor in a one-bedroom apartment in Westlake. Foo ate cans of beans for dinner, and was spending his days on Sunset Boulevard by the time he was eleven.

Foo punched Michael in the face so fast and hard it didn't make more than a pop sound, and the camera bag dropped to the floor.

"Foo, you asshole!" I yelled.

Michael didn't waste a second. He acted as if he wasn't hurt at all, as if getting punched in the face by a two-hundred-fifty-pound biker happened all the time. He lunged for the guy, and I thought that he would die today, because just going for a monster like that, well, it was the best way to get your ass kicked.

So I stepped up to pull them apart, all hundred thirty pounds of me. I must have felt like a leaf falling on Foo's shoulder. Michael was bent and twisted. Foo pushed him up against the wall by his throat. Michael's face was beet red from strain, and Foo pulled his fist back to pound that beautiful face into the wall.

"Foo! No!" I punched his back.

I heard a jingle of keys.

Michael held up Foo's keys by the carabiner. He'd grabbed them from Foo's belt loop when he'd attacked. Foo let go of Michael with his KILL hand, leaving his perfectly capable RIDE hand to hold down the smaller man.

Michael swung the keychain and threw it out the window. There was a moment of silence then a rattled clink as they hit the ground. "Fetch."

Foo dropped him to look out the window to the parking lot. I crouched next to Michael. He looked like hell but was still focused on Foo.

"Gracie's all alone down there," Michael choked out. "And in this neighborhood."

"Fuck!" Foo backed up from the window and looked at Michael and me. "I'll be back."

Was I sweating? Was my breathing shallow? I had to stop that. Stop. Project nothing but complete ownership of the world and everything in it. "Good, because I've got pictures of you and Jake doing enough shit to put you both away for a long time. I'm looking for reasons to go to First and Main."

Outside, a motorcycle went by. Maybe it was Gracie. Probably it wasn't. But that was enough to get Foo's ass in gear and out the stairwell door.

"Are you okay?" I asked Michael.

"Sure." As if telling the truth in a room full of lies, his nose started gushing blood.

"Jesus! Come on. Let me get you cleaned up."

I tried to help him stand, but he waved me off, getting to his feet by himself. Drops of blood splashed on the floor, and his white T-shirt was in danger of looking like a murder victim's. I grabbed the camera bag and put his arm over my shoulder even though he could walk fine. Like medic with a wounded soldier, I led him into my loft.

I kicked the door closed. God, I was so grateful to put a solid metal door between Foo Foo and me. I knew Michael had put himself in a terrible position, and my gratitude expanded my heart wide enough to press against the brittle bars of my rib cage.

I led Michael to the sink and bent him over it. "I'm so sorry, Michael. Do you think it's broken?"

"That guy?" he said, breathing without his nose. He sounded like a kid, and it was adorable. "You hung out with a tough crowd."

I pulled a cloth napkin out of the drawer and opened the freezer. "I did. But not anymore." I wrapped the napkin around a handful of ice. "Okay, turn around. God, I feel so bad."

"Why?" He closed his eyes and pressed his bloody hand over my hand, pushing the ice into his nose, and curled his fingers around mine.

How could I think about anything but helping him at a moment like this? How could I worry, with blood between us, if there was still a chance I could have him after what had happened in the hall?

"Because it's my past that came and broke your nose," I said.

"Not broken." He leaned back on the sink, and I leaned on him. He put his free arm around my waist, drawing me closer.

"Your mother would never approve," I said, half joking.

"Probably not."

"I feel like I should explain." I said it while hoping the reprieve he'd given me in the car was still good and he wouldn't make me explain a damn thing.

"Is he that not-first-love you can't talk about?"

"No, he's something else entirely." I blinked back a tear and swallowed a wad of gunk. I wouldn't cry over my stupid past when this guy was here bleeding for me. "I ran with his crowd after Breakfront. And I got out of it. I haven't seen any of them in almost nine years."

"You're hazardous, Laine. Have I told you that?"

"I think you said something about that."

"I like it."

I laughed. "We'll see how much you like it when your eye swells up."

"You should see the other guy." He removed the ice long enough to look at the bloody ice bag and shrug. "He looks fine."

"Is that what you're going to tell all your famous friends?" I put the ice back on him.

"I'm going to tell them I met this girl I used to know, and I had to have her. Even after I got punched in the face by some guy who was bothering her, I wanted her. And I'd do it all again just to have her put an ice pack on my nose and stand close to me."

"I hope it doesn't come to that. Come on. Sit down and take the pressure off."

He let me lead him to the couch. "Nice place," he said.

"Thank you. I had an exceptional month, so I bought it." I hoped I didn't blush, but I felt my face tingle with regret. I shouldn't have said that. My exceptional month had included a picture of him and his friends. Their images had sold for my down payment.

I sat him down and took off his shoes then turned his legs so he was lying down. He leaned his head over the armrest and laid his head back, holding the ice pack in place.

I saw something on my dining room table. Something that hadn't been there before. I walked toward it and breathed deeply.

Michael lay behind me with a face that would explode in the morning. That guy. That mark. That paycheck standing six one, he was all right. No one had ever done anything like that for me.

Looking at the table, all my gratitude and relief dropped out of me as if it were a lead weight in a wet paper towel.

Eight by ten, on monochrome rag paper. The stuff only students and artists used. The stuff you learn on when you're learning to do it right. The picture's surface was mottled like a granite countertop because it had been a test print. The exposure went from dark to light across the frame with hard lines between. The photographer had figured out the exposure and didn't bother letting it sit in the fixer long enough.

Past the destroyed silver gelatin, the subject was visible. On a mattress, bare legs crossed, sat a girl of sixteen with very long mousy hair and grey eyes like old coins at the bottom of a purse. In her hands were a Bic lighter and a cigarette butt that had obviously been salvaged from the ashtray to her right. She was too skinny, wearing a ribbed tank. Her nipples poked through the fabric, and the filthy sheets bunched between her legs covered only enough to show she wasn't wearing underwear.

"What kind of name is Foo Foo?" Michael said from behind me.

I glanced back. He looked like everything right in his jeans and bloodied white shirt, and I felt as if I needed to be drowned in bleach.

The girl in the picture peered across nine years of ambition, biceps dotted with fingertip-shaped bruises from the night before, beaten down but daring the camera to judge her for being who she was.

Foo's voice was fresh in my mind from the hallway, and I could hear him and how he liked it.

You like it, don't you, little slut? Say you like it.

He'd been the first to slap my face while he fucked me. Not the last. He said he didn't mean nothing by it, then he did it again.

Front hand, backhand.

Ain't you the sweetest whore. Fuck you, whore.

The camera never lied. The girl in the ribbed tank was a worthless whore, and until Tom had taken that photo and forced me to look at it so many years before, I hadn't been able to see myself.

My cheeks stung looking at her. Me.

I flipped the picture over to find the note in half-dry Sharpie.

You left a mess of these when you split.
$$ JAKE

"Laine?" Michael said from a million miles away.

"His name's Enid," I said, flipping the photo over. "We called him Foo Foo the Snoo." I shifted toward the kitchen, holding the picture behind me. "He's friends with my foster brother. Not the one you met. Not Tom. Another one."

I got to the kitchen island. It was spotless, like everything else in my house. Why did I notice that now? Had Michael noticed? Did he think that was who I was?

"This other brother? He was Jake, so we called him Jake the Pillow Snake. Which is from Dr. Seuss. *I Can Read with My Eyes Shut.* It goes…" Casually, I opened a drawer in the island. Inside, spoons and forks were nestled in shiny sleep. I slid the photo on top of them as if it was normal to keep damning evidence with flatware. "'You can read about Jake the Pillow Snake or Foo Foo the Snoo.' See, they were partners."

And they shared everything.

"Are you all right?" He looked at me sidelong, as if that would give him a better view of my troubles.

"I'm fine."

He sat up. "I'm putting a bodyguard on you."

"You are not."

"Oh, I am, Laine. I am."

"He'd better run fast, because I'm going to work."

His phone went off, as if on cue. He ignored it. "You are not going to hang around dark alleys."

My phone buzzed in my pocket. I'd forgotten to worry about its silence. Between us, the phones were on fire, and we just stared at each other.

"You gonna get that?" I asked.

He pulled his phone out of his pocket and silenced it before dropping it on the coffee table. "I mean it. You're not safe."

"Neither are you apparently." I sat next to him, and he leaned on me. I put my arm around him.

"Touché," he mumbled, kissing my neck. "But if you think I'm going to let you protect me—"

The napkin of ice threatened to fall, and I held it against his face. "I'm not going to sit here and defend my masculinity with a straight face. But I'm worried about you. And I feel responsible for you getting hit. If anything happens to you—"

"Nothing's going to happen to me."

"How do you know?"

"Everyone's watching me."

His weight became too much, and I leaned back. He adjusted himself as if his intention the whole time had been to get on top of me.

"You need a bodyguard as much as I do," I said. "You need to take these guys seriously. I don't..." I took a deep breath when he pulled up my shirt. "I hate putting you in this position. But he'll be back."

"Which is why I'm sending someone for you." He stroked my belly with his fingertip.

I turned to liquid physically, but a voice echoed in my brain.

Whore.

Slap, and a backhand.

Such a slut.

"He's from my world. I understand what makes him and his friends do what they do. I understand how to get rid of them." I hated saying it. I hated how true it was and how I would one day have to come clean about all of it, and I couldn't, not with the rolling arousal between my legs and the vivid memory of getting fucked and beaten by someone else. "You have more to lose."

CD REISS

"I do," he whispered, "I have you."

He slipped his hand past my waistband and into my panties, going right to my soaked seam. His fingertip brushed my clit, and I combusted, arching my back to get closer as my head shouted.

You love it you love it you love it like a good whore.

"God, Michael. I can't, I'm... I'm distracted. I—"

"You're so wet. Please. I want to see you come," he said. "My pants are staying on."

"I—"

I can't.

Don't.

But the words didn't come out, because Michael was on top of me, face an inch from mine, and he wasn't going to hit me and call me names while he fucked me so hard I cried. It wasn't in him. He just drew lazy circles with his fingertip, sending shockwaves up my back and gathering a lightstorm in the pitch dark.

I put my hands on his face, brushing the little hairless spot in his chin as if it were a talisman. The voice that called me a slut quieted, and the hands that stung my cheeks fell away. Michael was back for me. I was accepted again. Even past the swelling around his eyes, in the depth of the jade, I saw myself in him.

My pussy went white hot under his fingers. I tried to say something, some warning, but I could only open my mouth before my back arched against him. I tried to keep my eyes open, but they shut with the burst of pleasure. My hands squeezed his face as he put it against mine, and my body went rigid, then slack, then rigid, then slack.

"My God, Laine, you're beautiful."

"Did I hurt your face?"

"No." He took his hand out of my pants.

"Thank you." I brushed my thumbs along his jaw.

"I loved it."

"I can take care of you."

"No, I think my head is going to explode."

"You're fully erect. I can feel it. I have to finish it for you."

"I'm a grown man. I've had erections before. It's not a big deal." He slid down and put his head on my shoulder.

I stroked his hair, waist deep in peace, all worry gone for the moment, and floating in no more than an ocean of gratitude. I must have been more vulnerable than I realized, or he'd reopened some wound with his kindness, because though my sweet reverie stayed, as the minutes passed, a layer of need fitted itself on top of it.

I needed to tell him, if not the details, the outlines of who I was.

"I want you to know," I whispered, starting somewhere small, then everything I didn't want to say spilled out. "I have stuff. I've never been to jail, but you know, it's stuff, and it's ugly, and it scares me. Because, I mean, you're so perfect, and I'm... I'm just a mess. I'm not whole. I'm a bunch of pieces of a person I cobbled together." My eyes got wet when I thought of the comparisons between us and that picture in my silverware drawer. "So if you have to move on when you realize that, I'll understand. You have an image, and if anyone understands protecting a career, it's me. I mean, I'll be mad, don't get that wrong, but also." I swallowed and blinked, shifting my head so he wouldn't feel the tear on his forehead. "I won't blame you."

I waited for an answer. Anything. A change in position or a word on any subject. The weather. Sports. Something. But all he did was breathe.

I smiled so wide, tears fell into my mouth. He was sleeping. How hard had Foo hit him? Hard enough for a concussion? God, that asshole. I was going to give him a piece of my mind. He'd always called me stupid, and maybe that had been some little sheet-curling game he played, but it didn't turn me on. Being called a dumb whore because some big biker thought it was funny? Well, no. It wasn't funny, and it wasn't true, and when I was face to face with that moron, I would punch his face right back.

Michael's phone rang. I stretched to see it, but I couldn't move without disturbing him. I reached but couldn't get to it. He didn't move, just a breathing weight on one side. I could have slipped out from under him, even if I didn't want to get the phone. I could have gotten up and walked around, made coffee, done stuff until he woke. But I didn't want to get up. He'd fallen asleep with me, and I didn't want to insult the intimacy or the trust he'd put in me. I'd wanted to have sex with plenty of men, but Michael's breath on my neck, his foot tucked between the cushions of my couch, his arm draped over my stomach were more intimate than any sexual act. He'd laid himself bare before me, trusting me in the vulnerability of sleep.

I might have drifted off as the sun touched the horizon, or time might have gone faster than it should have, but when his phone rang again, he took a long, deep gasp and woke.

"I couldn't reach it," I said, my voice sharp and unwelcome, like a shrieking alarm ending an hour of sweet soft breaths.

"It's all right." He reached over me and looked at the phone. "Goddamnit."

I scooted up to a sitting position when he stood. He swayed, squeezed his eyes shut, and put the phone away, still ringing.

"I'm sorry. I was supposed to do a thing, and I almost slept through it." He jammed his feet in his shoes.

I got his jacket and helped him into it. "You look like you're still half asleep."

"I think I am." He kissed me once on each cheek then on the lips.

He tried to pull back, but I yanked him onto me. I might never see him again. He could easily walk out and decide I was too much trouble. He'd be crazy not to think that.

"I need you to wait here for an hour," he said into my cheek. "It won't take me longer than that to get you a bodyguard."

"Fine. One hour."

He put his hand on my cheek and slid it to the back of my neck, drawing me close. "Thank you."

"Your pleasure."

"Go out with me. Have a date. Tuesday night."

A date. So simple. Exactly what people did when they liked each other.

"Dinner?" I said. "In public? With a guy who's going to have at least one black eye?"

"A movie. Let me show you a little of my world."

"No."

He kissed me, and I fell into his urgency and his warmth, smelling dried blood. I didn't want to believe he could ever care about me. He was a dead end at full speed with broken brakes. He was a labyrinth with no exit, only starvation and the hope that there was a center.

But he was also sweet as spring, an explosion of poppies in Death Valley after a winter of rain. He was lightning before a rainstorm, drowning a dark road in white light for a split second before night soaked the way.

I pushed him away. "The clock's ticking, Greydon."

"I'll pick you up Tuesday."

"I said no."

He backed up toward the door. "Don't go anywhere. I'm sending a guy named Carlos. He runs fast, so give it your best shot."

"Get out. You bother me."

I closed the door behind him then ran to the window. I could see the exit of the Whole Foods parking lot in the stripe between two buildings. When I saw his little green Aston Martin drive away, I swallowed the worry I was holding in the back of my throat.

I paced the hard floor twice, roiled to the core by his absence, his presence, his possibilities, and his ability to hurt me. I snapped up the blue camera bag and dumped the contents onto the coffee table. I could get the thing set up in minutes. I called Tom while I unwrapped the boxes. There was no way I was waiting an hour for some guy named Carlos to show up.

Chapter 24

Michael

"Oh my god," Harvey said as I sat in the makeup chair. "What happened to your face?"

"Ran into a fist. You like it?"

"Oh, honey, you're falling apart like my nephew's Legos. First, you're late, and now? What am I supposed to do with this?"

"You got eleven minutes to figure it out."

He leaned back on the counter and put his fingers to his chin, stroking his goatee. He looked at me as if I were a crossword puzzle he couldn't solve. I worked with him whenever I was in Los Angeles, and today, for the Jack Rambling show, my face should have been a piece of cake.

"Don't hide it," I said. "Let's have some fun."

I winked at him with my good eye, and he winked back.

Mentally, I was working on a joke that started with "You should see the other guy," but Ken called as Harvey was working around the bruise. I rejected the call. I'd already gotten an earful from Gene for being late. He'd done everything he could to put something on my schedule during the weeks we weren't shooting, and his ladles of guilt over my lateness and lack of emotional investment were beginning to wear on me.

Once Ken found out about Mister Foo KILL RIDE, he'd probably call me an unmanageable risk and drop me. My face throbbed. My brain hurt. I remembered the shocking blow to my face and the lightning bolts creeping in on my vision as if it were happening over and over.

Yet all I could think about was how much I wanted to take Laine to bed. Feel her twisted under me, hear her cry out for me. I wanted to share sweat and skin, to blend a scent of our own making. And the big guy with the tattooed knuckles? He'd been with her at some point. I could tell from the way she reacted that it hadn't been love or anything like that, but it had been physical, and she was scared. Much had become clear, and for whatever it was worth, I wanted to kill him.

Focus, Mike.

Harvey stepped back to check his work. The phone vibrated. I wanted to throw it out the window, because ten things were happening at once.

A kid came in with a clipboard and walkie-talkie. "Mister Greydon! You're on in—" He stopped dead when he saw my face.

I smiled. "You should see the other guy."

Chapter 25

Laine

I had a rock in my shoe.

It had lodged between the soft flesh of the outside of my right foot and the leather of my brown stiletto as I ran down Wilshire Boulevard.

Still, I ran like a purse snatcher. Like the old days, when I didn't really know what was at the end of the run, when tips weren't guarantees and the phone never rang.

My bag cut across my right breast and banged against my lower back. I held a spanking-new four-pound camera aloft in my right hand, and my hair clips were doing nothing to hold my hair anymore but were bouncing against my scalp, hanging on for dear life.

I cut a corner into an alley. Voices around some corner, indistinguishable over the sound of my panting. Flashing lights that could have been my body giving out or cameras. A few days off, and I was lazy and out of shape.

The back of Kate Martello's was around the next corner. There wasn't a movie star on the planet who used the front entrance of anything and not a paparazzo worth his salt who couldn't find a back door. I slid on a pile of scree to get around the next corner, avoiding a twisted ankle by some miracle of grace and luck, and slammed full body into a shouting dog pack of photographers.

Wall-to-wall sweat, canvas jackets, lumpy bags, unshaven faces, car breath, and testosterone. My feet were on fire, and that rock in my shoe was getting shoved up someone's ass if I didn't get a shot I could sell. I squirmed to the front, giving as many elbows as I got. I knew those guys, and they'd step on me if I didn't step on them first.

The situation behind Kate Martello's was particularly bad. It was in the old part of Beverly Hills. The alley was narrow, and the only space in the front of the ropes for the paparazzi was a wedge between two black SUVs. It was a tight fit, but I was skinny. I elbowed my way forward.

"Is that the lens you're using?" Tom asked, not even looking at me as I crouched and stepped in front of him. He was taller and had no problem putting his camera above me.

"It's the one I got."

The lens that Michael had replaced was long, and I'd been in such a hurry to get out of that apartment I hadn't doubled down with something wider. I'd just grabbed a flash to fight the night and run.

"Fuck," I grumbled. "I need a wide angle." I twisted my body and reached into Tom's bag.

"Yeah, you do," he said, his eyes on the restaurant. He shifted so I could rummage around his bag. Flash. Battery pack. Long lens. Pepper spray.

"Don't you have an eight?" I asked.

"It's on my camera. My five six is in the car." He glanced at me. "Sorry."

"Who's in there?" I rooted around his bag. He wouldn't lie to me, but he could be mistaken, or maybe a jury-rig would come to me if I touched enough equipment.

"Brad. Jayce. Some girl. How the hell have you been?"

How was I supposed to answer that? How had I been?

Happy. That was how I'd been, but I'd die before saying that out loud.

"Fine," I said. "What about you?"

"Great. I want to show you the stuff I've been getting."

I let the flap of his bag drop. "Sure, I'd love to see it."

He beamed then snapped back to business. I guessed that was what he thought I wanted. "Can you see inside with that thing?"

Two paps whose names I knew I knew but couldn't recall pushed into me. Life sucked in the dog pack, but damn, it was never boring.

I put the camera to my face and looked through the diners for Brad and his crowd. It'd be nice to know whether they were paying the check or still working on salad, but it was hard to see past the darkness, and my thick lens didn't help. There was a huge TV in there, and all I had to do was find it on the lens, to orient myself, and…

I was hit right in the frame with Michael in crystal clear HD, smile as bright as the strip on a Saturday night and eye as black as the sky behind it.

What's the use of being with a paparazza if you can't get a black eye for her?

The closed captioning, streaking black bands with white type across the top of the screen, went only seconds behind the movement of his lips.

So, this is very interesting, tell me, is she standing outside the rear entrance? because we might want to stay away from her.

Oh, you will, Jack. Because I have one other eye, and she's mine, you understand?

I do, I do! I guess the other guy looks pretty beat up then?

He does. And let me know if you find him. About six three. Two-twenty. His knuckles are in pretty bad shape.

(laughter)

Okay, let's talk about Bullets Over Sunset. You're on hiatus because—

I put the camera down.

What the hell was that? Was he talking about me without talking about me? None of the paps seemed moved one way or the other, but they knew about the other night on the rooftop. I imagined they could smell the cinnamon of his skin on me, then I became convinced it was the truth.

I didn't have another second to feel shame about Michael and his busted eye. Brad Sinclair and his crew exited the back of the restaurant, and the pack broke. They didn't hustle or rush. Brad put his arm around a pretty blonde's shoulders and turned to Jayce with a comment that made his friend laugh.

I did what I was supposed to do.

I bolted ahead of everyone and leapt over the hood of a car to get in front of them. *Clickclickclick.*

Head to toe. Heels to hairpins. I had it. If I could separate Brad and Jayce into two separate frames, I could sell it twice.

"Hey," Brad called. "Shuttergirl!" He pointed at his eye. "That was you, wasn't it?"

I put down the camera. "Give me something to shoot, and I'll tell you."

He held out both middle fingers, smiling and looking over those stupid sunglasses. Everyone else had him from the side, but he posed for me. I shot it. You bet I did. Boots to bonnet.

"Well?" he said as his car pulled up.

I lowered the camera. "I'm left-handed. I woulda busted the other eye."

He pointed at me with a fake gun shot. I laughed. I forgot to be jaded and knowing. I forgot how it would look for me to have a friendly relationship with Brad Sinclair. I just felt unburdened and available for a stupid joke from someone I'd casually labeled a douchebag.

When Brad and his friends got into his car, I felt the car door slamming as if it were the closing off a portal to another world. I was in an alley with my peers in their smelly T-shirts and matte black cameras. I had always been an outsider, being a woman, but after being friendly with Brad Sinclair, I was worse than an outsider. I was a pariah. I saw it in their looks and their turned backs.

The shots I'd gotten of Brad should have gotten me high fives. Instead, I looked as if I had a leg up, and nobody liked that. Especially not the ragtag team of starkillers I hung out with.

"Laine!" Tom came jogging up behind me, having missed everything. "What did you get?"

"Good stuff."

I felt dead inside. I got no joy from it. Not from the accolades I'd get for doing my job, nor from the money or heated negotiation. I walked out of the alley, and Tom followed.

"Hey," I said, slipping out my phone, "can I see what you've been shooting?"

"Yeah."

I texted Michael.

—I'm worth getting a black eye for?—

"You seem surprised," I said to Tom.

—Definitely. I'd give my other eye in your defense—

"You never want to see what I'm doing outside the celebrity shit," Tom said.

"I don't know. You seem excited about it."

"I'm doing retouching I've never done before. I can't wait for you to see it." He practically skipped out to the street.

"Let me upload these, and we can go to Pasadena."

My phone rang. It was Michael.

"Hey, I—"

He cut me off. "I just got a call from Brad."

I heard people around him talking in serious voices, and through that, he was pissed. "Okay?"

"I asked you not to leave the house," he said.

"I'm sorry? Are you serious?"

"This guy knows where you live and how to get to you. Do you want me to take a picture of my fucking face so you believe it?"

"Your *face*? Your precious *face*?" I wanted to list for him what of mine Foo and Jake had bruised, but that would make him crazy.

"Laine, it's night, it's *dark*—"

"Tom is here. He'll protect me. He knows them."

"Put him on the phone." He was demanding and borderline discourteous. Who was he? This wasn't the funny, sweet guy I'd kissed hours ago. "Laine…"

"What is with you?"

"May I please speak with your brother?"

I handed Tom the phone with a sour face and got into my car, cursing.

"Yeah, I know him," Tom said from outside.

I plugged in my wifi and fired up the laptop, seething from the inside out.

"I know, I know, dude, I know…" Tom said as I ground my teeth.

I pulled up the pictures of Brad, half tilted, middle fingers up, and a big smile under his sunglasses. Not a pap shot. Not a bowed head or sense of discomfort that even the best of them got. No, he was a guy in his own element, and behind him was Renaldo with a sour puss, cradling his camera in his forearm.

"Believe me—" Tom said before I snapped the phone from him.

"You told Brad," I said.

"About what? You? Of course I told him, he's my friend."

"Now he knows me." I flipped through the pictures. It was amazing how they didn't work without the touch of shame and vulnerability. Even though Brad's comfort and smile were genuine, the pictures looked staged and phony. "How am I supposed to do my job if this is common knowledge?"

Tom got in and shut the passenger side door.

"You can't do your job and be with me. That's common sense."

"That's not going to work," I whispered, because the implications were painful.

Tom leaned over to look at my pictures then scrolled through, brow knotted.

"It is going to work, and you're going to stay by Tom until I can get

Carlos there to watch you."

I wanted to tell him I had a camera full of head-to-toes of Brad Sinclair and I couldn't sell one of them, thank you very much. But why would he care? He'd made his position clear.

"Can you not tell anyone else right now? Can you not make implications on talk shows? Can you respect my privacy? And do not even start to pick that apart because you will be as sorry as I am right now."

"Are you apologizing for being a pap?"

"No!" I said. "Not really." I took a deep breath. "Maybe."

"If you stay at Tom's place until Carlos meets you, I will be as silent as the grave."

My first reaction was to thank him, but I bit it back.

"We have a date," he said before I could think of something to say. "I'll see you then."

He hung up. I stuck the phone between my leg and the seat.

"These suck," Tom said.

"They're worthless." I snapped the laptop shut and started the car. "Am I driving you to your car, or did my nurse mother demand you be in arm's reach?"

"I am to be physically present at all times. Can you tell me what happened? Because I didn't think you saw those guys anymore."

I pulled out. "I didn't see them. They saw me in the *LA Post*. Who even knew they could read."

"Ah, and what did he want?"

"Money. What else?"

"I don't—"

"Do you remember the pictures? Those fucking pictures?" I slammed the heel of my hand on the steering wheel. He reddened, and I turned onto the 110. "Well, they have them."

"I'm sorry."

I put up my hand. "No! Don't even. Those pictures saved my life." I counted events on my fingers. "You leaving your camera at my house, Jake and them taking pictures of what was happening, you developing them and shoving them in my face… that… Saved. My. Life. But me leaving them there when I split? That was stupid. Damn stupid." I banged my hand on the wheel again.

I pulled off in Pasadena. Tom lived in a nondescript apartment building off Lake, and I knew the way by heart.

"What are you going to do?" he asked.

I'd spent little time asking myself that because I already knew the answer. "Pay them."

"You? You never give in to shit like this. You don't care what anyone thinks, and you don't get bullied. What happened to you?"

I guessed there was a reason I kept Tom around. He didn't let me get away with anything, and he didn't soft-pedal it. I'd done plenty wrong in my life, and though I rarely wanted to hear about it when I did it, Tom let me know every time.

This time, however, I didn't want to defend myself.

"Leave me alone." I pulled up in front of his building.

"No, I'm not going to leave you—"

I slammed the car into park. "Leave. Me. Alone."

"Do you even know how much they want?"

"I don't care." I gathered my things. Laptop. Camera. Bag.

"But you're just going to pay it?"

"Yes." I got out of the car and thumped the door closed. I walked up to the curb and toward the front doors of his building as if I wanted to be there. As if I was storming the gate to a golden city when in fact I was just changing the subject with my feet.

"Laine, come on, man." He jangled his keys. "What is this?"

"Would you want those pictures out? Two guys on me in crystal-clear black and white? Mascara all over my face. Socks on. Naked bodies everywhere. Do you remember them?"

"I'm not going to forget them," he said softly. "I don't want people looking at you, but I can't believe you're just caving because you're afraid of what Michael Greydon will think of you. I mean, that's the reason, isn't it?"

"I'm ashamed of everything about this. But he doubled down today. On television. What am I supposed to do? Let the world know he's with a whore?"

"You're not—"

"What's it matter what you think of me? If everyone thinks I'm a biker's fuckdoll, I am. And his career depends on what people think of him."

He jangled his keys and found the one he needed. He wanted to say something, I could see it, but he was holding back.

"It's not like it's serious," I said. "I mean, we're doomed from the start.

But for as long as it lasts, it's mine. And I don't want Jake the Pillow Snake killing it. Let it die of natural causes."

"Are you going to see him?"

"Yes."

"I'm going with you."

I glared at him. He'd been pushed around constantly by Jake and his buddies, but Tom was brave, the poor sad sack. Brave and stupid.

"Miss Cartwright?" A six-foot-four solid wall of man in a navy suit approached from a black Chevy SUV that was as big as a bus.

"You must be Carlos," I said, glad to be rescued from telling Tom he couldn't go with me.

We shook hands.

"I'm here to watch you," he said, "not to get in your way. If you tell me where you are at all times, I won't have to."

He said it so cleanly and professionally, it didn't ruffle any of my feathers. That was a talent.

"You coming in?" Tom asked, opening the door.

Carlos held open the door. "That's what I was hired to do." He smiled, big and wide. He could have been an actor himself. Of course, Hollywood couldn't tolerate even the slightly unattractive.

I realized I would have a hard time taking care of my business with Jake whether Tom interfered or not.

Deep breath. I could figure it out. I had to.

— — -

I didn't know when I became so dedicated to making Michael and me happen, or at least, not sabotaging the thing entirely. Probably when he fell asleep on me and the world outside stopped mattering. Or when he took me to his secret place. Or maybe when he tried so hard to protect me that I felt the need to step in and protect him.

Carlos was a pretty unobtrusive shadow, sitting outside Tom's apartment as I inspected every picture of Randee and her band. We broke down his retouch technique to the last pixel. Only when the woman herself showed up did I leave, and in the darkness, with the bus of a car behind me, I wondered what I was doing with my night, and I missed him.

I should have been out chasing something, someone, making myself available for an opportunity to make money. I didn't want to cross him or his friends again, and the phone wasn't ringing no matter how hard I stared at it. I could call Kill Photo, but why take two steps back if I didn't have to?

Could I continue to work with Michael, for however long it lasted? And if I wasn't a paparazza, what was I? Who was I?

I opened the silverware drawer, and I stared at me in poorly fixed black and white, scratching for a cigarette, pain everywhere down below. How hard had it been for Tom to develop this carefully enough to do an exposure test? And the rest of the pictures, where that shirt was pulled up and the sheet wasn't covering what was between my spread legs, how hard had those been to work on? How hard would they be for Michael to see? Would he ever look at me again?

I knew Jake's number. I just had to call him and ask him how much for the pictures. It didn't have to be more than that.

I sat on the edge of my bed and dialed four digits before another call came in. It was Michael.

"Hi," I said, relieved to put off Jake for the moment.

"Hey, I hear Carlos got there?"

"Am I supposed to feed him or something?" I lay back on the bed, suddenly relaxed, as if I had permission to not worry about anything.

"His partner will come relieve him. You're not supposed to even know he's there."

"Okay."

"About before?"

"You being a jerk?" I creased the sheets in my fingers, making a sharp edge of the fold. I caressed it against my knuckles

"That."

"You get a do-over."

"Thank you," he whispered.

I could almost feel his breath on my ear.

"You're not working?" he asked.

"No, you?"

"I'm at a thing. A boring thing."

"It's quiet," I said.

"That's how boring it is."

"You should come here."

"Ah, Laine, what I'd do…"

"What would you do?" It must have been the touch of the sheets and the dim light that made me ask. Or maybe it was the silence on his end.

"Kiss you, of course. But everywhere. Every inch of skin. I want to taste it."

"Oh." I had nothing more articulate. He'd never said anything like that to me, and the pleasant shock went right between my legs. "Michael..."

"Laine, the next time I see you... I'm taking you. I mean it. And then that's it. You're mine. I'm not kidding."

Voices came through the phone. Background noise, as if they'd entered the room.

"Tell me you heard me," he said.

"I heard you."

"What did I say?"

"You want me."

"What else?"

"God, I'm so turned on I can barely think."

"Good. I have to go. Let Carlos stay close. See you tomorrow night."

The line went dead, but I felt like an electrified fence. I was supposed to call Jake. Wasn't that what I had been doing? But I couldn't. Not while I could feel my underpants rubbing against me. The last person I should talk to in that state was Jake.

I stuck my hand in my panties. I was soaked from only a few words. Everything was wrong. Everything stood between Michael and me, but my body wanted an uninterrupted night with him. More than wanted it. My reaction was a response to need.

I closed my eyes and imagined him above me, groaning my name, unaware of anything around him but my body. I imagined him breathing in harsh gasps as he came, and my fingers moved enough for me to come with him, even though he wasn't there.

My hand cupped my ache as it built again. I wasn't making another call, and I wasn't accepting one. I fell asleep basking in the warm promise of him.

Chapter 26

Laine

I knew Michael was taking me to a movie, and that meant jeans and nice shoes, a short leather jacket, and hair thrown up in a nest. Not a big deal. But a short phone conversation with Phoebe shook me from my fog of stupidity.

"*Big Girls* premieres Tuesday," she said. "It's huge."

I sat on my balcony overlooking the newly gentrified street and threw back my head. I knew that. Nothing premiered in that town without my knowing, and somehow, I'd let that star-studded bit of Oscar bait drop from my radar.

"He would have told me," I said, bending at the waist until I was in crash position.

"Unless he thought you already knew. I mean, with him starring in it and all."

"This is going to be very public, Phoebe."

"What are you wearing?" she asked.

"They'll all be there."

"Laine?"

"This is it. It's all over."

"Laine?"

"I'm not going," I said.

"I have a few hours before I leave for Vegas. Meet me at Grandview."

When I saw Phoebe fingering a lacy thing in the dress department, I knew something was wrong. She was too sharp a woman, too crystal clear and energetic for that faraway dreamy look.

"Phoebe?"

"Would you show me this one?" The height of the rack prevented her from getting the dress off herself, and she'd probably shooed away three salesgirls already.

I pulled the cream, floor-length lace dress off the rack, and she stared not *at* it but *through* it.

"What?" I said.

"It's nice."

"Not my style."

"I have to get a wedding dress," she said.

"You're not getting off-the-rack at Grandview. Sorry." I clicked the hanger back in place.

"I have to get it made custom for, you know, the chair. God, I hate this. I'm going to hate every minute of it. I mean, I'd run away and get married if it weren't for my family and the whole concept of running, which I never got a taste of."

Phoebe rarely got depressed. She didn't spend a minute pitying herself. She'd put herself through law school and made a name as a tough negotiator and relationship-builder by using her girlishness not as a handicap but as a weapon. I admired her strength, and because of that, I respected her fragile places.

I sat on a leather chair next to the rack. "Do you want to go get some coffee?"

"No. I want to just do this. Flat out." She said it as if what was coming was hard, as if it had been eating at her.

"Go on," I said.

"You can't be in the bridal party."

"Why not?" She'd picked me as the maid of honor because she didn't have any sisters. We'd talked about dresses and responsibilities. I mean, maybe a demotion for whatever reason but to be cut out completely? "What did I do?"

"Nothing. You're my best friend. Ever since you tripped over me running after Rabine Johnansen. You know why? Because you laughed and helped me up. You've never treated me like a cripple, but you've never ignored it either. So this is the thing. I am a cripple. And I'm supposed to use different words, but this is the fact. And the happiest day of my life is in six months, and I'm going to be in this chair for it. I want... I want something else. I want it to be different."

I had the feeling from her run up that she wasn't cutting me out of the bridal party as much as she was letting me into something else. "What do you want me to do?"

"Wedding pictures are forever, and I don't want them to be ugly. If it's just the usual thing, me and Rob under a trellis, except I'm in a chair, I'm going to cry whenever I look at them. All I'll have of this day for the rest of my life will be the pictures, and I don't want them to look like an excuse, or half done, or fall short of the norm. Everything about it has to be different. Can you do that for me? Can you... I don't want a photographer. Can you not be the photographer? Can you be the documenter? I'll pay you anything."

"You want me to photograph your wedding?"

"Yes."

What was I supposed to say? *No, Phoebe, I think wedding photographers are failures.* Or *Sorry, that doesn't fit in with my vision of myself?*

Besides the fact that would be rude and break her heart, besides the fact that our friendship might not recover from such a rejection, I had to be honest with myself.

The idea was kind of exciting.

"I need complete creative freedom," I said. "You go all bossy lawyer on me, and I'm just going to drink and dance all night."

She slapped her hands over her mouth. "You'll do it?" she said from behind her fingers.

"I need full access to every step of this, so get Rob and your brothers on board. They can't get on my case to make it boring and normal."

"Yes. Anything."

"I can't guarantee you'll look like a model."

"No, no, the point is that it's real. And beautiful but—"

"Beautiful because it's real. I know. I get it."

"I'm so happy, I can't... this is better than... god. You have a date with Michael Greydon! What am I doing?" She wheeled her chair back. "All the stars wear boring black. You need a color."

Chapter 27

Laine

I own Hollywood. I own the dark corners and littered curbs. The shattered bottles, the half-full fast food containers, the broken toilets and ripped mattresses at the curb for months, they're as much a part of me as the spotlights crisscrossing the sky, the cobblestones of Rodeo, the Bentleys, and the private parties. Nothing shocks or scares me. I have never been star struck. Never at a loss for words. Never intimidated by the rich, the powerful, the glamorous any more than the destitute, the filthy, or the criminal.

How can you fear what you own?

How can you be intimidated by what's inside yourself? By a city that nursed you to adulthood?

How?

Looking out the window, I watched a limo pull into a loading zone on the nose of four thirty. A driver got out and let Michael out of the back. Carlos met him at the car and walked him to the front door.

I felt as if I were going to the prom. Not that I knew what that was like. I'd skipped that whole stage of life in favor of hanging out with drug-dealing dirtbags.

For Phoebe, it had come down to pink or yellow, and I'd thrown my hands up and gone with a pink dress. If I was going to be pretty and feminine, I was going all the way. Tight skirt, with lace overlay, that fell just above the knee. Sleeveless bodice with a scooped neck that was still modest and a shawl in a slightly deeper shade. Then shoes, and new stockings, and a matching hairpin, all of which had almost landed Phoebe late for a meeting with the SVP of Overland Studio.

"You look terrible," I said when Michael reached my door, because he looked perfect in a dark suit and tie. His black eye was still uncovered by a stitch of makeup, as if he was as proud of the wound as he would have been if he'd won the fight.

"Turn around," he said, looking at my body as if I wore nothing but the shawl and a smile. "Let me see this rag you bought."

"I knew you hated pink." I turned for him until I could only feel his eyes on me, rather than see them. "That's why I got it."

He put his hand on my waist and his lips on the back of my neck. "I can't even see the dress. Just the woman in it."

"Michael, I…" I drifted into a groan when he moved his hand from my waist to my breast, the edge of his thumb finding where I was most sensitive. I was about to tell him how long it had been since I'd been with a man and unzip exactly as much baggage as I needed to, but I couldn't, for the life of me, remember what I had been trying to say.

"We have to go." He stepped back, and I turned around.

"I lied before."

"You thought I liked pink?"

"I know you like pink," I said. "But you don't look terrible. You are obscenely handsome. It's not fair to all the other men in the world."

He drew his finger across my collarbone. "Lock the door behind you."

I did. Carlos waited by the elevator and stood silently by us as we put our backs to the elevator car wall, holding hands. Michael drew his thumb along the side of my hand, and I shuddered. Even that simple touch was electric.

"You were great on Jack Rambling's show today," I said.

"How did I look?"

"Like you were blasting a secret all over town without telling me first."

"It was a spur of the moment thing. I'm not usually impulsive. I had a simple joke set up, and then, I don't know."

I turned to look at him. He watched me, and I knew he was being honest. I couldn't be angry, even though I should have been about both Brad and the show.

When the elevator doors opened, I realized why I couldn't be angry.

I thought I'd understood the significance of our night out until we stepped outside. I'd thought it was about *us*, about us being official on some level. About accepting that we would proceed, one and the other, to hell with all of it.

But it was more than that.

Two more bodyguards waited past the glass doors, and they had a big job in standing between us and a dog pack of paparazzi.

I stopped. No, I didn't stop. I froze, thinking about the head to toe, the heels to hairpins; my posture, my face, the shape of my persona against the perfection of Michael Greydon.

"Hey," he whispered, "I thought I'd have the car ride to prep you, but—"

"Of course. Why would they bother with the opening? They'd have to fight the press there. Here, it's all them. These will be all over the internet with edited copy before we even get to the theater."

"Will you be okay?"

"Will you stay by me?"

"Always," he said softly, squeezing my hand.

"Damn you, Greydon. My heart just expanded three sizes."

"Let's have fun. Come on." He pulled me to the door, smiling as if he were a two-year-old on the teacup ride, delighted, unencumbered, and fully in the moment.

I tried to imitate his glee as we walked out, but I couldn't. They called my name, because they knew it, and every click of a shutter was a point of attention away from him. He held my hand, and my hand felt safe. Then he stepped in front of me and looked back, locking me in frame. He put himself as the calm eye in the storm of my fear, which then disappeared like water on the sidewalk at noon.

He pulled me to the limo. A man in a suit opened the door, and Michael let me in first. He got in across from me. The door closed, and everything disappeared.

"How do you do that all the time?" I said.

"It's not that big a deal. Not when I expect it."

I leaned back. It was just us, and the car hadn't moved yet. The paps were mostly gone. Having gotten their shot, they were either uploading, racing to our destination, or both.

"God, I feel so crappy right now," I said.

"Why?"

"My job. I feel... guilty."

The car moved, and Renaldo popped his shutter a few times as if he could sell a picture of a limo.

"I hate this, this regret. I thought the attention made you all feel good, but it doesn't feel good on this side. It feels ugly."

"Between us," he said, leaning forward, "I want to tell you something you should believe unconditionally."

I didn't answer because his hands covered my knees. They put a slight pressure on the insides of my legs, as if he was about to open them.

"Don't even believe it," he said. "Know it. You, personally, have never made me uncomfortable. You, personally, have never been anywhere I didn't expect you. And I always thought you had a beautiful body behind that camera."

My legs wanted to open. The insides of my thighs felt alive with desire, as if they were lit with klieg lights, and when he ran his thumbs along the insides of my knees, the buzz increased.

"I want you," I said. "I don't want to be unladylike in this dress, but I want you right now."

"I want every inch of you. Don't get me wrong, I'd like to tell Gali to spin around the block a few hundred times so I can be alone with you. But I'm not a boy. First, we're going onto the carpet. Let me lead. Then the lobby, which is just a movie theater lobby but full of people in the business, and they'll talk too long about nothing. I want you to trust me. All I'll be thinking about is spreading your legs and tasting you."

"How am I going to get through this movie?"

He laughed softly. "No one watches the movie. My God, I've seen it seven times already."

"Are you any good in it?"

"According to who?"

"You?"

He shook his head. "Not really. I think I overdid it in places and underdid it everywhere else. But everyone else is happy, so who am I to say? I just have to go into the theater with you and keep my hands off you for long enough to leave. Then it's in my contract that I have to go to the after party. It's three blocks away. We'll drive so we don't get mobbed. Then I'm taking you home, and I'm getting acquainted with every inch of you."

His eyes drifted down my body, as if imagining his acquaintance with those inches of skin, and I tingled. I wouldn't tell him anything about my past tonight. Not a word. I wanted a clean night. Just us.

164

There was a knock on the window soon after the car stopped.

"You ready?"

"We're going public, aren't we?"

"Right now." He took my hand.

I was shocked at how dry my palm was, and I knew it was because I was with him. He knocked on the window. Outside, everything was as I expected, as if set for a movie. Red carpet. Reporters. Fans holding little booklets and pens. The white facets of the Cinerama Dome were drowned in the lights.

"We're going in the front?" I asked. "No one goes in the front. What are we? Tourists?"

He kissed me through my smile. "We just run through this. It'll be fun. Just stay out of the camera's range."

The car door opened, and everything changed. I knew I'd never see my life, my job, or my city the same again.

Michael got out first and put his hand out to me. Behind him, the pathway to the ArcLight's courtyard was draped in red carpet and bordered by fans.

"Don't let go," I said before my feet hit the curb.

"Never."

The floods were blinding and too blue if you asked me, catching me in a tunnel of light that had voices at the end. Some had words, and some didn't. Some were simply long vowels. Some were his name. Some were spoken in a falsetto of excitement. They took my name and turned it onto a blade, opening me up.

A moment with Sunshine and Rover when I'd feel like this. On the beach. Late at night with all their friends in a drum circle. I jump in the middle and dance, and they clap in unison for me. All of them, eyes on me with approval.

"Hello, my name is Deanna."

I only saw her in silhouette. She had a clipboard and sensible shoes.

"Mister Greydon, you have DMZ first, to the left."

"Thank you," he said, putting my hand around his forearm.

"Miss Cartwright," Deanna said, "you can get off camera if you want by taking a step to the right."

"Thank you," I said, grateful for the instructions on getting out of the way. Nothing would make me happier than moving out of DMZ's line of sight. I didn't want them taking my picture or anything else.

"Michael Greydon!" Rob Bearston shouted both at Michael and into his microphone.

And Mister Yi, checking the linking on a sideseam with a magnifying glass that strapped around his head. Nodding. A warm glow that was mine.

I panicked. Instinctively, I thought they were stealing my memories. I knew it wasn't true, but I tried to stop remembering, which made it worse.

"Rob, nice to see you."

I think Michael said that. I was watching the photographers. They weren't my people. They were hired guns from the studio's publicity department, and I was in the frame. I took half a step to the right, and Rob pushed me back as if he was saving me from falling past the velvet rope.

"Miss Cartwright, not real often we see you on this side of the rope."

I am ten. Tom sits on the couch with me, watching Nickelodeon. We talk in a secret language about how we'll sneak out of the house and run the streets because we can, and the bio sister watches us as if she knows.

"You mean never? Right, Rob?" I said.

"Are you going to continue to shoot celebrities?" He put the mic just below my chin. "We'd hate to lose you. Everyone at DMZ wants you to keep up the good work."

Jake grabs me when I get home from school, sticking his hand up my shirt and pinching my nipple as if he's trying to unscrew it. I am only fourteen, but I get him off me, and he looks at me as if he knows it aroused me.

"You do pay awfully well," I said, "but I'll charge more if you don't get that mic out of my face."

Rob smirked. Michael laughed and put his hand over mine. I bit my lip, wishing I'd been able to take that half step to the right.

"Any questions about the movie, Rob?" Michael asked. "Because she'll cut you. Cut you bad."

"Oh, over at DMZ, we know that already. Good luck, Mister Greydon." Rob winked into the camera. "Good luck."

He couldn't see me. He didn't know me. None of them knew me. I kept repeating that to myself. They only knew what I showed them, and I had to show them nothing. It was the only way I could breathe.

Deanna appeared as if summoned. "Petra French from the Entertainment Channel is just this way." She led us across the carpet.

"You're cutting off my circulation," Michael said through a smile.

"Sorry." I loosened my grip on his forearm.

"You did great."

"They're going to play that quote on a loop for three days."

"After a while, you just stop watching television."

We stood in front of another camera, another host, but my half step to the right was allowed. I was in the safe zone. She asked Michael questions that seemed complex in the disorienting buzz, but I knew they would come off as simplistic on a screen.

Each stop was different, with a different expectation of me. I stood on my feet and said words thanks to his hand on my back. The pressure of his palm was a grounding wire to my physical balance and verbal skills.

Were you shooting him when you met?

Have you ever sold a picture of your date?

How did you two meet?

Do you have a camera?

Are you excited to be on the other side of the rope?

Can you tell us how Mister Greydon got that black eye?

I answered the yes and no questions, but Michael managed to steal the complex ones with a joke and a smile. He was home, but I felt as though I was at his parents' house at Christmas, tested with every question and slice of turkey, as he gently protected me from myself.

Deanna walked in front of us, pressing her earpiece. "Mister Greydon is entering the lobby."

Then we passed through the glass doors, and it was over.

His hand on my shoulder, my arm around his waist, he spoke close to my ear. "I'm sorry. I didn't expect that. They usually ignore the dates."

"I understand the rush," I said.

"That goes away, trust me. It's nothing compared to kissing you."

"Oh, shut up." I think that, despite my words, I flushed. He was wearing me down, layer by layer, like a heat gun peeling off coats of paint and toxic lead whitewash to the bare wood.

The lobby of the theater was nicely done but purely functional. The snack counter was open, but no cash registers were ringing. Everyone was busy talking in their evening dresses and snappy suits, voices and laughter echoing off the high ceilings and marble floors. I spotted three photographers in black by following their flashes. More hired guns shooting for crap pay.

I didn't have another second to take in the scene and see what was different about it, because Michael was approached with congratulations and handshakes. I knew most of them by name and face, but they didn't recognize me, or they pretended not to. Studio execs, talent agents, managers, hangers-on. Sometimes Michael introduced me; sometimes the exchange was so short, he didn't. I was courteous but said little, laughed when I was supposed to, and held on to Michael for dear life.

The word bandied about most was "Congratulations." The consensus I gathered was that this was more than a movie for Michael but something groundbreaking.

During a spare second, when he pulled me away from one glowing couple, I leaned into him and whispered, "This must have been the performance of a lifetime."

"They're all just working hard to not mention my eye." He looked at me as if memorizing the details of my face.

"What?" I asked, tingling red in the cheeks.

"Can't wait until later, that's all."

Brad walked sideways through the crowd to get to us. He was wearing plaid shorts and a suit jacket and tie. His sunglasses were transparent enough to make his eyes visible. As soon as he saw me, he put up his middle fingers.

"Hey, how did those come out?" he said to me as he shook hands with Michael and slapped him on the back.

"I'll send them to you."

"You're all right, Laine. I don't care what my agent says." He said it with a laugh, as if I was in on the joke.

Gene Testarossa, like a fly hovering over a plate of raw meat, came up behind Michael. "Can I talk to you?"

He didn't acknowledge me or Brad. Even when Britt, with a glittery sling on her left arm, tapped Brad's shoulder, and they hugged, Gene kept his focus on Michael.

"Hey." Michael poked Brad in the chest and gestured toward me. "Watch her."

"What do you think I'm going to do?" I said.

"You? Nothing. You're perfect." He pointed at Brad with two fingers and put the two fingers to his own eyes then back toward Brad. "Eyes."

"You got it, bro."

Gene pulled Michael away.

Britt made it a point to press her lips together until Michael was out of range, then she grabbed my shoulder. "I think I'm in love with you."

Brad cackled.

"I'm sorry?" I said.

"You are exactly what he needs."

"Oh, I—"

She slapped Brad in the chest. "Yes or no? Was he not the most boring little shit in the world?"

"You never met my parents," Brad said.

"Then when I found out he broke a window at the Fall Gala thing? I swear I applauded. Hug me. Hug me now." She held out her good arm and enfolded me in half an embrace. A flash went off.

Britt turned toward the girl with the cumbersome camera and kissed my cheek. Brad, as attuned to a lens as a shark to blood, got in the shot. Me in the middle of two badly behaving stars and Michael nowhere to be seen. I was seen inside the unit, caught at the edge of the vortex and sucked down the drain. I forced a smile.

Maryetta muscled through the crowd to take her lover's arm. "Who is this?" she asked

"This is the paparazzi I was telling you about," Britt said.

I shook Maryetta's hand, and we exchanged greetings. It wasn't until that moment that the surrealism of the situation hit me. Maryetta directed experimental theater, and she was the least famous of all those people, yet I'd photographed and sold even her image.

What the hell was I doing there? Where was Michael? I wasn't supposed to be there. I belonged on the other side of the rope, in the dark corners. Where was my camera? How was I supposed to do my job without it?

"I'm going to the ladies' room," I said. "Excuse me."

"Hey, no way," Brad said. "I gotta watch you."

"I have her." Britt took my elbow and led me away.

Maryetta walked close on my other side, but I wanted Michael.

In the twenty steps to the bathroom, Britt was pulled away to laugh and talk about stuff I didn't understand. Maryetta joined her, and I was alone.

I owned the city. Nothing intimidated me. Nothing, really, except being in a room full of people I'd self-righteously annoyed, or bothered, or hurt even. I never imagined I'd be in such a room, never understood that my high heels and camera bag had been a costume, my camera a weapon, and the night a shield. I had none of my gear, and I was in a room full of targets with eyes that stared, mouths that pursed in judgment, laughter that cut.

I was back at Breakfront. I was a reviled outsider clothed as a member but painted, tarred, and feathered in my wrongness.

The door out and the door to the bathroom were equidistant from me. If I went out, I'd be seen by the few photographers and reporters who were left, but I could get a cab home, where I'd cry. If I went into the bathroom, I could get myself together and reemerge to face the room.

The door out seemed most appealing. I wanted to be alone more than anything, but Michael would wonder what had happened to me. He'd chosen me to be with him tonight. It was important to him, not as an actor but as a man. If I split, I would make the event about me, and it was about him.

So I took a deep breath and went to the bathroom.

I'd been to the ArcLight before. Most of Los Angeles had, but that night, the bathroom looked different. It was lit with scented candles and soft lights that set off the glass vases of flowers. It looked less institutional and more luxurious.

Ute Herman and Gabrielle Sanchez chatted in the powder room. Garden Jones sat on a damask chair and chatted on her cell phone. The SVP of marketing from Overland Studios leaned kiss-close to the mirror and picked a false eyelash off her cheek. And Lucy Betancourt strode away from a sink, right toward me.

"Laine," she said gently, "how are you?"

"Fine." I swallowed.

"I saw you come in with Michael."

"So?" I said, unable to stop my venom. "You going to put a fiver in my bra?" If I'd realized how close to the edge I was, I would have left immediately, but it snuck up on me.

"No, Laine—" She glanced around the room.

Everyone was working hard to look at anything else but us.

"I'm not going away," I growled. "I won't be chased off."

She sat on a couch and twisted sideways, so she faced the space next to her. She smiled curtly and patted the seat, indicating I should sit by her.

When we were in school together, she was the queen bee, and as cruel as she'd been to me, I'd craved her attention.

Nothing had changed. Nothing ever changed. I'd shed my Breakfront persona years ago, yet in her presence, I shrugged back into the broken-glass-lined coat as if I needed to get cut.

I sat, but I didn't face her. I faced front, my one act of childish rebellion. I felt pathetic doing it, but I couldn't look at her.

"You look like a deer in headlights," she said.

"Lucy, is there something you want? Because Michael will be looking for me."

"He's a good man. You don't find too many of those."

"I know. On both counts."

A bell rang somewhere, and women started filing out.

"Why won't you look at me?" Lucy said.

I turned toward her. She was as patrician as she'd been as a teenager, with her straight turned-up nose and angular cheeks. People paid good money for her features, but hers had come free as a genetic gift.

"Because you're going to tell me I'm going to be a stripper when I grow up, and I'm all out of patience for it," I said.

"You shouldn't let other people tell you what you are. Especially insecure seventeen-year-old girls."

"I'll put that on a postcard."

"Does it matter if I apologize? I'm aware it's too little too late. I knew I couldn't keep Michael. He was on his way across the country and then you. Of all the things that worried me, you were the easiest target." She opened her purse and found a compact and lipstick. She opened the compact and looked into the little mirror, even though there were mirrors all over the room. "Being cruel to you made me feel good. I'm sure that reflects poorly on me, but I'm past worrying about appearances. I don't know if you even understand what appearances mean." She got her lipstick out and twisted it.

"What's that supposed to mean?"

"It wasn't an insult. It means I don't know you, and you're different. Different expectations. He brought you here, and everyone's talking about him losing his mind." She smeared color on her lips and pursed them. "I can defend him to everyone, but I can't defend you. You were a rat punk in school, a real viper. Every time we tried to talk to you, you practically spit on us. So no, I'm not defending how I acted, but I want you to know that if you bring him any trouble, I'll make you miserable."

"There's going to be trouble."

"I mean if you hurt him. If you disrespect what he's done tonight by being seen with you." She shook her head as if loosening the worst of the options. "If this is a business deal to you, I swear on my face, I'll make sure you don't sell another picture." She slid the cover on her makeup and snapped the compact closed.

"Nothing like spending a first date being threatened by the ex," I said, standing. "But I promise you, I'm not here on business. Up until now, it was strictly pleasure."

She snapped her bag shut and looked at me. "Tell me, how do you feel about him?"

"I haven't even told him that, but I'll tell you how I feel about you."

"This should be fun."

"You're a good friend. A little scary, but still," I said. "He did all right with his friends."

Michael swooped in as if dropped from the back of a white stallion, half breathless and impeccable, his motions proportionally attuned to a constantly shifting universe. "Here you are!"

"This is the ladies' room," Lucy said, standing.

"So I see." He took my hand. "Come on, there are people waiting everywhere." He turned to Lucy as he opened the door. "Are you going to the after party?"

"Good Lord, I'm not going to Mort's. I don't have to abide by a contract. It's not my movie."

"I want you to go and watch Laine."

"Oh, no way!" I said a little too definitively.

"No one else is qualified. Britt and Brad are already half drunk. And I'm going to get pulled away. The press knows you. I didn't realize it. But you won't have a good time if they're all over you."

"I didn't bring any fives," Lucy said in her most snooty tone. Without a break in her expression, she seemed completely serious until her eyes flicked toward me, then back to Michael.

I crossed my arms. "Nothing less than a ten goes in my G-string these days."

He looked between us. "What?"

Lucy mock-shuddered. "Fine." She stepped beside Michael and turned. "I'll run you a tab." She opened the door, brushed past Deanna and a huge guy in a red tie, and strode down the hall as if offended.

"What was that?" he asked, holding out his arm for me.

"What? We were reminiscing."

We exited the bathroom. I had to admit, I liked Lucy. She was consistent, and she cared for Michael. She acted like a prudish, middle-aged woman, which must have once made Michael feel secure. If anything bad happened between us, she didn't need to like me as much as make him safe.

"Right this way, Mister Greydon," Deanna said with a sweep of her hand.

"Don't talk to Gene," Michael whispered as we walked down the hall.

No one bothered him, took pictures, or asked for his autograph. It was as if, amongst these people, he was home.

"Why would I do that?"

"Because I just fired him."

I read his lips more than I could hear him. I stopped. "Why? Not because of me?"

He walked backward so he could face me, glancing around to see who was within earshot. "I hired him to be a dick because I couldn't be. He did his job for ten years. I'm done with it. I'm a big boy. I can be my own dick."

I bit my lips to keep from laughing, but I had never been good at that. The laugh burst out as if someone had let the air out of a balloon. He stopped walking and let me stride right into him, where he held me for a second as we laughed together. The big guy in the red tie and Deanna held the swinging doors open. Michael and I stepped into the dim, flat light.

"We're leaving after the second reel," he whispered to me.

"Why?"

"You know what it's like to look at yourself ten times bigger than you are? There's nothing more uncomfortable."

I looked at my normal-sized date and saw exactly how uncomfortable it would be. "All right."

A man in a tuxedo leaned into Deanna, who whispered something. Then he led us to seats at center front with a sign on them, printed on copy paper and tied around the backs with a red ribbon.

GREYDON +1

Michael shook hands and made a joke or two with the couple behind us, then he took my hand and led me into the aisle. He knew everyone and had a smile and a joke for all of them. When we finally got to our seats, he let me sit first. He adjusted his cuffs.

"You seem nervous," I whispered.

He put his arm around the chair and pulled me close enough to feel his lips move against me. "We're going to the party because it's in my contract, then I'm going to take you home and own you. You're going to be up all night."

My face got hot again. I wanted him to stop talking like that, and I didn't want it to ever end.

Andrea Rodenstein, the director, jumped up to the front of the auditorium. She introduced herself to applause, thanked her crew and agent, then named the cast with thanks. When his name was called, Michael stood, waved, and sat back down before they'd finished the ovation. It was loud and long, and someone in the back of the room chanted, "Oscar! Oscar! Oscar!"

Michael turned in his seat and pointed toward the back of the room then put his finger to his lips, asking for silence. Brad stood and chanted even louder. Britt stood and, like a bunch of fans with their faces painted the team colors, got half the room chanting before it died down in a thunder of applause.

"Does that always happen?" I asked once Rodenstein got the crowd under control enough to continue.

He shrugged. "Brad. What can I say?"

"He's a good friend."

"Yeah."

The lights dimmed, and the movie started. Within the first few frames, I knew why Brad and everyone had chanted. The above-the-line cast and crew, as well as the executives from marketing and finance, had seen the movie already, and they knew what was now all over the screen.

Michael's work in *Big Girls* was the performance of a lifetime. The sweet man sitting one seat over, his palm over the back of my hand, scared the living hell out of me. He became a volatile abuser, capable of spurts of violence and passion, with no in between, and Claire Contreras, the actress playing his wife, became the focal point of his every emotion, even when she wasn't in the scene. I was terrified for her and engaged completely. Michael tapped my hand after about fifteen minutes.

"Come on."

"But I…" I pointed at the screen.

He sat back, and I felt him tense up. He wasn't even looking at the screen. I tapped his knee, and he looked at me from behind his hand.

I cocked my thumb and mouthed, "Ready?"

We slipped out the Exit door in the back. Michael knew everyone in the lobby and accepted congratulations and compliments. My purse vibrated, which I was capable of ignoring unless I got it in my head that it could be Tom in trouble.

Which got into my head because of Jake and Foo. They knew Tom, so seeing as Michael was walking and talking, shaking hands and air kissing while he made his way down the hall, I checked my phone.

I was hit face first with a black-and-white of young Laine on her knees, doe-eyed, looking at the naked man above her with her mouth open.

—Wanna hear from you girlie girl—

My surroundings closed in on me. The laughter, the noise from the indoor parking lot, the dog pack waiting for our exit, shouting names and clicking, was far away. I became a soft, slimy animal in a tight shell of shame and fear.

—What do you want Jake?—

"Laine?" It was Tom with his camera, still monochrome, still schlubbing along even when he was getting the shot. But his camera wasn't in front of his face; it was at his side. "Shut it off."

Had he heard from Jake? I was sure he had. He wasn't just telling me to stop looking at my phone in front of paparazzi. He'd never give me a lesson in poise. He put his camera up when Britt and Brad appeared.

Another buzz from my phone, and another picture came in with a message.

—We miss you, sweet angel. I'm trying to not upload these pictures all over but my hand's getting itchy—

I put it away.

"You all right?" Michael asked, hand on my lower back again, lips close enough to my ear to touch it.

"Yeah." I turned my head to face him, and he was just perfect with his scent of cinnamon. Even in the gross parking lot, he made everything beautiful. Even with the bruise under his eye that he'd gotten for me. Would he throw himself in danger again? Would he have to? "Just sick of this thing buzzing all the time."

"We'll get you a blocking service."

A blocking service? That must be what he had, where he had a short list and no one else got through. How was I supposed to get tips like that?

But of course, that was the point. There would be no more tips. They'd already dried up, along with my hope of forgetting my past. Maybe I should just block everyone but Michael, Tom, and Phoebe. Jake especially. Double block him. But then, God knew what he'd do with those pictures.

The driver opened the limo door, and Michael took my hand. It must have been shaking from seeing the pictures because he looked at me tenderly, as if he wanted to protect me from the paps and the flashing lights. But that wasn't it. As much as the exposure made me uncomfortable, it was nothing compared to those pictures.

I got into the back of the limo, and the door shut behind Michael. He sat across from me, a point of calm against the chaos outside. The sounds were shut out, the clicking, the shouting, the car engines. Paps leaned into the window to get a shot of us.

Except Tom, who leaned into the window, camera down, fingers to his ear, and lips moving. *Call me tomorrow.*

I gave him a thumbs-up as the limo drove away.

"I'm sorry, Laine," Michael said. "It's always like this, but I'm used to it. I wasn't thinking. I should have given you more time."

"It's all right."

"I wanted to show you off."

Me. He wanted to show me off to his movie star friends. He gathered my hands and pulled me into his lap. I straddled him, my hands on his cheeks. His eyes were honest and open. I didn't deserve that. I didn't deserve the guy I'd wanted in high school who'd gone off to make something of himself while I stayed home and let myself be used.

"I want to be honest," I said as he kissed me. It was hard to concentrate with his hands running up and down my back and his lips on my throat. "I have things." *Things?* "I don't want you to think I'm something I'm not."

"You're a woman, right? All woman parts? I'm not going to get your dress off and find stuff I can't use?"

"Don't be silly."

"Is there anyone else? Boyfriend? Husband? Late-night booty call? Because that's a deal-breaker."

"No one. It's been a long time."

"How long?" he asked into the curve of my throat.

"Almost a year."

He pulled away from me, and my longing pulled taut in the space that divided us.

"Why?" he asked.

I'd become attached to the idea of him, and I didn't want to let it go. Not yet. I was sure the whole thing would go down in flames, but God, I didn't want it to be that night.

At the same time, I knew I could wiggle out of answering by repeating that the right guy hadn't come along, stuff hadn't worked out, nothing was wrong anywhere in my world.

But I couldn't lie to him again.

"I don't trust men or anyone," I said so low I could barely hear it. "I have a past."

"I know. It was at your door yesterday. We all have a past. So I'll ask you again. Is everything in the past? That's all I want to know."

"Yes." Was that the truth? With Jake sending me evidence of my wrongdoings as we spoke, was it really all in the past?

"I know you had a hard time," he said. "If it's that, I don't care. I mean, I care, but it won't stop me from having you tonight. Or probably any other night. If that guy bugs you again, we'll deal with it. Okay?"

I nodded. He didn't know what he was agreeing to, and I owed him explanations on top of explanations, but I couldn't. I'd ruin everything for him as well as me.

"Okay," I said, half kissing him.

He shifted against me, and I felt his body under his clothes, the hard curves of muscle and the sweet intention in the press of his hips.

"I want you to trust me," he said into my cheek.

"I do, and it scares the hell out of me."

The car stopped. Flashes blinked through the window. Those lenses hadn't been bought and sold. Those were my people. I'd been on the other side of the rope, watching the line of limos and half done catching the first car door open before I was tracking who was in the next. I knew they were talking about where Michael and I were, and a couple of the guys had noted the license plate. They didn't share the information though. They'd just make sure they were in the front of the pack when our door opened, acting calm and collected until they got a good spot, then they would be all elbows and inertia.

I sat back and straightened my skirt.

Michael put his hand up the outside of my thigh, touching up to the lace tops of my stockings. "I like these."

"Good, because I wore them for you."

His reaction was pure instinct, as if I'd pared down his intentions into their most basic. "Okay," he said, brushing his fingertips inside my knees.

"We go outside, you stand and look gorgeous, we go in, stay as long as we have to, and I'll take you out back. Got it?"

"Got it."

The car crept toward the front of the line.

"Ever hike Griffith Park at night?" I said. "There are mountain lions, for real."

He ran his hands up my legs, past where the stockings ended. "We should go."

"What about your contract?" My back straightened as his fingertips brushed my crotch. My panties would have to get wrung out over the sink.

"Tomorrow night."

We kissed in the promise of a tomorrow and a next day, twisted until he was on top of me. He pushed my bag out of the way, and it spilled on the floor in a spray of lipstick, cards, money, and phone.

Which was lit with an incoming message.

Which was a photo.

Of me.

In black and white.

On my hands and knees.

Naked but for socks.

I reached for it too quickly, breaking our rhythm.

Why wasn't I slick and sneaky? I could barrel through anything. I owned the space around me, except when I didn't. Except when the one thing I didn't want Michael to ever see was on the floor of our limo and he was on top of me, reaching for my phone to help me.

I pushed him off me and snapped the phone from his hand.

"Laine…"

"Don't you know you shouldn't look at someone else's phone?"

I wanted to curl up and die. I wanted to hope he hadn't seen it. I wanted it to be three seconds ago, when I could have put the bag down carefully, or half an hour ago when I could have shut off the phone, or three days ago when I could have called Jake and ended this, or ten years ago.

I couldn't breathe. The space between us was suffocating. He was silent. That was bad. If he hadn't seen it, he would have just put his hands back up my skirt. I pulled it down and readjusted myself.

"What just happened? What was that?" he asked.

"Can we forget it? You can just drop me home." I couldn't look at him, so I couldn't detect what he was feeling. I wanted to look up and see him, but partly, I was afraid I'd see disgust and disappointment, and partly, I didn't feel worthy of being in anyone's sight.

He slid his hand over mine, brushing my fingers and lodging his in between them, just as he'd done on our last day at the bleachers, before he told me he was leaving.

I snapped my hand away. "I'll take a cab."

He grabbed my jaw and turned my face toward his. "Talk to me."

The limo crept forward, and the blue light from outside moved across his face in a hard line. He didn't scare me. His hardness actually soothed me. But I didn't want to be soothed. I didn't want to be comforted. It made me weak and needy. I bit back a hitched breath.

"I can't," I croaked.

He reached behind me and hit a button with his fist. "Gali?"

"Yes, sir?" came the driver's voice.

"Drive around the block until I say stop or we run out of gas."

"Yes, sir."

The car broke out of the line, and the paparazzi got small in the distance. I stared out the window, clutching my phone in my lap. I imagined opening the door at a red light and running. Running forever, cutting turns across lawns, leaping over cars, my butt sliding over the hoods, hopping fences, and climbing a ladder to the top, the top, the top of anything.

Michael reached for the phone, but I held it.

"Just tell me," he said.

I shook my head. Cleared my throat. Drew my fingers under my eyes to catch the tears before they fell. "Listen, this was fun. I like you. You're a better guy than I deserve, as anyone will tell you. Probably you should go back to the party. People are expecting you. I'll go home, and we can just remember this very fondly. Okay? Can we do that?"

"Was that you in the picture?"

I looked down, turning the now-dark phone in my hand. "No. That girl is about sixteen. She's a…" I swallowed. Breathed. "She feels alone all the time, and she's young and immature, so she's not okay with it. So a little bump in the road, and she gets with a guy. And this guy? He's a sleaze, but he makes her feel taken care of. He gives her a roof over her head and a kind of family. He protects her, and he doesn't let her take any of the drugs he sells. But he…"

Breathe.

Breathe.

"He lets his friends fuck her. He uses her to make deals, and just… if they're all bored and drinking, they'll just use her for fun. She lets this happen for over a year, because if nothing else, she feels safe. It doesn't matter who fucks her as long as he knows, and he's watching over it, and he says it's okay. Because he took care of me."

I hitched a little when I said "me" instead of "her." Pretending she was someone else was a useless ruse. I was a whore and worthless and the owner of nothing but my shame.

"Why now?"

"Pictures of me around, in the paper, on the internet. He was reminded, and I'm sure he thinks I'm rich now."

"And this is the guy from the hallway?"

I couldn't look at him, but I imagined he was turned off and just getting the facts straight.

"No," I said.

"Jake? Jake the Pillow Snake?"

"It doesn't matter. But yes. He was the son of the family I was with before the Hatches. Before Breakfront. He was twenty, maybe twenty-one when I ran away from Orry and Mildred, ran back to him. Right after you left."

"That's statutory rape, Laine."

I turned to him as if I wanted to bite him. I recognized the viper Lucy spoke about in the first two words out of my mouth. "I knew exactly what I was doing. I consented to everything, and don't you take that away from me. Fine world you live in, where my life was illegal. Cute. Real cute."

It was a low blow, playing the foster child card. But Michael would not be shamed by his privilege.

"He's peddling child pornography? Posting those? And you consented to that?"

"I have to go." I went for the door handle despite the fact the car was still moving.

"Stop!" He held the handle. "Just stop. You're giving me whiplash."

I pushed him away. "I don't need you to take care of me! I don't need *anyone* to take care of me. Do you hear me? I can take care of myself!"

"Okay, I got it. You're capable. You know what you're doing. You're a fine, upstanding whirlwind of ambition. Then why are you shutting down? Why are you hiding? Why are you trying to get out of a moving car?"

"I'm trying to not hurt you."

"Hurt me? You're fucking killing me," he shouted, face tight in the moving lamplight. "I see this picture of you, and you're in pain, I can see that, and you tell me this story, and it hurts to hear it. And now you're running away because you think I'm looking to get away from you. You're trying to do me a favor because… what do you think of me?"

"I think you're normal. Just cop to it—"

"Cop to what? Wanting to go to a *party* instead of being here for you? Laine, I want you. I care about you. You give me something I've never had before. You're a devil in high heels, but you… God, I want you. You. Your body, yes, but everything else too. I want to make everything in your world right. I can't help it. Let me in. Just let me in."

I leaned back on the seat as if my neck couldn't hold my head. "You're a good person. Don't make me something you have to fix. I'm fine. I earned my life the hard way."

"Let me in."

"Why?"

"Because I won't hurt you."

"But you will." When I blinked, the tears that had hung over my eyes fell onto my cheeks. "Jake is going to put these all over the internet, and you'll have to protect what you've built. They won't tolerate you with a whore. You'll stand by me out of obligation, and you'll blame me. How could you not?"

"None of that is true." He took a handkerchief from his inside pocket.

"It'll ruin you unless I give him what he wants." I brushed my hands over my cheeks, but he pulled them away and handed my face the handkerchief.

"What does he want?"

"Money. Which I'll give him." I sniffed. Wiped.

"Is that it?"

"Probably a nostalgia screw. He's come around few times since I left. And no, he never got what he came for."

Michael leaned back and looked out the window as we drove down the dark expanse of deLongpre for the fifth time, turning back toward the colored lights of Hollywood Boulevard. I assumed he was coming down from the drama-high of our conversation and was putting together what being with me meant. Finding a loophole. Strategizing a way to break it to me.

I'd had a couple of parent-sets look me in the eye and say it wasn't me, it was them. I knew how it went. They needed to do it that way, but for me, it didn't matter.

I was happier being single, to be honest. If I dated anyone, he should be a pap or a criminal or something. Michael was a liability. He was going to end a career I loved.

I was okay.

Chapter 28

Michael

She was going to end me. Even if the thing with that picture—and who knew how many more—blew over tomorrow, she was trouble. I'd known that from the start and had continued as if she wore a costume that could be peeled off, as if she was *acting*. But she wasn't, not a bit. Her hurt was real and disquieting.

I could get out of it. Having said too much, too soon and having made little promises I couldn't keep, I could still get out of it. Save her and me a lot of trouble. It was better that way, really. I'd existed before I knew her, and I could exist after. Over time, we'd go back to the way we were, with her hidden behind a camera and me hidden in front of them. I'd stop being a magnet for her past, and she'd move on safely.

Excusing myself from her life was the only sensible thing to do.

"Laine," I said so low I could barely hear myself.

"Yeah?"

"How many pictures are there?"

"A roll. Thirty-six."

I looked at her for the first time since she'd mentioned a nostalgia screw. Her chin was an eighth of an inch higher, and her mouth was set tight.

"A roll?" I asked.

"Negative film and paper. Tom was learning. He left his camera, and the guys thought it would be funny to leave him a present."

"It's not funny."

"Tom didn't think so either. He said he threw up when he developed them, then he made me look at them. It was awful. But it doesn't matter how many, does it? One or a hundred, how many will it take to ruin your life?"

She was so guarded. She was braced to take a blow and beautiful in that. I was sure I could let her down easy and never see her cry over it. I'd walk away without a drop of guilt, only an ocean of regret.

Once I saw her tears fall and heard her admissions, her shame, and her self-blame, the idea that I could leave her was a distraction. She could take care of herself, but I didn't want her to. I wanted to take care of her. I wanted to be that man who was more to her, the one who treated her like the jewel she was. I wanted to be the one to protect her.

I touched her cheek. She pulled back a hair, still girded, her hand on my arm as if she wanted to draw it down. I slipped my fingers to the back of her head and pulled her toward me.

"Michael, really, I—"

I put my weight into it and kissed her because I had to. Her face knotted then relaxed, and she kissed me back.

I was unqualified to save her. My black eye proved it. But I was also unable to abandon her, because I wanted her with every cell in my body. I admired her strength, her dignity, her very spirit. She'd broken free of her situation through sheer tenacity and effort. The only care I had about her past was how to release her from its effect on her present and future.

She was no whore. She was a queen.

The seat vibrated. She pulled away and went for her phone, but I got it first. She grabbed for it, but I pulled it back. It was a call, not a picture, and it was from an unknown number.

"Stop," she said.

I answered it. "Hello?"

"Who is this?" Male voice.

"Laine's phone."

"Where's she at?"

Laine looked as if she was going to explode. I put my finger to my lips, and she flipped me the bird. I was crazy about her. I had no reason not to be.

"She's indisposed," I said.

"What the fuck kind of word is that? Hey, wait. I know that voice. Man, are you that actor? 'Cos I will beat your ass."

"How much do you want, Jake?" I asked.

Laine pressed her knees together and put her forehead on them. I rubbed her back.

"Foo!" Jake said into the room, away from the phone. "It's the guy whose face you busted! He wants to know how much!"

I couldn't hear what Foo said. I just stroked Laine's hair.

Jake got back on the phone. "I'll text you a number, bitch. What the fuck happened in *Dead Lawyers*? That explosion was—"

"I need a place and time, Jake. Thirty-six prints and negatives."

"Test prints," Laine said between her knees. "Tom did six test prints. I have one. So five more."

"Five test prints," I said. "If you can add, that's forty-one prints. Thirty-six negatives."

The moment of silence following concerned me, but then Jake said in a low, conspiratorial voice, "Hey, I know why you're doing this. She sucks dick like a fucking champ. I taught her that. You're welcome."

I hung up. I didn't want to hear another word, and he and I were done with business. And the personal part? I wasn't in a position to kill him and get away with it. I hit the intercom behind the seat. "Pull over, Gali."

"I'm going to die," Laine said.

"Not tonight."

She sat up straight, her face red from being in crash position. "I can take care of this."

"Let me do it. I want to. I need to know you're not going to see him."

The car came to a stop on a side street.

"How am I supposed to not worry about you?" she asked.

"Don't. Look around. Tell me if we were followed."

She peered out all the windows, leaning over me to see out mine. I couldn't help but touch her when she was near me.

"Looks clear."

I kissed her just as her phone vibrated in my hand. She tried to look, but I kept the screen away. A number and an address. Perfect.

"Stay here for five minutes." I got out of the car.

As soon as I closed the door, Carlos got out of the passenger side. The street was residential and unpopulated in the moonlight. Even two blocks away from Hollywood Boulevard, the crickets made a racket.

"I have a thing for you tonight," I said. "I need you to pick up some cash from my business manager and make an exchange out in Venice Beach."

"An exchange?"

"Double rate. And you should be carrying."

"I don't do nothing illegal. It's in my contract," Carlos said.

"It's not illegal. It's not drugs. It's pictures. Forty-one of them. And thirty-six negatives. I need you to count, and do it without looking at them, as much as you can."

He looked as if he was suspicious but agreed when I gave him my word. I called my business manager, connected the dots quickly, and got back into the limo. At least this one thing would be put to bed once and for all.

Chapter 29

Laine

When he got back in the car, he looked relieved, and joyful because of it.

"Done," he said.

"What does that mean?"

He took my hands. "Carlos will bring him his money and get the pictures for me. Then we can burn them, or hide them, or whatever you want."

"I don't want you to pay for this."

"If I pay, I know it's done. Pay me back if you want. I don't care. All I care about is making sure this is gone by morning."

I didn't know what to say. I was grateful, humbled, and unworthy. The better he was, the more unworthy I felt, and I knew it was wrong. I knew it wasn't helpful, and I knew it wasn't true, but I had no idea how to stop feeling like that.

"Are you going back to the party?" I asked. "It's in your contract."

"Fuck the contract. I told Gali to drive us back to my place. I hope that's all right."

"It's all right."

He drew his thumb over the line of my jaw, the pressure just enough to make me want him despite everything.

"Can you ever get that picture out of your mind?" I said.

"It wasn't you."

"It was."

"That picture was of a confused, lost girl. You aren't any of those things."

I considered letting him off the hook by telling him he didn't have to take me home. He didn't have to spend the night with me. But he was a grown man, and if he didn't want to, he wouldn't choose to. I wouldn't assume I was unwanted or a pity fuck. I would take him at his word. So I kissed him, and we kept kissing until the car took a sharp turn into a driveway. I looked away from him, out the window. It was getting dark, but I could still see the modern house that was as big as the Hatches' had been. Everything about it was clean and trimmed and perfect.

I sat back and straightened my skirt. "Thank you."

"I haven't even done anything yet."

"For helping me. Thank you."

"I'll say this once, but it should be obvious," he said. "If you want to wait because of what happened tonight, I'll wait."

"Damn right you will. Except I don't think I can."

There was a quick knock at the window. Michael knocked back in response, and the driver opened the door.

"Thanks, Gali," Michael said, getting out. "I think that's it for the night."

Michael held out his hand for me, and when I took it, he led onto the driveway I'd glanced at through layers of glass. Gali closed the door with the *thup*. Our fingers looped together as we made our way up the walk.

"Nice house," I said. The windows were warm against the flat light of the Los Angeles sky, and the ground swept up and away in the distance, like the ocean decorated in tea lights.

"It's bigger than any one person needs, but it'll do in a pinch."

We stopped at the front steps to kiss, and he jangled his keys.

"Keys?" I said.

"Yeah?" He stood in front of the huge wooden door, its size proportional to the rest of the house, and the detail in the glass matched the expense.

"It's funny the mundane things I think people like you get to skip."

"People like me?" He punched numbers into a keypad, disabling the security system, and turned the key.

"Magic people. You know."

He laughed, opening the door. "Yeah. Me. Magic."

He stepped aside, and I walked in, my heels clopping on the wood floor. A few strategically placed lights were already on, revealing only what needed revealing. He had a perfectly balanced and furnished home full of right angles and masculine colors. The walls were soft grey, and there was glass everywhere, showing off the view and the turquoise, bean-shaped pool in the backyard.

"Can I get you something?" He passed me, walking backward into a kitchen that, like mine, was defined by an island, the open space around it, and its spotless lack of use.

"Water?"

"That, I have."

We went into the kitchen together. He filled a glass from the fridge door. His perfect hand gripped the simple glass, his beauty shattering the ordinary nature of his task. I leaned on the counter, looking out onto the living room, the painting over the fireplace, the view. The stairway to the second floor was exposed wood and metal with just a railing. Was his bedroom up there? What would be different when I walked down those stairs?

"You were pretty amazing tonight," I said. "In the movie. I thought you were going to jump through the screen and sit in my lap."

"Scary guys are my specialty."

He handed me the glass, and I drank. He stood so near to me that only the distance of the tipped glass separated us. When I was done, he took it and put it on the counter. As I drew my hand across his cheek, I flicked his stubble under my nail. His eyes, jade and blue, were so close to mine, and his hands on my body, unmoving, waiting.

"I have a confession," he said.

A lump grew in my throat. Were we doing confessions? Did I have to drop my life at his feet? I didn't want to. Not tonight. Not ever, but especially not tonight. "Let's confess stuff later."

"This is a *now* kind of confession."

"Okay." My voice cracked, because I didn't want it.

"I don't live here."

"Excuse me?"

He stepped away. "Let's do this quick before I lose my nerve."

"What?"

He didn't explain or even give me a chance to utter another question. He pulled me out of the kitchen, through the living room, through another room with chairs and a rug and couches, another room with a television, another functional room with storage, another that looked like an entryway of sorts, and out of the house.

"Where are we going?"

He didn't answer as he pulled me along a stone path. The drop-off into the Hollywood basin was to my right, and this man ahead of me, saying nothing, pulling me across his property, around a wall, and to another doorway with flowers planted all around the entry. He pushed me into the door, and his passion accelerated, lips on mine, tongues meeting, twisting, hands finding the boundaries of my clothing.

"I want you," he said, gravel in his throat. "All of it. Nothing between us."

"Where are we?"

He opened the door behind me, and by force of inertia, we were through the door.

"The guest house."

I didn't have time to see much. Just leather couches, paintings. It was neat but warmer, with blankets and exposed stone. One story. And there were his lips, his hands, his hair in my fingers, the rush of fluid between my legs as I pushed his jacket off his shoulders. He yanked off his tie, his eyes on fire. He was the guy in *Big Girls*, all heat and perfect lips set to a task as he stepped forward.

I gasped. "Nice house."

"One bedroom," he said. "Nine-hundred-twenty square feet."

The ravenousness in his voice took the strength out of my spine. I turned around to face the view. Same as the big house but cropped by shrubs. Somehow, it was less grand. More manageable.

"I can imagine you here," I said. "More than the other."

He brushed my hair away from my neck. "This hair," he said into my ear. "Never cut it."

I would have agreed to anything when he kissed the base of my neck. He slowly pulled down the zipper of my dress and slipped the straps off my shoulders, drawing his fingers over my arms until the dress fell to my feet.

With slight pressure to my shoulder, he turned me around and looked me up and down. I'd worn the pale pink underwear for him, and it got the exact reaction I wanted and feared.

"You like it?" I said, trying to sound normal, but I sounded breathy and nervous.

He scooped me up so quickly I squeaked. His right arm was under my knees, his left arm holding up my back. I looped my arms around his neck and let him carry me to the dark bedroom. It was small, lit only by the glitter of the city below. He laid me on the bed and turned on the lamp.

Details blurred around him. A closet door. A photograph of the Hollywood sign from the back. Pale blue walls. And him, a focal point so strong it was impossible to see anything outside him standing over me with his shirt unbuttoned halfway and a hungry look in his eye.

I was propped on my elbows with my knees pressed together by instinct or training, because the pinpoint of arousal where my thighs met felt vulnerable.

"You're beautiful," he said, putting one hand on my knee, "and you're mine."

He put his hand on my other knee and parted my legs. I threw my head back as every sensation made my body react. He slipped his hands inside my thighs and got on his knees at the side of the bed.

"Michael?"

"Laine?" He kissed inside my knees, working upward with his lips and tongue.

"I want to tell you something."

"Yes?"

"I don't want you to be disappointed, but oh God, that feels so good."

He looped his fingers under the sides of my panties and slid them down before tossing them off. "I won't be disappointed."

"I've only ever come one way."

"Tell me." He put his lips back on the inside of one thigh and drew his hands up the length of the other.

"Myself. I can only make myself come. Or sometimes fingers like the other day but never—"

I couldn't finish, because his lips reached home, and his tongue took me, luscious and soft, gentle and firm, while he spread my legs farther, exposing me completely to his mouth.

I looked down. His eyes watched me over the horizon of my body, protecting me, making sure I was with him. He brushed a finger over my nipple as he sucked on me gently, and he stretched his arm until he cupped my chin in his palm. I turned my head and took his fingers in my mouth. He groaned into me, vibrating, sucking harder, and the impossible seemed possible.

I was five, running the length Venice Beach with Sunshine and Rover. We went every early morning, the night rain over and leaving the air thick with salt water. I tasted those mornings on Michael's fingers. His tongue was more than a surface but the promise of a mounting wave that rose higher and higher, curling into foam at the top.

I remembered the seagulls on the wet sand, a clustered pool of rippling white feathers, and I remembered running into it as if I would splash in a puddle. When I got to them, they broke apart, flying upward in a squawking cacophony, and me in the center of it, the space around me no more than the beat of wings, splitting upward to the grey sky; the disordered but peaceful pool of birds I'd intended to wade among, gone, dynamic, and purposeful.

I broke apart like those seagulls when I came, losing all sense of place and time, overtaken with kinetic blackness, breaking apart into his mouth, lying flat on the sand in a carpet of foam, slowly forward then back into the vibrating stillness of the sea.

I opened my eyes. The white ceiling looked back at me, crackling with the last of my orgasm. "Jesus, Michael." My eyes fluttered closed again.

"You were saying something about me being disappointed?" He crawled up the bed until his lips were right above mine.

I smelled myself on his face, and I kissed him. "I forgot everything I was trying to say about anything."

"Good."

I wedged my finger between the placket of the next shirt button and slipped it through. He got up on his knees above me and undid his cuffs, tossing the cufflinks onto the night table. I yanked his belt free of the buckle as he pulled his shirt over his head.

I'd seen his body on film, flat and huge like some fake, painted shape and blowing through the frame like an icon of perfection. I was glad he had to stand to get his pants off, because it gave me a second to connect what I'd seen already with the reality of what was before me, which was just as perfect but real.

He wasn't a big guy but taut and toned, every bow and bend a piece of a flawless whole. And, of course, the part of him I'd never seen, which was erect, sent a new shudder of anticipation through me.

I covered my face. I heard him rip open a condom wrapper.

"What?" he said.

"You're so perfect, I can't even look at you."

He laughed and fell on me, pulling my arms away and pinning them over my head. "Look at me, please. I love it when you do."

I did, but all I could see was his face, the stubble on his cheeks, and the blue flecks in his green eyes. I relaxed my legs, and they opened for him. He shifted until his shaft was against me, sliding as we kissed and frictionless against my arousal. I wanted him as I'd never wanted anyone.

"Please," I moaned. "Let's go. Let's do it."

"So impatient." He let my hands go and reached between us to run his fingers over me.

My back arched.

"And wet. Very wet." He got on his knees and looked me up and down, then he put his hand over my face, moving it over my lips. I kissed his hand, but he kept moving it down, over my neck, my breasts, my belly, watching me squirm as he put it between my legs. He put his dick against me. "You ready?"

"Yes."

He entered me with purpose and strength but not any faster than necessary, stretching what hadn't been touched in so long. I thought he was going to break me, and I thought when I cracked, pleasure would fill the fissures. I pulled him on top of me, wrapping my arms and legs around him.

His weight on my body, the pressure of his arms around me, trapped me in a cocoon of his flesh and surrounded me with his scent of cinnamon. Even when we rolled and changed, he enfolded me, and I felt safe. I just lived that security, that release of anxiety, pushing against him because I wanted to crawl inside him.

I didn't expect to come—I only expected to enjoy his body—but I felt as though I might. He must have felt it in the way I tensed and gripped his back.

"Laine," he whispered, looking me in the eye, "come for me."

"Oh, Michael. I…"

"Yes," he said, continuing the affirmations until everything went black and electric, and I said his name.

He groaned and sped up his strokes, his face tightening. I put my hand on his cheek, feeling his tension and release, and realized I didn't just want him but loved him.

I loved him. Without regret, washed in the unguarded moment of our ultimate pleasure, I loved him.

Chapter 30

Michael

We'd spent the night bound together like matching shapes. I'd sensed nothing but the sound of her voice and the scent of her skin, thought about nothing but how to please her. I didn't want to leave an inch of her body untasted or a thought unexpressed. I didn't know her, but I did. In a way that was bigger than a simple life's narrative, more important than the facts and figures of what had happened, I knew her. The planes of her face, the curl of her lashes, the line of her lips, I could memorize the beauty of them, but the expressions that flashed across her face were a surprise to my mind at the same time as they were familiar to my heart.

For the first time in my life, I felt three-dimensional. For a man whose life and work depended on feeling every part of his body from his fingertips to his heartbeat, the feeling was new and worth defining.

I'd spent half of my first year in the Yale drama department learning how to pour a cup of tea. It was insulting. I'd already worked with the best director in the business the summer before. The picture was in theaters with my name blazing across the top, yet there I was, getting berated daily because I couldn't pour a cup of tea without looking as if I was "acting" as though I was pouring a cup of tea. Brad nailed it on day one and was on to bigger and better things in the first week. I had to work at it and get frustrated, hate tea, love tea, learn to *not think about the tea* then to think about it, and fill my head with anything but the muscle memory of pouring.

I had been the worst actor in the department. I aced math, history, every core course, but at my chosen field, I was a bust. My father thought it was hilarious and the reason I should do something else. My mother thought I was wasting my time in school at all, since I could just land parts based on my name. But what Yale taught me was that I needed training if I wanted to be any more than a hack.

But I'd been a hack. I'd made stuff up, invented a reality from a fantasy life. But there I was with this sleeping woman in my arms, not thinking about what I was feeling while closely observing the three-dimensionality of it.

My life had been written at birth, a list of opportunities read out loud to the world. Beginning, middle, and end. I had found security in that room to make decisions, yet the safety of limits. Laine had come and folded the paper, creasing my expectations in high school with her life story. Now, with her breath on my shoulder, she folded my life into an airplane and shot it out the window. The writing was the same, but the choices had changed, become wider and yet more limited. I'd gone from fake to real. From painting to sculpture. From acting as if I was living to actually being alive.

Every explanation fell short. Maybe some things weren't meant to be captured and acted out later. Maybe some things were just meant to be lived. And lying next to this woman, I was living.

Laine took a sharp little breath that meant she was waking up. I wanted her to, because I wanted to spend time with her, but I didn't want her to, because she was comfortable on me. Her eyes opened. She hitched herself up on her elbow and looked at the clock then fell back down with her head on my chest.

"Got a date?" I asked, moving her hair from her face.

"I dreamed about you in *Big Girls*."

"Was I still scary?"

"Yeah. But then I woke up and it was you," she said.

"Do you want breakfast?"

"I want to sleep."

"How late do you usually sleep?"

She didn't answer right away but stared doe-eyed out the window, her cheek pressed against my body. Then she got onto her hands and looked at me from above. "I'm not rich. I do well, but… the reason I sleep late is because I work late."

A paper airplane, once folded, is always creased. The perfection of its beginning, its pure potential, can never be regained. When she reminded me of what I already knew, she'd picked up the plane and tried to flatten it, but it was changed forever. I could see it, but I didn't know what she saw.

"This wasn't a casual thing," I said.

"I know," she said, looking away from me.

"Things have changed."

"For you? What's changed for you?"

"I'm with you. That's what's changed. And I'm serious about that."

She slid away until she knelt between my legs with her hands in her lap. Her nipples were hard in the cool morning air, peeking through the curtain of her hair. I wanted her again.

"I don't know how to do anything else," she said.

I didn't know what to say. What would I want to hear if I suddenly couldn't act? It was the only thing I knew how to do except rip up my elbow playing tennis. It was the only thing my father had known how to do before he dug himself a hole of drunken inactivity, and I didn't know what to say to him either.

"Maybe," she said, "when I'm working, I can shoot anyone else. None of your pack. There are enough celebrities in this town."

"I don't know if that'll work."

"No," she said, staring into the middle distance, her limbs twisted and taut around each other. She was a ball of elbows and knees under a curtain of dark hair. "You're right. It won't. I took a picture of Brad the other day, and he knew me, and it just didn't look right." She scratched her head and rested her cheek on her knee. "I think I kind of screwed myself."

"You can lean on me until you figure it out."

"Are you offering me money?"

"You make it sound like something it's not," I said.

"What is it then?"

"A bridge to whatever comes next for you."

She sighed and gave the middle distance her attention again. "I thought this might happen, but now that it's here, it's kind of, well… it's still scary."

She seemed so frail, a balls-to-the-wall street kid with sharp wit and a twisted posture. I'd put her in the exact position that terrified me. I'd taken from her the one thing she depended on. I was the one with the privilege. The pedigree. The one with his future written on a creased paper. I could find her a way out of it somehow.

I took her by the back of her neck and pulled her to me. "I'm sorry."

"Don't be. After all this, having these guys outside my house and being followed and everything, I don't think I could go back to it anyway. I know it's legal and I know it's a business, but I don't know if I could go on knowing

I made people feel like that."

"Even A-listers?" I asked.

"Especially A-listers. You're a bunch of pussycats."

"You won't starve, Laine. You won't be alone."

"I've survived worse calamities than you," she said. "But you? I don't know if you can handle me."

"You're Calamity Laine."

She smiled and kissed me as if she liked the name.

"You know what would make me happy?" I rolled on top of her, pinning her wrists. "Fucking you again."

"That's it?"

I wedged myself between her legs and kissed her. "I'm going to miss you taking pictures of me."

"I can take them, I just can't sell them."

"Why not? Because you like me now?"

"Because it's not the same. The pictures I took in the loft upstairs? Remember those?"

I put my lips on her breast, sweet with sleep and the previous night's indulgence. "I remember."

"You should see them. They're not the same. They're intimate. Even the way they're framed, and the light is so soft on them. No one wants that. At least no acquisitions person I know would want them. And besides, I wouldn't sell them without your permission. I couldn't…"

I looked up at her. She stared at the ceiling, and though her thumb stroked my shoulder, she went far away.

"Earth to Laine."

"Let me show you them."

I took my mouth off her body and rolled over. "Go, before I change my mind and take you again."

"Empty threats," she said when she was out of reach, looking over her shoulder and smiling.

As if on cue, my phone rang as soon as she was out of sight.

Chapter 31

Laine

I loved him. The thought of selling his image, even with his permission, seemed like a violation of our intimacy, of us. It would be willingly letting everyone into my life. Not just leaving the door open but putting a big "Open for Business" sign out front.

I should have been able to sell the pictures from the loft without his permission or anything else. I should have been perfectly comfortable shipping the digitals off to *YOU* mag, collecting coin, and seeing him the next day. He'd asked for his life a hundred times over, and I was just harvesting the leftovers of his fame.

But I'd changed. I'd had more than a few intellectual runarounds about why I should continue to be who I was and do what I wanted, but all the usual arguments fell flat against the texture of who I was becoming.

And who would that be?

I'd resisted it as long as I could, but looking at him, with his hair flattened on one side and a touch of sleep lingering in his eyes, I couldn't imagine being a paparazza. I'd heard how deeply he groaned when he came and felt his touch in the middle of the night. He was just a man and a better man than most. I hadn't captured that betterness until the pictures in the loft upstairs, and those were mine alone. They were private.

I didn't know what to do. I didn't know how I would figure out who I would be, but in the moments before I had to worry about money or identity, while he was still with me, I let myself get excited at the prospect of reinventing myself.

His phone rang from somewhere in the bedroom, probably inside a pocket. He reached for me, and I taunted him with a laugh, running naked to the living room to get my bag. I grabbed it from the guest house door, taking a second to admire the view. I pulled the pictures off my server and put them onto my phone. They were film, so they had defined grains that looked tactile, even on digital.

He was already on the phone when I got back to the bedroom. He stood naked against the door to the patio, his body as flawless from the back as the front. I crouched on the bed, my back to the headboard. Michael didn't look happy with what he was hearing.

"Okay, I'll be right there. Thanks for letting me know." He tapped off and stared at his phone for a second before looking at me. He tossed the phone on the bed. "Last night, I sent Carlos to take the money and get the pictures. He did, but he got stopped at a DUI checkpoint. He had to tell them he was carrying a weapon, and so, because it was Tuesday or for whatever reason, they checked the car and arrested him for possession of child pornography."

I covered my face with my hands. "Oh, God. What should we do?"

"You shouldn't do anything. You're the victim. You don't need to show your face anywhere, and you shouldn't. But I need to go take care of this."

"I'm so sorry. Can you tell Carlos I'm sorry?"

He was already getting dressed. "You didn't do anything, Laine."

I didn't do anything. Nothing but get Carlos arrested because I hadn't taken responsibility for Jake earlier. I should have gone to give him his money and been done with it. Now Michael had to go explain that *he* had wanted the pictures, all because I couldn't see what I'd been given when I was fostered by Orry and Mildred Hatch. I only saw that the sweet boy I liked left me. Now that sweet man had to step in front of his bodyguard to get him off the hook.

"You're going to have to say you were the one who wanted them," I said.

"Yep." He buttoned his pants with a faraway look. "I don't know if there's a way to keep your name out of it. They're going to ask me why I wanted them."

"What if I say I was eighteen when they were taken?"

"Lying will only make it worse, and I don't want you involved."

"Michael, really? I couldn't be more involved."

He crawled onto the bed, shirt half buttoned, until he was close enough to kiss me. "Really. You're protected until you speak. So just hush until someone with a badge asks you a question."

"I hate this. I hate that I caused you trouble."

"I knew you were trouble when I saw you on that balcony at NV. I wanted you then, and I want you now."

He had so much to lose, and I was poised to take it all away. He kissed me tenderly, and I wondered who he cared for: the screwed-up paparazza who was nothing but trouble or some fantasy of a woman he was going to save from her past?

I wasn't comfortable with either option, but I didn't know what I wanted to be loved for either. What was it about me that I wanted to hold up and say "love me for this and not that?" Nothing I could think of. I had nice hair. I could run in heels. I took a good picture quickly.

"Laine?"

Michael snapped me out of my trance.

"Sorry. I should go. They're going to come find me and ask me questions." I gathered up my things. "I had this friend. Sister. Whatever. The cops found out about some shit her dad had done. Her fosters opted her into notifications, and the rest of her life, the phone rings every time he has a probation hearing or her picture shows up somewhere." I gave a fake little laugh that sounded hollow and nervous. It seemed to echo off the walls and unfamiliar corners. Not my bed, not my pillows, not my pictures, not my view.

This was going to explode. Michael Greydon, official famous person, found trying to obtain pictures of me as an adolescent. His intentions had been innocent, and no one would care.

I was a victim now. I wasn't the sole owner of my life. I wasn't in control, and I didn't have power over the land. I was weak and wrecked, a puppy on the yellow line, waiting to get hit or be saved but unable to move. I hated it. I hated feeling like a target someone had hit and everyone else wanted to rescue.

Naked in the middle of the room, hugging my bundle of clothes, I must have been a sight to Michael in his movie star jeans and celebrity smile. I must have looked like a lost china lamb.

"It's going to be all right," he said, putting his perfect hands on my bare shoulders. "They're on paper. He told Carlos the versions he sent you were the only digitals, and he took them with his camera phone. They won't be around. I'll explain what happened. It'll be done."

"No, it was supposed to be done years ago, when I left. And it was. Now

I have to explain everything to strangers. It was hard enough to explain just to you. And once I walk out of here, they won't let me near you until you're cleared. Trust me. I know the system."

I stared straight in his face, but I couldn't see him. I had no idea what he was feeling or thinking. I couldn't feel past the need to run away and do something, anything.

"I'm sorry," I said, trying my best to be comforting when all I wanted to do was leave. "This is going to be a pain in the ass for you, and it's my fault."

"You need to stop saying things like that."

"Well, it's because of me. You can't deny that. So listen, thank you for helping me with this. You're a good guy, and you did something amazing for me that you're going to pay for. You have to go, and I have to go. Let's just get on with it."

As if on cue, there was a knock on the door.

I jumped out of my skin. "The gate?" I gasped half a sentence.

"My damn publicist." He kissed my cheek tenderly and walked to the front.

I went into the bathroom to dress. Through the door, as I hitched up my lace-topped stockings, I heard voices, not the whisperings of two men who worked together but something else. Something more terse and businesslike. I wrestled with the zipper on the back of my dress, contorting myself into a knot rather than walk out the bathroom door undone. When I did walk out, a new scene awaited.

The bedroom door was closed. The sheets were twisted all to hell, as if two people had been entwined in them all night long. A middle-aged woman stood in the room with her hands folded in front of her. She wore a blue sweater with beads around the neck and a navy skirt that ended right below the knee. Her light brown hair was darker at the roots, and her black shoes had a sensible low heel.

"Are you Laine Cartwright?" she asked.

Could I say no? Could I deny everything? Could I laugh and ask how anyone could think a man like Michael Greydon would knot up the sheets with Laine Cartwright?

"Maybe," I replied, unable to hide my hostility.

"May I speak with you?" She pointed at a chair as if she was the one who had fallen in love in that room a few hours earlier.

I realized she was going to tell me about the pictures. She was going to say Michael had bought them. She was going to ask my age and about Jake and why I'd been a fuckdoll when I was fifteen. I didn't want to answer any of it. I didn't want to hear a bad word about Michael, and I didn't want that room tainted with those years. I wanted that space, that bed, the air, and all of it to only hold love.

"No," I said. "If you want to talk to me about the pictures, you have to take me to First Street. I want all of it recorded, because I'm not repeating it."

She nodded as if the request wasn't unusual.

"And I'd like to call my lawyer."

"You're not being accused of anything," she said. "But of course, that's fine. Would you like to call a friend to come with you?"

I hadn't expected that. I figured I'd go alone to the precinct like a criminal, get questioned in a cold, hard room, and take a cab back to my empty loft. But I did want someone to go with me. I wanted to lean on another human being for strength and comfort, and I wanted it to be Michael. I pressed my lips between my teeth, holding back the choke and blubber that gathered in my throat. He was the last person I could ask for, and he was all I wanted.

Who would a normal person ask for? Their mother. I barely remembered mine. I'd visited her twice in a grey room with aluminum folding chairs and a card table. She'd tried to squeeze all of life's lessons into half an hour, and I remembered none of them. Stay out of trouble. Value yourself. Don't let a man run you. Blah blah blah. Goddamn her. What useless high-handed crap it all was.

My mother was supposed to teach me to do something, cook, get an apartment, go on interviews, balance a checkbook. But Irving had taught me how to do that, and how to pay quarterly taxes, calculate focal length, go on an interview. He'd cosigned my first checking account, helped with the deposit on the apartment I got after I left Jake, gave me a trade I could use to support myself.

"I do," I said. "I do have a friend I want to bring."

Chapter 32

Michael

Here's a secret the LAPD keeps pretty close to the vest, and one they'll deny to your face. If they want to get into your house, they'll get into your house no matter who you are or what security system you have. They didn't need Ken to give them my maid's key. They had tools.

My gate was broken, and the door to the main house had been broken in. I couldn't believe they'd even knocked on the door of the guest house when I saw that, but I had no time to ask before I was put in a squad car and driven away.

Outside the broken gate, they waited. I'd never resented the paparazzi before, with their cameras and catcalls. But that day, with everything in my life interrupted, a day of explanations ahead, and ugliness between Laine and me, I hated them. They stood a respectful distance from the police car, but they caught me there. I'd be stuck in a room explaining things while they guessed at the truth and made up lies about Laine.

And it was so titillating. What could be better than Michael Greydon staring at child pornography with his hands in his pants? It explained why I hadn't had a long-term relationship since Lucy, why I didn't stay out late or do drugs. My vice was worse than a simple substance abuse problem. It was the story of the year, and they'd ignore the truth for as long as they could, because the truth was honorable and real.

The LAPD didn't book me right away. They took me into a room and asked questions, the most pertinent being, "Did you or did you not arrange for the purchase of sexually explicit photographs of an individual you knew to be under the age of eighteen?"

Once my lawyer, Joe Barnett, showed up in his suit and aftershave, I told him the truth, because that was what I knew how to do. Then I admitted to the LAPD that yes, I'd arranged for the purchase of the pictures, and yes, I knew that the girl in them was under eighteen.

They booked me without hearing the rest of it. Barnett had told me that was what would happen. I asked about Carlos. They told me he was being held but not arrested. I asked about Laine. No one would tell me if she was all right.

"Find out," I told Joe. "I don't care what you have to do."

"If she's implicating you—"

"I don't care. Make sure she's not alone. Make sure she's not upset. Go to her house and make sure she's okay."

He agreed, but he lied. I knew it from the way his mouth moved. He was as invested in protecting me as I was invested in protecting Laine. There was nothing in it for him to check on her and report back to me.

So I sat in the quiet cell, which was comfortable enough with its soft seat and frosted glass, as if designed with a pending apology in mind. I thought about what I'd done, and not done, and the foolhardy arrogance that had led me there. Laine's past had been her secret. She'd protected it, and because of me, it was no longer a secret. It had the potential to go horrifyingly public. Guilt lay on top of regret, whispering potential ammunition in my ear.

You arrogant, overconfident ass. This is her life. It's not a movie. It's not a story you're telling yourself about yourself.

"She's fine," Ken said after my two-hour wait in the apology room.

We sat across a table in a white room with a wood table. Portraits of dead cops looked down at us.

"How do you know?" I asked, infuriated by his casual posture, his legs crossed and foot shaking at the ankle as if he needed to be somewhere else.

"If she'd killed herself, we'd have heard."

"You know what, Ken—"

"Don't you even think of firing me." He put both elbows on the table. "You need me, and I'm not wasting my breath convincing you of it. I don't care if you admit to me that what you did was stupid, but once you're out of here, you'd better admit that to the public. They want your head."

"It was stupid," I said.

"Good. That's progress."

"Did the pictures get out?"

He didn't answer.

I slammed my hand on the desk. "Answer me."

"Yes."

A vacuum opened in my chest, and my heart fell into it.

Ken continued. "Her brother—"

"Foster brother."

"This Jake guy had them scheduled to post to a porn site," he said. "He was going to use that to pressure her, but they went up while he was being questioned."

"We can't stop it, can we?"

"Look, she'll get over it. You, on the other hand, might not."

"I'll be fine," I said. "I want resources behind getting those pictures taken down. I know it's impossible to get them all."

"It's just plain impossible. If she were nobody, I could contain it. But she's not. She's your girlfriend."

My girlfriend. The word sounded infantile.

"So here's what we have outside these walls," Ken said, "and try not to get discouraged by the fact that it's all bad news. On one hand, you've got a news media cycle that only knows why you were arrested. They haven't found out that you sent your bodyguard to get pictures of your girlfriend to protect her. All anyone can envision is America's Boyfriend beating off to shots of naked little girls. On the other hand, Laine's pictures are taking a slow tour around the porn world tagged as 'vintage teens.' They'll get drowned out in two weeks by the flood of shit on the internet. But when you explain publicly what happened, people will start searching for the pictures, and she doesn't look that different. They'll stop being a fetish tag and start showing up on CelebrityOgler.com with blurred nipples."

I must have made some move with my hands or some expression that betrayed my immediate rage. I didn't have a word besides *No* for the invasion that would be.

As if Ken saw an opening, he leaned forward. "If you don't want to get run out of town, you have to explain what happened. If you want those pictures to die a quick, painless death by irrelevance, you have to quietly yet openly dump her now. No one will care about her enough to search."

"Quietly yet openly? What the hell is that?"

"Call her a girl you used to know, had a short thing with, then start talking about the movie."

"What movie?" I was biding my time in asking that. I didn't know what to think, so I asked a meaningless question.

"Any movie. Just make the studio happy, because Bob Rice is cancelling contracts. You're already in breach for not doing the PR you agreed to."

I shook my head. There was no use in talking further to Ken. I wasn't leaving Laine. If there was a third way out of this, I would find it. Breaking up with her wasn't an option, even if it was the best way to protect her.

Chapter 33

Laine

Phoebe was in Las Vegas to see a client, but she promised to get back by morning. She gave me the number of a colleague, but they didn't pick up.

The lady in the blue sweater said I didn't have to talk to her until my moral support showed up, which pissed me off. I was a grown woman and didn't need backup. She kept treating me like a victim, incapable of consenting to anything. As if my being a little older would have changed my ability to make a decision about who could stick what inside me. I'd consented to the sex. Yes, I'd hated it, but I consented. And I consented to the pictures, and yes, I hated that more, but I consented.

"We may find they were distributed over the internet," she said softly.

"I didn't consent to that," I said, crossing and uncrossing my legs. My stockings had started sagging, and I felt out of place, with my fancy pink dress, in a room decked out in jeweled colors and decorated with the alphabet. An indoor play structure sat in one corner, and in another was a child-sized white table stacked with anatomically correct dolls.

"Miss Cartwright, we can prosecute a distributor of child pornography whether you consent or not."

"So do it. Just not Michael. Hang Jake out to dry. I don't care."

She handed me papers, and they all had the word victim on them. I wouldn't sign them. I wouldn't even look at them. Before I could shove them up her ass, there was a knock on the door.

A man stuck his head in. "Your family's here."

I didn't waste a minute before walking out to the lobby. Tom was there, his monochrome face in a room that finally matched him. Irving had shown up like a beat-up knight on an old brokeback horse, so quickly that traffic must have parted before him. I didn't know what family meant to me until they came when I needed them. I was so surprised and relieved to see them, I hugged them both so hard I thought I'd break them.

"He didn't do anything," I said after the first greeting. "He was trying to get them so we could burn them. And I keep telling them that, but they won't let him go."

"I shouldn't have developed them," Tom said.

"You saved my life. If you hadn't put them under my nose, I don't know what would have happened to me."

"Yeah, well. I came to see you, but also…" He rolled his eyes, indicating the room at large. "Gotta tell them my side."

"They wouldn't put you away for it," I said with an edge of desperation.

"I was a year younger than you, dorkhead."

"Still are," Irving said. "Go talk to the fuzz and get it over with." He nudged Tom toward the sign-in desk then pulled me to a plastic chair.

"Can we not, I don't know, talk about this?" I said.

"Sure." He picked a magazine off the little linoleum table. "Personally, what you did when you were fifteen is your own business. Are they letting you go?"

"I guess I can go any time. I have to sign some stuff, but I want to wait for Michael."

"You like him."

I nodded. "If anyone else had gotten picked up for this, we'd laugh about it in a week, but him? This could hurt him, so I have to make sure we look like a united front. You know, so the public knows I'm not mad at him or anything."

"Speaking of the public, they're waiting outside. Your peers, I mean." He licked his finger and flipped a page of celebrity news. "I'm going to ask the obvious. How do you like being on the other side of it?"

I looked over his shoulder at the magazine. Britt with a roller in her hair. Brad wearing white in winter. Fiona with ice cream on her shirt.

"What should I do?" I asked.

"I don't think there's a precedent for this, so do whatever you have to. Do whatever is right."

We sat there another few minutes. Tom waved as they led him to a room to tell the story of his forgotten camera and an exposed roll of film. Irving didn't ask about the pictures, and I tried not to think of them being distributed. I hoped that they hadn't been. I didn't know how I'd function if people knew.

Yet it seemed foolish to hide. If they were out, they were out. I wasn't that girl anymore. She was scared and lonely, sensitive and breakable. I'd broken her and put her back together, myself.

Just me.

And Irv.

And Tom.

And Hollywood.

I wasn't that girl anymore, but I loved her.

Why shouldn't she have a voice in all this? Why should I leave it to Michael's machine and the police? Hadn't that girl been silenced long enough?

I took a deep breath and stood.

Irving looked up at me. "What's on your mind?"

I didn't answer, because I didn't want to be talked out of it. I knew what Irving would say. He'd say I didn't know what I was doing. He'd say I was being impulsive and that I'd get in trouble. So I walked out the door without saying anything.

I was still in last night's dress. The shawl had gotten lost somewhere. Michael's house, or the police car, or any of the ten rooms I'd been shuffled between. Didn't matter.

They saw me through the glass door, and twenty of them called my name, their faces obliterated behind flashes and cameras. There was a video camera among them—I could tell by the constant flare from the left. Fill lights on such a cloudy day would keep the pictures from being flat. Toby or Franco were behind the fill if I had my guess. I pushed the door open and stood on the precinct steps alone in my pink dress. I folded my hands in front of me and stared into the lights. *Clickclickclick* a tempo in unexpected rhythms, like fusion jazz.

"Hi," I said.

"Hi, Miss Cartwright," a few said in unison like a third-grade class.

I laughed, remembering that I liked my job and I liked those guys. I got them. I shielded my eyes from the lights. "Who's got the vid rig?"

"Me," a voice shouted.

I recognized the accent. "Franco! Hi! Renaldo? You there?"

"Right here!" came a voice in the front.

I saw his bald head shining and waved. "Take your strobe down. It's not that cloudy."

Laughter.

"Laine!" shouted a voice I recognized as Bart's. "What's happening with Michael? Did he buy kiddie porn?"

"Technically?"

"Come on!" Renaldo said, adjusting his dials. "What else is there?"

"He was protecting the person in the pictures, guys. You know him. You've worked with him. He's not a pedophile."

Another voice piped in before I even finished. Kyle? Lennart? "You the moral support?"

What was it about being in front of those cameras that made me feel peeled open? I couldn't tell whether it was that I knew the men behind them or the universal desire to be seen and loved, but I wanted to answer what was asked so that it could be known finally. I felt the power to protect myself and him in just a few words. I could finish all of this nonsense.

"Yeah, Laine? Why are you here?"

"Because I'm the girl in the pictures."

I didn't have much else to offer. A bunch of explanations went through my head. In the split second where I decided to reveal more, I felt a hand on my arm. I looked over. A man in his fifties, in a suit, with a perfectly proportioned smile.

He turned to the cameras. "All right, guys. You got your pictures. You'll know what you need to, when you need to."

"Thanks, Ken!" Renaldo shouted as everyone put their rigs away.

I was led back into the building by Ken, who didn't leave me much of a choice. It wasn't until I was under the cold, hard fluorescents and Ken was in front of me that I lost the sense of control and ownership I'd clung to.

"What was that?" he asked.

Behind him, clusters of men and women in uniform passed by, making him seem as much a part of the system as the cops themselves.

"That was me. Why?"

"People like you keep people like me in a new Ferrari every year."

I crossed my arms, suddenly cold. "What's the problem?"

"Now that you told the world there are pornographic pictures of you? What could be the problem?"

"Michael got them."

"They were digitized. That's how they got onto your phone. No?"

They'd been crappy photos of photos, but yes. They'd been on my phone, which meant easily distributed. And found. I'd never trusted Jake, so it shouldn't even be a question that he'd upload the pictures if he could turn a dime off them.

I felt small, weak, and unprotected. I closed my eyes as if no one could see me if I couldn't see them.

"What should I do?" I whispered into the darkness.

"My job is to protect my client. But a bit of personal advice? If I were you, I'd go home and change out of last night's dress. And don't look at the internet."

Chapter 34

Laine

Irving pulled up in front if my building.

"Think of it this way," Tom said from the backseat, "everyone who gets the pictures was looking at an underage girl. They're going to catch a lot of real sickos."

I nodded and opened the door. I didn't want to talk about it anymore. "Thanks, guys. It meant a lot to me that you came."

"We should come up," Irving said.

"No, I just want to go to bed. Would you call me later?"

"Sure." He hugged me from the driver's side.

Tom got out to do the same. "Call. I mean it." His hair flopped in the wind.

A shutter went off behind me. I cringed.

"Lonnie!" Tom yelled. "You asshole!"

He brandished his middle finger and charged the pap, our friend and colleague, and Lonnie backed up. But Johnny, Red, Allie, and others I couldn't identify also scattered.

I went up the steps, Dave following on bent knees with a *clickclickclick*. I kept my head down and walked into my building. My head stayed down in the lobby, in the elevator, in the hall, and as I opened my door. I dropped my keys on the floor with a clatter. I locked the door behind me, stepped out of my shoes as I walked, peeled off my stockings across the room, and tried to unzip my dress but couldn't without stopping. So I kept walking to my bed. I pulled back the covers.

I hadn't hid under the covers in years. I hadn't hidden behind or under anything since I'd left my final foster home to tool around with the motorcycle crew out of their little dump in Whittier. When Mister Yi, the dad with the sweater factory, hadn't liked the way I linked a seam, I'd hidden. When the OCD mom in Studio City had yelled at me for leaving milk on the table or putting toilet paper in the toilet instead of the trash, I'd hidden. And in Westlake, where Tom and I were ignored, then moved, then moved again, I just hid when I had to and lashed out the rest of the time.

I'd stopped hiding so definitively at one point that I forgot I'd ever done it, until I thought about the pictures and people finding them and men looking at me like that. As I stood over my bed, ready to hide, I stopped myself. I wasn't hiding.

As safe as I felt under the covers was as safe as I felt with Michael. He was my under the covers. He was my Los Angeles. Let them all look at me. He was mine.

Chapter 35

Michael

I walked out of the precinct with an unblemished record, thanks to my legal team and Laine explaining what had happened to the LAPD. I walked past the paparazzi as they shouted. I fingered the phone I hadn't seen in hours.

"Hey, Michael! Have you seen Laine's pictures?"

I froze. Ken yanked my arm, and my lawyer nudged me so subtly no one would have even noticed in the photos. A black car waited with an open door. Gali nodded at me when I got in.

"She's about to be more famous than you," Ken started before he'd even sat all the way. "They're finding the pictures faster than we can send out DMCA notices."

"How do they know it's her?"

He poked at his phone then pocketed it again. "She told them."

"No. No, she didn't." I was filling space. Obviously she had.

He took the phone from me. "It's all over YouTube."

He handed back my phone, with Laine on it under a white triangle. She stood against the backdrop of the concrete police station steps, her hands pressed together in front of her. I pressed the triangle.

—*Hi, Miss Cartwright*

She shields her eyes with her forearm.

She corrects their lighting.

Laughter.

—*What's happening with Michael? Did he buy kiddie porn?*

—*Technically?*

She stalls, but it's obvious she's looking forward to telling them something. The cameras are eating her alive. She looks stunning, larger than life. Like a rare, escaped bird perched proudly over the city. Star quality. She had it.

—*He was protecting the person in the pictures, guys. You know him. You've worked with him. He's not a pedophile.*

She loves her big reveal. It's all over her face. She loves telling them I'm innocent. The camera sees all of it.

—*You the moral support?*

—*Yeah, Laine? Why are you here?*

—*Because I'm the girl in the pictures.*

And just like that, it ended on her complete lack of fear in the truth, and the triangle reappeared over her.

"She didn't know they were out," Ken said. "That Jake is a real piece of work. Stupid and smart at the same time. The prosecutor is making jail time his life's mission."

"How did you let that happen?"

"Let it happen? She's a free agent, Mike. You knew this."

I leaned back in the seat. "I'm starting to want to do things her way. I'm getting bogged down in the rules."

"You're already in breach of contract with *Big Girls*. A party's not a party for you. It's an obligation. And the big stuff? Conduct unbecoming. You're turning into a liability on *Bullets* in the middle of a schedule killer."

"I didn't do anything," I said.

"It doesn't matter. You're a public relations nightmare right now. That's not what the studios bank on."

I had no answer, because he was right. I was the good guy. I didn't get taken in for buying kiddie porn, and I didn't fail to do one interview, one junket stop, or one party. That was a big part of the reason I was paid so well and hired so easily. No one had to worry about me. No one had to spend money covering my tracks. No one had to spin my Saturday nights into Sunday's public apology.

All of that was about to change.

Would I become like my father? A dead weight for a decade or more because I couldn't find work? He had all the money he needed, but he wasn't *working*, and I was about to have the same problem.

I dialed her number. I needed to hear her voice. I needed to tell her to wait for me, to not do anything or speak to anyone until I came to her. She didn't answer the phone, and I found I was glad. I had to think, and I couldn't. I hung up. I didn't want to leave a message in front of Ken and my lawyer, who only pretended he wasn't paying attention.

"I need her pictures to go away," I told Ken.

"Keep associating with her, and they'll keep looking for her pictures. They'll never die."

"You're not getting it. That's not an option."

"Mike, you hired me for a reason. This kind of thing? It's chaos, and chaos happens to everyone at some point," he said. "I manage chaos. I calm it down, or I turn it to my client's advantage. That's my job. That's why you need me. And believe me, I don't need your money. Fire me the way you fired Gene, and as a businessman, I won't care. I have plenty to do. But you've been with me since you were eighteen, and I care about what happens to you. The stakes are high now, and if you go off the deep end now, if you spiral into a pit, and I can't stop you, I'll feel…" He motioned with his hand, spinning it at the wrist.

"Guilty?" I offered.

"Close enough."

"And in your professional opinion, I should no longer see Laine?"

"If you want to protect the both of you."

"And if I continue to see her anyway?" I asked.

"There might be more chaos than I can manage and more than either of you can handle. That's my professional opinion. You can have any girl you want. Just pick another one. A pretty one who won't sabotage your career."

I respected Ken. He knew his job, and he wasn't the biggest jerk I'd met over the course of my career, but what he was suggesting simply wouldn't work for me. I couldn't imagine thanking Laine for a nice time and walking away. I couldn't imagine never seeing her again, never being surprised by her, never witnessing her delight and her darkness, her impulsiveness and her cynical wisdom.

My phone buzzed. I was sick of it. I was about to shut it off, but it was my mother, who was probably worried sick that she'd raised a pedophile. "Mom? Hey, I—"

"Gareth is at Sequoia Hospital. His liver. He didn't even take a damned drink, but it's failing."

I forgot about everything but getting to the hospital on time.

Chapter 36

Laine

That blanket over me was cinnamon-scented and invisible. I padded around on bare feet, in my robe. I felt better, slightly untouchable, and inside a sphere of safety.

I'd gotten a text from Michael.

—Wait for me—

I could do that. As much as I wanted to run out and shoot frame on top of frame, that was the wrong thing to do. I needed to lie low for his sake and wait until it could be sorted out. I didn't look at the internet. I exercised a level of self-control so rigid I pulled the cable out of the wall. If I saw myself on the feeds, I knew I would be paralyzed.

I felt good about that. Relaxed, even. I knew what to do.

I pulled up the photos I'd taken of him in the upstairs loft. He was so perfect on my screen in all his thirty-inch glory. I'd forgotten what he had been explaining at that moment, but he looked calm, yet on edge, as if anything could happen. I smiled, a warm feeling radiating from my chest to my fingers and toes. I edited the digitals on autopilot, wiping away imperfections with my stylus, little marks and flecks, the little chapped spot on his lower lip, gone gone gone.

Those lips, on my body, moving between my legs and on my mouth, the scent of my arousal on them. My bones liquefied as I thought about it, as if the scaffolding that held me up had gone viscous and warm. When he looked through the screen, I realized he wasn't looking at the camera. He wasn't looking at an audience. He wasn't acting or faking. He was looking at *me*, and that elation in his eye was mine.

I undid all my changes and went back to the raw image. Those blemishes weren't imperfections. They were perfection itself. They were part of my experience of him, which was three-dimensional, alive, dynamic, and flawed.

I layered the image on itself and blended it so the defects weren't covered but more apparent. I touched up the image until I could practically smell him, and his skin was as textured as it seemed when his face was an inch from mine.

It was dark when I finished, and I sat back and looked at my work. Through the reality of who he was, one thing was abundantly clear.

He wasn't normal.

Even with every imperfection uncovered, he was perfect. He jumped out of the frame from the way his mouth was set against his jaw, to the expression in his eyes, to the tilt of his chin. Not everyone had that. Not even every actor could make his face work as a whole. I remembered the moment I took the pictures. He'd been unprepared, yet his face and body worked in such a way as to make me feel as if he sat in the room with me.

Michael Greydon was a star, a regular guy inside a body that would shoot across the sky.

I looked out the window at the moon rising over downtown, and I saw a couple of paps standing outside the Whole Foods. Likely, they were either waiting for me to leave or for Michael to arrive.

This was his life. This was a problem he faced. I'd face it for him. I'd tolerate anything to be with him, but the paps outside Whole Foods would be our smallest problem. I had a ten-ton past that was already coming between us. He was a star, and I was dragging him down. He was meant for a perfect life, and I would always be the girl in *those* pictures. If we got married tomorrow and had babies, I'd always have an asterisk by my name.

—Are you all right?—

It was Phoebe. I called her. She picked up on the first ring from someplace loud and crowded.

"I have to be honest," I said, sitting in my chair by the window, "this sucks."

"Oh, honey—" The sound cut off as if she'd wheeled herself into a closet.

"Are you sure you still want me to take pictures of your wedding?"

"Why wouldn't I?" she asked.

"All your clients will know me as kiddie porn girl."

"You stop it, do you understand? You stop that right now. You're a good person, and talented, and a bunch of things that I'll be happy to brief anyone on. Should I come over and make you a list?"

"No, I'm good," I said. "I'm just going to go to sleep and wake up and try to feel better."

"Can you call me tomorrow? I want to really talk this through. I want to hit it from all angles."

I recoiled. God, no. The last thing I wanted was to look at the situation from all angles. I wanted to close my eyes and make it go away, and Phoebe, with her analyst's mind under a rainbow glitter shell, wouldn't allow that.

"Let's talk tomorrow," I said.

We hung up, but I knew I wouldn't call her in the morning. Just the thought of dissecting my reckless actions made me want to run in all directions at once.

Chapter 37

Michael

I never had to go into the main entrance of anything. I flew charter and had staff and a special liaison to manage things like the DMV. I only knew what other people did because I had to get in front of a camera and act like other people.

It was sad, really sad, that I'd never been a citizen of the world. I'd never thought I was too good to stand in line at the DMV. I lived the way I did because the one time my father and I had gone through the regular gate for a commercial airliner to Australia, we were mobbed. He'd signed everyone's boarding pass, and the plane was late. He grumbled afterward, but at the gate, he was a pure gentleman.

I admired a lot about my father, and that incident was one in particular. I hoped I wouldn't have to reprise it at the hospital, because Ken dropped me off in the parking lot and took off to spin pornography into heroism.

—Wait for me—

I texted Laine as I walked quickly, eyes on the phone. If I avoided eye contact, I could move through public spaces faster. But there were no mobs, no paparazzi. Though I felt eyes and camera phones on me, no one stopped me in the stairwell. Everyone had their own cares and troubles, and by the time I got to the ICU nurse, I felt as if I could walk at a normal pace with my head up.

"Mister Greydon," she said when I was a few steps away. She grabbed her clipboard and walked me down the hall before I could even stop.

Brooke sat in a small waiting area outside a bank of private rooms. I'd never seen my mother look so worried.

"What are you doing?" she said. "No, don't answer. I'll tell you what you're doing. You're killing your father." Brooke was shaking. Her face couldn't express much past the collagen injections, but the trembling in her arms told me she was upset.

"Just stop and tell me what happened." I had neither the desire to defend myself against her anxieties, nor did I have the time to explain that I wasn't a pervert. I was still out of breath from ignoring people while I ran up four flights of stairs.

"It did. It was stress. All this in the news, he just broke down."

"Don't look at the internet, Mom. That's, like, a rule."

"The calls coming in. They asked if you showed any signs of a sociopath as a child. Did we know you were a molester. And the girl, her pictures are all over the place. They crop them, but you know where everything is. Gareth, he just… running around the house yelling and cursing. For someone who did this his whole life… he didn't know what to do, and then he just… I thought he was acting." Her eyes filled up, red-rimmed and shiny, until she blinked. When her tears fell, not a speck of mascara or liner moved. "He said he had a pain and was acting confused. And see, I said it. Right there. *Acting.*"

I put my arms around her. She was a bag of cold bones, all wire and tension, a dead weight shaking against me. I'd always assumed she never gave a damn about anything. Maybe I'd been wrong.

Chapter 38

Laine

He'd said to wait for him, but I didn't know what that meant exactly. I couldn't wait anymore. I'd waited all day. I had enough money socked away to last a couple months, but eating into my cash reserves gave me palpitations. It was night, and that meant it was time to make money. To get my life back, I had to start from scratch. Though I felt a thread of excitement from the prospect, I felt mostly fear, because I wasn't going to stake out the right restaurant or personal trainer. I wasn't after the right celebrity doing the wrong thing. I didn't know what I was after, but I wasn't going to find it in the house.

Simple things first. There would be no tips. I was the tip. I was the mark. They were waiting outside my building's front door and the garage exit. I had to avoid the paparazzi to be one. I laughed at the very thought then got on a pair of sneakers. I would run faster and quieter than ever. If I could get out the door, I could get something. I knew this city like a lover, and she'd whisper her secrets to me.

I slung my bag over my shoulder and climbed the stairs to the top level. A sign warned me that the emergency alarm would go off if I opened the door to the roof. I reached into the front pocket of my bag and removed a little circuit board the size of a stick of gum. I screwed a silver rod into the bottom and reached for the top of the door. I jammed the circuit board between the beige box connected to the top of the door and the one connected to the doorjamb. When I opened the door, the alarm had no idea anything had happened, and it slept like a good child. All I had to do was grab it on the way back.

The cold night air swept through my hair as I traversed the roof in my high tops. I crossed my building and jumped onto the next, avoiding the shafts between the buildings and the little fans and vents that waited to trip me.

Before heading down the fire escape around the corner, I took a moment to stand at the edge and look over the city. Every blinking light over the landscape serviced a person. How many were looking at my pictures? How many wondered about me and what Michael saw in me? How many were outraged on my behalf? How many wrinkled their noses?

I'd never know. Their opinions were relevant as a whole, but as individuals, their importance diminished. So Mrs. June Snowcone in Encino thought I was a whore? What did that matter? She wasn't even a speck of light in the flat plaid grid of the Valley. I could ignore her. I could stop caring about her by no more than deciding to.

When I was the one with the opinions, they seemed valid and real, but from the outside looking in, or maybe the inside looking out, they didn't matter. From this view, I had the sense that they didn't know me. Those people knew nothing of my struggles or what went into my decisions. From this view was peace, because I understood that I wasn't a two-dimensional black-and-white photo but a woman, in full color, who moved in time and space, who had relationships, a sense of humor, a past and a future.

It didn't matter.

June Snowcone couldn't touch me.

Beneath me, four floors below and across the street, I caught a movement as smooth as marbles rolling across a suddenly tilted table. Four, six, nine dark shapes followed a pale suit and blond head. I couldn't make out what the voices were saying, but I backtracked to my building's roof to get a closer look.

They followed her as if she was the Pied Piper. When she got to my side of the street, I recognized her.

"Lucy!" I called.

She stopped and looked up.

"Wait for me!" I said.

When I opened the stairway door, the alarm went off, and I didn't care. I ran down, taking turns at high speed, thankful for my little black court shoes. I skipped steps and bounded down the last two, three, five steps until I got to the lobby.

I slapped open the glass door. "Back off, assholes."

They barked my name and took pictures. I was no longer their friend. I recognized them by their facial hair and rigs, their outfits, and the way they held their equipment, but I'd become a mark. I didn't hate them for it, but that didn't make it less true.

Lucy came in with her head high and her bag at her side.

"Hey," I said, pulling her out of range of the cameras. "Are you all right?"

"I'm used to them."

"No, I mean... what are you doing here? You're not going to give me a hard time about the pictures, are you? I was just a kid. I'm not trying to hurt him."

"Stop one minute," she said, sitting on the old leather couch.

The lobby had been done in modernist furniture and poured concrete, with large black-and-white photos of the neighborhood when it was being built. Her eyes flicked over the details then back on me.

"Do you want to come upstairs?" I asked.

"Another time." She patted the seat next to her as she'd done in the bathroom, and I sat.

"I know why you're here," I said.

"Really?"

"I know it's hurting him."

"What? Those pictures?" She looked incredulous.

I felt peeled open. She wasn't Jane Snowcone. She was right in front of me, breathing the same air, and she had nails and teeth that could hurt me.

"Yes," I said.

"Oh, please. When I said hurt him, I meant *hurt him*. I didn't mean create an inconvenient sideshow." She put her hand over mine. "I'm not saying what happened is an inconvenience to you. I'm saying, he's not hurting the way you think. Not if I know him. Not over that."

"Over what then?" I said suspiciously.

"Don't you watch the E channel or something?"

"Not today, I don't."

"Wise." She stood, hitching her bag over her shoulder. "We might as well go out the front. Do you mind if we take my car?"

"Where are we going?"

"Gareth Greydon is in the hospital for liver failure. Michael is there, and you should be with him. You'll never get through without me, so... come on."

I didn't think much past that. Fathers were important. I knew that verbally. I could say it to myself with conviction and feeling, but I didn't know what I was talking about. So I was grateful for Lucy. If I'd heard about Gareth any other way, I might not have known what to do.

As Lucy and I walked through the bank of paps with their crack-exposing flashes and name-calling I was learning to ignore, I steeled myself to walk back into Michael's world.

Chapter 39

Michael

Gareth Greydon was a tough bastard. He'd be happy to tell you all about it. He'd tell you all the parts he'd played and the famous scenes where he did his own stunts. He'd tell you which tough-guy lines he was famous for and how he'd changed them from the script to be even better than they were, even if he didn't change more than the tense. Even if it was a mistake. Even if he broke his ass doing a stunt and hobbled back to his trailer, aching from head to toe.

So when my mother brought me to him, I was thrown. I'd grown up with him. He'd been around most of the time, even if he wasn't sober, and I'd never seen him look as trapped as he did in flat cotton, his body tied down with clear tubes.

"Jesus, Dad. Did you get the plate number?"

I offered my mother the chair next to the bed, but she wouldn't take it. She just stood behind me, wringing the manicure off her fingers.

"I was too busy lying on the floor like a damn patsy."

"You were reeling, sweetheart. It's not your fault." Brooke patted his shoulder and glared at me.

"Dad," I said, "I'm sorry. I know this was upsetting, and I—"

"Oh, for the love of Christ, forget it," he said.

"This could tank *Bullets*," I said. "It's tainted."

"You hush, Michael Greydon," Brooke barked in a whisper.

"No, no." My father held up his hands. "It's all right."

"The doctor said no upsetting news," she said.

"This isn't news," Gareth said. "Listen, Brooke, sweetheart, just give me a minute with my son, would you?"

"Michael, you have to promise not to upset him."

"I promise."

"No!" Gareth shouted. "Stop it. Get out. He'll say what he wants."

I sat in the chair. Brooke kissed Gareth's forehead, and he shooed her away, grumbling.

She came around the bed and kissed my cheek. "Be good, all right?"

"Yes, Brooke."

She clicked the door shut behind her.

"She's going to make me nuts," Gareth said. "She was harping on the whole thing until I collapsed."

"Gareth, really?"

"Swear to it."

"What's the verdict? You going to die from it?"

"Oh, please. This was the little girl version of liver failure. I got it beat already. I'm not going to let her kill me."

I laughed.

He took my forearm and squeezed. "I want to say something to you. You're a good kid. Trying to save that girl from what happened to her, it was honorable. That was how I wanted to raise you. I'm proud of you."

"Thanks, Dad."

"The studio won't see it that way if I know those assholes, and I know those assholes. I've done things with Bob Overland no one should even talk about. But you know what? I don't care. I know you put everything into getting that movie made so I'd have a second chance. But you risking it to do the right thing? That's the man I made. That's the important thing. I might not get another chance to make a movie, and you know, fuck it. I made you, and I love you." He ran his hands through what was left of his hair. That gesture used to make the girls crazy, but it had become a tell for when he was uncomfortable.

"That was hard for you, wasn't it?" I said.

"You have no idea."

I patted the part of his arm with no tubes sticking out of it. "We'll act like it never happened."

Chapter 40

Laine

It was funny what I learned on the other side of the ropes. Lucy wasn't much of anyone in the grand scheme. She wasn't Michael Greydon or Britt Ravenor. Despite running her own agency, to the industry, she was just a model five years past her prime who was waiting for a reality TV show or an acting gig to appear. But in my business world, where documenting the right disaster could mean millions, she was worth following. Her showing up at my house was pure gold to the paps outside the Whole Foods, because I was Lucy's ex-boyfriend's new girl, and a picture of me getting gangbanged at fifteen was on the internet. The web of relationships was just perfect.

We pulled up in front of the Hotentot Bistro. Lucy gave the valet her keys and a hundred dollars while I waved at the paps and called them by name. We went into the restaurant but did not sit. We walked through it, into the kitchen, and out the back door, where her car waited for us. The hospital was a short jump across town.

"Nice trick," I said as we drove away.

"I try not to use it so much, but we don't want them following us to the hospital, trust me. Those people are parasites. They have no regard." She glanced at me. "Sorry."

I shrugged. "It's fine. I never won any popularity contests even without the camera."

"You have a nice look, you know," Lucy said. "I could have done something with you if you were a couple of inches taller."

I laughed, half nervous and half charmed. Soon after, we pulled into the hospital parking lot. Like normal people, we parked, got out, and walked through the glass doors.

"It's dead," I said. "When something like this happens and I don't find out about it, I get pissed at myself. I think, what did I miss?"

"Nurses aren't waiters. They don't have paps on speed dial."

As we got into the elevator, I didn't mention that I was on a few phones in that very hospital. She didn't need to know how many times I'd hidden in the bushes outside.

We got out and turned a few corners, went through a narrow door, and came into a well-appointed room that was no bigger than a regular doctor's office's waiting room. Brooke Chambers stood when we entered, and a list of adjectives went through my head. Tough and graceful and vulnerable. Kind, generous, compassionate. Everything. She'd been everything and anything she wanted to be. I almost stopped dead in my tracks at seeing her face to face.

"Lucy!" she exclaimed.

"Hi, Brooke. This is Laine."

She held out her hand, and I shook it.

"I'm such a fan," I said. "In *Love in Between*, you were so amazing. I always thought those rotten kids were lucky to have a mom like you." Then without a second to breathe, I did something I didn't understand, because I wasn't any celebrity's fan. I hugged her, and I couldn't believe it when she hugged me back.

I was overwhelmed. Could I cry on her shoulder? Could I tell her everything? Could I tell her how all these years, I'd looked forward to meeting her? And could she, would she, make it all go away for me? The pictures. The eyes on me. The years of non-consensual consent. How could any of that rule me when she hugged me? She was so warm, and her shoulder fit my cheek, and when she rubbed my back a little, I felt loved. Purely and truly loved.

When Lucy cleared her throat, I woke out of my dream state.

"I'm sorry," I said. "It's been a rough day."

"That was very kind. I don't get that much anymore."

"You're just amazing. I'm sorry. You were, I mean, are so talented. And I'm sorry to meet you with all this terrible stuff happening." I willed my mouth shut.

"How is he?" Lucy asked. I felt rescued.

"Stable," Brooke said. "He's in there telling his son the meaning of life right now. Apparently it only comes to you when your internal organs fail."

"I hear that happens. You only figure out what's important at times like that? I've heard that's the case." I thought I'd willed my mouth shut, but like a lousy dieter seeing friends at a restaurant, all my self-control went out the window in front of Brooke Chambers.

"It's a bad time, Laine," Brooke said. "Just a bad time all around, with the movie falling off schedule and my son being arrested."

"I'm sorry about that."

Lucy put her hand on my arm.

"You didn't mean any harm," Brooke said. "Everyone has the best intentions. You know, my son never does things the easy way. He makes everything an uphill battle. But it's his career."

Best intentions. I didn't like the sound of that. Best intentions meant everyone was misguided. It meant everything had gone wrong and people were hurt. It meant that no matter how much everyone involved wanted to be upright and strong, some situations were dead in the water.

I was probably being oversensitive. I was probably only hearing a reprimand because that was what I chose to hear. Brooke wouldn't be at her best in a hospital waiting room. She didn't know me, yet she knew what I'd been through. I was in a fishbowl where she could see me, but I didn't really see her.

I eked out a smile. I wanted Brooke Chambers's approval, and asking what she meant or defending myself at fifteen or twenty-five wouldn't be helpful. We were there for a family, not petty insults. She was making a point about something bigger than three women in a tiny room.

I got it. I got it loud and clear, a message developed in boiling hot chemicals, clustering the silver grains into lumps. I saw the image of what she meant, though the details were lost in the contrast.

And I found that image was perfect in the frame. Uncomfortable and unpleasant but somehow more real and accurate than anything with the details burned in. She was right, even in what she didn't say.

She didn't say that the pain was inevitable despite our best intentions.

She didn't say that he and I were an uphill battle.

But she did. She'd said I'd break him in the course of loving him. I was just another choice that made things harder than they had to be. I'd end his career.

My career was over. Was I going to make sure his was too?

Michael came into the room, and I felt a longing for something I didn't have, even though he was right in front of me.

Chapter 41

Michael

I didn't expect her. I'd expected my mother and Lucy and no one else, because my father wouldn't want anyone to know he was in the hospital until he was back on his feet and growling at doctors.

"Hi," I said to Laine as I hugged Brooke.

Lucy piped in, "I brought her, so if you didn't want her here, you can blame me."

"Nice to see you too," I replied, kissing her cheek.

"How is he?" she asked.

"Getting his curmudgeon back."

I put my hand on Laine's shoulder and pulled her into me, expecting her body to feel the way it always did: pliable, soft, and luxurious against me. But though she made all the motions of affection, she was stiff and distant.

"Excuse us a second," I said to my mother.

I pulled Laine out into the hall. The lights were brighter and the floors more scuffed. She looked tired and wrung out.

"How are you doing?" I asked, touching her face. "We're trying to get the pictures taken down."

She didn't look at me. "I don't care about the pictures."

"Really?" I didn't believe her, and my tone let her know it.

"No, I care." She let her gaze drift up to me. "But how are you doing? You look tired."

"Long night. For both of us. Want to go to bed?"

I didn't know where my sudden playfulness had come from—maybe the fact that my dad would be all right and seeing Laine wasn't broken about the pictures. She was miles away, but she was in front of me. I was relieved that

I could do something, and that she was there, and I needed her.

Yes, I needed her against me. I admitted that. So I said quick good-byes and hustled her into my car. I may have been too wrapped up in my own happiness and despair to realize she was pensive. Or I may have expected any normal person to be a little off after the events of the last twenty-four hours. I can't imagine we weren't both completely scrambled.

But I took her hand in the car and she put her head back on the seat, looking out the window.

"We're getting as many of the pictures taken down as we can," I said as we crossed La Cienega.

"What does liver failure mean? Will he be all right?"

"Ken is on it. And the police are doing what they can."

"Your mother, she was upset, she couldn't hide it. Is she always like that?"

"That Jake guy, I swear if they don't lock him up and throw away the key…"

"Lucy's all right," she said. "I really thought she was the worst person in the world, but she's thoughtful, and she loves you. I guess people change."

"I think they do." I turned into the hills. "I mean, they don't really. But they do."

"They improve." She turned her head to face me, her cheek on the back of the seat. "*We* improve."

"Yeah."

I didn't ask her where she wanted to go, but I brought her home. There may have been a practical matter of her clothes or a camera. I didn't ask if she had to get to work. She didn't object. I assumed she needed me as much as I needed her.

Chapter 42

Laine

He got out of the car and came around the front. The front lights of the little house clicked on when he passed.

Was he my last chance at happiness? Was the disaster of those pictures going to break me? Or would we find a way through it? Because his hips swung around the car and I thought if I lost him because of Jake, I'd never recover.

He opened the door for me and stood with his hand out, framed in the triangle between the door and the car, half lit by the porch light. I hadn't thought about sex, or more accurately, I hadn't thought about good sex, since the previous morning. But as I put my hand out for him and we touched, I couldn't think about anything else. I was body slammed with arousal, and I wasn't the only one, because I was barely out of the car before Michael pushed me against the car in a bruising kiss.

And it was good, exactly what I needed. I wanted to be swept away in his hands, his mouth on my face and neck, pulling groans from me. I kicked my leg around his waist to feel his erection against me. He pushed. I pushed back. If I could just make the fabric between us disappear, rub it away with friction until the threads frayed and popped, getting to the skin, the fluid and blood, until he was inside me.

"I have to have you," he said, cupping the back of my head, mouth to mouth.

"Yes."

It must have taken twenty minutes to get to the front door. He pushed me against every stable surface, kissing me, fondling me, yanking buttons and zippers. I could barely get a foothold long enough to touch him. By the time we got to the door, my shirt was hiked over my breasts and his pants were unbuttoned.

The door swung open, and we tumbled in. My pants were undone, I don't remember when or how, but he stuck his hands down them. I let loose with a long vowel when he touched me.

"Christ, Laine."

He slapped the door shut and got on his knees before me, pulling my pants down. I stepped out of them. He got a condom from his back pocket before lowering his pants below his hips. I opened for him, hitching one leg over his waist and my arms over his shoulders. He pushed me against the wall, driving into me.

"Say you're mine," he growled.

He felt so good, pushing on me just the right way, holding my legs apart so he could go deeper. Light and heat gathered where we were connected.

"Oh, Michael, I'm so close."

"Say it."

"I'm yours." I pulled him to me, not doubting the words as they escaped my lips, because no man had made me feel like this. No man had made me feel so safe, so wanted, so valuable. We could do this, and if I didn't believe we could get past our troubles, my world wouldn't have exploded in pleasure. I pulled him close with my legs and came for all it was worth, letting go of everything for that moment.

He came right after me with a bark and a groan, panting as if he'd just been for a run. We didn't move, didn't say a word. He hitched me up and I gripped him tighter as he carried me to the bedroom.

Chapter 43

Michael

I'd fallen asleep wrapped around her, which felt as natural and right as any place I'd ever fallen asleep. Once I got her into my bed, we kissed, touched, talked, and made love twice more. She asked about my parents as if she were asking about an exotic trip I'd taken in the distant past. She was fascinated, as if the silliest details were important, and the parental idiosyncrasies I took for granted were the cornerstone of my relationship with them.

She was still guarded about her time with those assholes who'd hurt her, but she told me about Sunshine and Rover, and I remembered the faraway look on her face when she'd spoken of them during our conversations in the bleachers. I wanted to find them for her, to reunite her with the only people who had been parents to her.

We acted as if nothing had gone wrong in the previous twenty-four hours. We twisted together in the cocoon of my bed until the sun blasted through the guest house window and my phone woke me. In the previous night's haste to get naked, I'd forgotten to turn off the damned ringer.

I untwisted myself and walked out to the living room. My jacket was half under the couch, in a ball with the sleeve sticking straight out as if it was hailing a cab. I yanked it, and the phone slid out of the pocket. I plucked it up to shut it.

But I saw who it was from and felt compelled to take the call. "Hello?"

"Mike. It's Steven."

"Good morning. Is it morning? The sun's barely up."

"I've been up all night," he said, and I heard it in his voice. The guy never lost a minute's sleep for anything.

"Good thing we're not shooting." I threw myself on the couch. I was completely naked, and it was my house, yet I felt as though I should put something on. I knew what this was about.

"Last night," he said.

"Wasn't me."

"Stop joking."

"What do you want me to say? I didn't do anything wrong." I heard Laine behind me, but I couldn't look at her. The house was so small I couldn't go anywhere to have the conversation where she couldn't hear me.

"Look," Steven said in his director voice, "I don't want to get into a big battle over morality."

I sat up straight. "Morality? Are you—?"

"I don't want this to go bad. I respect you as an artist. But hear me out. This shoot's already compromised. I have the Overland thing bumping right up against it. The delay was going to eat into my pre-production. And now this?"

"This what? Say it."

"I can't work with you."

My heart sank as if sucked into a vacuum. He was bailing. Losing an actor was the worst thing that could happen to a project. That killed it immediately. But losing a director was the second worst thing. That killed it in a slow, wasting death. And my father needed *Bullets*. He'd been waiting for this chance for ten years, and I'd put everything on the line to make it happen. Gareth was in the hospital because production had paused. How bad would he get when the project died?

"I've got Ken on the PR," I said. "It's going to go away."

"I have daughters."

"You have daughters?"

"I have to think about them. I'm sorry. But they're going to be the same age as that girl soon."

"So? I…" I stopped.

He wasn't worried about the public relations nightmare. He wasn't worried about what people thought of him or me or *Bullets*. He thought I liked teenagers, and he didn't want to work with a predator.

"Fuck you, Steven." I threw the phone on the couch and turned around. Laine stood in the doorway, fully dressed and looking skittish and nervous. I was so annoyed with Steven and so worried about my father that I threw up my hands. "Don't even ask."

"Okay." She sounded small and anxious.

I just wanted everything and everyone to go away so I could throw something. "Steven quit right to my face, and I'd normally say, hey, brave move not having his agent call me. But his bravery doesn't make this less screwed up."

"It's because of me."

"No." I paused then told the truth. "Yes."

"I figured." She looked out the window, crossing her arms.

We'd been so close the night before, and that morning, with the taste of her still on my lips, she was a million miles away. She sat on the edge of the couch, looking into her lap. When I put my hands over hers, she didn't move them.

"I thought about this all night. After you fell asleep, I was up, thinking about what your mother said. And I slept a little and woke up thinking it would all be all right. Because I'm just... you. It's always been you. I look at the past nine years, and I don't think anything I've done that hasn't been because of you in one way or another. And it seemed that being with you was somehow... like it had a purpose. Like it was the end of a long journey. But I woke up uncomfortable and convincing myself it would all be all right. Your mother said you make everything an uphill battle, and I started thinking, 'Is that me? Am I his uphill battle?'"

"Come on, really?"

It was the wrong time to show impatience. It was the time to come together with her, but I was overwhelmed, hurt, and worried about my father.

"I think we had a good time, and now we have to move on." Her breath hitched, and her voice had an odd flatness to it, as if she'd opened a valve at the bottom of her throat and let the emotion drain out before speaking.

"What?" I sat up straight, feeling my nakedness for the first time. "Why?"

"Don't you see? I've been nothing but trouble to you. I walk into your life, and you get beat up and your movie is in trouble. People aren't talking about you and your work, they're talking about *me* and who *I am*. You break your contract, then you do something borderline illegal to help me, you get arrested, and your father winds up in the hospital. Nice, right? And this morning, Steven quits. Nice how I enrich your life. Nice how I add something instead of taking away."

"Hold it." I held up my hands. She was talking crazy. She just needed to hear sense. "You're looking at this all wrong. That's all external stuff. We can get through it."

"We couldn't have done anything better. We couldn't have worked harder to make it right, and we still fucked it up," she said. "My best chance was with you, and if I ruin you in the process, then it's me. All I've ever wanted to be was no worse than anyone else, and it's uphill every day. I wasn't born to be normal any more than you were, but I can't drag you into my version of not normal."

"Laine, can you just stop and let me think for a minute?" I put my hands on the sides of her face so she had to look at me, because this was important. "How is it you can get shuttled through twelve homes as a child and cope with everything you've coped with and not deal with this nonsense?"

Did I sound angry? Maybe I was. Maybe I didn't want to deal with this right now. But I knew from the flatness of her expression that I wasn't giving her hope. I wasn't telling her anything she wanted to hear. I was talking into the mirror. I'd never felt this frustration mixed with despair before. She was gone to me, and I had no idea how to make it right. Was this feeling hopelessness? It was new and awful beyond measure.

"I'm so fucked up," she said, emotion back in her voice. "I mean... so fucked up. I shouldn't be with anyone. I should be alone and happy with my friends. I should play with their kids and be the aunt everyone loves. That's what I want. I don't want this. It's too complicated."

I should have answered her tears with kisses, should have held her or said something to cut off the next line, because before it, everything was salvageable.

"Do you love me?" she asked. "Can you honestly say you love me?"

I was too squeezed. Too many things were happening, and all of them closed and locked my heart.

"That's not a fair question," I answered. "It's only been a couple of weeks."

She nodded, her face a mask of stone and ice. She was gone, and I realized I should have said something else. But I couldn't take it back, even if I wanted too.

"So sensible," she said.

"What is that supposed to mean?"

"I'm sorry." She stood. "And thank you. Thank you for everything."

And that was that. The fact that I'd never experienced that before notwithstanding, when a woman said it was done, it was done. As if I could hear a gate clang closed, my defenses fell into place.

"That's fine," I said, as shut down as I'd ever been.

"Can we still be friends?" she asked.

"Sure. I should go. Let me put you in a cab."

She put her shoulders back and held her head high. "I can get myself a cab, thank you."

"I can get Gali here in three minutes."

I took her arm to stop her and she jerked it away, then held her hands up as if stopping an oncoming train. I felt ashamed to have touched her. Even after all the intimacy of the night before, I'd somehow physically overstepped.

"You're a good man, Michael. You'll see it's the best thing."

She didn't wait for an answer. She just turned on her high-tops and walked for the door without looking back, head down as if she were looking for dropped change. I didn't sense that anything had shifted until she fussed with the doorknob, and when I jumped to help her, she put her hand up to keep me away.

"I got it. Just open the gate for me."

She walked out and closed the door. She trudged to the front, and just before she got to the gate, she put her chin up, her shoulders back, and walked as though she meant it. I pushed the button and opened the gate so she didn't have to break her stride, and that too was a mistake.

I was supposed to shut it off like a faucet, as if I'd been acting the whole time.

I hadn't been. I'd meant everything I ever said to her, and I didn't know how to un-mean it. But maybe she was right. Maybe I should admire her strength to do what had to be done. I didn't know how to have a relationship any more than she did. I'd never learned how to work for it. I'd left my name to do the heavy lifting.

My life was my life. It wasn't changing. Whatever my ability to expose myself while exposing none of myself was, it was something I'd been born into. I couldn't change it any more than I could make myself shorter. She saw that. She was wise beyond her years and strong beyond her stature.

She was right. It hurt, but she was beautiful, and she was right.

Chapter 44

Laine

Nothing was right. Nothing was exactly wrong, but nothing was right. I had things to figure out, and I didn't even know what they were. I should have been out getting work, but I wanted to go to bed. Not to lie under the covers but to sleep. Forever.

I'd done the right and honorable thing. I knew immediately why so few people bothered with it, why so many just went where their heart pulled them. Because doing what made sense hurt. I had a physical pain in my chest. Doing the right thing wasn't supposed to feel like that. It was supposed to be uplifting. But the loss of him... well, the only word I had was pain.

I pulled an ice-crusted container of French vanilla out of the freezer. Maybe I'd just freeze out the sad. I opened the drawer for a spoon, and I stared back at me in black and white.

Jake had already copped a plea for two years behind bars, and still, the problem of that old me was nestled with the spoons.

I took the picture of sixteen-year-old me out of the drawer, ice cream forgotten. Look at that kid. She was tough. She did what she had to. She'd been given nothing and turned it into something.

I didn't flinch from the photo. That girl had screwed up any chance I'd had at happiness, but she had given me that chance in the first place. I didn't hide the picture or try to not think about it. She was mine. She was a part of me.

"I forgive you," I said, then I started crying.

I think I cried for two days. Two and a half. Normally I viewed every tear shed as a sign of weakness, as a lack of ownership and control. But I gave up on that in the first ten minutes. I'd been through a lot. I earned my tears. This snot-shooting, breath-catching blubber was mine, and I deserved it.

Irv called, and I texted back that I was busy. Tom emailed me an invitation to a Razzledazzle show, and I texted back that I couldn't make it. No one called to tell me who was eating at what restaurant without their underpants.

Sometimes I called up memories of Sunshine and Rover, with their brightly colored everything. I knew they loved me. I had been with them for two years, and I had to be ripped away from them. I remembered the funky smell of the van, sweat and love and something else.

I'd always thought they'd abandoned me, but maybe it was more complex than that. Maybe I shouldn't have grown up in a van. Maybe they thought I could do better than them. At six and a half, I had no idea what it meant to leave behind someone you loved.

It sucked.

Michael was the only person who could soothe me, the only one who could make my crying stop, but I'd abandoned him. I had no right to call him to comfort me.

But what I could do was look at him. I thought it would hurt to pull up the pictures I'd taken of him, from the loft upstairs to the first pap shot I'd gotten by the valet of the WDE Agency. I'd filed them by how handsome he looked, how happy, how engaged he was with the camera. I had one where he was scratching his head and looking pensive, and I stared at it at three in the morning, trying to understand him. I couldn't. It was just a picture.

In the evening of the third day, I realized I'd stopped crying. I felt clean. I felt powerful again, and though I hadn't slept, I was wide awake.

So I went to see Razzledazzle at the Thelonius Room. It was so dark I couldn't see a foot in front of me. Even the foot-high candles didn't cut through the murk.

"Where have you been?" Tom yelled over the music of the opening band, Spoken Not Stirred.

"Home crying."

He looked away from his camera. "You?"

"Yeah. You got a problem?"

"You should have called me."

I shrugged. "I'm sorry. You like doing this. I shouldn't have distracted you with being a pap."

He nudged me with his shoulder. We had more to talk about, but Razzledazzle came on. He disengaged to do his job.

I knew enough people around the room to hold conversations, but by the third song, I was alone at the bar, trying to get away from the noise. I ordered a glass of crappy wine from a skinny girl in black jeans. She'd done her hair in a fancy twist, but after hours of work, she looked worn out.

Though I felt strong, I knew it was a moment of weakness when I called Michael.

The call bounced. I was off his list.

Sure, being cut off hurt, but the worst part was knowing I'd upset him enough to get pulled. I hadn't expected hurting someone to feel like this. I thought leaving someone behind would be okay, not a big deal, because I'd be the one in charge. But it wasn't like that at all. I felt sorry. I'd done the right thing, but it came with a flavor of regret I hadn't tasted before.

I left and stalked the streets of downtown, taking pictures of… I didn't even know what. Corners. Garbage. A broken water main. Doorways. A club let out, and I took pictures of the drunks. I did it the next night, and the night after. I didn't know what I was doing but avoiding my own sadness, but I was doing something.

Chapter 45

Michael

Gareth, who had wanted to do *Bullets* more than he wanted to breathe, took Steven leaving pretty well. He called it deathbed perspective and did a few talk shows explaining himself. The studio found a new director who was half as good and twice as fast, and we were back on track, more or less, after another week and a half of shooting with Britt keeping her arms down.

The furor over Laine died down. I didn't call her. After a few days, I took her off the accept list, but whenever I saw a pack of paparazzi, I looked for her. I thought about what I'd do if I saw her. Give her that perfect shot or give her the finger, I didn't know. I alternated between being grateful for what she did and resenting it.

I pulled onto my street after one of the last days of shooting on *Bullets*. One, two, three, five paparazzi at the entrance to my driveway. No, six. Six paparazzi on the street, cameras up. *Clickclickclick.* None were Laine. It was as if she'd disappeared. I couldn't even find a candid of anyone, anywhere, in any magazine with her byline.

I ignored the paparazzi. I didn't even wave as I pulled in and closed the gate. Call time on *Bullets* was after sunset, and I needed a shower and a nap, in that order, but Brad's car was in the drive.

He stood in the doorway of the guest house in his underwear and a tuxedo shirt. I forgot when I'd given him the keys, but he was a welcome sight, even half dressed.

"The fuck?" he said. "Seen the time?"

"It's eight in the morning. You should be sleeping. At home. In your own house." I went up the walk and onto the steps of the small house. I was fully surrounded by hedges and walls, but I wanted to get inside and out of sight.

"Dude, these two girls I was with? Started fighting right there. Like, skin under fingernails. I had to go."

"You could have put pants on."

"I was going house, to car, to house," he said. "I drank the beer in the fridge, by the way."

I waved him off and went inside. Brad slid his nearly bare ass onto a barstool. I dropped my bag onto the counter.

"You want coffee?" I asked. "I have instant."

"Sure." He turned the sound up on the little TV. "They're talking Oscar for you on Cinema City."

"The nominations aren't for two months."

"The posters went up all over the city. You haven't noticed your face looking down at you?"

All over Los Angeles, before a turkey graced a Thanksgiving table, billboards went up with "For Your Consideration" across the top and a list under it. It was the studios' way of reminding the industry of the year's great films and performances while their Oscar ballots were in front of them.

"I don't even see my face anymore."

"See it, dude. Overland put, like, seven million into an ad campaign for *Big Girls*. And they can't even stand Andrea."

"It was a miracle they even released it."

"The miracle was you, asshole. You were a fucking powerhouse in that thing." He poured water into a cup while he spoke, thinking about not burning himself, the trajectory of the water, putting in enough but not too much.

"Remember in school," I said, "pouring the tea?"

He laughed. "Oh, man, I felt so bad for you. You couldn't pour water and talk at the same time." He put the pot down.

I was amazed by how our minds multitasked only when we didn't think about it. Like a switch flipping on, Laine popped into my mind again. Whenever I thought of experiencing life firsthand, I thought of her. One day it would stop. One day.

"I can't do this," I said, shutting off the TV.

"What's that mean?"

"I don't want to be considered. I don't want an award. I'm done. I need a break. A something."

"Dude."

"Dude, nothing. I'm burned out. I don't know what to do with myself, but I have so much to do I can't even think."

"You know what we used to do at home when shit got bad? Like when there was too much?" Brad asked.

"Tip cows?"

"Fuck you, that's the Midwest, asshole. We went on a road trip. Drove up the mountain to look out over shit."

I whispered, "Road trip."

It was a ridiculous idea. Absurd. I was booked for the next eighteen months. I had one week in August with no work, and the slightest hiccup would fill those days. I couldn't possibly travel. People counted on me. My new agent would scream. My dad would call me irresponsible. Ken would have to spin it. The press would assume I was on drugs, and the Hollywood machine as a whole would hate me for making them scramble.

Yet it was the most appealing idea I'd ever heard. An hour after I'd considered the idea that I couldn't pour water without overthinking it, I was making calls to get out of town. I didn't know where I was going, except *away*.

I wanted to go to places where my face was just another face, to do things I'd never done. I'd learned to mountain climb for a movie, but I'd never done it. Not for real. Not on an actual mountain. I'd only acted like a mountain climber and a ski instructor and a race car driver. Acting was done.

On set that night, Gareth said, "You go after you fulfill your commitments." He looked at me through the mirror as we both got our makeup done. It was our last day of shooting, and my obligation to my father would be done.

"You're lucky I'm finishing this movie," I said. "I should leave tomorrow."

"They'd never forgive you."

"Fuck them."

He laughed.

"You're bailing on Harvey Worth?" Ken asked on the phone as I crossed my property.

I'd avoided making any industry calls until I'd told Gareth I was leaving. Ken was the last of them. I had a ton of stuff to do and no time to do it in, and for once, that felt exciting. "Yeah."

"He makes a movie once every ten years."

"My agent mentioned that to me repeatedly," I said, coming to a garage only my staff had seen the inside of. I jerked the door open.

"You're going to get killed, kid."

"Fans don't care."

"Fans? You need to make a movie to have fans. I told you, even you need to get hired. Even you need to keep your reputation."

I was surprised at how dusty the garage was, considering how spotless the staff kept the big house. I found my mountain climbing stuff with a broadsword and shield. I'd learned how to use a nunchaku for a part. I found a box of spray paint. When I was nineteen, I'd played a New York graffiti artist and learned to handle a can of paint.

"My virtuous reputation will remain intact."

"You're not getting it," he said. "No one cares if you sleep around. It's your professional reputation, your ability to deliver that matters. It's the industry you have to appease."

"I have a message for the industry." I hung up.

I left the equipment. I wanted to be unencumbered.

Chapter 46

Laine

I watched one YouTube video over and over. Michael Greydon, America's Boyfriend, pulls his Alpha Romeo out of his driveway and gets out. Seven paps jump on him. He doesn't smile. He lets the gate close. He swaggers a little. Sunglasses. Leather jacket. Jeans. He has a spray can in his hand, and he steps up to his gate. He assesses the size of it. The paps ask him what he's doing while they shoot him. They ask where his driver is. He doesn't answer. He raises his arm and, with turquoise spray paint, puts a long vertical line on the leftmost side of the gate. Then a shorter horizontal one. He doesn't stop, and the paps get silent as he paints his gate with two words.

I was proud of him. I watched that video a million times. I didn't know who he was flipping off, and I didn't care. The paparazzi, his staff, Brad, Britt, his father, his mother, me. I had no idea, but I was pleased for him. He'd cancelled two films and split.

He was traveling as if he was the happiest, most grateful little bird ever, jaunting off to faraway places and filming everything. From the sky over Tunis, the waters of the Nile, and the sheer cliffs of Tibet, he posted it all on the internet. Everyone followed him and his journeys as an anonymous traveler. Especially me. I'd gone from his secret crush, to his nightmare, to his lover, to his problem. In the end, I'd wound up a fan, not of his acting or his stardom but of the man he was. If he never made another movie, I would have still admired him.

"You keep saying you don't care about him, but if you ask me, the lady doth protest too much," Phoebe said, staring at my computer. We'd taken some test shots for the wedding, and she was noodling through the unedited batch.

"I don't even know what that means." I wiped the inside of a pot.

"I'm being bitchy. I'm sorry. Nevermind. It's just that I'm sitting here looking at your computer," Phoebe continued, "and you have, like, ten files with his name on them and his YouTube tabs open."

I slammed the pot down. "So?"

"Can you call him?"

I put the pot away. "No." I walked around the desk and discovered Phoebe wasn't looking at the folder with her wedding test shots.

"I clicked by accident," she said.

She looked meek, but I knew her too well. Behind her was a YouTube box with the sky flying across it. The shooter was behind a little camera mounted on his shoulder, invisible to the viewer.

Snap.

Some crowded city with stands right up to the street and sounds I couldn't even decipher.

Snap.

Back to the parachute jump. The ground getting bigger. Michael's voice, turned low, laughing in excitement and terror.

Snap.

A shot of unidentifiable street food.

Snap.

The skydive. The parachute opened with a whoosh, and his velocity to the ground was cut to a drift.

"It's fine," I said, pausing the video. "I shouldn't keep that stuff on my desktop when Miss Sneaky Boots is around."

When the video window disappeared, the pictures from the loft upstairs, when Michael had made me eggs, came up. He came through the frame, same as always, with a half smile so intense it burned through the lens.

"These are really nice. You should sell them," she said.

"I can't. It would be weird."

"Is this why you haven't been doing what you used to? The paparazzi thing? Because of him?"

"No," I said in a way that was too definite for what I felt. "It's just… it just lost its allure, I guess. The excitement is gone, and I have this yucky feeling."

"From taking pictures?"

"No, from stealing. As if they were never mine to sell in the first place. But these?" I pointed at the ones of Michael that Phoebe had pulled up. "These feel good. Bad, because it's him, but good, because they're mine. And I can't sell them, because talk about yucky." I waved it away. I didn't want to talk about Michael anymore. "The whole thing. Just because someone wants to buy something doesn't mean I need to degrade myself to produce it. I mean, yes, there will always be paps, and there will always be celebrities, and in a way, they do ask for it because they're smart people, and they know what's involved with success. And the magazines ask for it because millions of people ask for it. And the money goes around and around. It's a snake eating its tail then complaining it's choking." I paced away from the computer and fussed in the kitchen. "Everyone's degraded because we're treating people like objects, like marks. The stars. The magazines. The readers. And me. I was degraded. Just because I did it to myself doesn't make it less degrading."

"What does that mean for you exactly?"

"I have no idea."

Chapter 47

Michael

I got profoundly lonely and profoundly bored, but those weren't the times I thought of Laine the most. I thought of her when I shot awake as the Imams chanted a prayer over a loudspeaker in the middle of the night. I thought of her when I saw a sunrise worth photographing. I thought of her when I walked a crowded street and no one noticed me as anything but a white American. When I wanted to share a moment, I wanted her there, so I photographed those moments and filmed them. It was a shallow cure for a pervasive disease. Loneliness. It was at once empowering and debilitating.

But I thought she might see them, and I felt less alone. That connection created with a shared photograph—was that what she had been doing with her work? Creating connections between people? From my perch at the top of the media food chain, I couldn't see it. Maybe my face created a connection between people, gave them something in common. Maybe she hadn't been a parasite but a facilitator.

I wanted to talk to her about all of it, to get her take on those connections, but I was far away, and she'd left me. So I went about my days doing things I'd had to think about. Speaking with my hands. Getting a roof over my head. Surviving. I didn't need approval to do any of that, so despite being alone, I felt like a free man.

I hadn't thought about certain things in what seemed like forever. How to be in a public space. How much eye contact to make. Calling ahead so all the right people and none of the wrong people would know where I was.

I felt as if I'd gotten normality down to a science. A few weeks past Christmas, I sat in a shop, drinking mint tea and reading a little Kurt Vonnegut book I'd found outside a hostel. The main character had decided he was the only real person in the world, and everyone else was placed there by God to see how he reacted. When someone was out of his sight, they ceased to exist.

The guy was crazy of course, but his perspective wasn't totally foreign to me. I smiled as I read, because I was so grateful to be in that little tea shop with a moment to read a crazy book I'd found in a cardboard box.

Chapter 48

Laine

I went out that night, same as always, stalking the streets in my sneakers. I took hundreds of frames of I-didn't-even-know-what, waiting for something good and worthy to appear. Sometimes I climbed a fence because I was curious or got on an empty eighteen-wheeler docked at a warehouse to get to the roof just to see what was there. The corners of downtown embraced me, but they revealed nothing. Not yet. But if they showed me anything at all, I'd be there to see it. That was the important thing. Showing up.

I found an alley I hadn't seen since I was ten. It was the little strip behind Mister Yi's sweater factory. I remembered the patterns in the bricks and the slope of the cobblestones into the iron drain. The paint on the exit sign was worn out and lit by a new, up-to-code exit sign. I took a picture of them together, the old and the new, because I could, but I knew it wasn't special.

A grey metal door slapped open, and the sound of thumping techno poured out. Two, three, five people burst out, laughing and screaming. I gasped in surprise.

"Shit!" a girl in a boob-exposing top said.

"What?" a guy in sunglasses shouted.

Brad Sinclair laughed. "Aw, man! You are so damn good."

"No fucking paparazzi!" Sunglasses Guy said.

Two girls stepped back and hovered over a flame and something small between them.

"I'm not—"

"Get over here!" Brad said and enfolded me in a hug.

Britt and Maryetta bounced out too, giggling. Britt froze when she saw me.

I held up my hands. "I'm not—"

"Laine! How did you find this place?" she asked.

"I wasn't looking. I—"

More hugs. Who were these people? They were always nice, but this? It was almost as if they were real and a little high but normal for people their age.

"I ain't seen you in how long?" Brad said.

"I don't—"

"Since before Mike left!" Britt interjected. "How are you?"

"I'm—"

"Take my picture!" Britt squealed, embracing Maryetta. "I love this woman! I love her so much!"

Maryetta rolled her eyes, and I captured it in a flash.

Too bright.

I adjusted. Caught Brad making a gang sign. Then him with his arm around Britt. Then Sunglasses Guy looking sullen. Brad tying his shoe. Sunglasses trying to run up a wall and losing his shoe. Britt pulling his waistband. Maryetta lighting a cigarette. The alley became a studio, the tight corner of the city a backdrop to a scene.

"We gotta blow! Come with us," Brad said.

"Yes!" Britt added. "I got a driver. It's so much better!"

"I can't, I—"

"Why not?" the guy in the sunglasses asked. He'd had the most fun in front of the camera.

"I'm running out of memory, and I want to see what I have. I know that's lame," I said. "Next time?"

A little convincing sent them on their way. They walked down the alley to a small lot on the other side.

"Wait!" I shouted.

Maryetta and Britt turned.

"I need releases!" I said, running toward them. When I caught up, I continued, out of breath. "I need you to sign releases so I can sell these, if it's all right. I'll clear them with you first, in case there's anything you don't want seen?" I jerked my thumb at the two girls putting a lighter and a foil packet away.

"Yeah," Britt said. "Call me tomorrow, and I'll get you everyone's contact info, okay?" She gave me her number and said to Maryetta, "Remind me to put her on the list."

"Yeah. You sure you don't want to come?" Maryetta asked me.

I thought of all the shots I could get. I lived five blocks away. All I had to do was go home and grab a memory card.

"Next time," I said. I was tired and done pushing myself.

They all trotted off to their cars, unencumbered by worry or fear, and I went home feeling the same way.

I sat in front of my screen, where Phoebe had opened all the pictures of Michael. I spent a minute looking through them for the millionth time. I loved him. Maybe I would always love him, but for the first time, I saw a life outside him.

Chapter 49

Michael

I didn't care about the Academy Award nominations, but I saw the start of the announcements in the hotel lobby on a screen the size of a headshot. I'd forgotten about them, but once I saw a man and a woman stand at a podium, I knew what it was. They spoke English, and squiggly, indecipherable captioning ran underneath them. I'd worked with her on some blitzy action thing that was releasing in two months, and he acted in mostly fussy period pieces.

I sat on an uncomfortable chair and ate a roll with tea. I'd stopped pretending I wasn't curious.

They announced the nominees for the small categories, and I watched, rapt. I cheered to myself when *Big Girls* was nommed for sound editing, followed by music, director, and screenplay.

Then actress—six nominees, with Claire Contreras among them. I was happy for her. She'd been wonderful to work with, and for the first time, I missed being on a movie set.

I wasn't supposed to expect a nomination. I wasn't supposed to even watch the announcements. I should have been running around Kowloon and making plans to move into mainland China. Anything but staring at the TV, waiting for something that promised fulfillment but would never deliver. A reward for doing everything right when nothing had felt right.

But it came, my name and my face, and I felt exposed again. Minutes after, when I was leaving the hotel with my bag slung across my back and my head down, my phone rang. I only accepted calls from my parents, and as expected, it was Gareth.

"Congratulations," he said.

"Thank you."

"Where the hell are you?"

"Kowloon."

"What's it like?"

"Crowded," I said. "Rainy. But if I don't tell them who I am, they don't know and don't care."

I heard muffled voices from the other side, some rustling, then Brooke got on. "Sweetheart, come back, would you? The whole thing's died down. No one even talks about that girl anymore. They just talk about your internet things. You can make it back for the ceremony."

The ceremony, where I wouldn't win because no one would vote for a man who may or may not have been a pervert. Everyone else from *Big Girls* would win, because they'd been excellent. Claire and Andrea, Max, who'd written the hell out of the thing.

"I can't," I said, and that was that.

She'd stopped arguing with me a month ago. I headed to China because I could and because they didn't have televisions.

In the end, my father brought me back, that old son of a bitch. He was getting his liver transplant. When I'd called him, he said, "I don't give a rat's ass if you come home. I'm going to be unconscious. But if I croak on the table while you're in Asia, you'll feel like crap about it."

I'd been huddled by a pay phone. I'd forgotten to charge my phone.

"You're not going to croak," I said.

"Damn right, I'm not. I want to see all their faces when you don't show up to get your Oscar."

I hung up thinking maybe I should go see my father pinned to a bed. I could watch everyone I'd worked with and respected win something. It would be fun. Then I could return to going wherever, whenever.

I hadn't booked a charter. I wanted to be normal for another three quarters of a day. I wore sunglasses, a too-long beard, and a hat. That had never fooled anyone for long, but it would get me to baggage claim.

As soon as the plane hit the ground at LAX, my chest constricted, and I felt such a weight on me, my hair felt heavy.

I fell into old patterns: looking away from crowds, seeming preoccupied, rushing, wondering who would do what for me instead of me doing it myself. I wanted to get back on the plane.

A photo mural twenty feet long stretched across the concourse, showing a perfect blue sky and the word in white, the bottom tilted to the planes of the mountain.

HOLLYWOOD.

Seeing it like that, I didn't think of the industry or the things I'd run from. I thought of the last time I'd been up there. With her.

I thought about her all the time. How much she'd like climbing a mountain in Cashmere or learning the infinite corners and cobblestone back ways of Hong Kong. She'd been so far away, I hadn't thought of calling her, but there I was in LA. I could call her.

But she'd let me go. She'd been the one to walk away, and she'd dropped off the face of the earth afterward, which was for the best. I was poison for her. I couldn't call her. Pride, or emotional self-preservation, stopped me.

I got in a cab. There was a magazine on the seat, an arty fashion thing, with Georgana on the cover, wearing makeup no one should be seen out of the house in. I casually flipped through it as the driver got on the 105.

I smiled when I saw Brad's picture. I could stand to see that nutjob again. He was hamming it up in a grainy black-and-white spread while Arnie tried to run up a wall and Britt kissed Maryetta. The detail in the picture was enthralling, seven stories at once, with the alleyway itself a fully-developed character. I couldn't look at it without smiling. I kept coming back to it and seeing new things. I moved my thumb to examine some detail in a corner and found the photographer's credit.

Chapter 50

Laine

Pictures had become cheap. If my hard drive got full, I tossed stuff. I took so many frames that storing every single one digitally would have been unmanageable. My attitude was, if I couldn't find it if I wanted it, it had to go. So I threw stuff out.

But film? No one threw out actual negatives, or at least Irving didn't.

"Is this George Clooney?" I held up a clear plastic filer of 4x5 negatives.

Irving put his face next to mine and looked at it against the window. We'd been organizing his piles for weeks, and there still wasn't much to toss.

"Yeah," he said, taking the folder and looking closely. "Handsome guy. Unreal handsome." He flipped me the folder. "This is pre-ER."

"All of these were under it." I held up a stack of folders with more negatives. "All Clooney?"

"We had three shoots, so yeah. You know, I bought the guy lunch each time. He ate like a horse. Actors, man. No money."

I marked a fat file "George Clooney" with a Sharpie.

Gareth Greydon's liver failure two months before had put a bomb under Irving's butt. They were the same age and had known each other at Breakfront when Gareth was a student's parent and Irving was a teacher. Irv didn't want to die in a pile of dust and negatives that would get thrown away.

"I have no children, but I have a legacy!" he'd said.

So we started organizing his house. The treasure went deep and wide. I had to stop myself from looking at everything so carefully we stopped working.

"Laine!" Tom called from the front room. "Your phone's ringing!"

"Who is it?"

"Blocked number. Ignore?"

"Get it, would you?" I called back, moving a pile of boxes to get Clooney in alphabetical order. Brad and Britt were always blocked numbers, and I thought they might call me when their pics were published in *Underground*. I took another pile and held them against the window. "We need to get another light box."

"We have one. It's called the sun, and it's free."

"I can get you a light box, you know."

"Miss Hotshot gets a few spreads with 'culture' magazines and what? She's buying the teacher stuff?"

"Oh," I said, looking at the next set of negatives. "Oh, my God."

"What? You found Prince Harry?"

"Michael."

Not just any Michael. My Michael. My Michael from the bleachers. Varsity tennis Michael. How he got mixed in with pre-ER George Clooney was an illustration of what a mess Irv's house was, and it added to my shock.

Irv snapped the negatives from my hand. "Nice-looking kid. Move along. Go over there." He waved me toward the piles on the other side of the room.

I plucked the negatives out of his hand. "These are mine."

We faced off for a second before Tom came in. "There are four boxes of prints with water damage under the sink."

"Toss," I said.

"Keep," Irving said at the same time.

"I'll put them to the side," Tom said. "We can do rock, paper, scissors later."

"Here," I said, giving him the clear plastic folder with Michael's pictures. "Can you put these in my bag?"

"Sure."

As he was walking away, I asked, "Who was on the phone?"

"They hung up."

I attacked a new pile and didn't give the call a second thought.

Chapter 51

Michael

Brad had a huge crackerbox in Bel-Air, because that was what he was told famous actors lived in. He'd been wrong, but like most things he was wrong about, he didn't care one way or the other. He just emptied the place of any potentially adult trappings and put in stand-up video games, dart boards, three huge televisions, and a pool table. All it was missing was a dark wood bar with brass beer taps.

"What are you wearing tomorrow?" Brad asked, lining up a combination shot that would tap the three and sink the nine if he were a better player.

"A tux."

"By who? I have an Armani jacket, but I'm wearing shorts." He shot and missed.

"I have one in my closet. I don't even know who." I chalked my stick.

"You could get a comp last minute."

"Nah. Hey, I saw that pic in *Underground*."

"Yeah." He leaned on his stick, cracking his gum.

"Laine took it." I leaned over the table, lining up the three for an easy sink into the side pocket.

"Yeah."

"How is she?"

"Fine."

I missed and scratched. "Fine?"

"Yeah. She's fine." He plucked the cue ball out of the rack. "She runs around at night taking pictures and caught us at Grassroots. She's got a nose for it, you know. Found Dave at Crawlers last night. He told me they hung out and got some cool shit. I'll tell her you asked about her."

"Alone? She runs around downtown alone?"

He lined up his shot. "Yep."

I didn't know what bothered me more: her toting ten thousand dollars' worth of equipment around downtown Los Angeles at night or the fact that Brad Sinclair had intimate knowledge of her life when I didn't. "I called her the other day," I said, trying to sound casual. "Did she change her number?"

"Dunno, never had it before. She's a hot shit photographer now. Maybe she's not taking calls from nobodies." He sunk the four in a tame shot that was beneath him and did nothing to set up his next move. "What's the face?"

"A guy picked up."

"Look, dude," he said, dropping the five. "You tossed her."

"She tossed me."

"No…"

"Yes, Brad. I was there." I wanted to punch him, and I hadn't wanted to punch anyone in a long time.

Brad, for his part, looked unflustered, swaggering around the table looking for his shot. "Did you fight for her, bro? Or did you just let her walk out? You know, she says she's leaving to protect your precious career, and you just let her go? That what you did? 'Cos to me, that sounds like it's easier to let yourself think she did it when, in fact, you broke it off. You let it happen because you were scared of all the shit going down." He leaned over for his shot. "It's cool, man. People do shit like that all the time, but don't act like it was any different."

He knocked the six into the nine in a shot that looked like pure, stupid luck. The nine spun and barely made it into the corner pocket. Brad fist pumped.

I had the sinking feeling that he was right.

I tried to shake it off, but I thought about it all the way home. Was he right? Had I let her do the dirty work I was too scared to do?

I couldn't sleep, replaying what my father had said in the hospital, and how I'd failed to live up to what he thought of me on every level. Then I looped the scene in my house over and over. How Laine had walked out and I'd allowed it. I told myself I'd fought for her, but I was a liar. I'd snapped under the weight of people's expectations.

I got up and sat on my patio. The view mocked me, reminding me that I was nothing, powerless, a speck in a monstrous city. I'd felt like that in plenty of cities across the Pacific, but it had been comforting. That night, the spiked lights of downtown jabbed me in the chest.

Maybe I needed to head down there. Maybe I needed to test out that sixth sense of hers. No one really knew I was back yet. I hadn't made a call. I was still just a guy in the city. That would last another day but no more. I got into my shoes with anticipation and laced them up with hope.

Chapter 52

Laine

I own this city. I walk with its rhythms, run with its breath, speak its language. Los Angeles is my lover. It knows I'm a survivor. It knows what I've done and has found no reason to forgive me, because there has never been a sin. I am brave and strong. I have a good sense of humor. I am loyal and friendly. I have friends around every corner. Celebrities and homeless people, priests and con men. The Mexican dudes playing dice in the loading dock, the guys with the boom box outside the abandoned buildings. The businessmen and actors, the models and personal trainers. The hookers on Sunset know my name, and I know theirs. We all live here. This is our Los Angeles.

— — —

"I want two with extra…" I tilted my head and snapped my fingers. "Look, I don't speak Spanish. The cabbage with the carrots? It's like in vinegar or something?"

The lady in the hairnet leaned out of the food truck, three feet above me. She was bathed in floodlights inside the truck, and the rest of the street was washed in the black of a streetlamp-free night. "*Curtido?*"

"That! I like it." My back pocket buzzed with a text.

—Gusta, gusta!—

The text was from Maryetta.

—Where are you?—

I looked for a street sign and couldn't find one. Just fifteen or more people at hastily placed card tables with white plastic backyard chairs.

—East Hollywood. Food truck
in a parking lot off the 101—

—We're near 18th and Alameda at
a thing. Paul Messina is here. He
wants to meet you like now—

Paul Messina, the fashion magnate. A photographer did not turn down a meeting with him, no matter who they thought they were.

—I can be Downtown in ten—

The reply came as I was leaning over the hood of my car, shoving *pupusas* in my face. It was an address I knew well, the Messina Inc. global compound. I got in my little Audi and headed back Downtown.

Chapter 53

Michael

I felt as if I'd never seen downtown Los Angeles before. I'd run through it the way I'd run through everything—head down, noticing things in snippets. I saw it for the first time that night. I drove into the deepest part of the city and parked by the Whole Foods. I wasn't lying to myself about what I was doing. I was testing myself and her, practicality against hope, just throwing the dice and hoping for sevens.

I walked the streets. No one followed. No one chased. I didn't see a camera anywhere. The night embraced me, and when I saw a crowd, they were heading into a club hidden behind matte black paint. It was about ten p.m., and the city was alive.

I'd walked a dozen foreign cities in much the same way, hands in pockets, living in the dark places, the hidden byways and underpasses. But I'd never done it at home.

My pocket dinged with a message from Brad.

—Hey, dude. Big thing at the Messina compound—

I didn't want to go. I just wanted to stand on street corners and listen, but the compound was a block away. Maybe if I went, that was listening too.

—Yeah. I'm in—

—I'll get you on the list—

"Get me on the list?" I said to the phone, even though Brad couldn't hear me. "Give me a break." I put the phone away. I'd been gone too long if I needed to get on a list to go somewhere. Or maybe I'd been gone just long enough.

The Messina compound was four warehouses in a row behind twenty-foot razor-wire-topped fences. It was ugly as sin most of the time, but that night, the acres-wide parking lot had been turned into an outdoor club where people danced on the parking lines. Dozens of nine-foot-high tube lights that changed colors encircled the dance floor, and tables of food ringed the lot. The bare walls of the buildings on either side had light shows, and the offices inside were spotless and brightly lit.

Everyone knew Paul Messina could throw a party, and he never disappointed. Needless to say, the lot was packed with people.

One chain-link gate was open, and a velvet rope sat in front, a burgundy smile between two chrome poles.

"Can I help you?" asked a woman with a clipboard. She wore tight bellbottoms and a midriff shirt that tied under her breasts, doubtless the next season's offering from Messina Couture.

"I, uh… I'm on the list." There was no way Brad could have been there already, but I'd been alone for months. I could go to a party by myself.

She cocked her head and looked me up and down. "Name, please?"

"Greydon."

She froze. I was outed.

I put my finger to my lips. "*Shh.*"

She let me in.

Paul threw parties for his employees and shareholders, so everyone knew everyone, except the loner with the beard. I was sure they were too jaded to say anything about me though, and I was sure Midriff Girl had told someone. I didn't know if I'd been recognized, but I was unmolested as I went to the bar. I got ready to text Brad my location when I saw Britt at a table with Paul, then I saw *her*.

Her.

With that hair and a way of sitting in tension, as if she wanted to curl her limbs around solid surfaces. In the flashing pink and yellow lights, with the music so loud I couldn't hear myself think, she was divine. My tongue tensed against the roof of my mouth.

I wanted to taste her. I wanted to be that chair she wrapped herself around. As I stepped closer, I wanted more. I wanted to talk to her, to hear her life from her lips, her laugh. After another step, I wanted her eyes on mine. I wanted her to recognize me. To know me. I wanted her to be mine again. In my body, I felt her. My skin went sensitive and electric.

She was talking to Paul. Her hands were animated as she drew her fingers across her picture in *Underground*, explaining something. He nodded and asked a question, and her knees contracted, coiling her legs tighter around the legs of the chair, as if she couldn't wait to answer. She was working, and there I was, wanting to bury my face in her neck. I had no way to approach without screwing with her.

No. I'd done enough damage.

Chapter 54

Laine

Paul Messina knew how to throw a party. I'd heard about them, but they were at odd times and never publicized. Celebs didn't usually show up in droves, and there was no parking on the block, so the events were too much trouble for paparazzi.

I'd stayed until three. Paul wouldn't let me leave, meaning he kept feeding me drinks and asking when I was shooting his fall line. I was too drunk to answer intelligently, and he seemed all right with that.

I woke up at noon the next day, my head under the covers with a brain that felt broken and a mouth that tasted like glue.

I took a Tylenol and drank a quart of water, then I loaded my shots from the night before while I drank my coffee. I'd got some slightly interesting stuff with Paul, but he was uncomfortable in front of the camera. The great thing about working with actors and celebrities was that, even if they protested, they loved the camera. It fed their inner child. Paul was a fashion designer. He didn't know what to do with his body.

I flipped to the news. More of the usual. I was thinking of going back to sleep until Phoebe's Oscar party when I saw him.

Michael, eating breakfast an hour before at Terra Café with Lucy. Clean-shaven and wearing something that fit so well, I could tell he'd lost weight. I froze. My nerves tingled. He was back. I couldn't read the copy fast enough. My eyes skimmed over everything, and I comprehended nothing. I took a deep breath and a sip of coffee. I tried again.

He'd been back days already.

I'd held onto the thin hope that when he got back from wherever in the world he was, he'd call me right away and say he wanted me. He'd say he was done running, done getting his head together, and just wanted to be with me.

Well. That was that, wasn't it? He was back, and our little one-sided love affair was over.

I threw myself back into my desk chair, found the blue folders with his name on them, and dragged them all into the trash.

I crawled into bed. I tried sleeping. Couldn't. I paced in bare feet and pajamas.

My map of Los Angeles towered above me. I touched Monterey Park and dragged my fingers to Rancho Palos Verdes. RPV. The concrete behind the map had a hairline crack, and the map had pulled and ripped there. I fingered it. I pulled. The green expanse and part of the bay came off like a piece of sunburned skin, leaving a curled sliver of map in my hand and a wound with upturned, grabbable edges. I took one of those and peeled. It came off in an arc. I let it fall. The next bit was still partly stuck. I worried it away and let San Pedro from Trinity fall to the floor.

I got all the water off, then Santa Monica and Topanga, until the entire west side was gone to Brentwood.

To hell with it.

I got my stepstool and peeled off Holmby Hills, Bel-Air, and half the Valley into Studio City. West Hollywood all the way to Silver Lake, and down into Wilshire Center. Done with it. Done. I peeled the entire map away, leaving Downtown for last, which I took off in a swath of sticky paper.

I stepped back and looked at what I'd spent hours doing. The wall had streaks of sticky stuff and a few shards of the city on it, but otherwise it was clean. The floor wasn't so lucky. It looked like a bed of white paper flowers in full bloom.

I didn't clean it. Not yet.

The only thing you had to bring to one of Phoebe's Oscar parties was a twenty for the jackpot. She supplied booze, food, pencils, ballots, and a year's worth of magazines to help you research your choices.

I'd only won once. Seven-hundred-sixty dollars. I'd guessed every winner except the sound editing category because I'd thought the movie was too loud. When I'd said that while hugging my fishbowl full of twenties, everyone in the room shouted until my ears hurt from the vibrations and my sides hurt from laughing.

Rob lived in a half-fixed, half-dead Victorian in Angelino Heights. He'd done the first floor in period-appropriate detail but modernized the layout with a big central room and ramps for his future wife. He intended to fix the house, remove the ramps, and sell it so they could buy a place that was more comfortable for her.

The landscaping was being redone. Everything was dirt. I went up the walk with a bottle of wine and a bag of chips. I always brought something so no one could accuse me of not being raised well, even though the accusation would have been true.

Roger opened the door. "Hey, Laine." He hugged me, and I went in.

I was late, so I walked into the middle of arguments over film scores and discussions about how much each studio had put into advertising. The people who worked for marketing departments at the studios were very popular at this point in the evening, because everyone knew the amount of money a studio spent on advertising to voters was a huge factor in whether or not a nominee won.

"They killed advertising for best actor when the pedo thing happened," a guy in a button-down black shirt said. The front tail was tucked in to show off his belt buckle, and the rest hung out over his white jeans.

The guy he was talking to pointed his pencil. "That movie was an ad in itself. Do you know what it grossed its first three weeks?"

That could go on all night, and I had my own opinions—I just didn't know what they were. I stopped to say hello to a few people on my way to the kitchen, where Phoebe sat at the table with a glass of wine. As soon as she saw me, she held up a glass for me. We kissed hello, and I greeted everyone else at the table before sitting.

"Well," I said, pencil aloft, "what do we have?"

I never researched but voted by feel, memory of the movie, and instinct. It was easy. I didn't have to vote for the best or what I liked, only what people had been talking about. I got a sense of who the front runners were from that. In this crowd, the winner never got more than one wrong, and I came close each year.

Of course, as I got to the end of the ballot, I knew I would struggle with one category. Best actor. I wanted to vote for him. He was the best, no doubt, but the campaign had been tainted by me and my past. Also, after months, I was still hurting. I had to admit it to myself. Sure, I'd been the one to leave, but I was still weak and sensitive when it came to him.

Phoebe peered over my paper as my pencil hovered. "What are you going to do?"

"There's no way they voted for him. Ballots went out before it died down."

"Yeah."

"But he was the best," I said.

"You voting your heart or your mind?"

I looked at her. She smiled a knowing smile, and I ticked the box next to Michael's name.

"Atta girl."

The question at the end was the tie-breaking bonus. *How long would the show be?*

I tapped my chin with the end of my pencil. "What do you think about this one?"

"Short," Phoebe said. "They're cutting people off no matter what."

"They always say that."

"My client runs the band. They're serious. Anyone who stops playing gets docked. It was in his contract."

I scribbled a number and took a picture of my ballot. The procedure was to take a picture of your paper then hand it in as the opening monologue started. Mine went in last, and the show began.

The opener was filled with Hollywood insider jokes and knowing shots at the nominees. This year, Donny Bauer presented fake movies on slate for the following year, which included Gareth Greydon in *I Lost my Liver in San Francisco*, Britt Ravenor in *Crash 2*, and... drumroll... Michael Greydon in an NC-17 version of *Romper Room*.

My face went hot. The show did a quick shot of Michael sitting next to Brooke, his mouth pursed, shaking his head a little and trying to be a good sport.

Rob's living room went dead quiet.

"That is so freaking rude," said a girl in a little skirt.

"Bauer's an ass," someone said.

"He's reaching," someone else said.

The woman next to me punched my arm. "He's wearing a weave, you know. I screwed him, and it came off." She made a flopping motion with her hand.

I laughed and nudged the woman, a comedienne who, long ago, had had a regular part on a sitcom.

"It's fine, everyone. It was totally worth it," I said.

I got some high fives, but thankfully, the room moved on in a few minutes. Clusters of people talked through the "Dead Actor Segment." We made fun of the dance number, checked our ballots for sound editing (yes!), costume (another one!), and art direction (nailed it). As director and screenplay came up, all eyes focused on the television. By the time Andrea stood to thank the Academy and her agent, the room was quiet, and everyone whispered about *Big Girls* sweeping. Andrea thanked Michael for the performance of his life, and the camera stayed on Michael's beautiful face for so long, I thought I'd melt into the couch. Andrea went on and on for so long the music came up to stop her. Phoebe watched me, and I gave her a discreet thumbs-up. I was fine. A little wistful, but fine.

Actress next. Claire Contreras got up and did her thank yous. Her agent. The studio for believing in her. God. Her husband. Tears flow. Michael Greydon, who… well, without him to play against, she couldn't imagine…

And his face again, with the "someone is saying something nice about me" look they all gave. I wondered what he was really thinking. I wanted to ask. I wanted access to his heart and mind again.

I was holding together nicely, I had to say, but when they said his name in the nominations for best actor, I felt as if someone had removed my sternum and taken my heart in their fist. I swallowed the feeling. I promised myself I wouldn't be disappointed if he didn't win, and I'd be happy if he did. The presenters made a stupid joke then opened the envelope.

It was him. He'd won.

I cheered, standing by myself and clapping. The audience in the auditorium stood with me as he kissed Brooke, shook hands with Gareth—who yanked him into a back-slapping hug—and headed for the front. He kissed Claire, high-fived Andrea, waved to his friends, and got up in front of everyone.

They sat, and when I realized I was the only one who had stood, I sat too. The sitcom actress next to me patted my knee, and I realized everyone was looking at me.

"I'm twenty-three for twenty-three!" I said.

"Thank you," Michael said.

Phoebe turned up the volume.

"This is… I didn't expect it. I came to support the cast and crew and… Andrea, Claire, Max for writing it so I could see it, and…" He stopped himself and looked to the side, stage left. "The *Romper Room* joke."

The camera went to Donny Bauer, who stood on the sidelines in his tux, hands folded in front of him.

"I get it," Michael continued. "I really do, and I hope the laughs were worth it, but"—he waved his finger at Donny—"there's a person attached to that story, and it's not funny." He turned back to the front. "Thank you all for your faith in me, that I wasn't what they said. Thank you. I'd do it all again. If I had the chance, I'd do it all again, but…" He looked at his statue. And looked.

He was silent way too long. He held everyone in the room in the palm of his hand. Everyone in the auditorium. Everyone in the nation. And me. I was his. He owned me in those five, ten, twenty seconds.

"If I could do it all again," he looked back at the audience, "I would have scooped her up and taken her with me. Because—"

The music came up, cueing the end of his speech.

He put out his hands. "Don't! Don't cut me off!"

The music got louder.

Michael gave in and just shouted over it. "Laine Cartwright, I love you. I've always loved you."

I gasped so loud everyone looked to see if I was dying. But in a second, the cello stopped, then the keyboard. The camera stayed on Michael, who didn't move. He just looked down at the orchestra, making a "stop" sign. The music died piece by piece.

As if realizing he'd been given a reprieve, Michael straightened and looked at the camera again.

Me, he was looking at me.

"I hear you," I whispered into my hands.

"I went to a party last night, and I saw you. You were… how can I say this? Perfect. And you looked so happy. I walked out because I thought, what would she want with me? She's fine. She doesn't need me. It took me a minute to realize how ridiculous that is." He looked down again, then he put his statue on the podium and laid his hands flat on it before looking at the camera again.

He had more to say, but how much more would they allow? On the one hand, I needed to hear it, and on the other, I was breaking apart from him.

"I'm glad you're happy," he continued. "But if there's no one else, if you still want me, meet me at the corner of O and W for a do-over." He smiled, as if embarrassed, coughed, then finished. "Thank you."

The screen blinked to commercial. I looked away.

Everyone was looking at their phone.

"There's no corner of O and W," said the guy in the black shirt.

"I keep getting something in Palmdale."

"You'll never have two letters crossing. Try Oh, like O and H."

"West Virginia."

"Ohio."

"This can't be right."

"I know where it is," I said, standing. A few dozen eyes looked away from their phones to me for an answer. "Not telling."

I had to step over people sprawled on the floor as the announcers for best picture came on. "Thanks, everyone."

The woman who had screwed Donny Bauer stood and held out her arms. "Good luck, kid,"

I kissed her cheek. I was embraced, kissed, and wished luck by people I barely knew. I ran a gauntlet of love to the front door, where Phoebe waited with my jacket.

"You deserve this," she said as I hugged her, "and I don't mean a rich movie star." She pushed me away and held my shoulders. "You deserve to be loved."

"Thanks, Phoebe. I love you."

"Go," Phoebe said. "I'll call you if you win." She rolled to the front door and opened it. "Get out."

I ran to my car. It was night and cold, and I didn't care. How long would it take him? Would he do his post-win interviews first? Would they let him out without a hundred Hollywood-sanctioned softball questions?

I wanted him back. I couldn't believe it was even possible, but I hadn't misunderstood him. No one could misunderstand that. He loved me, and God knew I still loved him.

The streets were dead. I hit a little bottleneck at Fern Dell, but I headed up the mountain undetained. The park was officially closed, meaning I could get towed if I parked, but I kept moving up past the Observatory, going by the memories of my childhood and the last time I'd been there. I got to the end of Deronda, where the gates were closed with signs that threatened certain arrest and prosecution.

The one to the left was wide open. I went past without slowing, but I had to take it easy up the hill. It was dark, and I nearly took the short way down the mountain.

"Slow down, Laine," I said. "You're getting there first anyway."

I took it easy, turn by turn in the silent night. Dirt and pebbles crunched under my tires, and crickets competed with the rumble of my car's engine. I made it to the electrified fence and expected to be stopped there, but it was open. Had he planned this ahead of time? There was no way he'd done all the post-award activities and beaten me up the mountain.

I pulled in. No car in the spaces. I cut the lights and took a deep breath. I was there, and I'd wait half the night for him to show, because I knew he would. He wouldn't dump or abandon me, and wherever he needed me to be, I'd show. I knew it in my gut.

I got out and navigated the hill in the dark, the soles of my sneakers steadier than the heels but still imperfect. I was on the WOOD side, the letters black spaces against the bright lights of the city and the dull, starless grey of the sky. I slipped. Rocks rattled down, and I had to grab a branch.

"Are you all right?" a voice asked from above. Michael. He sat at the top of the first O.

"You're here."

"I ran out of there as fast as I could."

I hitched my leg on the support poles of the O and climbed to the top, feeling rather than seeing the cold metal bars. He reached down for me, and I took his hand.

"Almost there," he said.

I got my head over the top of the letters and stopped myself. "This view…"

"At night? Almost as breathtaking as you."

I climbed up and straddled the top of the letter, and he held my face and kissed me.

"Michael, I—" But I couldn't finish. I fell into his kiss, his warmth. His intensity was like a blanket over me, scented in cinnamon. I breathed his name, owned by that kiss more than any other. "I never told you…"

He pulled away and put his nose to mine while cradling my jaw. "Whatever it is, it's all right."

"I never told you I loved you."

"You came. That's all I need."

I kissed him. "As if I could resist you. Can you stand it? That we're so different? Just say yes."

"Yes. I love you because of it, and yes."

"I'll never chase you away again."

"I won't be so easy to chase away, because I'm never turning my back on you. Never again."

I couldn't get enough of his lips, but he backed up long enough to let me swing my leg over until they both dangled in front of the O. We sat, hand in hand, watching the lights blink and move over the boulevards like right-angled waterways. I put my head on his shoulder, and we presided over our domain, under the starless sky of Los Angeles.

THE END

Acknowledgements

I don't think of myself as a lone gun, but this book in particular got more help than any book before it. So, as many people as you see here, double that number for all the people I'm forgetting.

Shuttergirl began as a conversation between myself and my agent, Maura Kye-Cassella, and I'm grateful for her decisive honesty. For instance, her main note on the first draft of *Shuttergirl* was, "This is really bad." That was a year ago, and my level of irritation matched my level of glee when she said of this version, "You nailed it."

Angela Smith, I don't have enough words. She took late calls from me, read my shitty attempts at a story numerous times, and suggested, "Look, they need to have a good time together. He needs to seduce her." So I wrote the Hollywood sign, and everything fell into place from there.

Cassie Cox, as usual was my perfect line editor (she did not line edit the acknowledgements so if there are typos in here do not write me letters), and Lynn always fits me into the schedule. Always.

LRB, KB and DW, your tireless support and the way you allow me to own the chat with my whining is precious to me. I have girls in groups, FYW and BGP who are a goldmine of support. Nothing happens without the support of other writers. I know writers out there who reflexively one star competitor's books on Goodreads, leave bad reviews and undercut fellow authors. But my sisterhood wouldn't, and they are a treasure.

THANK YOU:

TRSOR for being the BEST promotions company in the business.

All the authors who wrote and blurbed this book ahead of time.

Sarah Hansen – patience of a saint. Thank you for staying with me until we got the cover right.

Kaylee, my assistant, thank you for loving this book from jump, and attacking the promotions like a tiger.

Diana and Tony for your tireless work in Goodreads. I have such a hard time taking on more than one social media outlet, you maintaining my presence there is so important.

SueBee – you are a true fan and friend. Thank you for your forgiveness and gentleness.

Erik – Still love the inner-chapter separators. You're an epub ninja.

Special Forces – With a team like this, failure was never an option.

D-sleepy, Lady Nono, A-Bomb – thank you for Saturday and Sunday mornings.

Starbucks stores all over Hollywood have turned a little crazy, but I still write there and all over Los Angeles. I want to thank my city for being my office.

MOST IMPORTANTLY:

I want to thank everyone in New York who made this release possible.

About the Author

I can be reached at **cdreiss.writer@gmail.com**

I'm also on Facebook pretty frequently on my personal profile and my fan page. If Goodreads is your thing, my fan group name is **CD Canaries**.

I'm on Instagram, Tumblr, Twitter, and Pinterest with varying degrees of frequency. My handle is my name. I'm pretty easy to find.

To find out about upcoming releases, sign up for the mailing list on **cdreiss.com**.

Thank you for reading.

Other Books

You may or may not know that I'm known for erotic romance.

The Submission Series

Jonathan Drazen.

Gorgeous. Check.

Charming. Check.

Smart. Check.

Rich. Hey, I'm not gonna complain.

All the ingredients for a few nights of mind-blowing pleasure are right there. He's made it perfectly clear he can't love me, and I'm not out to fall in love either.

But I can't stay away from him. He's got this bossy way about him in bed. The word "Sir," falls from my lips, and when he tells me to get on my knees…well, my knees have a mind of their own.

I got this. I can be his slave for a few nights and walk away unscathed.

We get in. Get it on. Get the hell out. Done.

He knows the line between love and lust. It's right between my legs. Now, let's see if that line blurs for me.

The Submission Series has 9 books: *Beg, Tease, Submit, Control, Burn, Resist, Sing, Dominance* (Jonathan's POV's), *Coda*

You can also buy the bundled versions: 1) *Beg/Tease/Submit*, 2) *Control/Burn/Resist*, 3) *Sing/Coda/Dominance*

The Corruption Series

If you love hot Mafia men, check out my *Corruption Series*, Spin and Ruin are full length and ready.

Theresa Drazen wants to know one thing.

Is there something wrong with her?

Because from what she can see, she has money, brains, a body that does the job. Yet, she keeps getting shelved. Most recently, by her fiancé who happens to be the DA.

And she'll get over it, really. No problem. She'll just have a nice, short encounter with a mysterious Italian named Antonio who may or may not be involved with some kind of alleged criminal activity...blah blah...

Let's call a spade a spade.

He's a mobster.

Let's face a few more facts.

He's hot. He's smart. And if anyone breathes on her the wrong way, he's got no problem beating their head against a Porsche until they're willing to lick up their own vomit to make it stop.

Just about everything about that turns her on.

Yeah. There's something wrong with her.

**MATURE AUDIENCES--Rough sex. Dirty talk.
Criminal activity. Cursing. Fisticuffs. Closed course.
Professional driver. Do not try this at home.**

The Perdition Series

Fiona Drazen's life as a celebutante and submissive slave in *The Perdition Series* starts with *KICK,* and continues with book two, *USE.*

You know what a celebutante is. It's a Paris Hilton. A Kim Kardashian. Someone who's famous for existing. That's me, and in case you were wondering what it's like...trust me, it's the best shit ever.

I like coke and I like sex. I have the money to buy the first and the looks to get the second. No one needs to know where I am for days at a time and no one gives a fuck. That's just the way I like it.

You got issue with that?

Good.

Because you think I have problems, and I don't. A problem would be defined as some situation in my life I didn't arrange. Like having no money. That's a problem, and I don't have it. Like having a ton of sex I don't totally enjoy. Also not my problem.

Now that we understand each other, you and me, and we understand that my life is exactly how I want it, you have to know that you don't have the right to hold me here.

Right?

Right.

The Perdition Series starts with *KICK*, and continues with book two, *USE*.

CPSIA information can be obtained at www.ICGtesting.com
Printed in the USA
LVOW08s1538120615

442281LV00006B/631/P

9 781626 818804